SHOTZ FIRED
and
DEADLY WIRED

TWO NOVELS IN ONE

By Jim Warren

SHOTZ FIRED and DEADLY WIRED

Books may be ordered through booksellers,
Lulu Marketplace at Lulu.com
or at Amazon.com.

This is a work of fiction. All of the characters, names, incidents, organizations, and the dialogue in this novel are either the products of the author's imagination or are used fictitiously.

ISBN: 978-0-557-41770-4

For the men and women
in law enforcement

SHOTZ FIRED

CHAPTER ONE

BANG! Boom Boom Boom Boom Boom! Sporadic gunfire could be heard everywhere. Boom Boom Boom Boom! The running gun battle between turf-warring gang members was at a fever pitch, with the police caught in the middle. Paramedic units gathered two blocks away, waiting to be called forward to give aid to the winners and losers. Gunfire continued as officers sought cover behind bullet-pocked vehicles parked in front of the city's Civic Auditorium.

The three-story brick building was probably state-of-the-art 50 or 60 years ago, but now it was just old. It had once stood proudly amid the businesses and upper-class residences of downtown. Over the years, the area had changed. Urban blight took over and the auditorium, like the inner city, was just old. If the battling police officers needed reinforcements, they were just a shout away. The show must go on!

This was National Law Enforcement Week and a cadre of police officers in their dress blues were participating in the department's annual medals awards ceremony, inside the auditorium. Invited guests were nervous, the continuing gunfire was unnerving and the program was running long.

My partner was called forward. As Chief Riley pinned on the medal, his aide read from the citation. "Officer Joseph Wayne Beveltnik is awarded the Purple Heart for injuries received on duty. *On October 18th of last year, Officer Beveltnik and his partner, Officer Griffith Park, stopped a vehicle for a traffic violation. The driver suddenly and without provocation, shot at Officer Beveltnik. Officer Beveltnik sustained serious facial injuries due to shattering cruiser door glass and bullet fragments from the hostile gunfire. Due to his duty-related injuries, Officer Beveltnik is hereby awarded the department's Purple Heart.*"

As the Chief was shaking Joe's hand, I was called forward. While Chief Riley was suspending my medal from my neck, his aide read from my citation. "Officer Griffith James Park is awarded Capitol City's highest honor, the Medal of Valor, for eliminating a hostile fire threat thereby saving a life.

"*On October 18th of last year, Officer Park and his partner, Officer Joseph Beveltnik stopped a vehicle for a traffic violation when the driver suddenly and without provocation opened fire on Officer Beveltnik. Officer Park did not hesitate. Officer Park shot, striking the driver and eliminating the hostile fire threat, thereby saving Officer*

Beveltnik's life. Officer Park's actions bring great credit upon himself and the Capitol City Police Department."

After the applause died down, Chief Riley said, "This concludes our medals awards ceremony. Thank you for joining us. Now, you're all invited to join our honorees in the Heritage Room for refreshments. Also, you may wish to stay inside until the situation outside is contained."

The rest of the morning was a blur of congratulations and adulations as fellow officers, families and friends mingled over punch and cookies. Gung ho young officers ran out to join the waning fire fight.

Outside, the distinctive thrumming of the WUND News helicopter could be heard. While several people turned on radios to get the latest word on the hostilities from Mr. Wunderful, my mind drifted back to the incident that brought Joe and me here.

We were working our usual overlapping evening shift. Things were going slowly and my mind was wandering—not a good thing for a cop on duty. I had been thinking back to the beginning of my career. I'd always wanted to be a cop, not because of the portrayals of shoot-em-ups or steamy sex; I truly believed that it was my calling.

Most cops are dedicated and hard working people who really care about helping others. There are always a few bad cops who make us all look bad, but they have always strengthened my resolve to better myself in the eyes of the public. It's true, but sounds like a lot of horse hockey -- even to me.

I missed out on doing military service and thought I'd fight my war in the urban jungle. At 25, I was one of the older police recruits. Most were real gung-ho and couldn't wait to be promoted up the ranks to chief. All I wanted to be was a street cop, cleaning up my little section of the world. I'm not John Wayne or Sister Theresa, I'm just a good cop and have been for 15 years. Some say I'm a throwback to an earlier age.

"Hey! Zoo Man! Snap out of it! Your mind is wandering – I can tell!"

"You're right, Joe. You caught me." Now I was edgy.

"That car's got bad tags, I'm going to pull him over."

As Joe pulled our black and white in behind the Lincoln, I said, "I know it's been a slow evening, but a license plate violation? What's the violation, felony stickering?"

"Expired tag," Joe said sheepishly, "something to do. We don't have to write him, just make sure his license is good and do a warrant check. If he's OK, we can give him a warning. Will that make you feel better?"

"It's not about me, I just think it's a cheap pinch, that's all. That is a pretty clean Lincoln, though I'm more interested in finding out why such a clean car has such a dirty tag on it." Fifteen years on the street and little things like that make me edgy. I was already edgy, now I was just downright jumpy. Some call it a sixth sense, all I know is that I get a funny feeling in the pit of my stomach.

"The L.E.A.D.S. computer is down. I tried to run it before I shook you back into reality. What do you think is going through his head while we sit back here? I know I'd be sweating bullets."

"Let's not keep him waiting. Be careful, partner," I said. "Talk this one back while I move up on his right." My gut feeling was to treat this stop like an academy ambush scenario. When I approached the right rear of the car, I made sure that the trunk lid was securely down. While the driver watched his door mirror, I watched him through the right rear window; nothing seemed amiss. The male white driver in a business suit did not appear to be nervous.

Joe opened his driver's door, keyed the mike and using the cruiser's external speaker, ordered, "Exit slowly and walk back to the sound of my voice—do it now!" The Lincoln's door opened and the driver stepped out. As soon as his feet hit the ground, he wheeled and started peppering Joe's door with shots from a small semi-automatic.

I never saw where the gun came from nor do I remember drawing my weapon. Suddenly my service weapon was in my hands and instinct took over. At waist level, I fired a barrage of .45 slugs through the Lincoln's front passenger window, striking the suspect several times in his left side. The driver bucked and jerked and dropped like a rock; a heavy rope chain around his neck snagged the door latch post and he hung there like a side of beef. It seemed like everything was happening in slow motion. I ran to the driver's side and kicked the small semi-automatic away from the suspect's reach.

"Joe, are you OK, partner?"

"I took some glass and stuff to the face, missed my eyes though, and I'm going to need a change of underwear. Other than that, I'm OK, I guess." My bloody and shaken partner said, "Thanks for the heads up, Zoo Man!"

Fifteen years on the street and the first time I have to drop the hammer, I kill a guy. It's not a good feeling. I've always hated the ongoing fire arms training sessions, but they sure paid off this time. The next few months were emotion-packed. You think you know how you will react to a shooting situation, but really, you don't.

The firing of my weapon was enough to start an in-depth investigation, but I had killed a guy—this was going to be intense. All I could do was sit and watch as the investigative scene unfolded in front of me. After the medic took Joe to the hospital, he would not be allowed to return to have contact with me. Joe would be interviewed at the hospital. It's the same tactic that we use with the bad guys so they can't work on concocting a story. Joe and I didn't have to worry about that, what happened was pretty straight forward. Homicide detectives wanted a letter of information as to what happened, and since I was the shooter, that task would fall to Joe.

My long night was just beginning. I was escorted to the homicide squad, where I was to be interviewed by Detective Ike Goldstein.

"How are you holding up, Zoo?"

"OK, I guess."

"Is this the first time you've been involved in a shooting?"

"First time, and I hit the jackpot!"

"Does it bother you that you killed someone?"

"Nope, he deserved it. He was trying to kill my partner. Aren't you supposed to be reading me Miranda rights?"

"Patience, Zoo, I'm not the enemy, I'm on your side, remember? How about a cup of coffee?"

"Yes, please, black." The coffee was strong enough to curl a strong man's toenails—just the way I like it.

"Before I start being official, let me give you this." He handed me a list of lawyers. "This is the current list of attorneys used by the FOP. I suggest you pick one and call him."

I picked one who had a good reputation and called him at home.

"Call the FOP and tell them to put me on the clock. Secondly, make no statement on the advice of your attorney. What do you have planned for tomorrow morning?"

"Sleep, but I'm available in the afternoon."

"Great, meet me at my office at 1:00 pm."

Detective Goldstein said, "From everything I've seen and heard, it was a righteous shoot, nothing you need to worry about, but we still have to go through all of the formalities so that none of the bleeding heart, liberal, second-guessing groups can say we were taking short cuts or covering for our officers. If we don't dot every I and cross every T, it gives them ammunition to find fault with us. Be thankful that you didn't shoot a minority. That has its own set of problems."

He pushed a form in front of me which I recognized as a Formal Miranda Rights form. He also took out a portable tape recorder and placed it on the interview room table. “As I’m sure you know, this interview and all subsequent interviews will be tape recorded and transcribed by one of our secretaries.”

What he didn’t say was that the interview was also secretly being videotaped. Goldstein caught the eye of another Homicide detective and waved her over.

“Griff, this is Detective Phyllis Abel. She’ll witness my reading of the form to you.”

“Hi Phyll.”

“Hi Zoo Man.”

Goldstein missed the little wink she gave me as he tested the tape recorder. “This is Detective Isaac Goldstein and I am about to read Miranda rights to Officer Griffith Park, fifteen-year veteran of the C.C.P.D. in regards to the homicide which took place earlier this evening. Also present is Detective Phyllis Abel. Officer Park has in front of him a copy of the Miranda Rights waiver which I will now read to him.”

After being read my rights and refusing to make a statement on the advice of my attorney, my session was over. Ike Goldstein said I would be getting a call later from Lt. Dingell, to come in and make the statement.

I set my alarm for 11:30 am and awoke five minutes before the alarm was to sound. After a nice, hot shower, I got dressed for my appointment. I didn’t figure that Attorney Tennenbaum would expect me to arrive in sartorial splendor, so I chose a pair of Dockers and a light blue and black checkered sport shirt. I drove my old beater to the courthouse district and parked three blocks away to avoid the $5.00 parking lot fee. I arrived right on time.

Mr. Tennenbaum’s secretary said he was with another client and swept her hand toward the waiting room, with a “have a seat.” Wilson Tennenbaum’s name had been the only name on the list of attorneys that I recognized, and I’d heard good things about him from other cops. Ten minutes later, my attorney appeared.

“Mr. Park, I’m Will Tennenbaum, sorry to keep you waiting,” he said, as he extended his right hand. Wilson Tennenbaum appeared to be in his mid-50s, 5’8”, 200 lbs. with a pot belly. He had a full head of brown hair which was graying at the temples. As we walked down a hallway and into an interview room, he aside, “Are you a coffee drinker?”

"Yes sir, black please." Mr. Tennenbaum got me a black coffee and one with cream and sugar for himself from the coffee maker on the credenza.

"I made an inquiry this morning about last night's situation and it sounds like there's no problem but we can't be lax, we'll do this by the numbers. What I want you to do is sit here and write out the incident in detail, like whoever is going to read it has no previous idea of what happened. Take your time, think it through, and don't leave anything out. We have lots of legal pads. When you're finished, push the white button by the door and I'll come back in. Help yourself to the coffee and if you need it, that other door leads to a restroom." With a nod and a wink, the attorney left.

As directed, Griff took his time and as he focused on the incident, more details emerged, little things that were seen or done and just taken for granted. He had to focus and put on paper not only what he had done automatically, but he also had to justify it. He had to break down his split-second decision.

Griff remembered a little trick that his sister had taught him. Write on every other line. It makes it easier to read and make corrections. After two hours of printing in departmentally-mandated block printing, he was finished and pushed the button.

"All done, are we?"

"Yes sir," Griff said as he was helping himself to another cup of coffee.

"Let's see what we have here," the attorney said as he sat down to read the statement. The two of them sat together for another half hour, going over the document and making minor changes. "Officer, I've been doing this for years, and no one has ever written out their statement double spaced. This is the easiest to read and amend that I've ever seen. I'm going to make this mandatory."

"Thanks Sis," I thought.

"OK Officer, put this statement in this manila envelope and don't open it until the detectives want their statement. I've found that if one keeps opening and reading it they want to make changes and then it won't seem genuine. Trust me, I've seen it happen. When your Homicide Detectives ask for your statement, just open the envelope, take out the statement and read it verbatim. This is kosher, expected, and it's in your own words. Any questions?"

I had none, so I was dismissed with an admonition that if I should be charged, to contact him. This was definitely a learning experience. When summoned to the Homicide Squad, I read my statement which was accepted without question. The case was eventually presented to the Grand Jury which issued a no bill. From the beginning, I knew that I had done right, now it was official.

The Executive staff, which forms the Firearms Review Board, and evaluates all shootings, also gave me a clean bill of health.

My on-again, off-again girlfriend gave me up for good. She no longer wanted to be around someone with "blood on his hands." The holidays sucked too since I have no family in town. My small family consists of my two parents and my sister. My parents are retired. Dad won a multi-state lottery, so they are cruising around the world—again. An occasional letter postmarked from somewhere out of the country is my only contact. I honestly expect someday to get notification from some sea captain that my parents have died and were buried at sea.

My sister is another story all together. Agnes gave up a successful job as a hospital administrator to "find" herself in the wilds of Oregon. I received a postcard from her a year ago, in which she wrote that she had married and referred to her husband as Sasquatch and her young son as Hairy. I'm pretty sure this was just her Park sense of humor.

I'd always enjoyed Halloween. It was fun to have the neighborhood rug rats roaming the floors of the apartment building, accosting every door for candy. I could hear kids and even some adults telling the ghosts and goblins to stay away from the "killer's" door. A night's worth of candy was going to last a year.

With no family in town, Thanksgiving was a bummer. I didn't let on to my partner. He had lots of family and I didn't want to bring him down. Christmas was better. Joe and Bev took me under their wings and I spent Christmas with them, eating dinner, exchanging gifts and trying to act normal.

Holidays are tough when you've been through something traumatic. You really have to work hard at not second guessing yourself when you're alone. I celebrated New Years Eve alone in my apartment watching Dick Clark bring in the New Year. New Years Day, it was pork and sauerkraut at Ma's Diner for good luck, and then back home to watch football on TV. Happy New Year to me.

Things did not ease up much. The taunting, name calling, innuendos and the mention of wrongful death suits all contributed to sleepless days. Not to mention, all of the investigations, "Monday morning quarterbacking," psych interviews and a Grand Jury hearing. After what seemed like an eternity, I was finally cleared of any wrong doing and Joe and I were decorated. The announcements of the awards ceremony brought renewed letters to the editor about use of force and police brutality.

Detective Ike Goldstein was assigned to investigate the death of the shooter that Griff had taken out. The deceased's drivers license indicated that he was one Burke Shotz from Topeka, Kansas. Also found in the victim's wallet was a hand-written conceal carry permit and business cards which indicated he worked for Topekagem Jewelry Wholesalers in Topeka.

A Topekagem audit had shown that the books had been cooked and thousands of dollars worth of jewelry and loose stones were missing. Burke Shotz was their prime suspect. The Lab boys found no jewels or anything else of interest in Shotz's Lincoln. Likewise, nothing of interest was found in his room at the Capital Motel. An FBI fingerprint check found no sign of, or warrants for, Burke Shotz. No relatives could be located either.

The case was finally closed and Mr. Burke Shotz was buried in the Potter's Field in the rear section of Capitol City Cemetery. Eventually, things returned to normal and the guys at the precinct house stopped calling me "killer" and again referred to me as "Zoo Man." I would prefer that the boys just call me Griff, but once you're tagged, you're stuck.

My given name, an old family name, is Griffith Park. I was on my first permanent assignment when one of my fellow officers realized that my name was the same as that of the Los Angeles Zoo and the rest, as they say, is history.

CHAPTER TWO

"Item Last: Everybody from six on up seems to have some type of video recording device, so let's be extra careful with what we say and do; we don't need to get caught up in some 'Rodney King' type scandal. That's it men, have a safe shift." Roll call was over.

"Zoo, Joe, see me before you head out."

Joe and I gave our cruiser the once over, stored our gear and shotgun, then marked in service but busy with the Sergeant. Our Sergeant's name is Jerry Atrick, but no one has stones enough to make fun of his name.

"You wanted to see us, Boss?"

"Sit down boys, let's have a chat."

That didn't sound good and often it meant get out the Vaseline; maybe I'm just cynical. Apparently the Sarge read the look on my face.

"Relax your sphincter, Zoo. You and Beveltnik here are my two best guys. I just want to give you some info. I got a memo from one of the patrol captains that there may be something strange brewing in the rundown Mission District in your area, but he doesn't know what. Any ideas?"

"Not a clue, Boss, nothing seems out of the ordinary."

"Either of you got any contacts down there?"

"We've got a couple of snitches," Joe said, "but we never get anything but nickel and dime stuff from them – usually just enough to give them some beer money."

"Give the area an 'extra look-see will 'ya? I doubt it'll be anything too exciting. Besides I wouldn't know how to handle you guys if you got medals again."

"Just like always, Boss, kiss our feet and buy us a steak and we'll be just fine." I dodged a box of paper clips as we left his office.

Joe and I speculated about what might be happening in our seedier section as we patrolled that evening. We saw Ole Breezy, one of our regulars, holding up a light pole, and pulled over. "What's up, Breeze?"

"Not much, what's up with you and Officer Ballsack?"

"That's Beveltnik," Joe yelled, only slightly perturbed. "Anything strange going on around the soup kitchen?"

"Nothin' that the Big Guy's money can't fix," Breezy said.

Joe and I looked at each other and we both said, "What Big Guy?"

"I dunno – just some overgrown Palooka who's been holdin' down a cot at the Holy Roller's Mission – he's always got money. He can pay his own way, why's he takin' up a spot that's for us legit bums? Why is that, Zooey?"

"I don't know but maybe we'll look into it – what's the Palooka look like?"

Breezy gave us a description. "He looks like a bear in a baggy suit and he walks 'goofylike,' like a cowboy with a sore butt – ya can't miss him."

We gave Breezy some beer money. "I don't know if this has anything to do with anything, but a soupy shouldn't be flashing cash – we'll watch for him though."

After a couple of non-descript hours, we took a dinner break at one of the area's finer dining establishments, Ma's Diner. Joe and I sat on both sides of the counter corner so we could watch each other's backs as Ma herself waddled up behind the counter.

"What's good tonight?" I asked. "Why, I am Zoo Man but you can't afford me." Ma laughed so hard, I thought her 400 pounds would cause an earthquake.

"Hey Joe, I see you guys got new pretty pretties on your shirts – are those ribbons because of that shootout thingy you guys had?"

"Heck no, Ma, these are for not allowing any bank robberies to occur on our shift."

"Impressive!" she said, and she waddled off to get us our coffee.

"Joe, do you think she'll ever figure out that there are no banks open to rob in the evening?"

"Naw, but it's better than having to brag to her about our medals. By the way, thanks again for saving my life."

"Oh, was that you working with me that night?" I dodged a handful of sugar packets – seems like people are always throwing things at me.

Being a slow learner, I again ordered Ma's chopped steak. I'm not sure where she gets her beef but it's always tough and chewy. The side dishes are always better than the entrée.

Joe got his usual order of "radioactive" chicken. This consists of a half of fried chicken which usually has extra body parts; Joe enjoys the extra meat. On our shift and in our area, we are limited to eating establishments. Ma's isn't the best, but she does cut us some slack on the bill.

Soon after our ration of indigestion, we got back to work and answered a disturbance call at the God's Holy Mission, which is more than just a flop house. It's been around for as long as anyone can remember and has been run by a variety of men over the years. The Mission is in an old high school which had long since been closed. The third floor classrooms had been converted to dormitories for homeless men. Each room had the potential of sleeping twenty men on cots. The second floor was basically the same, but set aside for homeless women with or without children, and is also a haven for battered wives who had fled their homes.

The first floor school offices had been set up as the Mission's offices and the administrator's residence. The first floor also had a large room which had formerly been a gymnasium; now it was just a make shift recreation area. This room also doubles as a place for overflow sleeping accommodations during bad weather.

The basement is divided into furnace, maintenance and storage areas, and houses the old school's cafeteria. It is now the neighborhood soup kitchen with rows of mismatched tables and folding chairs, serving 50 to 75 people daily for lunch. Hopefully, cash and food donations from restaurants, bakeries and grocery stores will increase so they can open a food pantry.

The current director of God's Holy Mission is a Reverend Wagner. We met him in his office. "What's the problem Reverend, what can we help you with?"

"Oh, it's all over now. One of our semi-regulars was picking fights over cot space but he's already gone, probably wandering the streets looking for someone to harass. He has a bad temper."

"We'll watch for him," Joe said. "What does he look like?"

"Like Quasi Modo. No, that's unkind of me to speak that way. He's a big man, white, late 40s to early 50s. He walks, no he shuffles, and he's hunched over, real bow legged too. You can't miss him, he's wearing an oversized brown baggy suit." The Reverend had just described Breezy's big palooka.

"You wouldn't happen to know his name would you?" I asked.

"They're all God's children, we don't ask them their names."

We left the Reverend standing there with his hands folded and his eyes looking up to heaven.

"Kind of creepy, don't you think? Reminded me of John Carradine."

"Who?" Joe asked, as he pulled our ride into traffic.

"The actor who played the undertaker in *The Shootist*. You don't watch many movies, do you?"

"I'll bet it was a John Wayne movie – he's your idol."

I was just about to answer when a loud explosion shattered our rear window. Joe made a hard left into an alley and we both bailed out, guns drawn. We peeked around the corner where we had been, but saw nobody. Joe radioed "shots fired" and we could soon hear the sirens of the cruisers coming as back up. Soon, officers flooded the area.

No shots had been fired, but we had taken a 40 oz. bottle of beer to the rear window--probably from a rooftop.

"What's with – with me and car windows, Zoo?" I noticed he was rubbing the window-glass scars on his left cheek—his own personal shootout memento.

"What's with people throwing things at me?" I thought.

A thorough check of the area did not turn up our own personal beer distributor. The other cars headed back to their own sectors and we headed for the body shop. That was our last official act for the night; apparently we had somehow ruffled somebody's feathers.

Several nights later, things were exceptionally slow, so Joe and I decided to swing by Ma's Diner for some coffee. As Joe turned down Badgely Road to catch a short cut, we saw a fast-moving shadow crossing the road ahead.

"What the hell was that, Joe?"

"Damned if I know, but I'm going to find out!" Joe raced forward. The shadow had come from one warehouse gate on the right to go into one on our left. We drove in the open gate and started to go along the right side of the warehouse. Suddenly, a blacked out motorcycle came roaring out from the opposite side. By the time Joe got our ride turned around, the bike was through the gate and was gone! Even the sound was gone. We aired it so other units would be aware that there was a shadow rider in the area.

"Pretty spooky huh, Zoo?"

"Spooky all right and fast! Let's check behind these warehouses and see if we can figure out what the phantom was up to." Nothing seemed amiss behind the warehouse, not that the spook had much time to do anything. A check behind the warehouse where we first saw the shadow also revealed nothing.

"Maybe that was the big Palooka we've been looking for."

"It didn't look like a circus bear on that bike to me Joe, but maybe."

The monotony had been broken but we still wanted coffee. Joe put us back on course to Ma's. Maybe this has something to do with what that patrol Captain was talking to the Sarge about. In any case, we have someone else to watch out for.

Three more weeks went by with no problems in the Mission Area and no big Palooka. We were just about to give up on the area when we got a call.

Radio: "Patrol 17, check on one down and out behind a warehouse on Badgely Road."

"Patrol 17, could you be a bit more specific? There are at least a dozen warehouses over there?"

Radio: "Sorry fellas, that's all we got, anonymous caller."

We'd been checking behind and around the buildings when our spotlight picked up something in a fenced-in area. The sign on the fence read "Waverly Forms 808 Badgely Road." The lock had been cut and the gate was open. We trained our spotlight on the figure we had seen. We had found our big Palooka--dead.

The body was in a kneeling position, forehead on the ground and hands flex-cuffed behind his back. We stopped and checked the scene closely before we approached the body. The surface was concrete with nothing strewn about – only oil stains. As we got closer we saw the small caliber bullet hole behind the left ear.

The Palooka died wearing a cheap suit with the pockets turned inside out, raggedy tennis shoes and mismatched socks.

Somebody had sullied our area with an execution and we were determined to solve it before the paper pushers did. We wrote out a statement about our find for the homicide detectives and handed it to the lead detective. We told the homicide dicks that this was the damndest suicide we had ever seen—they were not amused.

As the scene was self-contained inside a chain link fence, we let Homicide and the Crime Lab boys take over and we continued on patrol.

Two days later, we found out that the victim had been one Benjamin (Big Benny) Bigwell, a small-time crook from New Orleans. We also heard that he'd had six one hundred dollar bills stuffed in his sock.

We looked up Breezy. We found him sleeping off a drunk behind the Qua King Duck Chinese Restaurant. He had a hundred dollar bill and another thirty dollars and change in his pockets.

"Where'd you get all that money, Breezy?"

"I jush found it offishur Biljac." He was too drunk to be corrected. We took him to Ma's Diner, sat him down in a back booth so we could have some privacy. Ma was busy with other customers so Ruby took our order.

"Bring us a whole pot of Ma's special strong, black coffee and three cups. You might want to start another pot, we may need it."

When Ruby turned away from the table, Joe lightly grabbed her arm. "And some cream please?" Ruby winked at Joe and said, "I remembered, I was going to bring it for you." Joe blushed. I think Ruby likes Joe a lot!

We didn't even ask Breezy how he liked his coffee. We just kept filing his cup with hot and black. After half a pot, Breezy's tongue started to loosen and we started to question him.

"Breezy, where did you get that hundred dollars you've got in your pocket? Did that big Palooka give it to you?"

"Yep." At least, he appeared to understand the questions.

"Did he just give it to you?"

"Nope," It's going to be a long night.

Joe jumped in. "C'mon Breezy, why'd he give you money?"

"Made a delivery for him."

"What kind of delivery?"

"I dunno, it was heavy like a brick."

"Did you open it? Take a peek?"

"Nope."

"OK." I asked, "Could you at least tell us where you made the delivery?"

"Can't remember, haff to think on it."

We kept filling Old Breeze with coffee while he thought. Joe and I each made two pit stops, but not Breezy, he must be part camel, I thought.

Joe said, "I believe Ol' Breezy here is what we call a mule."

"More like a camel," I said as an aside.

"I heerd that and I think yer a jackash," and with that he clammed up. No matter how we tried to explain that a mule is one who carries drugs, he would have none of it. Breezy was insulted and refused to say another word, refused more coffee too.

"How much for all this coffee, Ruby?"

"For you guys, $15.00, and we'll call it square." I fished a twenty out of Breezy's pocket and gave it to Ruby. "Keep the change."

We dropped Breeezy off at the Mission and figured that we would attempt to question him again later, if we could find him, again. A hundred bucks can buy a lot of cheap booze.

For the next week, we canvassed the Mission Area, to talk to the lesser knowns that the suits wouldn't have bothered with. Maybe we could turn up something. We spotted Harry the Tooth lumbering down an alley and decided to talk to him.

"Hey, Tooth, c'mere, haven't seen you around lately."

"Ain't been around, Zoo." He flashed us a smile with a full set of choppers.

"What happened to your tooth?"

"Traded it in on these wonder grinders—ain't they grand?"

"Must have cost a grand," Joe said. "Did the Mission front you the money?"

"Nope, earned it, making deliveries."

"Who for?" I asked.

"Cain't tell you, he'll git mad."

"If it's Big Benny, you might as well tell us cause he's dead."

Harry's jaw dropped in disbelief. "No shit? Now, I'm in trouble. I still owe $400 on these choppers. Can they be repossessed?"

"Tell us about the deliveries, Harry."

"Buy me dinner so I can use my new teeth and I'll tell you all about it."

As we went in the door, I yelled, "Look Ma, it's your favorite customers."

Joe yelled, "Look out!" and I plucked a salt shaker out of the air just before it hit me. "What's that for?!"

"I had to reupholster the back booth after you brought that old drunk in. He pissed so much that the foam rubber under the fabric was spongy!"

"Since you're remodeling the back booth, we'll just sit at the counter then, so put down that pepper shaker."

Joe and I sat cross corner like we usually do with Harry in the middle. "What do you recommend?" Harry queried.

"If you really want to give those choppers a good test, I'd recommend Ma's chopped steak. It's full of gristle—DAMN Ma, you could have killed me with that hard boiled egg! If Cincinnati had a hurler like you, they'd be in the World Series! You got no sense of humor?"

Joe was rolling with laughter as I was wiping hard boiled egg out of my hair when he said, "And who says the truth doesn't hurt? Damn Ma, I was just joshin'—my shield is not supposed to be a target! We are NOT paying for those eggs!"

Harry looked left and looked right and then looked down as he said quietly, "I ain't saying shit!"

Once we composed ourselves, we got Harry a vegetarian meal, then got down to business. He told us that Big Ben recruited him and others at the Mission to make deliveries for him. "He paid us a lot more cash than we could ever get collecting cans."

We asked Harry about where the deliveries went and he became vague. "All over, but we was supposed to forget where. The deliveries were always to different places. I was supposed to eat the slip of paper with the address on it so I wouldn't remember."

"But you do remember, don't you Harry?"

"Naw, I always get stinkin' drunk with the big money. It helped me to forget."

"You're not being very helpful Harry! What's it gonna take to make you remember?" A piece of pie and some coffee got Harry talking again.

"Listen, guys." Harry looked sheepish. "I never learned to read, so I gave the papers to Rev. Wagner to read for me. Maybe he still has them. While you're there, you might check the soup kitchen. Big Benny always got the packages from there."

We cut Harry loose and then mulled over what he'd told us. He'd said he never met anyone at the drops, just dropped off the packages and left.

"Well, Zoo, ya think we got enough to get a search warrant for the soup kitchen?"

"No, I don't. First of all, we're only guessing about drugs and secondly we don't know if the good Reverend is involved. Let's talk to Wagner and see if he's got the papers though."

We visited Rev. Wagner at the God's Holy Mission and talked about a lot of different things. Finally, Joe said, "We were talking to Harry the Tooth and he said he had some papers he can't find. Did he happen to leave them here?"

"Just some addresses. I tossed 'em in the drawer just in case he needed them. He can't read, you know. Would you guys like to take them to him?"

"Not a problem," I said and we took off before Rev. Wagner smelled a rat.

We spent the rest of the day, between calls, looking for other mules. None of the other locals owned up to being a package carrier, so we decided to check out Harry's drops on our next shift.

CHAPTER THREE

Tuesday evening was slow which worked well for us. The first address on Harry's list was a closed-down gas station on Hansen St. The building was standing open and looked about the same as always, an eyesore surrounded by a chain link fence with gaps big enough to ride a Harley through. This was definitely a transients' hangout—40 oz. and wine bottles littered the interior.

"Look at this, Zoo. Broken crack stems and chore."

"Yeah, we'll have to check this place more often."

We shook the place pretty good, but to no avail.

"What's next on the list, Joe?"

"The closest place is on Badgley Rd. The old Tri-Way Mfg. Co."

The Tri-Way Mfg. building at 837 Badgley Rd. had been abandoned so long that few people remembered what was made there. The square two-story building was used mostly by kids having laser tag and paint ball battles. SWAT even used it for training a few years back. This would have been easier to check during the day because the broken windows would have let light in. Our flashlights would have to do.

The open front door invited us to enter. We could hear pigeons and the ammonia smell from their guano was strong. The roof must have a leak because water was dripping from the second floor.

"I'll take the second floor," Joe said.

"Be careful, partner. Sing out if you find anything."

I checked the ground floor with my trusty rechargeable Mag-Lite. The former work areas were dusty and paint ball spattered. The break room, however, showed signs of recent use. Some of the lockers contained clothes that were not dust-covered. Whoever was using this place had been using oil lamps-- I used them too--might as well save my batteries.

I was about to check out some butcher paper which might have once held a kilo of coke when I heard a scream that froze me in my tracks and made my blood run cold.

"Jeeesuss Fuu," followed by a loud thud and then silence.

"Joe, are you OK?" Still nothing.

I ran toward the stairs and almost fell in a hole where the water had been splashing earlier. I found Joe on his back on a pile of rubble in the basement. He was unconscious, I hoped.

"Patrol 17 to Radio, Patrol 17 to Radio, Emergency!"

Radio: "Go ahead, 17."

"837 Badgely Rd. My partner's down, fell through rotting timbers. He's unresponsive. Radio, we need paramedics and heavy rescue—tell them to hurry."

Radio: "CCFD. is rolling, 17."

"Patrol 17: Tell them to bring generators and portable lights. There's no electricity here."

Radio: "We copy, 17."

"I'm going to find my way to the basement. I'll shine a light up through the hole so they can find us."

Radio: "We copy, 17."

My heart sank when I saw my partner up close. Joe was lying awkwardly on his back on a pile of debris. He was breathing but out cold. The only blood I saw was from Joe's lower left leg where a piece of rebar was sticking through. I was at a loss as to what to do except maybe pray. I didn't dare to move him for fear of making things worse.

After what seemed like an eternity, the sound of screaming sirens filled the air and soon thereafter the hose hoppers heavy rescue unit was on the scene, followed by the paramedics.

Heavy rescue set up generators and spotlights and soon were assisting the medics in extracting my partner. They cut the rebar below Joe's leg. Removing that rough piece of metal would be up to the experts at the hospital. They started an IV, and these well-trained medics were slow and methodical in stabilizing my partner.

I felt like a fifth wheel but couldn't and wouldn't leave my partner's side. As the medics were removing Joe, he started to wake up, moaning at first and then screaming from the pain and was probably scared because he couldn't move. Joe was tightly secured to a backboard and was hoisted off the debris and out of the basement.

When I got to the surface, I saw what appeared to be every cop in the city standing vigil with grim faces. Sgt. Atrick took my cruiser keys and tossed them to another unit's shotgun rider. She would bring my ride to the hospital.

As I got into the ambulance with my partner, he groaned. "Did you get the number of the truck that hit me?" I thought he was delirious until his eyes met mine and he smiled weakly. "How bad is it, Griff?" I squeezed Joe's hand and told him, "It probably isn't as bad as it looks, but I think the puppy tattoo on your leg may be history."

As one of the firemen put an oxygen mask on Joe, I said, "Some people will do anything for a medal." Through the mask I heard a muffled, "Don't—it hurts to laugh."

At the hospital, there were more officers including the Chief. Joe's wife was also there with the department's chaplain. She ran toward me when I stepped out of the E.R. Bev Beveltnik hugged my dust-covered uniform and said, "Griff, don't let him die, don't let him die." I told her he was tough and would be OK, but she'd have to be strong for him. I tried to keep her calm, after all she was carrying their first baby Beveltnik.

An exhausting two hours later, I again exited the Emergency Room. I'd been keeping a vigil outside of the trauma suite. Sgt. Atrick was speaking to Chief Riley who was saying, "Sergeant, if you're Jerry Atrick, why do people keep calling me the old man?" The Sergeant just rolled his eyes and lamely said, "Good one, Chief."

Sarge turned his attention to me and asked, "How's he doing, Zoo?"

"He's a tough kid, Boss. He's got some internal injuries, back problems, and a punctured calf but the prognosis is good. He'll need months of recuperation and rehabilitation, but should eventually be as good as new. I'm worried about Bev though. She's in there now talking with the doctors. You know that she's pregnant."

"She won't want for anything. My wife's on the Ladies Auxiliary and she'll make sure that Bev is well taken care of.

"Here's your keys, Zoomer. Your cruiser's parked around the corner. Put Joe's equipment and cut up shirt on the desk in my office and lock the door. Hey, what's that?" He pointed to a hole in the back of Joe's ballistic vest. "Rebar—without this vest he wouldn't have had a chance."

Sarge said I should take some time off—on him. He knew I'd practically be living at the hospital anyway.

After a week off and with assurances that, with time and rehabilitation, my best friend would definitely make a full recovery, I returned to work. After my first roll call back, Sarge sat me down in his office. "Zoo, you know we're short handed and I won't be able to give you a partner until the next academy class graduates in a few weeks."

I had been a field training officer before but did not think that this would be the right time for me to introduce a new kid to the mean streets. The Sergeant read the expression on my face and held up his hand to stop me from speaking.

"Before you say anything, hear me out. You're the 'mayor' of your sector and you're tough enough to go it alone. I've spoken to the Homicide dicks and frankly, their case on this Big Bernie Bagwell homicide is going cold. We think you should work the case from this end as vigorously as you can, between runs of course, and see if you can shake loose some clues."

I was surprised but relieved. I had no intention of not pursuing leads anyway. I owed it to my partner to press on.

"I've advised radio to keep you off the domestic and other two-officer runs, if there is a two-officer unit available. Any questions?"

"No questions, but I will probably show up on those two-man runs anyway. Nobody knows the people in my sector better than I do."

Sergeant Atrick just smiled and said, "Get out of here."

I paused at the door and said "The victim's name was Big Benny Bigwell, not that you need to be corrected, and put down those paperclips—I'm tired of people throwing things at me."

CHAPTER FOUR

It has been almost four years since I last worked alone; no one to watch my back and to laugh at my lame, twisted humor. Joe is a good cop and a good audience. I picked up where Joe and I had left off. I wanted to have another look at the Tri-Way Building where Joe had gotten hurt. I put a second flashlight ring on my belt and carried Joe's light as well, in case mine failed.

My goal was to return to the break room. I wanted to see if there had been anymore activity there. Initially, I walked the exterior of the warehouse and found two open rear access doors. I closed the doors to within six inches and then loosely attached a piece of very thin dental floss across each opening so that I could tell at a glance if access had been gained, a trick I learned from my Field Training Officer.

Once inside, I returned to the break room where I had been looking around before my partner had crashed his own party. I was not disappointed. Things had been moved and one of the oil lamp chimneys was darker—I lit it to save batteries.

The oil lamp cast eerie shadows around the room, but the light was sufficient to see. I used a flashlight for up-close inspections in the lockers. The clothes in the two "occupied" lockers were generic—the type any street person would wear. The clothes were too neat, too fresh, too pressed to be those of a homeless person. One locker had about a three-foot stack of current yellow pages—odd! All of the other lockers contained small bits of dust-covered trash. I found no makeshift toilet facilities in or around the area, leading me to believe this was used for short-term stopovers.

After a half hour, Dispatch radioed, "Patrol 17, what is your status?"

"I'm OK, about another half hour at this location should do it; thanks for checking."

I briefly but carefully looked over the rest of the facility and got cold chills when I passed by the scene of Joe's accident. I cleared, knowing I'd be back. Something was nagging me about that break room, but I just couldn't put my finger on it.

Several more routine runs and my shift was over. If I was going to be effective and thorough, I would eventually have to be put on daylight special assignment.

Other nights revealed little and the rest of Harry the Tooth's location notes also turned out to be abandoned buildings, but they were all locked up tight. I prowled around the God's Holy Soup Kitchen but found it locked as well. I still could find no one else who would admit to making deliveries and Old Breezy was nowhere to be found.

I made two more trips back to the Tri-Way warehouse. The rear doors hadn't been used but the clothes in the locker had been changed. I was just about ready to leave when I remembered the phone books and I took a look. Bingo! I hit pay dirt on the third book down. The center had been hollowed out and there were six flex cuffs inside, just like the one found on Big Benny, and they were already fashioned into loops. I bagged one of the cuffs and took it with me. One more book had a hollowed out section that was empty. I put the books back and would check them later. It occurred to me that I might need help watching this place.

I called Narcotics and had them bring one of their sniffer dogs to the warehouse. There was no reaction to drugs or drug residue; maybe we were wrong about drugs in the packages.

Sergeant Atrick gave me permission to work daylight special but only in uniform and in a marked car, and I was to respond as back-up on runs if needed. I reported to daylight Sgt. Nobles. He wasn't too keen about having one of his cars tied up, especially if I wasn't going to take my share of paper runs. Oh well, he'd get over it.

I checked out the God's Holy Mission Soup Kitchen, mingled with the poor and downtrodden and spoke briefly to them as I eyeballed the interior. Most of the homeless were cordial yet dressed shabbily—not dressed in clothes like I found in the factory locker. Harry the Tooth (now Teeth) said he hadn't been contacted by anyone else for deliveries and he hadn't seen Breezy either. What was I doing wrong? What was I missing?!

The Crime Lab said that my only strong clue, the flex cuffs, were a generic brand used by many police departments and utility crews to bundle wires. There was no DNA found on them. I checked with Homicide. They had nothing and wished me good luck.

On my first day off, I volunteered to work at the Soup Kitchen. They needed the help. Not only was this good PR for the Department, but I got to nose around a bit too.
Reverend Wagner was setting up tables when I arrived. He was glad to have some assistance. I was given an apron and a trainee's badge and I went to work.

Billy Gardner and two other soupies worked the back and the serving counter. They were preparing and serving the food. They appeared to be very experienced. Today's repast appeared to be tuna salad, either on white bread or a bed of lettuce, green beans, rice pudding with raisins and a biscuit. Green Kool-Aid was served in plastic cups.

I was dressed in jeans and a sport shirt. No one recognized me as the beat cop. I worked the front, busing tables and assisting the elderly by carrying their food to the tables. While I worked the tables, I made casual inquiries about looking for part-timework and asking about Big Benny Bigwell. I came up with no new information, but I felt good about serving my fellow man. About a hundred souls were helped today.

When the lunch was over, Rev. Wagner spoke with each of the men and women as they left. I wiped down the tables and chairs, and folded them up. Rev. Wagner thanked me for volunteering and then left for his office. In the back room, Billy and I finished up. The other two volunteers left with the lunch crowd.

While looking for more cups, I spotted a large locked metal box bolted to the shelf of one of the closed cabinets. I confronted Billy Gardner, one of the "soupies" who was working behind the counter. "What's with the locked box?" I asked. Billy shushed me and pulled me aside. "That's Rev. Wagner's secret stash," he whispered. "He keeps his petty cash in there in case somebody breaks into his office; pretty sharp, huh?" I understood the explanation of the hidden box, but I have a suspicious mind. Too bad I don't have Superman's x-ray vision. After the kitchen was cleaned up, I looked up the good Reverend. I found him in his office and knocked on the door frame.

"Come in my son, thank you for helping out. When you and your partner were here, I never thought that either of you would be back to volunteer. Couldn't you talk him into coming with you?"

"He had a bad accident, Reverend, going to be laid up for some time, he sure could use some prayers."

"Say no more, my son. I'll put him on my prayer list."

"I really enjoyed helping out. I don't know why I never thought to do it sooner." I was being genuine. "How does one go about donating financial support for the mission?"

"We get primarily cash but we take checks and credit cards too. If you don't provide all the options, then people won't donate and donations are our life's blood."

"Maybe I can give you some security advice. How do you secure your cash donations?"

"I don't; I just throw the cash in a desk drawer. If somebody needs money bad enough to steal it, he can have it." My eyebrows must have raised like John Belushi's.

“Look Officer, the homeless who come here are kind of on the honor system. Most are good people down on their luck—not common criminals. If donation money disappears, they all suffer.”

“Reverend, have any of your unfortunates come into any money recently that you know of? Maybe made a donation to your cause? Frankly, Reverend, I’m investigating a homicide in the area and money was involved.” I couldn’t have been more vague if I’d tried.

“Do you suspect one of my flock?!” he challenged indignantly.

“Why, no Rev. Wagner – should I?”

“No, no, it just sounded funny, you know?”

“You still didn’t answer me about donations from your flock.”

The Reverend sat down in his swivel chair and began to rub his right eyebrow. “To be honest, Officer, two $100 bills wound up in my desk and I don’t have a clue from whom. I just accepted it as one of God’s miracles, a gift for the Soup Kitchen. Is the money stolen?”

“I don’t know, maybe it is miracle money. By the way, who all has access to your office?”

“Just about anyone. I have an open door policy but sometimes I’m not here.” He looked like a deflated John Carradine.

“If any more ‘miracle money’ shows up or if anything seems suspicious, call me.” I gave him my phone number.

I was certainly surprised about how loosely Rev. Wagner ran his shelter and could not understand the disparity between Wagner’s cash handling ability and Billy Gardner’s explanation of the locked box. And why does the Soup Kitchen keep coming back to the center of this investigation?

I phoned the Homicide Squad to update them about the possible money connection and spoke with Lt. Barry Dingell and got what I thought was short shrift. Lt. Dingell went on and on about how busy his detectives were and actually said, “People are dying to be investigated.” Dingell said he appreciated my help with the low-priority murder investigation and to “call me if you need anything.” He hung up so fast that I was left saying goodbye to the dial tone.

I shrugged off the feeling that I was just being used and decided to redouble my efforts to solve this thing. Tomorrow I’ll toss the warehouse one more time and maybe find my missing puzzle piece.

CHAPTER FIVE

Patrol 17: "Mark me busy on an investigatory follow-up at 837 Badgely Rd."

Radio: "Negative 17, please stand by."

Radio: "Patrol 22 and Patrol 19."

"Patrol 22. Go ahead."

"Patrol 19."

Radio: "Patrol 17. Please respond with Patrol 19 and Patrol 22 to 1212 Romero St. A neighbor heard what sounded like a loud gunshot from inside that address."

"Patrol 17, let's meet up at Romero and 11th."

"Patrol 19 copy."

"Patrol 22 copy."

When both units arrived, Griff approached them.

"Either of you guys been here before?"

Both officers shook their heads no.

"1212 is the address of the Toscic residence. Leon Toscic is a 25-year-old junkie who has been in and out of psyche units and drug rehabs numerous times. Dad's in county lock-up. Mom works downtown somewhere and does what she can for Leon. Leon is suicidal and there might be guns in the house. Dad is a hunter. Be ready for anything – any questions?"

Patrol 19: "Yeah, how do you know so much about these people?"

"I've chosen to work my whole career in this area. After ten or so years, you get to know who you are dealing with."

The residence at 1212 Romero Street was a single-story, post-war house with an empty carport. Patrol 19 went to the back door. Griff and Patrol 22 cautiously approached the front door. It was standing ajar.

"Mrs. Toscic, Leon, it's the police. It's Officer Park, may we come in?" No answer. Griff called out again, "It's the police; we're coming in!" Patrol 22 advised Radio and Patrol 19 that they were going in.

Cautiously and with guns drawn, both officers entered the residence. Patrol 22 Officer, Vince Sawyer, went to the left toward the bedrooms. Griff went to the right into a living room which was sparsely furnished. On one wall was a velvet painting of Elvis and on another, Martin Luther King Jr. and John F. Kennedy. Griff proceeded toward the kitchen, dining room and basement door.

"Police officers, is anybody here?" As Griff was approaching the dining room, he heard a blood curdling scream and turned to see Vince Sawyer running for the front door with his hand over his mouth. Sawyer just made it to the front porch before he heaved his guts out. A morning's worth of breakfast and coffee went flying into the yard.

Griff backed out of the house and went to Vince's side.

"What is it, Sawyer?"

"There's blood everywhere and, and, and there's no face!" With that, Officer Sawyer barfed again.

Patrol 19 Officer, Ed Smith, came running to the front when he heard the scream and barely avoided the splash of the second spewing.

Griff eased Sawyer's weapon out of his hand and secured it back into its holster. "Smith, take care of Sawyer, I'm going back inside; apparently it's pretty bad in there.. Sawyer, there's no shame in getting sick, just come back in when you're done."

Griff found the grisly sight in the back bedroom; it was about as bad as he'd ever seen. Leon Toscic had finally successfully committed suicide. As he sat in a chair, Leon had placed the butt end of a single-shot 10 gauge goose gun between his feet and the end of the barrel under his chin. When Leon pulled the trigger, he had indeed blown his face off. Flesh, blood and brain matter splattered the walls and ceiling. More blood than one would imagine being in a body was pooling on the floor.

Although feeling a little queasy, Griff held it together. This is one part of police work that the public never sees. At best, the 11:00 news will show a body bag being carried out – the news, sanitized for your protection.

Officer Sawyer returned, white as a sheet. "I'm sorry I made such a fool of myself. I've never seen anything that bad before."

"Don't apologize. Seeing things like this comes with the job. You came back in, that's what counts. This is where some young officers end their careers."

Officer Smith steeled himself and came in too. Before Smith became a cop, he had worked in the morgue and had witnessed bloody and grotesque things. Officer Smith took over. He notified radio and the Homicide Detectives, and had Sawyer put up scene tape.

Homicide Detectives handle all suicides and they would call for the Crime Lab for photos and measurements and the collection of evidence. They would also notify the next of kin. They wouldn't have to handle that last task. A neighbor had called Mrs. Toscic at work and she arrived just before the Homicide dicks.

The paramedics were just pulling away when a beat-up pick-up truck slid to a stop in front of the house. Ruth Toscic ran towards her home yelling for Leon; tears streaming down her face. Griff stopped her and wrapped his arms around her.

"Let me go! Let me go! My boy, Leon, is in there!"

In a lowered voice which sounded like a cross between Billy Graham and Mr. Rogers, Griff said, "Leon's gone, you can't help him now."

"How did he…what did he do?"

"He committed suicide, used a gun."

Griff held her tighter, as she buried her face in his chest, sobbing. After a bit, she looked up. "Officer Parks, why, why, why did he do this?"

"As yet, we haven't found any note but my guess is he just gave up fighting his demons."

"Can I go to him? Can I see him?"

"Ruth, even though Leon took his own life, the place has to be treated like a crime scene, the Homicide detectives will have to handle this. You don't really want to go inside anyway."

Griff carefully measured his words. "I'm afraid you wouldn't recognize Leon. It's an ugly sight and extremely messy. Remember him the way he used to look. Leon was a good kid, he just had too many problems. He couldn't cope."

"What do I do now, Officer Parks?"

"The detectives will talk to you. They'll contact the coroner, the funeral home, and call relatives for you if you wish. They can even contact a special cleaning service which is trained to handle..uh..messy scenes. Do you have anyone you can stay with?"

Ruth Toscic slowly nodded.

"I'm truly sorry for your loss. If there's anything I can do to help, please call me. Here's a card with my number on it."

As Ruth was putting the card into her pocket, Homicide detective, Phyllis Abel approached.

"Phyllis, this is Ruth Toscic, the deceased's mother. Her husband's in County lock up. Would you try to get an early release for him?"

"I'll give it a shot – anything for you, Zoo. She's in good hands; I'll take good care of her."

"Thanks Phyllis. I see that your lieutenant is here. I'll fill him in on the rest. Hang in there, Ruth."

Mrs. Toscic just nodded; her emotional tank was nearly empty.

Lt. Dingell looked over the scene and debriefed the officer. He then took Griff aside.

"How do you do it, Zoo? Day in and day out, dealing with these people and their troubles. I left the street years ago to get away from it, but you?!

"I think it's what I do best, what I'm cut out for, Barry. No offense, but I'm just not the type to wear a suit and push papers. I like working the streets, these are my people."

"Have your people helped you find Bigwell's killer yet?"

"Not yet, Lieutenant, but I'm going to do some follow-up as soon as I clear here." When Griff left Romero St., he again marked busy at 837 Badgely Rd.

CHAPTER SIX

I thought I'd take another look at that Tri-Way break room to check for any additional activity. One more look and then I'll review my notes over some Wor su Gai at the Qua King Duck; I'm always looking for a good Wor su Gai and theirs was supposed to be decent. Veteran officers become hardened to such scenes as the Toscic suicide; it usually doesn't affect their appetite.

One of the rear doors of the warehouse had been disturbed; I entered cautiously. I was half way to the break room and skirting Joe's hole when the lights went out.

I woke up shivering cold and with a splitting headache and retched like I had food poisoning. Once the waves of nausea passed, I tried to figure out where I was. My surroundings were pitch black and smelled burnt. I reached for my flashlight but it was gone—so was my gun belt. I was disoriented in the dark, but decided if I crawled in any direction, I'd find a wall or structure. I promptly put my hand in my own vomit. Instinctively, I wiped my hand on my pants and discovered my pockets were inside out. My badge was gone too, but I was not cuffed or shot behind the ear.

Endless crawling did not help my headache but eventually, my head found something – a large tire attached to something else. I hauled myself up and then relieved myself like never before. As I stood there relieved, hungry and cold, I felt for head wounds. A large knot on the back of my head hurt like hell when I tried to clear my head. Gradually, I became accustomed to the dark and could barely make out some images.

I was standing next to a tractor and realized that the burned embers had a ham smell to them. I must be near a smokehouse. I felt around the tractor but found no flashlight or flares. Hopefully, the tractor had been pulled straight in because I was now carefully walking away from the back of it, expecting to find a door.

A wall loomed up in front of me, and I felt around for a door and found one. I shook it but it was locked. When the door moved, an alarm sounded and floodlights filled the room. Even though the bright light made my head hurt worse, I was grateful to see and gradually confirmed that I was in a large barn. I had been lucky. Many sharp and dangerous items were strewn about the floor.

An electronically-altered, disembodied voice said, "My, aren't you the resourceful one. You'll make a fine slave."

"Oh, great," I said, "demoted from civil servant to slave," not even thinking about whether or not I could be heard.

"OK, Mr. Zoo Man, here are the rules. You do as I say, and you will get to live. If you cooperate, I will eventually see that you get moved to nicer quarters. As you look around, you'll find a Porta-Potty – no more pissing on my floor! You will also find a cot and near that, a passage in the wall where meals will be served to you – bon appetite."

"Who are you? Where am I? What do you want from me?" No answer. Maybe I couldn't be heard, but I was definitely being watched.

I found the Porta-John and was surprised to find that it was clean. Likewise, the cot had fresh sheets and a folded blanket which I wrapped around myself to ward off the cold. Once I feel better, I'll check out my "prison." The warmth from the lights and the blanket must have relaxed me and I nodded off.

The disembodied voice woke me up. "Time to eat, I hope you like Chinese." I heard the outer passage door open and close and then the door on my side opened. It reminded me of the milk delivery box on the side of my Mom and Dad's old house – big enough for bottles of milk, but not big enough to crawl through.

What I found was a bowl of warmed up, canned chop suey and a spoon. "What, no Wor su Gai?" I yelled. "Where's my fortune cookie?" Either my captors couldn't hear me or they had no sense of humor – I'm guessing the latter.

Having left me alive, I figured that the food hadn't been poisoned and ate it all. The chop suey was salty and I yelled out. "How about a Diet Coke the next time?"

After I ate, I began to check out my oversized cell. The barn was about half the size of a football field with a hay loft that ran along one side. Small pens made up one end of the building. They had dirt floors just like the rest of the building. Each pen had a small door in the wall but they were secured from the outside. I saw boxes in the ceiling corners and in the hay loft and assumed that these held cameras.

What a pickle! My first attempt at solving a homicide and I become the victim of a kidnapping. I don't know what state I'm in or if anybody has even started to look for me. Too bad my partner is laid up, otherwise he'd be looking for me. That voice had called me "Zoo Man." That information wasn't in my personal effects. I guess they knew who they wanted when they grabbed me.

Griff was missed and wheels were turning.

CHAPTER SEVEN

10:43 am

Radio: "Patrol 17, what's your status? Patrol 17?" Come in, Patrol 17. Patrol 9 and Patrol 12."

Patrol 9: "Go ahead."

Patrol 12: "Go ahead."

Radio: "Both units respond to 837 Badgely Rd., the former Tri-Way Mfg Co., and check on Patrol 17. I'm not getting any response."

Patrol 12: "Radio, what was 17 dispatched on?"

Radio: "Patrol 17 was not dispatched, he was doing follow-up on an investigation he was working."

Patrol 12: "Copy."

Patrol 9: "17's unit is here. When Patrol 12 arrives, we'll check inside."

10:51 am

Patrol 12: "Patrol 9 and I will be checking inside. We'll contact you as soon as we know something."

10:55 am

Patrol 9 Officer, Cheryl Winks and Patrol 12 Officers, Russ Simington and Calvin Rich begin the search of the warehouse.

Radio: "Both units, be very careful. That's where the floor gave way under Patrol 17's partner."

Patrol 12: "We all copy."

11:18 am

After finding Officer Parks' 8-point hat but no sign of the man himself, 837 Badgely Rd. officially became a crime scene.

Responding Supervisor, Sgt. Nobles, took charge. A perimeter was established, crime scene tape was strung and a crime scene log was started.

Patrol Administrative Sgt. Gomez was alerted to establish a rotation of officers to be used as crime scene guards. Patrol Lt. Drieson was advised. The Homicide Bureau was notified because those would be the detectives who would head up the investigation. Patrol Capt. Langley advised radio dispatchers to send out a state-wide alert to other agencies. Because of the supposition of kidnapping, the FBI was notified. Eventually, Capitol City leaders and the media were informed.

Things did not go as smoothly as hoped – the City had never literally "lost" an officer and they were treading on new ground. As each hour passed, fears worsened. The only ray of hope was that with no blood and no body, Officer Park was still alive. No one gave up hope.

The clock was ticking. Everybody was looking.

The Meeting

As the search and investigation continued, the new dispatcher known on the streets as the Georgia Peach, took over the console.

"Sahgeant NoBalls, Sahgeant NoBalls, are you on thu ayr, Sahgeant NoBalls?"

"This is Sargeant Nobles, N-O-B-L-E-S, if I'm the one you're calling then I am on the air!"

With that, the mike buttons started clicking—the equivalent of a computer LOL. Whenever this city's antiquated communications technology catches up so that the mike clicks can be traced, the days of harassment will be over.

"Sahgeant N-o-b-l-e-s, suh, you are to report to Chief Riley's office ASAP.

"Sgt. Nobles, I copy."

Sgt. Nobles had never been summoned to the Chief's office before and could only surmise that this would have something to do with the missing Officer Parks.

Upon arrival at the "Ivory Tower," Sgt. Nobles was ushered to the Chief's conference room, and was surprised to see so many others there. As he looked around, he saw Police Commissioner, Wilkinson, Mayor Muldrew, Sgt. Atrick and in a wheelchair, Officer Parks' partner, Joe Beveltnik.

Also in attendance were Councilman Daniels, Councilman Strieber, and Councilwoman Clayton, State F.O.P President, Gilbert James and a stenographer. Sgt. Nobels hurriedly took a seat at the conference table.

"Glad you could make it, Sgt. Nobles," the Chief said. "We'll dispense with introductions. Those of you who don't know each other can catch up later."

Chief Riley looked haggard and worried and finally looked down at his desk as if he were trying to compose himself. "I know how quickly rumors and half truths can spread throughout the department. This is a private meeting and what is discussed here is not to leave this room. Have I made myself clear?" All around the room heads nodded.

"Months ago, Comm. Wilkinson and Mayor Muldrew came to me with a proposal which I was dead set against. The proposal was that each officer have, on his person, a GPS tracking chip."

The room started to buzz with murmurs of disbelief and mentions of invasion of privacy. Before things got out of hand, Chief Riley loudly cleared his throat and held up his hands, gesturing for everybody to settle down.

"Hear me out. The Commissioner and the Mayor tried to sell me on the fact that this was for the officers' protection. It was my contention that this type of technology was an invasion of privacy and was subject to abuse."

F.O.P Rep. James jumped up. "You can't seriously be thinking of doing such a thing. This would definitely be a matter for contract negotiations and I for one would be totally against it."

Chief Riley said, "Let me remind you that I called this meeting and your invitation to it was a courtesy. This is not a debate. Please conduct yourself with a modicum of decorum. Now, if I may be allowed to continue! The Mayor, the Commissioner and myself had many heated discussions about ethics and the good of the department. What I am about to say now may sound like a confession and will probably alter some of your thoughts about me. The very thought that GPS technology could be used to spy on my officers was quite repugnant to me. But….how can I say this? The circumstances that were presented to me allowed for a compromise."

Once again the murmuring started and there was an undercurrent of disbelief and betrayal.

Police Commissioner Wilkinson spoke. "The Mayor and I are of the belief that such a tracking device would be invaluable in case of an emergency in which an officer got separated from his partners. We convinced the Chief that experimental "chipping" should be done—isn't that so, Mayor Muldrew?"

"Yes, yes, quite so. With the Chief's utilization of an experimental plan, I would see that City Council would free up monies for other projects such as new equipment and new training aids. Chief Riley acquiesced to our idea and monies were loosened—a win-win situation."

"Just when is such an experiment supposed to begin?" Gilbert James demanded. Just as Chief Riley was about to speak, the conference room door burst open and the Chief's secretary rushed in. Chief Riley abruptly stood up and in a chastising voice said, "Helen, this is a private meeting. You were told not to disturb us!"

Helen Steiner never broke stride. She went directly to her boss, grabbed his arm and pulled him aside. "Sorry to interrupt but this can't wait. This just arrived addressed to you."

Chief Riley glared at his secretary and then at the open envelope. When he removed the letter, a small piece of metal came out too. It was Officer Parks' name plate with the pins clipped off the back. With his back to the others, he read the note.

We have your officer, he is still alive. If you want him back, it will cost you $1,000,000 in circulated, non-sequential $20 bills.

Instructions to follow.

Chief Riley apologized to his secretary and then thanked her in a voice loud enough for all to hear. With that, Ms. Steiner left the room. Chief Riley slumped back into his chair, put his right elbow on the table, and leaned his forehead into his fingertips. The seconds ticked by as the Chief gathered his thoughts. There was an eerie silence in the room. Finally, Riley looked up.

"This meeting has taken on even more relevance. What I have here is a ransom note demanding $1,000,000 for the return of Officer Park. Further details about the payment will come later."

As the attendees sat in stunned silence, the Chief said, "This apparently will give us a little wiggle room, time wise. The Commissioner, the Mayor and myself will consider this option later." Chief Riley slowly turned to Gilbert James. "Now, what was it that you were asking?"

"I just wanted to know when your experiment was set to begin."

Now composed, Chief Riley resumed the meeting. "To answer your question, Mr. James, the experiment has already begun. Since the first of the year, whenever an officer was awarded a medal or commendation, a GPS microchip was imbedded in his or her award ribbon. In the case of multiple ribbons, only one would be chipped. We worked out a set of guidelines in which the tracking chip would be tested one time after issuance and not again unless an emergency arose. We have such an emergency—the taking of Officer Park."

"I don't mean to be out of order Chief, but if you have the capability of finding my partner by using this…this…this guinea pig experiment, why haven't you done it?!" Sgt. Atrick shot his officer a look, he would speak to him later.

"Officer Beveltnik, this is why we are here. We want input from all of you as to how to ethically proceed and what disclosure, if any, should be made to the public."

The main consensus of the body at hand was that although opposed to it, the GPS tracking should commence and the public be left out of the loop. If Officer Park is rescued, it is to be reported as the action of good police work.

"Comm. Wilkinson contracted with a private company to handle the tracking. Commissioner, please take Mr. James with you, show him everything and commence the tracking. If Officer Park is located, Sgt. Atrick will lead the rescue unit. Sgt. Atrick, SWAT team members will be at your disposal."

When the meeting broke up, Chief Riley asked Atrick, Nobles and Beveltnik to remain. "Officer, I understand your outburst about using GPS to locate your partner, for that you are forgiven. I want Officer Park found safe as much as you do, and to that end we must all work together."

The Chief then proceeded to debrief Joe and the two sergeants about the nature of Officer Park's investigation. Beveltnik and Park were close partners and the Zoo Man had kept his partner in the loop about how the investigation was going.

"Gentlemen," the Chief said, "let's brainstorm this thing. Maybe we can come up with something new that's germane to the case." As the session began, Chief Riley added, "Another thing we need to consider—this may not have anything to do with his investigation….this may be personal…may be revenge. I'm going to have our crime stats analyst and I.A. back trail Park's arrests and incidents to cover the revenge angle."

Nobody ever remembered the Chief having such a hands-on approach in an investigation. The Chief had never before had a member of his "family" taken.

CHAPTER EIGHT

Griff's barn/prison was very well made and any cracks barely let in daylight. Since the floodlights first came on, they remained on and days were measured by meals. Dinner will mark three days. Three days and no more contact from the disembodied voice.

Dinner arrived through the passage with no warning. A door opened, a door closed and there was food. Yummy! A cold over-cooked meat patty, an under-cooked half ear of corn and a warm Diet Coke (maybe they can hear me). No knife and fork—wouldn't want the "guest" to hurt himself.

"The food's cold and the soda's warm, I will NOT be leaving a tip!"

"I'm glad to see you haven't lost your sense of humor," said the electronically-altered voice.

"Are you comfortable?"

"As comfortable as can be expected I guess, under the circumstances. Being kidnapped and victimized by some maniac does not make me happy!"

"Only my friends can call me a maniac, are we friends?"

"If that's what it takes to keep me alive."

"Have you figured out why you are here?"

"I don't even know where "here" is and I'm completely in the dark—so to speak."

"You are here, Mr. Zoo Man, because you kept sticking your nose into my business—you were becoming a hindrance." Before Park could respond, the voice spoke again. "My partner got greedy and was skimming from profits so I had to eliminate him. I chose a small-time thug who wouldn't be missed and nobody would bother to investigate his death. Dingell got wise early, but you wouldn't let go. What made you think you were Supercop?"

"I never thought that. Someone, apparently you, littered my area with a corpse. It wasn't low priority to me! How do you know about Homicide Lt. Dingell?" The voice ignored the question.

"You will continue to be my "guest" until such time as I decide what to do with you. Best case scenario—you smarten up, give up your obsession with this case and work for me and I will let you live."

"You might as well have said, 'I am your father, Luke, come over to the dark side with me.'"

"Let's not get cute. I'm offering you a chance to live, think it over for a while—we'll chat later."

"If you honestly want me to consider coming over to the dark side, you might want to treat me better. How about some soap and water? I'm starting to get gamey—can't hardly stand myself. And hot food would be nice and some eating utensils too." No answer from the voice. "Hey! Hey, I'm talking to you! Hello?"

The voice was gone. Griffith Park was again alone with nothing but his mind to keep him company—so many things to consider, to remember, to puzzle over.

The Voice—how does he know my nickname? How does he know about Lt. Dingell? Why does he want to recruit me? Is it my connection with the Police Department? And where the hell am I? What about the investigation I was working on? What was I missing? What kind of smuggling or transporting is the "voice" into? And who the hell is this "voice" anyway?

Is anybody trying to find me? The frustration of not knowing was getting to Griff, starting to cloud his logic, making him want to lash out. Griffith Park finally lost it and started throwing things. After about ten minutes of ranting and raging, he was exhausted and sweaty. Mind racing, Griff laid down on his cot and quickly fell asleep.

Griff woke up smelly but refreshed. When he looked around and saw the mess he had made, he was embarrassed, not because of the mess but because he had lost control. He couldn't remember a time when he had lost control, not sober anyway.

Griff had a new resolve. He had to work on the assumption that he was not going to be rescued, he would have to find his own way out.

The opening and closing of the passage door startled Park. Was it "feeding time for the Zoo?" When he opened the door, he found a basin, soap, and a pitcher of warm water. A voice behind the other door said, "Wait a minute, Zooey, I got a toothbrush and some toothpaste for you—thought you might could use it."

"Breezy, is that you? Is that you out there?"

"Yeah Zooey, sorry you got caught up in this."

Griff starting firing questions like a machine gun. "Where are we? How can I get out of here? Who's in charge? What are they up to? Can you help me? Can I count on you, Breezy?"

"Shhhhhh! Shh! I'm not sposed to be talkin' to you," Breezy whispered. "I'm stickin' my chicken neck out talkin' to you. You jes whisper, OK?"

"I'm sorry, Breeze, I got excited—where in the hell are we?"

"On a farm."

"Can you be a little more specific? Where is this farm?"

"Out in the country—not much around here."

Between clenched teeth, Griff asked, "Where in the country, Breezy? Near what town? Are we even in the same state?"

"I don't know, Zooey," Breezy whimpered. "I was pretty drunk when I was brung here. Seemed like a long drive though. I'm not allowed to leave. They say I'm a gopher."

"Who says? Who's in charge? How many are there?"

"Burt and Mattie—it's their place I think. They let me camp in the cellar. I jes do what I'm told. The boss, he shows up every coupla days—I think he's kin to Burt and Mattie. Burt calls him 'Sam."

"How'd you get roped into this?"

"I started workin' for that big guy—he paid with hunnert dollar bills—until he got dead. His boss brung me here cuz he said I got loose lips, but he still pays me though."

"Is is just the three of them?"

"Yep! Mattie won't even cook, makes me cook."

Well, that explains the food, Griff thought "Who is the boss, Breeze?"

"I don't know—some guy—he comes and goes and wears a cheap dis-guys."

"A disguise?"

"Yeah, you know, wig, beard, mushtash. He's a big guy though, big like Conan the Brabanion."

"You know, I'm a prisoner here, Breeze. Haven't Joe and I always been good to you? Can I count on your help?"

"I dunno—I don't want to get me into any trouble."

"Can you make a call for me? Is there a phone in the house?"

"Nope."

"Nope, you can't make a call or nope, there's no phone."

"No phone."

"Breeze, I've tried to open the doors, but they won't budge. What's blocking them?"

"Heavy metal bars across the door, held in place with big ass locks on each end."

"Do you know where the keys are?"

"I dunno, I guess the boss has them."

"If there's a fire, how would you get me out?"

"I dunno." Griff was getting nowhere fast.

"Who watches the cameras?"

"What cameras, Zoo?"

"They've got cameras in here, watching my every move. You must have seen a monitor or TV in there."

"Maybe it's in the Boss's locked room. He shows up every two or three days and hides out in there but he's gone now. I gotta go, Zooey, before I get in trouble."

"Nice impression of a nervous Andy Devine."

"Who, Zoo?"

"Never mind. What else can you tell me?"

"Nuttin'–I gotta git back—bye."

Great! Griff thought, a light at the end of the tunnel and the bulb is dim. One light goes out and another goes on. If Sam, the "voice" knows Burt and Mattie, why is he wearing a disguise, and why is his voice altered? Bingo! Breezy and I must know the Boss; that's why he disguises his face and his voice!

Think man, think! Who do I know that's as big as Conan the Barbarian? The only thing coming to me was my own stench. While I was washing I was still trying to think of any gigantic men that I knew, still no luck.

With some hope of having outside help, I redoubled my efforts to find a way out; hopefully the cameras were not hooked up to recorders. I had pretty thoroughly checked the main floor walls but had not as yet ventured into the hay loft. Like the rest of the barn, the flat wood ladder leading to the loft was well made and solid. The roof had vents but no readily visible means of opening, but I could reach them by piling hay bales if it came to that. The hay loft was fairly straight forward, a large rectangular platform half filled with bales of hay. The large amount of cobwebs let me know that this space hadn't seen any activity in some time. At the far end, obscured by hay bales, was an air vent about 3 feet square in size; if I can get it open I'd have a way out. The vent was bolted in place from the outside with eight nuts snugged tight to the surface. Hopefully, I can find a wrench downstairs.

The closest thing to a useful implement was a large open end wrench in the tractor box, but it was obviously too large. I looked in, on, around and under everything in the place; with all of the junk in here, I thought I would find something useful. WWMD (What Would MacGyver Do)? I lay back on the cot. Maybe I would have a revelation.

CHAPTER NINE

During Chief Riley's brainstorming session, Joe told of the list of drops that had been put together from Harry's pieces of address notes. Unfortunately, the actual notes had been thrown away. They had been typewritten and seemed insignificant at the time. Chief Riley's hand-picked task force had visited all of the drops and found them secured. The Chief took the list, excused himself and left. He returned moments later. "I think you should come with me, Joe."

In Judge Robert Climes' chamber, Chief Riley introduced Officer Joe Beveltnik and then explained to the judge about their investigation. Joe told about Big Benny's execution and the list of secured drops visited by Harry the Tooth and possibly others.

"I can see where you're going with this, Chief, you want blanket search warrants for buildings which may or may not be involved in your investigation. I'm sorry about the taking of your officer, but I can't issue search warrants just because you think they may be involved. You'll have to bring me some tangible evidence; you know that, Chief."

A dejected Joe was wheeled out of the Judge's chambers and waited as a heated discussion took place between his Chief and the Judge. About a half hour later, Judge Climes called his bailiff into his chambers. Nearly another hour passed before a smiling Chief Riley exited the Judge's chamber carrying a handful of signed search warrants.

As they headed back to police headquarters, Chief Riley said, "Joe, I'm going to have to walk lightly for a while; I called in every marker I had to get these search warrants. Bob Climes had his Jimmy Olsen type whiz kid law student bailiff draw up the search warrants before he and I signed them. The Judge really wanted his ass covered before he went out on a limb."

"It must be nice to be the Chief, to wield such power."

"Power Schmower, when you get to be Chief, you learn how to play people. I'm just a glorified paper pusher. I've got to tell you Joe, I'm sure sorry about your partner, but damn, it feels good to be a part of doing some real police work again." With a renewed confidence, the Chief said, "We'll get him back Joe, we'll get him back."

The Task Force put together the perfect search team: two SWAT officers with a battering ram, two crime scene techs, two maintenance workers to re-secure the structures, and one uniformed officer as a visible symbol of authority. Patrol 22 Officer Vince Sawyer volunteered for that assignment.

The motor pool had an old fifteen passenger van which they cleaned up for use by the search team. The van was taken to the basement of police headquarters.

When the Task Force team came down to board the van, they saw that someone had hand lettered RILEY'S RAIDERS on the side. A now smiling Task Force left headquarters to begin their series of entries.

Riley's Raiders started first with another look at the site of "Joe's Hole," this time seeking evidence of contraband smuggling, not kidnapping. The work was slow, methodical and centered mostly in the most obvious spot, the break room. The Lab techs bagged and tagged everything-- the clothes, the phone books, the flex cuffs and even the oil lamp. All the items were sent to the crime lab to check for fingerprints or trace evidence. The tables and chairs were printed on site. With help from the SWAT team officers, the lockers were moved out and the areas behind and underneath were also examined. What a find! A pocket comb, two pencil stubs, a green gem stone, 19 cents, and a four year old lottery ticket. All were tossed in a bag and sent to the lab. Also located were strands of dental floss found by the doors. Their significance, if any, would be determined later.

Each of the secured drops had at least a table and chair and two had full ashtrays. Again, the tables and chairs were printed and the ashtray contents sent to the lab for trace and DNA testing.

At one of the drops, they hit the mother lode. In the basement with blacked out windows, they found a workbench covered in a velvet-type cloth. Stored in the drawers beneath were high intensity lights, magnifying glasses, small precision tools and jewelers' loupes. Several boxes revealed jewelry settings and small pieces of soldering equipment. The Lab boys meticulously bagged and tagged everything, vacuumed the velvet cloth and printed the larger items. As at all the other sites, they also printed the door handles, door frames and any other surface which may produce usable prints.

After contacting the Task Force, it was decided that this site should be put under surveillance, even though it was obvious that it had been compromised.

It was dark as Riley's Raiders headed for headquarters. One of the maintenance workers said, "Do you think it's just a coincidence that all those places had the same types of locks?" The cops and the Lab boys all looked at him at once. "What?" he said. Tomorrow all of the secured sites would be revisited.

Two days later, Helen Steiner entered her boss's office. "An envelope just arrived for you from the ID section."

"Go ahead and open it."

"I can't, sir."

"Of course you can, just slit it open with a knife. That is one of your duties, you know."

Helen Steiner didn't move, she just audibly cleared her throat. When the Chief looked up, she placed a manila envelope on the desk in front of him. The envelope was sealed with tape and it was addressed to Chief Edmond G. Riley. The envelope had two large red stamps across the front: TOP SECRET and EYES ONLY.

"What the hell? Did they hire James Bond in the ID section? I guess this must be really private stuff."

Chief Riley opened the envelope, read the contents and reached for the departmental phone list. The call was to Capt. John D. Rockefeller's office.

"Special Weapons and Tactics, Officer Stanhope." Judy (the body) Stanhope—she could kick your ass in a heartbeat.

"Why isn't the secretary answering the phone?"

"She's out to lunch, sir!" Stanhope snapped.

"Is Moneybags in?"

"If you're referring to Capt. Rockefeller, yes sir, whom shall I say is calling?"

"Just tell him it's the 'Old Man.'"

"Which OLD MAN would that be, sir?!"

"That would be Chief Riley, OFFICER!"

"Uh yes sir, right away sir, here he is, sir."

"Chief?"

"How fast can you get to my office, say ten minutes?"

"Can do."

"Great Rocky, I'll see you in a few."

Ten minutes later, Capt. Rockefeller was in Chief Riley's office.

"What's up, Ed? Are you ready for my officers to spring Officer Park?"

"Almost Rock, but I want to ask you about one of your officers first." The two were joined by Lt. Dingell.

"What can you tell me about Officer Sam Shotz?"

"Steroid Sammy? He's not the sharpest knife in the drawer but he's strong as a bull—good man in a fight. Why?"

"I just got a message from ID. Our investigation has come up with his fingerprints in the building from where Park was taken."

"That's not surprising. We did SWAT training in that building three or four years back and he took part."

"Shotz's prints were on current phone books. How do you explain that?" With that, Lt. Dingell excused himself and rushed out of the office.

"Furthermore, A.F.I.S. identified two other sets of prints along with Shotz's. One set belonged to the late Benjamin Bigwell and another set belongs to a convicted child molester, Speigel (the Spanker) Wanker."

"There must be some explanation for Sammy's prints being there. Unfortunately I can't think of one. Ed, do you think I've got a dirty cop in my squad?"

"What do you think, Rocky?"

"I admit it doesn't look good! What do you want me to do?"

Lt. Dingell returned and Chief Riley brought him up to speed on the information about the additional fingerprints found along with Officer Shotz's prints.

"Rocky and I were about to discuss what our next step should be. Why did you rush off so fast?"

"The Shotz name rang a bell and I wanted to check something. The last name Shotz isn't too uncommon, but what would be the odds of it turning up in our investigation?"

"Don't drag this out, Barry, what have you got?"

"The guy that shot at Beveltnik and who was killed by Park? His name was Burke Shotz!"

Before Rocky or Chief Riley could say anything, Dingell said, "Wait, there's more. Chief, do you recall what Burke Shotz did for a living? Wholesale jewelry rep."

Chief Riley just looked at him with a quizzical look, it hadn't sunk in yet. "The drop on Titus Rd.? The jewelry setting set-up in the basement?"

"Damn!" Riley said.

"What?" Capt. Rockefeller asked. "What are you guys working on? How does this tie in with Park?"

Riley and Dingell filled him in on the Task Force's investigation.

"Back to the question at hand Chief, Shotz certainly looks dirty. How do you want to me handle it?"

"Let's put a tail on him and see where he goes and see if we can catch him with his hand in the cookie jar, so to speak. We'll put a couple of guys from Special Ops on him—Dingell, you coordinate with them, get the ball rolling. Start by pulling his personnel file. Wilkinson and Atrick are about to move on Parks' location, Rocky, we'll need three or four of your people on a moment's notice. Make one of them Stanhope."

CHAPTER TEN

Griff (MacGyver) Park wished he'd asked Breezy to bring him some water; he was dehydrating under the hot lights. He sipped water from the pitcher and stripped off his uniform shirt and ballistic vest in an effort to keep cool.

The plan he had come up with was admittedly pretty far-fetched but not trying anything was worse! He took the oversized wrench he'd found and took it into the hay loft. Once hidden by the hay bales, our resident MacGyver laboriously proceeded to wrap baling wire as tightly as he could around one of the nuts on the vent. The idea was to build up the size of the nut so that the big wrench would fit around it. After about three hours of hand-numbing trial and error, it was time to actually try to unscrew the nut. To Griff's surprise, the wrench fit and did not slide off. Although nearly exhausted but buoyed up by an adrenaline rush, he attempted to turn the nut. Nothing! He tried again. Pulling with all his weight and with a yell that would have made a karate master proud, Griff started to make the nut move. Slowly, by millimeters, the nut loosened and finally fell off. A jubilant Zoo Man fell backwards, exhausted and dehydrated.

It took all of the reserve in his tank just to make it to the ladder and down to the floor. Bleary-eyed, Griff staggered toward his cot. At this rate, he thought another eight days or so and I'll have that damn vent off. Desperate for liquid, Griff shakily emptied the dirty wash water from the basin and treasured every drop of it. One gut-wrenching vomit spew later, he was out like a light.

As Griff drifted in and out of consciousness, he heard pounding and crashing noises like a surf crashing against the rocks. A bedraggled and smelly Zoo Man awoke to find an oxygen mask on his face and an Amazon in a SWAT battle dress uniform watching over him.

"Sarge, he's coming around!"

Sergeant Atrick trotted over and knelt down beside the cot. "Welcome back, Zoo Man, it's all over now, you're safe."

The Corinth County Fire & Rescue paramedics allowed him to remain on the cot while an IV of saline solution coursed through his veins. Eventually Griff came around and with assistance, sat up.

"Good Old Breezy, I knew he'd come through."

"What's that?" Atrick asked.

"How did Breezy contact you? He said there was no phone here."

"I don't want to dampen your enthusiasm, but I've never heard of a Breezy. The only contact we got concerning you was a ransom note. Do you know that you're worth a million dollars?"

"You big lugs paid a ransom to get me back?"

"Not exactly. There will be plenty of time for explanations later. First, you need to get cleaned up. Can you walk?"

"I'm a little shaky, but I can manage."

"Officer Stanhope, will you assist Senor Stinky up to the farmhouse so he can get cleaned up? I went by your place, Zoo, and picked up some clothes for you.

"You didn't happen to bring some big juicy steaks did you?"

"Sorry, Zoo, we'll find something for you to eat."

When Griff and Officer Stanhope stepped out of the barn, a mighty cheer arose—then clapping and whistling.

"Damn Judy, you must really be popular!"

"Not me, that's for you; besides I only know half of those guys."

As Griff waved to his fans, he noticed Capitol City officers, sheriff's deputies, highway patrol troopers and men in FBI windbreakers. He also saw cruisers from several jurisdictions, two armored personnel carriers and a sheriff's paddy wagon which appeared to be occupied.

The farmhouse was swarming with deputies and FBI agents searching the interior. Officer Stanhope spoke, to no one in particular. "Where can Officer Park clean up?"

A deputy pointed down a hallway. "Last door on the left, the bathroom's already been searched."

Griff whispered, "Care to join me in the shower, Judy? It's been a long time since you've scrubbed my back."

"Sounds great, Zoo Man, but this isn't the time or place. Besides, you're going to need <u>all</u> of your strength—a shower isn't going to be enough."

As Griff stepped through the doorway, Judy slapped his backside. "I'll get you a change of clothes and see if I can rustle up some grubb." She blew him a kiss and closed the bathroom door. About 45 minutes later, a clean, powdered, shaved and deodorized Zoo Man exited the bathroom wearing jeans and a Superman tee shirt—Atrick's choice.

A buffet of sandwich fixings was on the kitchen table. "No steaks in the house, Zoo Man—sorry."

"That's OK Judy, I've tasted your cooking…oh no…please put that mustard down, you know I'm just kidding. Besides, mustard wouldn't go well with my outfit."

Sgt. Atrick entered as Griff was finishing his last sandwich. "I thought you would appreciate your Superman tee shirt. Besides, Batman and Spiderman were in your laundry pile."

"Thanks Boss, this is fine. Now, when are you going to tell me how you sprung me?"

"Well, we can do it here and now while the search of the grounds and barns are going on, or we can do it on the long drive home."

"Let's do it here Boss, I'll fall asleep on a long drive. How far away from Capitol City are we?"

'Halfway across the state, Zoo. Now where do you want me to start?"

"At the beginning. Can Judy stay in here and take notes for me?"

"Sure, if it's OK with Judy." She nodded.

"Well, first of all your kidnapper is one of our own, SWAT Officer Sammy Shotz. This is his cousin's farm. We're in Corinth County."

"Why did he kidnap me and what were you saying earlier about a ransom?"

"He apparently kidnapped you because you were getting too close to his illegal operation. We're still putting it together, but it seems that he was smuggling jewelry and had people resetting the gems so that they could be resold without recognition. We're not sure if the ransom note was legit or just a smoke screen."

"Who's the 'we' you're talking about? Who do you have working for you?" Sgt. Atrick and Judy Stanhope looked at each other and smiled.

"I don't want you to get a big head about this Zoo, but Chief Riley himself put a task force together and ramrodded the investigation and your release."

"I'm confused Boss, I never found out anything about jewelry smuggling, why was I such a threat?"

"We believe revenge was part of his motive. Burke Shotz, the guy you smoked, was a half-brother of Sam's. He was a jewelry rep. who was ripping off the company he worked for. Shortly after the shooting, his company inquired about missing jewels but nobody put it together back then."

"Hey, I forgot to ask, how's my partner doing?"

"Joe's doing well, in fact he was part of the Task Force. It's a good thing that you kept him up to speed on what you were doing."

"What did Sammy say when you busted him?"

"He apparently found out that we were watching him and shook the tail that Special Ops had on him. Steroid Sammy is in the wind, but we'll find him. We do have the other three players in custody though!"

"Three?"

"Right, Mattie and Burt Shotz, it's their farm, and a third man named—uh, Briesen, Geofrey Briesen. They're being held in the Corinth County Jail."

One of the lab boys interrupted. "Excuse me, Sarge, where is Park's shirt?"

"It's in the barn, on the tractor seat."

"Don't worry about my shirt, damn it, find my gun, my badge and my hat!"

"Calm down, Zoo. He's only doing his job," Judy said.

"Yeah, easy big fella," Sgt. Atrick said. "They've found your gunbelt, your whole rig, but your badge and gun are gone. Your hat was found in the Tri-Way Building."

"Why's he so interested in my shirt?"

Sgt. Atrick leaned his chair back, interlaced his fingers behind his head and said, "You are not going to believe this! You were part of a super secret experimental program put together by the Police Commissioner, the Mayor and reluctantly, Chief Riley."

"What kind of experiment?"

"You and Joe and all of the other medal winners had GPS tracking chips imbedded in your uniform award ribbons. We tracked your shirt."

"What?! Is that legal?"

"I don't know, Zoo, but that's how we found you. The other stuff was an off-shoot of the investigation you were working on." Griff sat in stunned silence.

"I know this whole affair must have been traumatic; you know you'll have to see the departmental shrink again."

"I know, I expected that. Maybe I can get him straightened out this time."

"There you go; that's the old Zoo Man we know and love."

Officer Calvin Rich stuck his head in the door. "The Feds say they're done here, we can leave any time. Glad to see you made it, Griff."

"Thanks, Cal."

"This seems to be a good place to stop for now. We'll have plenty of time to get you caught up. You can ride in my car."

"OK Boss. Can you give me a little time first? I need to try to find something in the barn. It's like a needle in a haystack though."

"Sure Zoo, take your time; I want to make sure these guys got all of the video tapes of the barn anyway. Maybe we can make a sitcom out of them. Call it 'petting zoo" or something—whaddya think?"

Griff thought it over and said, "Sarge, I think you're a sick man. I'll let you know when I go to visit the shrink. Maybe he can help you too."

The two just looked at each other over the table. It looked like a staring contest. Judy broke the silence. "Can I help you find your needle?" Griff caught the twinkle in her eye.

"OK, but you have to behave. You heard the Sarge say that the barn is being video taped."

Once in the barn, they climbed up into the hay loft and proceeded to the hidden vent area. "This is cozy," Judy said, and was halfway out of her BDUs before Griff saw that she was undressing.

"What are you doing?"

"I'm going to bring back old memories," she said.

"Not tonight, dear, I have a headache, and besides, I really do need to find something." Griff dropped down onto all fours and rooted through the three inches of strewn hay. "Aha, I found it!" He stood up, stuffed his prize into his pocket and turned around. Judy (The Body) Stanhope was standing there, hands on hips, with her pants down around her combat boots. "That frilly, pink thong is definitely NOT city issue!" Griff pulled her to him, cradled her head in the crook of his arm and kissed her longingly and lovingly.

"OK, let's go," Griff said as he squeezed her butt cheek.

"What?! What do you call that?!"

"A down payment on a deposit later. Don't forget, there are cameras here."

"All right, a down payment. But just you remember there will be penalties for an early withdrawal." They both laughed as they left the barn and headed for Sgt. Atrick's car. Judy Stanhope gave Griff a wink and then climbed into the SWAT van and headed for home.

"Let's go meet your jailers," the Sergeant said. At 2:54 pm, they pulled up in front of the Corinth County Sheriff's office.

CHAPTER ELEVEN

"Steroid" Sammy Shotz had heard that his captain had been called to the Chief's office. This was not SOP. He couldn't remember a call-up on a moment's notice. Because he was dirty, he was worried. He was extra cautious.

Sammy was seeing movement in every shadow and a tail in every car. He started to think he was losing it. The big boy was sweating profusely when he became fairly sure that the dark green Ford Vic behind him was an undercover car. He made a right turn, went two blocks and turned right again. Another two blocks and another right turn confirmed his fear; he was being followed.

Sammy Shotz was so mad that he was in the cross hairs that he struck his steering wheel with the palms of his hands. The steering wheel bent under the assault by "Steroid" Sammy. Now he was really pissed; he loved his DeVille and now it was damaged!"

One more right turn and then Shotz punched it. He lurched forward and made a quick left turn into an alley. Again he punched it, struck a few garbage cans and barely missed a dumpster as he rocketed down the alley. A few swerves in and out of various streets and alleys, and he'd lost the tail.

Special Ops officers, Hunter and Tople, were also quite angry. They were very good at tailing suspects and they had been sucked in by the series of right turns.

"What do we do now, Rick?"

"I don't know, Tope, if we can't re-engage quickly, we'll have let the Chief down. Hell, we'll have let the whole department down."

"It's a damn shame that we're down a car, we could have taken turns dropping off and re-engaging; we probably wouldn't have lost him. Maybe we should head west. That was his initial direction. Maybe we'll get lucky."

"We'd better get lucky, Tope. I don't want to face the Old Man. All right, let's rethink him; what do we know about Shotz?"

"He's girl crazy."

"Duh, he's a cop."

"He lives east of here. If he's going to try to go to his place, he would have to skirt us on side streets to double back."

"It can't hurt to check, Rick,"

Hunter pulled the Crown Vic back into traffic and headed east toward Shotz' home. As they neared his place, they drove into a cross street and eased forward just enough to see the house. Tope grabbed his 10 x 50 binoculars and swept the property. "We got lucky, I can see the ass end of the Caddy from here."

While the Special Ops guys were settling in to surveil the house, Steroid Sammy was well on his way out of town on his jet black Harley. With any luck, he would be at Burt and Mattie's by 10:00 am.

Hours later as he was about 20 miles from his cousin's farm, he came up behind a caravan of police vehicles. Sammy put his tinted face shield down and passed the caravan. With any luck, he thought, he would beat the cavalry to the farm, grab his plunder and head out on a back road.

Too late! The main body of officers was already at the farm; the caravan was backup. Shotz pulled his Hog into a stand of pine trees and pulled his Bausch & Lomb Sniperscope from his saddle bag. He sat astride his bike and watched the circus unfold. The police vehicles had started up the farm lane and had stopped before the rise in the road. The officers stealthily approached on foot, both the main barn and the farm house.

Although the assault forces' main attention seemed to be the barn, they launched their first attack on the house. Shotz saw Burt and Mattie trotted out obviously in handcuffs and his simple drunken toady being marched out with his hands in the air.
Shotz was too far away to hear conversations and he couldn't read lips. Too bad, he thought.

The next assault was on the barn. Sammy watched as bolt cutters were used on his expensive locks. A small contingent of his beloved SWAT team approached. The statuesque "Body" Stanhope was obviously with them. He was surprised that they didn't enter the barn right away but waited for an armored personnel carrier to shatter the door open. The SWAT team then scrambled through the opening. Something must be terribly wrong, he thought, as an ambulance rolled up to the barn. "I hope they didn't kill my guest," he said to himself. The SWAT guys were then joined by a uniformed sergeant and the Feds.

Other officers came and went. About an hour later, Steroid Sammy saw the Zoo Man slowly exit the barn. He was escorted by Judy Stanhope. Oh, how he had wanted her! People swarmed all over the property but concentrated mainly on the house and the barn. Sammy saw many boxes taken from the farm house and saw his video equipment loaded into a van. Oh well, he wouldn't be coming back this way any time soon.

It was about 2:30 pm when the last of the police units left the property. He waited and watched for another hour before he came out of hiding. Sammy had guessed right. He'd lost everything from the farm house. The Feds had hardly glanced into the smoke house though—this made him smile. He removed a section of the dirt floor and then the floorboards. The backpack that Sammy pulled out would sustain him for some time on his run from the law. He inspected the contents. It was all there--$80,000 in cash and several pounds of loose gem stones. The pack felt heavenly against his back as Steroid Sammy Shotz took a back road and headed for the state line.

CHAPTER TWELVE

Being out of their jurisdiction and no longer in a crisis mode, Sgt. Atrick had covered the cruiser's beacons with a black shroud bearing the words OUT OF SERVICE stenciled in white. While Sgt. Atrick's driver du jour, Officer Calvin Rich, stayed with the black and white, the Sarge and Officer Park approached the Corinth County Justice Center. The large stone building was an eclectic mix of Victorian and Plantation architecture with tall white columns across the front.

As Griff and the Sarge approached the front steps, Griff stopped, bent down and picked up a penny. As he held it up for Jerry to see, he said, "Find a penny, pick it up. All day long you'll have good luck!"

"What was that, the miser's motto?"

"It was a line from the movie, *Grease*!"

"*Grease*?!"

"Yeah, you know, when they were racing their cars for pinks."

"Pinks?"

"Pinks—ownership papers. You're not a movie person are you, Sarge?"

"Only if it's a John Wayne movie."

"All right," Griff said, and gave his Sergeant two thumbs up. "Too bad I didn't find a penny before I entered the Tri-Way Building."

Griff and Sarge climbed the marble steps and found themselves in a large foyer with an ornate information counter facing them, about twenty feet from the doorway. Since he was in uniform, Sgt. Atrick approached the counter. Griff stood back, wearing a departmental windbreaker which Sgt. Atrick had provided. Behind the counter were six work stations, but only one was occupied. The name plate on the desk read, Deputy Caroline Monk.

"Can I help you boys?"

"We're from Capitol City. The Sheriff is expecting us." Griff moved up to the counter.

"While you're signing in, I'll tell you the ground rules," she whispered. "Sheriff Tolliver has been sheriff for over thirty years and he's pretty set in his ways. He's what we call eccentric. He's got a terrible temper so please don't get him mad. My husband is a strong and fearless man, but he cowers in front of the Sheriff." Deputy Monk continued. "Don't giggle or laugh in front of him, and if he asks you if you would like to meet Sgt. Fuzzybutt, just say yes."

Before she could continue, a booming voice came over the intercom. "Are those big city boys here yet?" Deputy Monk stood at attention when she keyed the intercom. "Yes sir, they're here."

"Well, send them in, girl!"

"Yes sir!" She pushed a button and the Sheriff's door popped open. As she pointed to the door, she said, "Daddy will see you now."

As they stepped into the Sheriff's private office, Griff and Sgt. Atrick were nearly struck dumb. Across from the door was the largest and most ornate desk that either of them had ever seen. Behind the desk was the outrageous reincarnation of General George S. Patton.

Sheriff Deacon Tolliver was a huge man and just about every inch of his huge beige shirt was covered with ribbons, medals and pins; his shoulder boards each held five stars. The Sheriff was also sporting a custom ordered, one-of-a-kind badge the size of a small hubcap. Both men had to fight back laughter when the Sheriff stood up to greet them. Deacon Tolliver was actually wearing a fancy two-gun rig of matching .44 cal. pistols with pearl grips.

"Come on in, boys, and set a spell."

As they introduced themselves, the Sheriff extended a ham of a hand and shook hands with a grip that nearly broke bones. "Sit, sit!" he ordered, pointing to two oversized leather chairs.

As they were sitting, the lowly boys from the big city glanced around the room. The wall behind the Sheriff's desk was covered with a huge American flag. Almost every other bit of wall space was covered with plaques, commendations, testimonials, and photographs of the Sheriff with a myriad of dignitaries. And then came the words they had been told about. In a voice that sounded like an overgrown Slim Pickens, he asked, "Say, how'd you fellas like to meet Sgt. Fuzzybutt?" Both men nodded enthusiastically. Tolliver indicated that they should stand.

Sheriff Tolliver boomed out the order. "Sgt. Fuzzybutt, front and center!" From out of a side office, bounded the biggest, blackest, scariest Great Dane that Griff had ever seen. The dog came to an abrupt halt and sat down on his haunches, facing the visitors. "Gentlemen, this is Sgt. Fuzzybutt. Sgt. Fuzzybutt, greet our guests," Tolliver boomed.

The dog walked over to Jerry Atrick, looked him up and down, then stood on his back legs putting his front paws on the Sergeant's shoulders. After he proceeded to clean Sgt. Atrick's face with one huge lick, he did the same to Griff. The Zoo Man wished he was back in the barn.

"Looks like he likes you boys. That's a good sign I like you too."

"You're not going to lick my face, are you?"

Deacon Tolliver roared with laughter so loud that the windows shook. As he wiped tears from his eyes, he said, "You boys are OK! Now, let's get down to business."

"Dan Daniels, Capitol City's D.A. would like you to hold the prisoners here until he can drive over to interview them; we'll pay for their food and lodging of course."

"No problem, fellas. Just have your people call my people. We don't get many prisoners here; haven't yet seen a need to build a jail."

"No jail? Where are you keeping them?"

"Don't you worry, Sergeant, we don't need cells, we have rooms upstairs."

"No cells?"

"This place used to be a mansion; the owner was a crackpot, a real eccentric."

Griff and Atrick had to force back laughter when Tolliver called someone else eccentric.

"There are small rooms on the fourth floor for the men and on the fifth floor for the women; we just took the doors off is all."

"How can you hold prisoners without doors?"

"That's easy," he grinned. "Private Fuzzybutt roams the fourth floor and Cpl. Fuzzybutt works the fifth. They're not friendly like their daddy. Oh damn, I'm running late for my cooking class. We're makin' soo-flay too-day."

"We thought we could see the prisoners today."

"No problem, boys, Caroline can take you to them – gotta go now!"

Deacon Tolliver could move fast for a big man. In nothing flat, he and Sgt. Fuzzybutt were out the back door. The pride of Capitol City sat in the office giggling like school girls. Sarge and Griff composed themselves and went out to see Deputy Monk.

"Daddy's a hoot isn't he boys?"

"Oh yeah! We're going to have to leave soon and Officer Park and I would like to see the prisoners."

"OK, let's go."

"Who's going to cover for you while you're away?"

"No problem. Major Fuzzybutt, front and center." An older Great Dane crawled out from under a desk and sat down by Deputy Monk's desk. "OK, we can go now."

The three of them took a rickety cage elevator to the fifth floor. The Sheriff's daughter exited the elevator first and calmed Cpl. Fuzzybutt with a kind word and a large dog biscuit. For the first time, Griff saw one of his captors. Mattie Shotz saw the Zoo Man and promptly gave him the finger and turned her back to him.

On the fourth floor, the biscuit scene was repeated with Pvt. Fuzzybutt. Griff and the Sarge looked into the first room; Burt Shotz was sound asleep. Deputy Monk said one Geoffrey Briesen was in room number four. "Hi Zooey, sorry I couldn't help you."

"That's alright, Breezy, at least you gave me a ray of hope."

"I'm glad to see you're OK, Zooey."

"Thanks Breezy. Listen, a D.A. will be coming here to talk with you. Cooperate and I'll see what I can do for you."

"Thanks, Zooey, I won't let you down. Hey, how's what's his name, Officer Belnap?"

"Beveltnik, and he's going to be OK, Breezy, thank you for asking. I'll tell him you were worried about him."

As they were bidding goodbye to Caroline Monk, Griff spoke. "If Ole Breezy becomes a trustee, for God's sake, don't make him a cook." Shaking his head, he thought, "Geoffrey Briesen – who knew?"

When they exited the Justice Center, Sgt. Atrick noticed that Calvin Rich was slumped over the steering wheel in the black and white. He hurriedly approached the cruiser, stopped and hesitantly touched Calvin's shoulder through the open driver's window.

Calvin jumped when awakened. A startled Sergeant stumbled backwards into Griff and they both fell, landing on their butts. As they sat there in the parking lot, both men burst into uncontrolled laughter. A bewildered Calvin Rich looked at his Sergeant and the Zoo Man as they rolled around on the ground like a couple of goofy school kids. At first, he just sat there transfixed by the sight and then he looked around to see if anyone else was watching the embarrassing display. Apparently no one was.

As they caught their breath and started to sit up, Jerry boomed, "Get over here, Fuzzybutt," and they again burst into loud, uncontrolled laughter. Their laughter was infectious and Calvin started laughing with them and at them. After a period of time, the two stooges were able to compose themselves and get in the cruiser, and then there were three.

The long drive back to Capitol City was occasionally marked by outbursts of laughter as Sgt. Atrick would tell Calvin about the one-of-a-kind Sheriff Tolliver. Griffith Park's roller coaster day caused the exhausted Zoo Man to quickly fall into a deep sleep.

During a pit stop, which Park slept through, Sgt. Atrick telephoned police headquarters. The latest information was that Steroid Sammy Shotz had been federally charged in the kidnapping of Park and that he was apparently on the lam. Local, state, and national APBs were already issued.

Also, Griff's partner, Joe, saw the mug shot of Speigel "The Spanker" Wanker and recognized him as the Reverend Wagner from the homeless shelter. The D.A. was moving toward getting a search warrant for Wagner's mission property to look for stolen jewelry, drugs and uncommonly large sums of money. Drugs had been added to sweeten the reason for the search warrant. Sgt. Atrick would inform his Zoo Man of this later. Since Griff was safe and Shotz was hiding out, debriefing could be put on hold until after Griff's well-earned days off.

CHAPTER THIRTEEN

Samuel D. Shotz was in the wind. He had made good his escape with a minimum of provisions and a maximum of booty. He had been preparing for this day for several years, starting when he first crossed the line of demarcation between good and bad. Sam headed west, his destination firmly fixed in his mind. He was, as he put it, a covert biker. His black leathers were plain, no colors or gang affiliations showing. Likewise, he wore no police-type gear, ball cap, tee shirt or even a belt buckle, and he put no FOP insignia on his bike.

Sam was heading west, way west. He would have preferred to be driving his beloved Cadillac, but sacrifices had to be made. After he had backtracked to his home, he had used his Cadillac as a decoy to throw off the cops who had been tailing him. He sure was going to miss that Caddy!

At the house, he had loaded his saddle bags with all the necessities of life; his department issued .45 and Park's as well. He brought along a change of clothes, mace, and his sniper scope – he'd have no problem finding a rifle. He could also buy clothes – money was not a problem. Almost as an afterthought, he grabbed the handcuffs. He could foresee no use for them but they could always be used like brass knuckles in a fight.

Sam put the rest of his police gear in his basement home gym; he knew it would be found later. He also cut up his credit cards; he wouldn't be needing them and their use left a paper trail. He put the credit card pieces in his pocket for disposal later, put on his ballistic vest and his leathers and slipped out by a back way.

Steroid Sammy was a schemer and not as dumb as he let on. He liked the name "Steroid Sammy" but in truth, he took no drugs at all; he was a true weight lifter. People were so sure he was a doper that they couldn't believe he kept passing the department's mandatory drug and alcohol tests. They just figured he knew a way to beat the system.

It was going to be a long ride and Sammy would have plenty of time to reflect. Shotz had always been a loner. He had few friends and even fewer relatives. To his knowledge, he had only two living relatives, his cousin, Burt, who owned a once-prosperous pig farm and a half brother named Burke.

Burke had worked for the Topekagem Company, a large jewelry and gemstone wholesaler in Topeka, Kansas. As he told it, he was highly trusted and filled his own orders from the massive walk-in storage vault. Burke Shotz worked a multi-state territory and would look up brother Sammy whenever he was in the area.

Burke always chided his brother about being a lowly police officer who could do better than making a government wage. Over a period of months, he kept telling brother Sam that he had nefarious plans that could make them both rich. Eventually Sam gave in, what could it hurt to listen?

Feeling certain that brother Sam would go for his game, he laid out his entire idea. Burke's plan was to smuggle jewelry and loose gemstones from his employer's vault and fudge the books to cover the loss. He would then bring them to Sammy. What his brother had to do was set up a way to secretly move the gems around so that no one could figure out who or what was involved. When Sam had a system in place and a location for work, he would provide discreet, almost legit jewelers to mount or remount the stones. He would provide the start-up money and split the profit with his half brother after he resold the altered goods. Burke could almost see the dollar signs in Sam's eyes. A partnership was formed.

Things had been going well enough until Sammy's nemesis, Griffith Park, stumbled into the situation. Not only did he kill Burke when the big dummy panicked and started throwing shots, but he was also a major snoop after Sam eliminated B. B. Bigwell.

Even in crime, Sam had a modicum of ethics. He had tried to eliminate "goody two shoes" Park without killing a fellow officer, but things fell apart. Now that he had completely crossed the line, Shotz, the criminal, had to burn his bridges and hide out. Sam knew where to go to hide.

Sam continued his trek west. He had ridden motorcycles since he was a child and loved them. His Cadillac had been his pride and joy but it never fit in with his alter ego lifestyle. Steroid Sammy Shotz was an outlaw biker at heart.

At home, Sam was a loner and no one wondered or cared what he did on his vacations. Every year, during Bike Week at Sturgis, South Dakota, he was just one of the boys. He rubbed elbows with the famous and the infamous. He'd even met Peter Fonda and Jay Leno on his trips to Sturgis. He also made the acquaintance of bikers with shady skills that he was going to need to establish a new identity.

Long before brother Burke changed his life, Sam was preparing for his eventual retirement. To that end, he had purchased a small ranch-style house outside of Deadwood, South Dakota. He had stocked the house with provisions; it had been his base of operations when on vacations and would now serve as his retirement home. Sam was headed west, way west. Big changes were coming.

CHAPTER FOURTEEN

Once a year, as mandated by departmental policy, each patrol sergeant is to ride one tour with each one of his officers. Patrol is the backbone of every police department and the sergeant must decide if his segment of the spine needs a chiropractic adjustment. Today it was Zoo's turn to get a Jerry Atrick check-up.

"Should I mark in service as one officer or two, Boss? Are you to be treated as a ride-along rookie or can I assume you know enough about police work to make us a two-man unit?"

Sergeant Atrick stared at the Zoo Man as he took the mike from his hand. "Patrol 17 in service, <u>two</u> officers!" There were no runs pending.

"How does it feel to be back in the saddle?"

"Feels great Sarge, this is my element, but I sure do miss my partner."

"He'll be fully recovered, eventually and then he'll be right back in this passenger seat."

"Oh no, Boss, he is my driver. Longevity has its privilege. Joe is one savvy partner and we sure do work well together."

"Don't worry, Zoo, I'm not going to split you up; by the way, he feels the same about you. You've had quite a year, Zoo. You guys survived that cruiser crash last spring when the drunk driver plowed into you, and of course, there's your famous shooting. Then you lost your partner to that freak accident and you got yourself kidnapped; you've had a full year. Most officers don't see that much action in their whole career and that's just one year. You have so much fruit salad on your shirt, you're starting to look like Sheriff Tolliver."

"Then you can be my Sgt. Fuzzybutt, Boss." They both laughed.

"Zoo, I don't want to seem nosey, but I want to talk to you about something."

"Go ahead Sarge, shoot."

"First, an observation. You're 6 feet tall, weigh about 200 pounds, you're 40 and could pass for 30 – why hasn't some girl snapped you up yet?"

"I guess I wasn't ready to settle down."

"Griff, I think you're married to the department. Wouldn't you like to have a family, some kids, something to look forward to when you retire?"

"Are you trying to marry me off to one of your ex-wives? What's this all about?"

"I care about you, son, I just want you to be happy, that's all."

"Not to worry, Boss, if you must know, I've recently re-established an old relationship. We used to live together but we split up for some reason."

"Maybe she couldn't put up with you being a cop—some women are like that."

"Nope, that's not it; but we're back together now, so everything is cool. As a matter of fact, if things work out, I may have to get a bigger place. Living in Zoo's Zoo, a three-room apartment with bars on the windows, may not be conducive to a long-term relationship. Not to worry, Sarge, but I appreciate the concern."

"Doesn't that car look suspicious to you, driving slowly down that alley?"

"Nope. That's just the widow Sandler – 86 years old and never had an accident or a ticket. She's a bit skittish about driving in traffic so she drives the alleys, works for her. It's her own personal slow lane."

"Now, how would you know that?"

"It's my business to know; it's my beat. But you keep looking. An extra set of eyes is like gold. Don't worry, I'll find something for you to do; make you feel like a police officer again."

Jerry mashed his lips tight shut; it was less painful than biting his tongue. Zoo and the Sarge rode in silence, multi-tasking. They were watching traffic, watching the environs around them for suspicious activity and keeping track of the other units' runs that were aired on the radio.

Zoo drove eastbound on Main St. As he was about to pass Winslow Ave, he heard a speeder with its engine wide open, and he slowed down. The speeder was northbound on Winslow and almost too late saw the stop sign at Main. The driver slammed on his brakes and skidded past the stop sign. The older yellow 'Cuda with Florida plates stopped just one foot from Sgt. Atrick's door.

"Damn Zoo, he came close to killing me!"

"Boss, close only counts in…."

"I know, I know – hand grenades and horse shoes!"

While the good sergeant blustered, Griff motioned to the driver to turn right and pulled in behind. The driver was very apologetic as he handed over his license.

"Please join me in my office."

Zoo did a pat down search before allowing the violator to sit behind him in the cruiser. As he called in a wants and warrants check on Mr. "Samuel S. Shotz, male white, age 25," Sgt. Atrick sat bolt upright. While writing the citation, Zoo asked. "Do you have any relatives on the police department?"

"Not that I know of; would it help?"

"No, but your name keeps popping up in an investigation."

"My name?!"

"Yep, tell me about your relatives."

"Not much to tell really, Mom and Dad, two sisters, aunts, uncles, cousins—you know, the whole nine yards."

"You come up here from Florida to visit relatives?"

"I don't think I have any outside of Florida—I'm just passing through, trying to get to Canada."

"Why Canada?"

"Why not? I'm on vacation. Are you going to give me a ticket or what?"

"I'm citing you for the stop sign violation; you scared my sergeant out of ten years of his life, which he can't spare. Why were you going so fast anyway?"

A sheepish Sam Shotz said, "Road Nazi's, those staties gave me a ticket for speeding, that stop put me way behind schedule."

"I'm afraid you're now even further behind schedule. You might want to rethink your priorities or else this could turn into a very expensive vacation."

"Don't worry, I can afford it."

"Can you afford a periscope?"

"I guess so, why?"

"It's just a suggestion; if you're going to drive with your head up your ass, it might help you to see the road."

Before young Shotz could answer, he was hustled out of the cruiser, given his ticket and told, "Drive safe now."

Griff checked the back seat for contraband and then got in behind the wheel. He noticed that Sarge was writing in a notebook.

"Not bad, Zoo, thorough and efficient and you didn't berate that driver. I'm not sure I can endorse that periscope line, but I believe it did get his attention."

"Another Sammy Shotz, what a coincidence. Lure in another one, Boss, and I'll catch 'em."

"I'm riding as an observer, I am not bait! By the way, nice reference to the Duke, that scaring me out of ten years line, from *Big Jake*, right?"

"Damn Sarge, you're good; if things get slow, we'll have something in common to discuss—John Wayne trivia."

The next two hours were fairly uneventful; another traffic violator, some business checks and a little harassing of some hookers to get them to move along.

"I'm starting to get a tad peckish, Zoo, how about some dinner? I'll buy."

"I never did get my Wor Su Gai, how does Chinese sound?"

As they were walking into the Qua King Duck, Griff grinned and said, "Have you noticed that there are no cats in this area?"

Sergeant Atrick was sure Zoo was kidding but ordered vegetable Lo Mein just to be safe. Griff savored every bite of the delicious Wor Su Gai, while they spoke.

"I think that Steroid Sammy should be in custody before long."

"What makes you think so, Boss?"

"The Feds are going to freeze his bank account and monitor his credit cards—almost as good as GPS tracking. And speaking of travelers, I noticed that you're taking the month of August off for your vacation. You deserve a good rest, Zoo. So, what are your plans?"

"I haven't decided yet. I'm torn between going down to Florida to watch the girls on the beaches and going west to visit historic sites. Right now, I'm leaning toward the latter. I was just a little kid when my family visited Yellowstone."

"No matter which you choose, Griff, you have a great time. You've certainly earned it."

Griff smiled and wondered if Moneybags Rockefeller was aware that Judy was taking August off too.

Before they paid and left, Griff spoke briefly with Ling Po, the owner. Whatever he said made Po laugh; he also pelted Griff with a handful of fortune cookies. Back in the cruiser as the Sarge was buckling his seat belt, the owner's cat jumped on the hood, startling him.

"Guess Ling Po missed one," chuckled Griff. The cat jumped off and the boys went back to work.

CHAPTER FIFTEEN

Sammy pushed his bike hard and fast. Previous trips to Sturgis had been leisurely if not luxurious; Sam would trailer the Harley behind his beloved Caddy. He would spend a night at a motel in Rapid City and leave the DeVille and the trailer behind. Sam would then don his leathers and wheel into Sturgis as just one of the guys.

His first major stop on this trek was Davenport, Iowa where he got a room and crashed for two days of R&R. He rode out of Davenport at night when it was cooler and tooled westbound on I-80 to DesMoines. The night ride was good, it was cool and he didn't have to look at the boring Iowa landscape. Sam skirted DesMoines and took I-35 north until he got on I-90 westbound. He didn't seriously rest again until he reached Sioux Falls.

Sam got a motel room next to a 24-hour full-service gas station. He took the saddle bags into his room and the bike to the service station. While he slept, the service guys gave the bike a thorough check to make sure everything was up to snuff. He told them not to top off the tank; he would personally gas up before he left.

At 5:00 am, Sam arose, put on his leathers and proceeded to pump his own gas. When he unscrewed the cap, it revealed a 3" knife blade which protruded into the tank. The tank dagger, a product of Sturgis technology, might have aroused the suspicions of an attendant who would possibly call the law. Nothing worse than a nosy cop and he should know.

Although subtle, Sam's transformation had begun. He hadn't shaved since he started the trip and his heavy beard had already begun to mask his features. A change of clothes at his Deadwood retreat would help to make him fit in. Steroid Sammy's long-range plan would not only help him establish a new identity, but also possibly fulfill a long-time fantasy.

Part of Shotz' past, before he came to Capitol City, he was as an amateur actor. He had played a variety of roles under different stage names. Once his identity transformation was complete, he envisioned himself as one of the gunfighter street performers who entertained the tourists on the streets of Deadwood. Hide out in plain sight was his goal; maybe even be good enough to play old aces and eights himself. That long-term fantasy would start with little steps; the first step was to reach Deadwood.

Hot, sweaty and ready to crash, Sam finally reached his new digs in Deadwood. He wheeled the Harley to the back of the house and parked it under the lean-to. He didn't remember the house being as dusty as it was, but house cleaning wasn't an immediate priority; rider cleaning was.

Sam stood his 6'2" heavily muscled body under the hot shower and washed away the road dust. The shower, he thought, was symbolic -- wash away the past life and start over clean. Things were going to be OK!

A quick dust-up of the kitchen table and he sat down with a cup of coffee. He started his shopping list – driver's license, birth certificate, passport.

Sam knew just where to go. His friend from Sturgis, Cogs Gearsly's tattoo shop was here in Deadwood, and he had other skills that he didn't advertise. First thing tomorrow, look up Cogs.

Sammy Shotz was up at the crack of noon, a man of leisure can sleep in. Hoofing it into town was good exercise and helped Sam work out the kinks after his marathon bike ride. Cogs Gearsly's place, S. T. Inkers, was a hole in the wall off the main drag. Cogs was asleep in his tattoo parlor.

"Is this any way to make money, Cogs?!" Cogs nearly fell off his stool, he'd been dozing deeply. He shook his head, put on his wire rim glasses and stared at the visitor.

"Sammy? Steroid Sammy? Is that really you?"

"In the flesh, Cogs."

"Hot damn, you're the last person I expected to see; what brings you to my slice of heaven?"

"Got myself in a bit of a jam, I'm here to use your unadvertised services."

"Like I said in Sturgis, 'you need the best, I'll do the rest'."

Cogs locked the door and hung his Out to Lunch sign. With a bend and a flourish, he pointed to the back room.

"Welcome to my web, master." They sat in the back with the curtain closed. "Now, what do you need, Sam?"

"I'm going to need it all. I'm putting Steroid Sammy to rest for good and all."

"Okay, who do you want to be?"

"I don't know. I don't want a name that's too catchy and draws attention, but I don't want something that's too mundane either."

"So if I said Studs Manly, you would say…."

"NO!!!!"

Cogs and Sam put their heads together and tried out numerous names until they both agreed on one. Once the phony documents are completed, Steroid Sammy Shotz will become Jacob Newman.

"New man, that fits the bill."

"Where do you want to hail from, Jake?"

"Someplace undistinguished, like Pigsnuckle, Arkansas."

"Why Arkansas?"

"The gullibility factor. Our national embarrassment came from Arkansas and people just looked the other way. I don't want people to settle in on me, just look the other way."

"All right, you'll need a birth certificate, a driver's license, a library card plus miscellaneous IDs and membership cards. Anything else?"

"How about a passport, Cogs?"

"Can do. Sit over there and we'll take a series of photos; don't want to use the same one on each piece. Is that it?"

"How about credit cards?"

"What do you think I am, a crook? By the way, how will you be paying me?"

"Do you give a discount for cash?" Cogs ignored the question.

"How about $500 for the whole shot, tattoos are extra!"

"I'll pass on the tattoos for now; how long to do the job?"

"Gimme a couple of days."

Sam/Jake decided to take a leisurely walk around town, look it over from the prospect of a new man. He thought, "get used to it, Jake, this will be your home for a long time." As he walked, he deliberately tried to let his new persona of anonymity take over. He had enjoyed being a stand-out cop, a self-assured SWAT team leader, but now he must learn to be the background.

The new Jake stepped out of the drug store and was brushed by a man going in. With cat-like reflexes, Sam's arm shot out and he grabbed the man by the throat. People stopped to watch. Damn! Sam quickly released his grip and shrank his full erect stature into a less imposing figure.

"Sorry, Sir, I didn't mean you any harm, I was day-dreaming and you caught me by surprise." Sam, now Jake, brushed the man off and patted him on the back. "Sorry about that."

The man blustered and squeaked, "That's OK, I wasn't paying attention, my fault, my fault.." With that, the man hustled into the drug store without a backward glance. Damn! What a way to blend in. Anonymity is hard! Jake sat down at an outside restaurant table, stretched his legs and thought about ways to become less jumpy. "Coffee, black," he said to the approaching waitress.

CHAPTER SIXTEEN

The phone rang four times before Joe picked up. "Beveltnik's," he answered.

"That's an impressive way to answer the phone, whatever happened to good old hello?"

"You don't like that Zoo? I'm trying to sound more family like, what with the baby and all."

"How are Bev and Baby Beveltnik?"

"They're both doing great. Bev's in the back changing Junior's diaper as we speak."

"Out back? Is she hosing him off?"

"In the back bedroom, Zoo, in the nursery."

"Oh, right. So how are you doing Joe?"

"Better, the doctor says at least two more months. The darndest thing though, my back starts to hurt every time Junior needs to be changed."

"I think I'll tell your pretty little wife that you're a scam artist."

"You do that and I'll rename him from Joseph Park Beveltnik to Joseph Wayne, Jr."

"OK, I won't tell; I like the thought that there is a Zoo II running about."

"How are your vacation plans coming along?"

"That's why I called, Joe. Do you still have that tow-along camping trailer?"

"Sure do. What with the new baby, we won't be needing it for quite a while; would you like to borrow it?"

"I'd appreciate it. We'd have a little more privacy than in a tent."

"We? I'm not well enough to travel yet, but I appreciate the invitation." Joe smiled knowing his partner was on the ropes. "So, who's the lucky passenger, Zoo?"

"Just another officer, you know somebody to conversate with, to tell my jokes to."

"Who is she, Zoo, do I know her?"

"What makes you think it's a woman?"

"Because I'm the only guy that listens to you and can stand your lame jokes."

"Partner, you cut me to the quick."

"So, are you going to tell me who it is or do I have to guess?"

"For now, you'll just have to guess. My ball game's coming on, so I gotta go now. How about I stop by tomorrow to check out the trailer, we'll talk about it then."

"Okay, Zoo, what time tomorrow?"

"How does 1:00 sound? I can play with Baby Beveltnik, you can feed me lunch and then you can give me the once over about the trailer."

"Lunch, huh? I think we've got some onions and limburger cheese kicking around. Yeah, we can feed you; see you at 1:00."

I felt bad about not confiding in Joe about my travel mate, but he'll find out soon enough. I just hope he doesn't blab it all over the department. The voice from behind me asked, "Who were you talking to, Zoo?"

"My partner, Joe, he says we can use his trailer, gonna check it out tomorrow."

"Are you really going to watch a ball game, cause I had something else in mind."

When Judy comes around the end of the sofa and stands in front you—you listen! "Nice smile," I said. It was a nice smile, sweet and demure and with her batting her eyelashes seductively, it was just like a scene from a movie—a porno movie! That smile was all she was wearing. They don't call her "the body" for nothing.

Judy pulled me up off the sofa and pulled me to her. As we embraced, she whispered in my ear, "I thought we'd discuss my wardrobe for the trip."

"What you're wearing is just fine."

"Mr. Suave, always with the snappy line. I want you to give me some hands-on pointers," she said as she nibbled my ear.

"I can do that!" I said, and with that I picked her up in my arms and headed for the bedroom, penguin style, because my jeans were now down around my ankles.

"Take me like Dracula," she said in a Romanian accent as I put her on the bed.

"You want me to bite your neck?" My voice sounded like the Count from Sesame Street.

"No, impale me!"

True to her word at the barn, she indeed rekindled old memories. Five years prior, Judy and I had been very close, in fact we'd lived together. Unfortunately, we grew apart. It had taken me five years to get over losing her; now that fate reunited us, I hope I never lose her again.

"Impale me," she had said. Although unfamiliar with the term, I understood what she meant. I spent the rest of the afternoon and evening learning about other nomenclature that was foreign to me. I was a slow learner but neither of us cared.

After all of that glorious, ravenous sex, we fell asleep in each other's arms, exhausted, and slept through the night. The next morning, we shared a shower and breakfast and settled down to plan our vacation itinerary.

As we sat at my kitchen table discussing our upcoming trip west, my mind kept wandering to just one thing–mountains. Finally, I convinced Judy to at least put a top on.

We spent the rest of the morning poring over maps and brochures, planning our western getaway. We made lists of provisions and clothing needed. Being cops, we also listed the personal weapons we owned and which ones to take with us; you can never be too careful.

At noon, we hopped into Judy's pick-up truck, since it was parked next to my beater in the basement garage, and took off to visit Joe. "Judy, don't you think our provisions list seems a bit long?"

"Maybe, Zoo, we can always pare back, but let's wait and see how much room there is in Joe's camper before we finalize."

When I got into her truck, I noticed a small leather bag behind the passenger seat. My cop's curiosity wanted to know what was in it and I had just the subtle way to find out.

"What's in the leather bag, Judy?"

"Toys," she said, straight faced.

"Toys?" I asked.

"Yeah, just in case I needed them, I wanted to have them handy. You noticed that I didn't come out to the truck last night."

"Aha," I said. "I like toys, we better take that bag along on the trip." Judy's great big grin said it all.

We arrived at Hacienda Beveltnik a little before 1:00 and were met at the front door by Bev. "Good to see you Griff. Joe said you would be stopping by for lunch," she said as she gave me a hug.

"You're looking great," I said. "What's your secret?"

"Dodging B.S. from you and Joe is the only exercise I need. Griff, are you going to introduce me to your lady friend?"

"Bev, this is Judy Stanhope. Judy, Bev."

"Welcome, you two, lunch is ready. I'll just have to set another plate. Joe didn't say you were bringing someone with you." When we entered the kitchen, Joe was washing his hands and his back was to us.

"Joey, our guests are here."

Joe turned around as he was drying his hands. I'm not sure if he saw me but he sure saw Judy. "Judy," he stammered. "This is a surprise. Zoo, why didn't you tell me you were bringing Judy along?"

"I guess it slipped my mind, what with the ball game and all." Joe didn't miss the wink to Judy. Light conversation about the vacation dominated the meal. After lunch, Bev brought out Junior and introduced him to me and Judy. Little Joe was certainly impressed with Judy. Just like most males, he drooled.

The camper that Joe had was smaller than I remembered, but adequate. It had a small fridge that ran on propane and water and electricity when hooked up at a campsite. Toilet facilities would be found at the campsites or, for emergencies, a thunder jug was located under the bunk. It had a fold-up table for two with storage under the seats. There were other cabinets containing dishes and a hot plate, and a small closet for hanging clothes and of course, Joe's surprise.

"Check this out, Zoo, I put this in for security purposes." Joe lifted the false floor in the closet to reveal a locked area for storing valuables.

Judy said, "That's a perfect place to store our toys."

"Our guns, too," I said, smiling.

After receiving a basic course on how to hook up and use the various features, Judy backed her pick-up to the camper and hooked it up. When I checked the trailer plate to make sure it was current, I spotted some more of Joe's handiwork. The attached sign read, "Piece to all who enter here." I didn't know if the sign hadn't been proofread or if it was a holdover from his bachelor days.

As we were pulling out of the driveway, I rolled down my window and said, "Nice sign on the back." Joe smiled and we both winked at each other. Two days later, the trailer was packed and Judy and I took off on what seemed to be the vacation of a lifetime.

CHAPTER SEVENTEEN

I took the first turn at the wheel as we left Capitol City. It wasn't long before Judy was questioning my driving.

"Where are you going? This isn't the route we planned. Have you taken leave of your senses? What is going on?!"

"Calm down, Sweet Cheeks, we're on vacation, we're going to have fun. Just relax and enjoy the ride."

"Ride to where? This isn't what we planned!"

"Trust me, Judy dear, we're starting off with a pleasant little side jaunt, there's someone I want you to meet."

"Who?"

"It's a surprise, just relax and enjoy the scenery. In a couple of hours you'll even start to recognize some of the landscape."

Judy sat in silence and did not appear to be enjoying the ride. After some distance, she finally spoke. "This is prettier than watching from the back of the SWAT van. I saw the Corinth County Line sign – are we returning to the hay loft? I've got toys," she said gleefully.

"Cool your jets, Sparky, we don't want to expend all of our energy on the first day."

Another twenty minutes found them in the parking lot of the Corinth County Justice Center. Judy had a quizzical look. "I want you to meet someone special, he's expecting us."

"Zoo, you should have told me sooner. I'm not properly dressed to meet anybody. These are casual traveling clothes."

"Judy, you look just fine, c'mon. Oh, just remember, no laughing, no giggling and watch out for Sgt. Fuzzybutt."

"What?!"

As they approached the counter, Deputy Monk spotted them. "Officer Park, good to see you again. Daddy's expecting you. Have you explained the rules to…Officer Stanhope?" She read Judy's name from the sign-in ledger.

"Briefly, on the way in."

"Good, I'll let Daddy know you're here."

As Caroline Monk spoke on the intercom, I looked for Major Fuzzybutt, but couldn't spot him. Caroline pushed the door button and the visitors went in. The flamboyantly uniformed Sheriff Tolliver rushed to meet them at the door. "Officer Zoo Man, good to see you, good to see you," he said as he pumped Griff's hand. "And who is this vision of loveliness?"

"Judy Stanhope, this is Sheriff Deacon Tolliver."

"Welcome, welcome," he said while giving Judy a much too friendly hug.

"I thought that was Sgt. Fuzzybutt's job," Griff said. Sheriff Tolliver laughed and slapped Griff on the back.

"I like you, boy. You two have a seat. I was pleasantly surprised when you called."

"We're starting off on vacation and I wanted Judy to meet a true legend, over thirty years as Sheriff."

"Hardly a legend, boy, nobody will run against me. I keep getting re-elected by default."

"My bet is that you're such a good sheriff that people don't want to be embarrassed by losing to you," Judy said.

"Well then, that must be the case," Sheriff Tolliver blustered, "Nice of you to say so."

Griff looked around and asked, "Where is Sgt. Fuzzybutt?"

Deacon Tolliver scowled. "Sore subject. Those pin-headed, slick-sleeved excuses for County Commissioners have banned pets from government buildings."

"Pets? Aren't they employees?"

"That was my argument but they didn't buy it."

"What about the Private and the Corporal? They were jail guards!"

"I'll have the last laugh yet, kids. If I can't buy this building and run it my own way, I'll make the County build me a jail. That will cost a pretty penny."

The next hour of conversation was genuinely pleasurable and Griff saw Sheriff Tolliver in a whole new light. "If you ever want to leave the mania of the big city, I could use a good deputy. You, too, Honeybuns."

Judy glowered, but the Sheriff chuckled. "Just funnin', don't go gettin' all sour on me now, I like you."

Before they left, Deacon called his daughter in. "Caroline, honey, I want you to take some pictures of me and Officer Park, the celebrated kidnapee of Corinth County." Before the pictures were taken, Sheriff Tolliver retrieved his six-guns, which had been hanging on a coat tree and strapped them on. Many photos were taken that day of the Sheriff with Griff and Judy.

"I would be honored if you would send me some copies," Griff said. "I have a rogue's gallery of distinguished and important people and your photo would have a prominent place." With promises made to send photos, the meeting was over and the vacationing big city cops were on their way.

"Your turn to drive," Griff said as he climbed into the passenger seat.

Judy got in behind the wheel, then leaned over and lightly kissed Griff on the cheek. "Thank you, Zoo Man. Meeting Sheriff Tolliver was a pleasant surprise, too bad we couldn't have met the Fuzzybutts though." Judy checked the map, found a connector road and pulled out, ready to continue their trek west. The Zoo Man, comfortable with Judy's driving, dozed. About four hours and one pit stop later, Judy pulled into a wayside campsite. While Griff handled the water and electrical hook-ups, Judy made a light supper of cold cuts and macaroni salad, fine fare for weary travelers.

As they were preparing to turn in for the night, Griff commented, "It's starting to get chilly, I forgot to ask Joe how to heat this thing."

"Don't worry, Zoo Man, I'll keep you warm," and with that she got into the bunk and patted the space next to her. As Griff got undressed and crawled into the bed, he smiled and remembered Joe's sign, "Piece to all who enter here." "I hope I don't get too overheated," he said as he snuggled in next to his bunk mate.

The next morning, the frost caught them by surprise as they hot-footed it to the restroom and shower facilities. Back in the camper, showered and refreshed, Griff said, "Note to self, park closer to the potties."

Thirty minutes later, they were back on the road and looking for breakfast. Now everybody knows that breakfast is the most important meal of the day and who better to know this than truckers – fuel the rig and fuel the body. Several dozen big rigs at a truck stop is a glowing endorsement that the food is good and the vacationing cops stopped to eat.

Both Griff and Judy were dressed similarly in jeans and flannel shirts, but that's where the similarity ended. Judy (the Body) Stanhope can fill out a pair of jeans better than anyone in the world; if there were a prize for jeans wearing she would win hands down every time. If that wasn't enough, her almost too tight shirt was showing off her other generous assets. Every pair of eyes in the place was on her, lady truckers as well as men. Griff didn't mind the attention she was drawing. He reveled in it. After all, he was with the dream girl that they all wanted. Griff was on vacation and living the fantasy.

After a leisurely meal, Griff went to the counter to pay. The cashier just shook her head and refigured the check at half the expected amount.

"That can't be right," Griff said, "you're cheating yourself."

"No, that's right. A half dozen truckers almost got into a fight to see who would pay your lady friend's part of the check. I should have taken the money from all of them. We would have made a boatload. Too bad nobody offered to pay your half."

Note to self, Griff thought. The voluptuous Judy and I should eat only at truck stops. One meal and already we're dollars ahead. As they pulled back out onto the highway, Griff told Judy about the fiasco over her half of the check. Judy turned beet red. "Next time, wear makeup, maybe we won't have to pay at all."

Judy's punch to Griff's shoulder took him completely by surprise and was so hard that he nearly lost control of the truck. As the morning wore on, the incident had become funny to Judy and really lightened the mood.

The trip had a definite route mapped out but the itinerary was flexible. They were going to enjoy themselves just like regular tourists. If a sign post boasts the world's largest ball of string then they would look at string. Hour after hour, the same boring landscape; thank God for rest stops and gas stations.

"Maybe the landscape will be more appealing if we get off the interstate for awhile, eh Zoo?"

"Couldn't hurt, we're flexible—you're very flexible!"

"And you love every minute don't you, Zoo?"

"Amen Sister, Amen!"

At Waterloo, Iowa they exited I-20 and took lesser roads through such places as Hudson, Holland and Owasa. A wider loop was made so that they could stop at Stanhope just so Judy could have her picture taken in front of the "Entering Stanhope" sign. The back roads of Iowa were a refreshing change from the Interstate but time was lost. At Fort Dodge, they picked up I-169 and headed for an overnight stay at a park outside of Algona.

Too weary to travel any longer, Griff crawled into the bunk to sleep away the exhaustion. Judy brought her nakedness to the bunk shortly thereafter and brought her bag of toys with her. The couple expended every last bit of energy and fell into a stupor-like sleep until past noon the next day. Griff was the first to rise thanks to nature's call. He opened the camper door, squinted into the sun and tried to orient himself to the location of the restrooms some quarter of a mile away. Thank God for the thunder jug. Judy arose to what she thought was the sound of rain on the roof, but was surprised to see that the sun was shining.

The excitement-weary travelers decided that the park site was a good place to rest and recuperate and just relax for one day. Griff retrieved a couple of lawn chairs from the covered bed of the pick-up and then stripped off his shirt to catch some rays.

Judy (the Body) wanted to sunbathe also and exited the camper wearing the tiniest bikini Griff had ever seen. The three triangles of fabric did little to hide her modesty and news of the sight went through the camp like a wind-fanned brush fire. The steady stream of men going to and from the restroom via their campsite started to worry Judy and Griff; maybe they shouldn't drink the water.

CHAPTER EIGHTEEN

It got to be laughable watching all those men trotting by to catch a glimpse of Judy's magnificent body without being obvious. She didn't mind, she was proud of her body, and she worked hard to keep it well-toned and blemish-free. Being on vacation and not encountering anyone she would know, Judy let her hair down. It felt good not having to hide her assets behind a ballistic vest and uniform.

The show had to end sometime and Judy was starting to feel the burn. She didn't want to overdo her bronzing regimen. "I'm going in, Griff, I'm starting to cook too much."

"OK, Hon, I'll be in in a little while. I'm going to ask some of these rubber-neckers if they know of a good place to eat around here."

Judy came straight up out of the lawn chair with a painful shriek followed by one of the longest continuous strings of muffled swear words that Griff had ever heard. Judy ran into the camper and let the door slam. Rubber-neckers fled like they were under attack; Griff followed Judy. "What the hell?!"

Another round of expletives through clenched teeth followed by, "That damn chair bit me!" This was a whole new side of Judy that Griff had never seen. With tears streaming down her face, she was looking at her backside in the closet door's full-length mirror. "Look at my tush. Just look at my tush!"

Griff had looked at her perfect tush every chance he got, but this time he noticed the blood-red welt that was starting to form. "Ouch!" he said, "That's going to leave a mark!" That was the wrong thing to say.

"I work damn hard to keep this body perfect and now it's defaced! This body is a temple!"

Griff nodded in agreement, he loved worshiping at that temple. "Don't worry, Sweetie, a little make-up and no one will ever notice."

"You can't hide this with face make-up, we're going to have to find someplace that carries body make-up."

So, body make-up became a quest at each stop. At an information center just inside the South Dakota border, the information counter girl was very helpful by checking area yellow pages.

"We found it, Griff, the Thespius Theatrical Make-up and Costume Shop in Rapid City; they're only open until 5:00 pm. We'll stop there tomorrow, it's on the way."

About four hundred miles west, Jake Newman was thinking about his good luck. With the help of a very resourceful Cogs Gearsly, he was fleshing out his bogus identity. Jake knew that Cogs wouldn't be cheap so he had been surprised at reasonable. He had been happy to pay $500 for new documents. For another $500, Cogs was able to have Sam's deed pulled and replaced by one in the name of Jacob Newman. Cogs was a wizard and worth his weight in gold. He had a contact in the Hall of Records to switch the deeds and assist with changing over Sam's bike title.

Jake Newman seemed legit, Cogs Gearsly cleared $900 and Mr. Inside made a hundo – everybody won, everybody was happy and the ace in the hole hadn't needed to be played – yet.

When Sam had first heard of Cogs' unique sideline, he checked him out. Several years ago, during a meeting in Sturgis, Biker Sam lifted some of Cogs' fingerprints. Back home in Capitol City, Officer Shotz ran the prints through the computer's data bases. Lo and behold, Cogs Gearsly was a nom de plume. Cogs turned out to be a multi-state offender, mostly theft offenses but what had really jumped out was his federal conviction for forgery. His real name, or at least the one that the feds knew, was Jorge dePrada. He must have had plastic surgery too because Sam had seen no trace of Cogs in Jorge's mug shot. This information was stored away just in case Cogs decided to get greedy.

Jake, with his new South Dakota bike plate, was free to roam around without fear of being stopped by some local yokel cop with nothing better to do than stop and harass out-of-state motorists. According to his new ID, Jacob Newman was from Spencersville, Arkansas. To go with his buff physique, he claimed to have been a bouncer. Nobody messes with a bouncer.

To legitimize his standing in the community, Jake applied for several jobs with no intention of taking any, and definitely at no place that took fingerprints. He figured having applications already on file might be a hedge against financial security, if and when his cash ran low.

Jake was getting used to his new persona but still needed a confidence booster. He biked up to Spearfish and tried out for a play with the newly-formed Spearfish Players. Not many people tried out and everyone got a part. Now Jacob could reconnect with his past and hone his acting skills.

The play being planned was a non-musical version of The Wizard of Oz and because of his stature and beard, he was cast as the Wizard. Every child in the area got a part as a munchkin and were subsequently dubbed Spearfish Fry.

The play was plagued by too many young children who were easily distracted or could not take directions. The frustrated director gave up after just three weeks and cancelled the production. Jake, having had previous acting experience, benefited by the rehearsals and interaction with the other players. With confidence now renewed, he was fairly certain that, with the right costuming and make-up, he could be hired on as a Deadwood re-enactor.

On his way back from the rehearsal, Jake came around a blind curve on a rural road and almost plowed into a serious three-car crash. All of his police training kicked into gear and the once good cop administered first aid to the injured victims. Realizing that a barroom bouncer probably wouldn't have the skills of a police officer, he pared back his assistance and crudely bandaged the injured. When he was satisfied that the parties were safe, Jake took flares from a victim's trunk and put them below the blind curve. He then rode on until he found a pay phone and notified the authorities about the collision.

Jake had not identified himself at the accident scene but one of the victims had recognized him and his black bike and told the newspaper about his helpfulness. Deadwood's local paper ran the story and looked him up for a comment. With renewed assurance, Jake granted an interview but did not allow himself to be photographed. Since the opportunity had presented itself, he also spoke about his made-up background and his wish to be a street player; he figured it wouldn't hurt locally.

Having been around bikers and their jargon, he embellished his story about being a bouncer in a series of rough, biker roadhouses. He declined to name the establishments because, he said, he didn't want to give them notoriety. Getting into the part, he described how he was able to handle rowdy bikers and that he even had the opportunity to bandage stab and gunshot wounds. Jake also told the reporter that he thought he would make a good re-enactor because he had a proficiency with period firearms.

Circumstances had presented themselves for the new Jacob Newman to be introduced to the people of Deadwood. For his plan to hide in plain sight to work, he would need a little help in disguising his chiseled features. Jake decided he would need re-enactor costuming, make-up and some facial latex to form a broken or misshapen nose.

Jake checked back with the director of the ill-fated Wizard of Oz, Vance Morrison. Vance knew just the place for his needs and gave him the name of a company in Rapid City.

Griff and Judy found the South Dakota landscape more appealing than Iowa. Flat and boring was gradually replaced by rugged and exciting with obviously more opportunities to do "touristy" things. Judy was especially taken by the wildlife that roamed free. Had she not seen it with her own eyes, she would not have believed that mule deer, antelope and wild mustangs could be seen from the highway. This leg of the trip was so enjoyable that time seemed to fly by and almost before he knew it, they were in Rapid City.

The Thespius Theatrical Make-up and Costume Shop was located in a warehouse district in a more depressed area of the city. Judy was a big girl who could handle herself so Griff stayed with the truck and camper.

When the stunning Judy Stanhope walked in the front door, the clerk/cashier gave out with a low wolf whistle which alerted nearly everyone in the place to her presence. A customer in the period Western costume section looked between the shelves to see what was going on. The customer couldn't believe what he saw. There in all her voluptuous glory, was the object of his lust. Jake Newman couldn't believe that the beautiful, tough-as-nails SWAT cop had found him, or had she?! Jake ducked down and stayed very still.

Judy took her time picking out just the right shade of body make-up that would go best with her bronze tan. After she made her purchase, she lingered to look at the other fascinating items on display. As she passed the costume section, she failed to see, cowering in the shadows, the wanted felon who had fled Capitol City.

When she emerged from the shop with her prize, she stopped dead in her tracks. Parked two spaces behind the camper was a jet black Harley totally devoid of marking. Judy had only seen one bike like that and it had belonged to Steroid Sammy Shotz. She looked all around and then slowly approached the bike. It sure looked like Sammy's ride but it had a South Dakota tag. Excitedly, Judy told Griff, "I almost thought we'd found him."

"Who?"

"Steroid Sammy. He had a bike that's almost identical to the one that's parked behind us, but this one has a South Dakota plate on it."

"We're on vacation, try to stop thinking like a cop and enjoy yourself."

"You're right as usual, Zoo, it just seems so odd – that's all."

"I know how to put you back in vacation mode. Let's find a campsite and then I'll help you put on that body make-up." They both grinned broadly as they took off down the road.

Looking out of the costume shop window, Jake saw Judy checking out his bike. When she walked away, she went to a pick-up and spoke with the driver. There, behind the wheel was Jacob's arch enemy, The Zoo Man!

Why were they here? Things were happening too fast. He would do anything he had to in order to stay free. After the pick-up and camper left the parking lot, Jake exited and saw that they were heading in the direction of Deadwood. Jake thought, if they're here for me, I won't go back and I won't be taken alive!

CHAPTER NINETEEN

In just a matter of minutes, the new Jacob Newman's world had been turned upside down. He had been so intent on establishing his new identity, he almost lost sight of why he needed to do so. He was a felon, he was a killer, and he was on the run.

He thought, "Is this the beginning of the end? Not hardly! I'm Steroid Sammy, I can outthink those rubes, they'll never take me! I'll bury them!" He had worked himself into such a rage that he now had tunnel vision. Follow! Find! Kill! He was going to end this now!! Sammy was starting to fall apart.

He fired up his ride and flew out of the parking lot in an effort to catch up with his enemies. Due to his self-induced tunnel vision, he never saw the police car and rode right into its path. The local officers' quick reflexes and disc brakes saved both of their lives. The black Rapid City police officer exited his cruiser with fire in his eyes. He quickly strode up to the bike and demanded, "What the hell are you doing, trying to get us both killed?!"

Jake stammered, "Calm down, Brother!"

"What kind of racist remark was that? I am <u>not</u> your brother! Let me see your license and registration."

After Jake handed over his license, he let his left hand slowly fall to the flap of his saddle bag. When he put his hand in, the officer quickly stepped back and drew down on him. "Freeze! Now slowly bring that hand out here where I can see it!" Jake slowly brought his hand out. Between his thumb and forefinger, he held a badge case by one corner. "Before you do anything rash, maybe you should look at this." He opened the case and showed the officer Griff's badge and his Cogs Gearsly-created Capitol City ID card. "This is what I meant when I called you Brother, no offense meant."

The officer studied the driver's license, registration, badge and ID. "Wait here," he said as he gave back the badge case. The officer went back and sat in his cruiser.

Jake had noticed that the officer was not wearing a ballistic vest. If things go badly, he thought, I'll just do what I have to do. While he waited for the officer to come back, Jake straddled his bike and threw his right leg over top of the gas tank like a woman riding side saddle. The gas cap was now in the crook of Jake's knee; he unscrewed the cap and rested his hand on it.

The officer came back to the bike, he was not carrying a ticket book, but he didn't look happy. "I'm confused, Mr. Newman. You carry a local registration and an Arkansas driver's license, yet you carry a badge and ID from an agency in a different city and state. Something ain't right, something stinks, what the hell is going on?!"

"Well.......," Jake started to answer when he suddenly ducked as if a bird were swooping at his head. That made the officer turn his head to the left to look up and behind him, while he instinctively ducked also. When he ducked, Sammy grabbed the cop's shoulder to pull him down while thrusting upward with the gas cap dagger. When the two movements met, the dagger plunged into the cop's heart. With a surprised, pained expression and a loud gasp, the cop died, impaled on Sammy's dagger. Sammy looked around and saw that no one had seen the act.

Since Sammy became Jake Newman, he hadn't done much weight lifting but he was still strong as a bull. He put one arm around the dead officer's back and walked him back to the cruiser like they were side-by-side buddies. He put the officer in the passenger seat, turned off the beacons and came around to the driver's side. Sam moved the cruiser to the side of the road, made sure none of his information was written on the officer's clipboard and wiped off the steering wheel. He pulled the officer's lifeless body behind the steering wheel and propped him up. He leaned the officer's head back and tilted his cap forward to make it appear that the officer was napping. Almost as an afterthought, he took the officer's weapon and extra magazines; can't have too many weapons.

That's it, he thought, you crossed the line big time when you murdered Bigwell but with this murder, you crossed the double yellow line. Jake had lost a lot of time playing good cop, bad cop with the local yokel and he needed desperately to catch up with Stanhope and Park. He had no remorse, he was past remorse. This last act solidified his status as public enemy number one.

The only two people who could put him away at the moment were just ahead. He rode like a madman but somehow missed them. Jake went home and tore into a bottle of bourbon while trying to clear his head and think.

Meanwhile, Griff and Judy were parked in a campsite outside of Deadwood. Even though she wouldn't need it until at least tomorrow, Judy wanted to try the body makeup and, of course, Griff was more than willing to assist. After the make-up dried, Griff suggested that they check its wearability with a little romp in the camper bed and Judy was quick to accommodate.

After their playtime romp, they decided to take a nap before checking out Deadwood at night. Griff did not have a restful sleep.

When he awoke, he found Judy sitting at the fold-up table working a crossword puzzle.

"You okay?" she asked. "You were tossing and turning like I've never seen before."

"My mind had a case of the "what ifs" and it messed with my dreams."

"A case of what?"

"The "what ifs." My mind kept asking, what if that motorcycle wasn't a coincidence, what if it was Shotz' bike with a stolen tag attached? What if Sammy Shotz is actually hiding out near here?

"Now, who's thinking like a cop?" Judy asked.

"It could happen. Stranger things have happened. I'm going armed from now on just in case."

"You're serious, aren't you?!"

"You're damned right I'm serious; I've been feeling a little naked lately anyway."

"You've been naked lately, and it had nothing to do with being armed," she said with a playful smile.

"Just in case, I'm going to carry a back-up," and with that he produced a 2-shot Derringer from their hidden trove of weapons.

"Ooh, that's scary, a .22."

"It's a .22 Magnum, thank you very much. Up close, it is scary, it sounds like a .45 and shoots a flame the size of a basketball from the barrel."

"Just be careful how you carry it, we wouldn't want you to have an accident."

"Let's go get something to eat and then check out the night life in Deadwood," Griff said as he dropped the Derringer in his right front pants pocket.

Griff unhooked the truck from the camper and they drove about a mile to a roadside café. They sat at a picnic table and ate a hearty meal of steak, potatoes, and baked beans; they both had an extra helping of beans. While Judy enjoyed a refill of iced tea, Griff went to use the pay phone.

When the operator asked if they would accept a collect call from a Mr. Zooman, Bev Beveltnik hesitated, "I don't know, he still owes us money, oh OK, but just this once."

"Real cute, Bev, when did you become a stand-up comic?"

"Since hanging around with you and Joey. How's your trip going?"

"Pretty well, once you're past Iowa. We're going into Deadwood tonight."

"Where exactly is Deadwood anyway?"

"In South Dakota, it's where Wild Bill Hickok was murdered, it was in all the papers."

"Good old Zoo, always the snappy comeback. I suppose you want to talk to Joey, he's up to his elbows in dirty diapers, I'll go take over so you guys can talk."

"Zoo, Buddy, you're a life saver. That boy's pumpin' out poo faster than I can keep up. How's the vacation going?"

"Real well, now that we've put Iowa behind us. That is one boring state! We're in South Dakota now and this is much better. What's new on the home front?"

"Not much, the gang bangers tried another little turf war but CCPD took care of it with less problem than the last time, and no casualties."

"What's the latest on Steroid Sammy?"

"Maybe he's dead, who knows?! The Feds say he dropped off the face of the earth, no bank activity, no credit card use, nothin'."

"That is weird, his name came up in a conversation, so I thought I'd ask."

"So, how are you holding up, Zoo? Has your bunkmate worn you out yet?"

"Not for lack of trying. By the way, Joe, how do you heat that camper?"

"Oops, I forgot. The heater went haywire, it's in the shop. Sorry about that. If it gets too cold, you might have to pick up some extra blankets."

"No problem, Joe, body heat's been working just fine."

"You old hound dog, you. You leave that innocent young thing alone, do you hear me?"

"Yes, Mother!"

"Oh hey, I know what I wanted to tell you, 'Back Alley Alice' died."

"Mrs. Standler? Nice old lady, how did she die, heart attack?

"Traffic accident. A packer truck backed over her, she never saw it coming."

"How ironic, her first accident was her last. I'm sorry I wasn't there to pay my respects."

"Not to worry, Bro, I sent a large basket of flowers; charged it to your account."

"Oh, thanks a heap, Joe, what would I do without you?"

"Save money?"

"No doubt! Well, Judy's waiting for me. We're going into Deadwood tonight."

"You two have fun and be careful. Tell Judy I said Hi!"

"You be careful too, Partner, give my best to the boys at the precinct and give Junior a hug for me."

When Griff returned to the table, Judy was just finishing her iced tea. "How's everything back home?"

"About the same as usual. Joe tells me the Feds are doing their usual sterling job, they can't find a trace of Shotz, no credit card use or anything."

"Don't worry, Zoo, he'll turn up sooner or later. He's cagey but he's not the sharpest knife in the drawer. He'll slip up."

"You know, dear, that denim blouse and skirt fit right in out here, kinda makes you look like Dale Evans. Yeah, it's a nice outfit all right but I bet we'll have to pay full price."

"Oh, Zoo," she said. Griff ducked the half-hearted left jab but never saw the right cross coming. He rubbed his jaw as they walked out of the restaurant.

"You know, Judy, you'll have to kiss this and make it better . . . . .all night long." The happy couple jumped in her pickup and headed for town. They left their truck in public parking near the CB&Q train engine house and started to walk old Main St.

There were a lot of costumed characters about, who tried to instill the Old West feel to the historic city. No sooner had they entered the street, a cowboy passed Griff and fired a gun into the air. Without thinking, Zoo took cover behind a barrel and jammed his right hand into his pants pocket. Before he could pull out the Derringer, the crowd laughed and applauded thinking he was part of the show. The cowboy patted him on the back and whispered, "Sorry about that, didn't mean to scare you, partner." With that, he strolled down the street to meet up with other re-enactors.

Judy pulled Griff over to a bench in front of one of the emporiums and sat him down. To the normal eye, the tourist was fine, but Judy knew otherwise. "Are you OK, Zoo? I've never seen you jump like that. You've been through enough firearms training scenarios. That shouldn't have shocked you. What's up?"

Griff puffed out his cheeks, exhaled loudly and allowed his heartbeat to settle down. "I don't know," he answered. "I guess it just took me by surprise."

"You're a bit too edgy right now, Zoo. How about you slip me that popgun, I'll carry it in my purse." Griff did not question the request; he just dropped his Derringer into Judy's purse; it settled in right next to her Colt 6-shot .38 detective special. A few more moments of sitting and looking at the Western ambiance and Griff's pulse rate was back to normal. The couple continued their walk down the street.

Of special interest to them, was the former site of Saloon #10. Below street level, at the back of a casino, they viewed a card game tableau at the actual spot where James Butler (Wild Bill) Hickok had been gunned down. Judy enjoyed visiting the historic spot, Zoo was sobered by it. On the way out of the casino, Griff dropped a few quarters in a one-armed bandit and won $20.00. This seemed to snap Griff out of his funk.

Back out on the street, a re-enactment of a crowd scene about the capture of Hickok's slayer was taking place. When the gun-firing players had moved on down the street, Griff suggested they go back to the camper. "Let's come back tomorrow and do the town in daylight." Judy agreed.

Daylight found the couple back on the streets of Deadwood. They enjoyed each other's company and perusing all of the shops. As soon as they entered one shop, Griff spotted a nickel on the floor in front of a 10-foot wide glass showcase, and bent down to pick it up. As soon as he did, the glass front of the case shattered and Griff jumped up, startled.

"Sweet Mother of God!" Judy said. "What did you do?"

"I didn't do anything, it just broke."

A clerk came running up. "What do you think you're doing?!" she barked.

"I didn't do anything – it just broke."

"A likely story. Who's going to pay for these damages?"

"Not me," Griff said. "I didn't break it. I just bent over to pick up this nickel, and the glass shattered."

"Then it <u>is</u> your fault!" the clerk said.

Judy stood back, embarrassed and too shocked to speak. A crowd was gathering.

"How do you figure it's my fault?!" Griff asked.

The clerk ranted, "That nickel's been there all day and no one picked it up and do you know why? Because it was tails up, that's why. Everybody knows not to pick up a coin that's tails up, it's bad luck. Bad luck for you—it's your fault."

"You've got to be kidding!" Griff stammered. "A bad luck superstition makes it my fault?!"

Judy stepped up and pulled the advancing Griffith back. "Calm down, Zoo Man."

"I am <u>not</u> going to pay for something that I didn't break."

"What we need here is a referee." Everyone turned to see who spoke and saw a large, uniformed deputy filling the doorway. "What's going on here?" the deputy queried.

The clerk launched into a tirade about the broken case, the nickel superstition theory, and a demand that Griff pay for the damages. Before the deputy could say anything, Griff spoke up. "Now listen, deputy," he looked at his name tag, "Tolliver, I didn't break that case. I don't know what made it shatter. I'm on vacation, I came in here to shop, not to destroy things."

Deputy Tolliver said, "I know Joanie here, she owns this place, but I don't know you. Let's see some ID." Now we're getting somewhere, Griff thought, as he produced his badge and ID card. "Are you the Zoo Man?" he asked.

Griff and Judy's jaws dropped simultaneously. "How would you know that deputy…Tolliver?"

"My daddy knows you. He says you're one straight-up cop. That's high praise coming from daddy."

Griff glanced behind the big deputy and saw the head of a Great Dane looking in the door. Griff was dumbfounded. "Are you Deacon Tolliver's son?"

"Yep, I'm Dean. Too much excitement back home so I came out West." To the crowd, he said, "Move along folks, just a misunderstanding here, I'll handle it. Joanie, go back to helping your customers. I'll be back with you in a little while."

As the crowd dispersed, Deputy Tolliver asked, "Do you have any enemies around here?"

"Not that we're aware of, why do you ask?"

"Unless I miss my guess," Tolliver said, "that's a bullet hole in the back of the case and I'll just bet we'll find a slug at the end of that furrow in the floor behind the counter."

The vacationing officers had been so focused on the upset clerk. They hadn't thought to examine the display case. As the deputy dug the slug out of the floor, he mused, "Probably a careless hunter, I'll check it out." While he looked out of the door toward the foothills, he asked, "Are you staying in town long?"

"Actually, Judy and I are camping but we planned on staying around here for a couple of days."

"Good, here's my card and my phone number. Call me before you leave the area. I'd like to show you some South Dakota hospitality; now excuse me."

Judy stopped Deputy Tolliver. "Uh, excuse me, we both noticed that you're wearing a mourning band on your star, did you lose a man?"

"Not us, Ms. Stanhope, Rapid City had an officer killed. Only other officers notice the black band, or care."

"How did he die?" Judy asked.

"The officer was working extra duty for some warehouse owners who were having a problem with taggers. They found him stabbed to death in his cruiser. The son of a bitch who killed him posed his body in the cruiser and took his weapon. That officer left a wife and three kids."

Judy said, "That's terrible, I hope they get the S.O.B."

"And you know what's worse, the cheap bastards who hired him tried to dicker over the price. How about the price that officer paid? I hope they sleep well at night," he sneered.

"If you have the opportunity, please give our regards to the officer's family."

"I will, Ms. Stanhope, thanks for your concern." Deputy Tolliver spoke briefly to the owner who was directing the janitor on the clean-up of the glass, and then stuck the slug in his shirt pocket, tipped his Stetson to Judy and walked out the door. When he reached the sidewalk, he said, "Come on, Recruit." The pinto pony of a Great Dane fell in beside him as he walked away.

CHAPTER TWENTY

"I don't believe it! I don't believe it!! I DO NOT BELIEVE IT!!!" The man who would be Newman spoke out loud. A lizard sunning itself on a nearby rock, cocked its head as if listening. Sam saw the movement and started speaking to the lizard. "500 yards, 500 yards! I could make that shot in my sleep. That Park must have a strong guardian angel, I've <u>never</u> seen anyone duck out of the way of a bullet before."

Sam carefully leaned his newly purchased rifle against a large rock making certain not to damage the scope. Years ago, he had spent too much money to buy the sniper scope but it was the best one on the open market. C.C.P.D. let him use it because he was so good.

He had spotted Stanhope and Park and noted that they were going from shop to shop at a leisurely pace. For a hunting party who was looking for him, they were sure acting like tourists.

An hour and a half earlier, Sam had ridden his Harley out to the foothills. He had hidden his bike behind some boulders and had climbed to his current vantage point. He had sighted in on the target area, a store doorway. It would be a tight shot, shooting between two buildings on this side of the street, but Sam knew it was a doable shot. Sam had successfully taken more difficult shots as a SWAT sniper.

The sun was almost too much for Sam and his khaki clothing was too heavy for summer, but he had endured because he was focused. He would have mere seconds to get a bead on Park when he entered the shop; one shot would take him out. If he was lucky, he might get a second shot off at the girl.

Things couldn't have gone better if they had been scripted. His prey had entered the store and stopped at the first display counter. Sam had lined up the shot, exhaled lightly, and squeezed the trigger. Then the unthinkable happened. For some unknown reason, Park suddenly bent over. That slug couldn't have missed him by more than a tenth of a second, and then all hell broke loose. People were milling about and Sam had difficulty setting up on the target for a second shot.

"Did you see that big Sheriff, the one with the big dog?" The lizard didn't answer. "He would have made a perfect target, but then cops would swarm the place. The fewer cops, the better." The lizard had had enough, it scampered down off the rock and bow-leggedly waddled away.

Sam took that as a sign that he should leave too, no use staying around in case that nosy big cop showed up. He packed up the rifle and scope in a hard case, picked up the brass bullet casing and picked his way down through the rocks to his bike. Sam slung the gun case strap over his shoulder and let it rest against his back like an idle guitar. As he motored toward his home, he passed a sheriff department's marked SUV driving out into the foothills area. The unit had a K-9 plate on the front and that big sheriff was driving.

Deputy Dean Tolliver was scanning the berm for signs of recent disturbance, and he found it. The spewed gravel indicated that a vehicle, possibly a motorcycle, had been here and had gone. He looked up at the hillside and tried to visualize where a sniper's nest might be, and saw several areas to check out. Even though he said so at Joanie's place, he knew he was not looking for a random hunter. That Zoo Park fellow had been a target, he was sure of it.

Dean Tolliver pulled the SUV onto the shoulder of the road and remotely opened the right rear window. "Okay, Recruit, let's go to work." As he watched Recruit work, he thought to himself, with a black on white, spotted Great Dane like Recruit, Anheuser-Busch could save money. They could retire their Dalmatian and one of the big Clydesdales. Tolliver chuckled at the thought of a beer wagon being pulled by Great Danes.

Recruit was working fast, sniffing the ground from place to place until he found what he was looking for, took up a position and promptly took a dump. Tolliver just leaned back against the SUV and shook his head. "Well, now that you've cleared your mind, let's go to work," and the big dog bounded up the hill. The team searched for nearly an hour before finding Sam's hiding place.

The clues were sparse but they were there. The sharp-eyed Tolliver saw where the sniper had sat with his back to a large rock facing the town and had dug his heels into the ground. He surmised that the sniper had rested his elbows on his knees and had used a sling to steady the rifle. Tolliver found no physical evidence, no cigarette butts, no food wrappers and more importantly, no expended brass. This guy must be a pro, he thought. He thoroughly picks up after himself. Before leaving, he took several photos of the site with his disposable camera.

The shot that just barely missed Park was a good shot, one that Tolliver knew he could not duplicate. When he gets back, he will book the slug into evidence. Hopefully, they'll eventually find something to match to it.

As he drove back to town, he admonished himself for not asking where Park and the girl were staying. Now that he was sure that Park had been a target, he needed to warn him. If the Sheriff would allow it, he would work solely on locating Park and the girl.

When Sam reached home, he parked his bike in the lean-to and took his rifle inside. In his bedroom, he opened his closet door, moved his hanging clothes aside and opened his hidden treasure room. Being two feet deep and five feet wide, it technically was not a room, but more of a secret place to store his weapons and valuables. Sam put the gun case on a shelf and visually took stock of his growing cache of weapons and, of course, his locked box of gems. Sam looked over the narrow shelf which held boxes of ammunition and full magazines. Below the shelf, he had installed a series of dowels, angled downward at a 45 degree angle on which he had hung handguns by the trigger guards. Sam's absconded C.C.P.D. .45 semi-auto was hanging next to Park's service weapon. Recently added to the collection was the Rapid City officer's .40 cal. Glock.

Concerned that he'd tipped his hand by missing Park, he sat down at the kitchen table to try to come up with a new scheme to murder the C.C.P.D. officers. This time, he would have to do his thinking sober. He had polished off his bourbon and had no more alcohol in the house.

Steroid Sammy had gotten a fairly good look at the couple's truck and trailer, and of course, they had state plates which would stand out to him. The new scheme that he hatched would be easy enough to pull off, if he didn't get caught. He would scour the area campsites looking for the cop's transportation. If he didn't spot the truck, he would hopefully stumble across it and follow it to the campsite.

In the wee hours of the morning, he would nick their truck's brake line so it would leak slowly. With any luck at all, those brakes would go out in a nice hilly area. "Let's see how good your guardian angel is then, Zoo Man!" Sam would need no special tools; his Barlow knife would do the job and not draw attention; he would, of course, also carry some concealed weapons, just in case.

Sam started at the campsites closer to town and worked his way outward. He was surprised at how often he saw that big dog deputy driving around. As he entered one campsite, he saw that deputy entering the office. He crossed that K.O.A. site off his list, he would check it later. His search was hit and miss and lasted two days before he gave up. He'd probably missed them. Well, back to the drawing board. He might get lucky yet.

Dean Tolliver's search was more methodical; he was checking campsite offices for the couple's registration. He hit pay dirt on his ninth stop, the Scrubby Pines campsite. The couple had pre-registered to return in three days to stay for two more nights; Tolliver would have two days to hopefully run into them and suggest to them that they arm themselves for the rest of their trip.

Two days later, Tolliver was on patrol at 1:00 pm. He was not particularly hungry but Recruit was and he let his driver know it. When the big boy speaks, Tolliver listens. It was lunch time. The K-9 unit pulled into the nearest Taco Waco and ordered a snack, four Gut Buster Burritos and a double order of frijoles. While his order was being put together, Dean got out a large bowl of healthy dog food and sat it on the picnic bench next to him. While he picked up his order, his faithful partner devoured all of the food in his bowl. When Dean sat back down and set to work on his lunch, Recruit moved to a position parallel to the bench directly behind his partner. The devilishly clever dog waited until the boss had a mouthful of food and then flicked the tip of his long tail, just barely touching Tolliver's ear. Tolliver turned to see what had redirected his attention. When he turned back, his burritos were gone, only the frijoles remained. Tolliver looked over at Recruit, who was innocently looking up at the sky with his head cocked.

"You're nothing but a vacuum cleaner in a dog suit! Am I now on a forced diet? If the refried beans is all I get to eat, you'll suffer with me. I'll just roll up the windows. Get your fuzzy butt in the car." The big dog easily jumped through the SUV's window and was sleeping contentedly by the time the deputy returned.

The K-9 crew pulled out of the Taco Waco and stopped at the first red light. Dean was pleasantly surprised when he saw Park and Stanhope cross his path, heading for Scrubby Pines. The light was just about to change when an all-black motorcycle and rider dressed all in black just made the yellow light going in the same direction as the camper. The bike looked familiar but Dean couldn't remember from where. He would think on it.

The bike entered the Scrubby Pines campground and slowed as it passed Park's parking trailer. The bike then circled on the camp road and headed for the exit.

Recruit's driver turned their unit into the entrance drive of the Scrubby Pines campground and was surprised to see the black motorcycle leaving the exit drive. "Now I remember, the morning we found the sniper's nest, we passed it when we were heading out, remember boy?"

"Woof."

"You say that about everything, don't you?"

"Woof."

As they pulled up to Lot 56, Park was just finishing hooking up the water line. Deputy Tolliver honked to get his attention.

"Dean, good to see you. Slumming?"

"No Zoo, working. Can we talk?"

"Sure, Judy will be glad to see you too."

The big deputy opened the driver's side rear window. "You stay here and guard the truck, Recruit, I'll whistle if I need you."

At the door, Griff called, "Judy, are you decent?"

"No, come on it, Stud."

"Real nice!" Griff said. "I'm serious, we have company."

"In that case, I'm still dressed, come on in."

Deputy Tolliver ducked to get into the camper door. "Glad my partner stayed outside; not much room in here."

"It is cozy," Judy trilled as Griff walked in.

"Have a seat, Dean, would you like a drink? Beer? Iced tea?"

"Nothing, thanks," he said as he eyed the two small seats at the fold-up table. "How about I just sit on the edge of that bunk?. You smaller folks will fit better at that table."

When they were all seated, Tolliver spoke in a serious tone. "I didn't want to alarm you at Joanie's shop the other day, but I had to check something out to be certain. Now, I'm certain that it wasn't a hunter's stray bullet that missed you. You were targeted. I found the shooter's hiding place."

Judy and Zoo stared at him in stunned disbelief. Griff said, "We haven't had time to make any enemies on this trip. Okay, we bad-mouthed Iowa a lot but that's not a killing offense."

"How about back home? Cops naturally make enemies. How about that fellow who kidnapped you, could he be stalking you?"

"Not hardly, he's on the run for murder and kidnapping. He wouldn't have stayed around just to stalk me. How about you, Judy, any jealous boyfriends?"

"Sure, tons. Just kidding."

"Judy was spooked the other day thinking he was around. She saw a bike similar to his."

"A bike similar to who's?"

"The bad cop who kidnapped me, Steroid Sammy Shotz."

"Judy, what kind of bike did you see?"

"It was a black Harley, no chrome, no detailing, but it couldn't be his, that one had a South Dakota plate on it."

"Did you ever see him ride it? If so, how was he dressed, denim jacket with a dragon on the back?"

“Oh, hell no, he wore black leathers and a black helmet. I figured it was a tribute to Johnny Cash, you know, the man in black?”

Deputy Tolliver said, “I’m sorry to deceive you with that denim jacket question, but I didn’t want to lead your description. My daddy taught me that ploy. Let me tell you what I know. When I was looking for the sniper’s nest, I passed a bike matching that description. Today, I saw the same bike and black-clad rider behind you as you passed through town and then he was leaving this campground as I pulled in to see you. Coincidence? What do you think?”

“I think we’ve fallen into a hornet’s nest,” Griff said.

“Oh Griff, Sammy was a sniper in SWAT, one of the best.”

“Are you two armed?”

“To the teeth, if we have to be,” Judy said.

“Arm yourselves and sit tight. I’m going to be busy, checking with my boss, the FBI, and your own department. I have to amass all we know before putting out an APB. I’m going now, but if we can get this guy, I’ll take you up on that beer.”

No sooner had Dean Tolliver left when Griff and Judy broke out their weapons. They both wore .45s and it was amazing how Judy could conceal such a big gun. Griff strapped a tactical dagger to his left ankle and then asked Judy for his Derringer. His eyes bugged out when he saw Judy’s .38 Colt come out of her purse with his .22 Magnum Derringer.

“The Tackleberry’s are ready for work,” he quipped, referencing the *Police Academy* movies.

When Tolliver returned, he had a walkie talkie for them along with an extra battery and charger. He also brought news. “Our department, in conjunction with the FBI, issued an APB for Samuel Shotz based on all of the information we patched together, but I have more.”

“Don’t keep us in suspenders, Dean, what have you got?”

“Yeah,” Judy said. “Spill it.”

“Before Officer Hairston was killed in Rapid City, he radioed in a license and registration check for a local resident, Jacob Newman. A follow-up at Newman’s home came up empty but they found the black bike. They don’t believe he’s in the house but they’re waiting for a search warrant to enter. And now for the good part, the Sheriff has assigned me and Recruit to be your personal bodyguards, in soft clothes, so you can continue your vacation, tourist style. Neat, huh?”

“Too neat, Dino, drop the other shoe.”

“The Sheriff figures that if you’re seen in public, it might draw Shotz out, what do you think?”

Griff looked at Judy and said, “So instead of being called tourists, we can now be called **bait**!” He and Judy said the last word in unison.

CHAPTER TWENTY-ONE

"Beveltniks, this is Joe."

"Joseph, how are you?"

"Uh, fine," Joe said hesitantly, "Who is this?"

"It's Ed Riley, Joseph, don't you recognize my voice?"

"Chief Riley? I'm surprised to hear from you. What can I do for you, sir?"

"I'm coming out your way in about an hour to check on one of my rental properties and I thought we might meet for coffee, if you're not busy, that is."

"I'm not busy, just surprised that you'd be calling me, that's all."

"Joseph, you were one of Riley's Raiders, why wouldn't I keep in touch? Besides, I'd really like to have a chat with you. Is there someplace you can recommend for good coffee?"

"Yes sir, a new place just opened up. It's called The Last Drop. The coffee's very good and you'll really like the barista."

"I'm a married man, Joseph."

"So am I, Chief, but everybody likes this barista."

"OK, where is it located?"

"On the corner of Race and Cain."

"How about we meet there in about an hour? I'll be in plain clothes so don't call me Chief."

"OK Chief, one hour, I'll be there."

Joe pulled into the coffee shop's parking lot just as Chief Riley arrived. Joe approached the Chief with the help of a cane and they shook hands. As they walked in the door, Ed Riley turned and whispered to Joe, "You were right about the barista." Her name tag indicated that her name was Cheri.

Chief Riley stepped up and ordered first. "I'll have some Guatamalan and espresso."

"One red-eye coming up. How about you, Joe, the usual?"

"Yes, please."

"Right," Cheri said, "one peppermint patty coming up."

"That sounds interesting, Joseph, what's in it?

"Uh, it's espresso, chocolate, peppermint and steamed milk, sir, I'm not a strong coffee person."

"You were certainly right about the barista, she really is a looker."

Cheri was a looker alright—5'7", 128 pounds, strawberry blond hair and beautifully buxom. The men flocked in for her coffee.

"Have you heard from your partner?"

"Oh yeah, collect, you know he'll never pay."

"We can take it out of his wages."

"That's OK, I was just kidding, he's good for it. He said they were in Deadwood, South Dakota."

"It hasn't made it to the media yet but there's an APB issued for Shotz, he's been spotted in Deadwood."

"That's where Zoo and Judy are, they could be in trouble. We need to warn them somehow!"

"Not to worry, Joe, they're in good hands. The sheriff out there has one of his best K-9 teams guarding them. Shotz knows they're there and has already taken a shot at Griff."

Concerned, Joe started talking a mile a minute. "We got to help him. What can we do to help him? I have to go there. My partner needs me. I need another drink." And with that, he jumped up and headed for the ordering station to order another peppermint patty.

"I'm sure glad we're not in a bar," the chief thought. When Joe returned, the Chief said, "Calm down Joseph, just calm down. Let's be rational about this. Your partner is in good hands. The Sheriff's department is looking after him. I know that this is an emotional thing for you, but you don't need to cry."

"That's not it," Joe blubbered. "The coffee's too hot, I burned my lips."

The Chief went to Cheri for some ice for Joe. "Burned his lips again, didn't he?" Cheri said.

Chief Riley and Joe parted company. The Chief went back to headquarters. Joe stayed behind to nurse his lips and watch the barista eye candy. Joe was also thinking about his partner. If Griff were here, he'd be drinking his coffee black and strong just like it's served at Ma's Diner. I wonder if he's found any really good coffee out west.

As a matter of fact, Griff had found good coffee thanks to Dean Tolliver. Dean had chosen a roadside diner as the place where they would plan their strategy over a cup of coffee.

"What do you want to do today? What would be on your agenda if you didn't have a target on your back?"

"Judy and I had hoped we could visit Mount Rushmore. We can't be this close without experiencing it. Can we do that, Dean?"

"You can do anything your heart desires, so long as you tell us in advance. Let's shoot for 2:00 pm, that will give our special task force time to set up and keep watch."

"What about you and Recruit. Where will you be?" Judy asked.

"I'm not sure yet but trust me, we'll be close by."

"There's no hiding Recruit, why don't we leave him to guard the truck and trailer so we don't pick up a spare killer while we're off trying to act normal."

"Good idea, Zoo, we can leave him in the truck with the windows down. I can put him on alert and he'll stay in there until a threat approaches or he's taken off of alert.

"I have to admit, it's a better idea than the first one I was kicking around," Dean said. "I was actually thinking about carrying a white cane and using Recruit as my guide dog."

Judy shook her head in disbelief and ordered a second cup of Earl Grey tea. "Hey Dean, if we're being used as bait, do we get compensated?"

"Good question, Judy, I'll be sure to ask the Sheriff. Maybe we can validate your parking." Dean Tolliver smiled.

"As long as I'm validated and not violated," Griff said.

"That was pretty lame, Zoo Man," Judy said as she playfully pelted him with sweetener packets. When she noticed the counter man glaring at her, she sheepishly picked up her ammo.

Dean suggested that as part of their Mt. Rushmore adventure, they should walk the Presidential Trail for a close up look at the massive mountain sculptures. "I'm sure I can get the Pennington County Sheriff's SWAT team to have snipers trained on the area, ready to take out Shotz if he shows and if he tries anything. We will also alert the National Park Service rangers and have them provided with Shotz' photo; the only problem is that officers found a new traveling theatrical make-up kit in the house. They said there were wigs, mustaches, the whole works, so there's no telling what he might look like, assuming he took some of the stuff with him.

"Did you say Pennington Co. Sheriff? What's up with that?" Zoo wanted to know.

As he signaled for another cup of coffee, Dean said, "We are coordinating but Mt. Rushmore is in their jurisdiction. They've pledged full cooperation if we come that way.

"We'll all be on high alert," Griff said, "but I hope I'm not too distracted by being bait that I can't enjoy myself. After all, I am on vacation."

"I feel the same way," Judy said. "I'm really interested in learning more about the artist, Gutzon Borglum. I think I read somewhere that he designed or worked on the Stone Mountain sculpture in Georgia too."

At the suggestion of a sheriff's aide, it was decided to lock the trailer in the impound lot, one less thing to guard and driving would be easier. By the time they had stowed their camper, it was 12:10 pm.

"Are you ready for this?" Dean asked, and was assured that they were.

"Good, turn your walkie talkie to channel 11. All of the jurisdictions in this caper will work off of there."

Griff dropped the walkie into his interior windbreaker pocket and they all mounted up. Judy drove, Zoo navigated and Recruit slept in the truck bed. Dean followed about a half mile behind. They took state Route 14A to Sturgis and backtracked on I-90 to Rapid City. From there, it was a leisurely drive down State Route 16 for about forty miles; the drive was winding and beautiful, nothing like flat and boring Iowa.

Just prior to the Keystone/Mt. Rushmore cut off, they came across a bad one-car accident in which a small sports car for some unknown reason, had crashed into a large boulder. There were no skidmarks. Zoo grabbed his walkie and alerted Dean then ran to the scene to check on the occupants.

"Too late for this old bird." Griff told Judy. "This older European sports car has no air bags, it appears that the steering wheel sheared off on impact and the driver was impaled on the steering column, what a mess."

As Dean was pulling up, Judy was yelling frantically from about 15 yards away. "There's a blood trail over here, there must have been a passenger."

The trail led into a heavily forested area in which the canopy was so dense that it shut out a lot of light. "Dean, we're probably going to need a tracking dog. Can Recruit do it?"

"Unfortunately, no. We tried to train him in tracking but he wasn't interested. The local PD is on the way. I'll radio them to see if they have a tracking K-9." Shortly, he spoke again. "The nearest unit is a K-9, I hope they can find the passenger in time. It looks like some significant blood loss."

Griff said, "Dean, where did you find a Hawaiian shirt big enough to fit you? Aren't you supposed to be inconspicuous?!"

"Now, don't <u>you</u> start, it's the only touristy type shirt I've got that's big enough to cover my hardware. When it comes to being stealthy, I'm a ghost. Just you wait and see."

The first local unit on the scene was indeed a K-9 followed by two other marked units and an ambulance. The ambulance crew ran to the car. They checked the body and made a death pronouncement and said they'd notify the coroner.

Deputy Tolliver identified himself to the K-9 officer and showed him where the blood trail began. The officer said, "I wish we had their vantage point, we could probably see into the woods." The officer had gestured with his head when he spoke and Judy and Griff looked in that direction.

"Wow," Judy said. "Mt. Rushmore must be even bigger than I imagined, I didn't think you could see it this far out."

Tolliver said, "What's really neat is that when you come out of one of the tunnels in Custer State Park, it looks directly onto the monument. I don't know how many miles away it is, but it's there, right across the canyon."

The K-9 officer returned. "Good news and bad news. The good is it wasn't a person, the bad news is, it was a cocker spaniel, torn up pretty good. It didn't make it. I retrieved the collar, we'll give it to whoever claims the driver's body."

Recruit, lying on the ground, looked sad when the news of the cocker spaniel was mentioned. Having turned the scene over to the locals, they prepared to leave when Judy said, "Well, this puts a damper on the day. I hate it when a pet dies." Recruit whimpered in agreement and hopped into the bed of the pick-up truck.

At the National Memorial, our tourists were awe struck at the size of the sculpture as viewed from the grand terrace. While they watched, a ranger leading a tour walked by and they heard her say that the mole on Lincoln's face was 16 ft. square.

"Did you hear that Judy, those presidents are even bigger than they look. C'mon bait, let's hit the Presidential Trail."

The trail went down and below the sculpture, the midden of fallen rock left over from the sculpting was fascinating too because of the size of the rocks. "This is quite a view Griff, everybody should see the sculpture from this angle."

As they were looking up Jefferson's nose, a child on the trail broke a balloon with a loud pop. As if one body, Griff and Judy wheeled and drew down on the four year old. Needless to say, the parents were more than a little upset. Things went downhill fast when five heavily armed SWAT officers and a large floral tent materialized to rescue them.

"Well, that tears it!" Tolliver raged. "This is a major FUBAR. If Shotz is here, he won't try anything now. Damn kids with their balloons. They shouldn't be allowed out in public. You should've shot the little bastard."

"Judy, this is the kind of temper tantrum I would have expected from his father. His sister warned me about their father's temper."

"Griff, that National Park pass we purchased will let us back in; we can finish our look around another day."

"Judy, dear, let's retrieve the trailer, go to the campsite and see if we can't salvage this God awful day."

"Not today, dear, not for several days, sorry."

"That's it, close down the carnival, the ride is out of order."

"Not so fast Big Boy. There are other games on the midway and other talents too."

It was decided that Dean would meet with his boss and they would meet again in the morning to lay out a new game plan over cups of coffee and tea.

CHAPTER TWENTY-TWO

Griff stopped by the local Stop and Rob and purchased a bunch of helium-filled balloons for Dean. Dean was not amused when he saw the kids walk into the diner. Judy excused herself and went to the powder room.

"I got these just for you Deputy, I know how much you like balloons," Griff snickered as he handed over the balloons.

"Bah," Dean grunted as he watched his gift float to the ceiling.

"Money well spent," Griff said, "Money well spent."

"Hey, who's going to get those down?" the stern-faced counterman asked.

"You want me to shoot them down?" Dean growled as he flashed his deputy sheriff's star.

The counterman backed down with a sheepish grin.

"That's OK, I'll get 'em later."

When Judy showed up at the table, they told her about the counterman's gruff reaction.

"I've been thinking about him since yesterday. He seems better fitted to work in a saloon than a coffee shop. I thought up a title for him," she said, "from now on he's the Barroomsta, get it, barroom? Not a barista, but a barroomsta?"

It was funny but they wouldn't give her the satisfaction of laughing. "I'll remember that snub tonight," she said. Griff came out with a long, loud and exaggerated belly laugh until Judy pleaded with him to stop.

"I heard from Daddy last night, he gives his best and said I should give Judy a hug, with permission of course."

"Permission granted," Griff said.

"He was talking to me," Judy said as she let fly with more sugar packets. To the barroomsta, she said, "I know, I know, I'm picking them up."

A chuckling Dean said, "Daddy says it was karma that brought us together. I didn't even know he knew that word. He also said that I should treat you like my brother. I told him that was my plan; I really do like you guys."

"We like you too, Dean," Griff said. "Your Daddy brought you up right, he can be very proud."

"All right, Stan and Ollie, let's get down to business. Where do you want to go today?"

Griff responded, "I'd really like to see the Little Bighorn Battlefield, but without the cavalry, pun intended."

"Right," Judy echoed. Yesterday was a fiasco, we think we can handle things by ourselves."

"OK, if you're sure, but I'm assigned to you. It'll be a threesome and I'll drive."

"What about Recruit?" Judy asked.

"He goes where I go. I guess we're now officially a foursome."

Dean made a phone call and was on the phone for quite some time. "The battlefield is in Montana, so I had to get permission to go. Once I cleared that hurdle our department contacted the National Park Service at the battlefield site and got permission for all of us to go armed. The circumstances were explained and Sammy's photo was FAXed to them – we're good to go."

As they got up to leave, Griff spotted a quarter near one of the counter stools and bent down to pick it up. It didn't budge, it was cemented to the floor. The barroomsta was howling with laughter and yelled over his shoulder, "We got another one, Helen!" A red-faced Zoo Man mumbled under his breath as they went out the door, "Next time, I'll bring a putty knife."

After stowing the camper and Judy's truck, they all climbed into Dean's Suburban and took off to see the site of Custer's last stand. With Tolliver driving, the "tourists" were free to take in the rolling landscape and marvel at all of the catchpenny places and souvenir shops.

"Obviously, there's lots of money to be made out here. When I retire, I think I'd like to relocate out here and open a frozen dessert shop. I even know what to call it."

"What's that, Griff?" she asked seriously.

"Custard's Last Stand."

Judy and Dean just shook their heads, they'd been suckered in again. Dean said, "Now I know why people are always throwing things at you." Griff ignored the remark and kept looking for the battlefield. He knew they were getting close, but couldn't figure out where it was. Everything was too hilly for a proper battlefield as depicted in the movies. Dean had been here several times before and knew what to expect but Griff was taken by the enormity of the place and the fact that the battlefield itself was not only widespread but also a sea of hills and valleys, certainly no place to launch a decent attack.

A road across the top of a ridge allowed one to get to the various engagement sites and overlooked others in the valley below. All along the way, by the road and on the hillsides, were individual stone markers exactly indicating where a soldier had fallen. Although some survived, some 210 officers and troopers, including Custer himself, perished.

The most sobering sight was the actual location of Custer's last stand, an area near the top of a hill and no larger than the foundation of a large house, where Custer and the last of his men fought and lost their last battle. One large marker just above Custer's last battle site listed the names of all the men who fought and died with Custer. A somber Griffith read every name.

Perhaps the Reno-Benteen marker summed it all up best:

This area was occupied by Troops A, B, D, G, H, K, and M,
7th U.S. Cavalry, and the pack train when they were
besieged by the Sioux Indians
June 25th and 26th, 1876

A quiet Zoo Man taken in by the solemnity of the site, entered the battlefield museum, hoping to find something to shake him out of his doldrums. In a glass case, was the small uniform of Lt. Col. George Armstrong Custer, "The Boy General." Griff called Judy to his side and as they stood looking at the uniform, Griff leaned over and whispered, "You know Custer wore an Arrow shirt." Judy could only shake her head, but Griff smiled; the doldrums were gone.

Before they left the grounds, the four of them gathered for the flag lowering ceremony. The sound of the cannon being fired covered the sniper's shot and Griff fell to the ground. Judy and Dean drew their weapons and visually scoured the scattering crowd but could not locate the shooter. The shot could have come from any one of the many trucks, campers and RVs assembled in the parking lot.

They turned their attention to their downed comrade who now had the big Great Dane straddling him, keeping guard. "Good boy, Recruit, we've got him now," and the big dog backed up. One ranger ran for a first aid kit while another phoned for help. Griff was alive, lying on his back with his life's blood soaking into the soil. He had been the target of a head shot that had just missed. The bullet dug a furrow across the top of his shoulders from left to right and disappeared into God knows where. While Dean and a ranger were applying pressure bandages to the wound, Judy Stanhope was trying to communicate with her Zoo Man.

"Griff, Griff can you hear me?" she kept repeating while squeezing his hands. Finally, Griff opened one eye and raspily between breaths spoke. "I can hear you, are you guys OK? Is anyone else hurt?"

"Everyone's all right, he's getting closer though. This time he actually clipped you, Brother Park."

"How bad it is Dean? It hurts like hell."

"I'm no doctor, but I can tell you that it's not life threatening. You're going to need stitches just below your neck and a lot of antibiotics would be my guess."

Griff tried to rise to meet the ambulance crew but they made him lie still and treated him for shock. Once the bandage was secured and an IV started, they carried him to their squad. Judy was allowed to ride in the squad, but they had to leave their weapons with Deputy Tolliver. As Judy was climbing in, one of the attendants heard Griff say, "Isn't this ironic, the carnival and the Zoo are both shut down for a few days." Judy blushed and Griff chuckled wearily.

The squad left and a floral-shirted deputy was left to explain who they were and why they were armed. He even produced a picture of Shotz and referenced the APB. The troopers and rangers accepted the explanations and assured Deputy Tolliver that roadblocks would be put up immediately.

The Montana Staties were good to their word because he and Recruit were stopped no less than four times on the way to the hospital. Twice his credentials were questioned and one officer even gave him a wink and said, "Nice shirt!"

Griffith James Park was admitted to the Shriner's Hospital emergency room for treatment while fellow officer, Judith Stanhope, completed the C.C.P.D. generated insurance forms. Judy was not granted entrance to the ER but was told that an employee would be out to see her. Some 45 minutes later, an ER nurse sought out a surly Judy Stanhope who was not used to waiting.

"Ms. Stanhope, your, uh, boyfriend is going to be A-OK. That was a nasty wound, what happened?"

"Back scratcher accident," she snapped.

"Really, are you serious?"

"No, not really, it's a gun shot wound," she said and under her breath added, "you twit."

"Damn, I wouldn't have guessed that. Anyway, Dr. Singer put in 31 stitches to close the wound. Because of the nature of the injury and the pain involved, Dr. Singer administered anesthesia to put Mr. Park to sleep. He will be assigned to a room and he will have to stay at least one night. As soon as I know the room number, I'll be back out to tell you."

Judy was sitting in the waiting room contemplating her situation. Her fellow officer and boyfriend is the walking target of a rogue cop and she is just as susceptible of being on his hit list. She was so engrossed in her thoughts that she didn't hear Deputy Tolliver coming up from behind. "How's our favorite target?"

Judy jumped like she was shot from a cannon. "Damn, you're quiet for a big man! Are you trying to give me a heart attack?"

"No, but what better place to have one? Sorry if I scared you Judy. I didn't realize that you were so deep in thought. How's our boy doing?"

"They put him out so they could use a Singer sewing machine to put in some thirty chain stitches. They're going to send him to a room shortly."

"A sewing machine? Are you sure?"

"Ms. Stanhope, Mr. Park has been moved to Room 302, you may go up if you wish, just use the left bank of elevators."

"Uh nurse, what was the name of that sewer-upper again?"

"That would be Singer," she said walking away. Dean Tolliver sat down hard with his mouth wide open in disbelief.

Judy went over to Dean and patted him on the shoulder. "It's all right Dean, I'll explain it to you later, let's go up to Park's room and check on him." Judy led Dean to the elevator and steered him into the car. People looked at his stupor-like gaze and were told by Judy, "His friend's been hurt, he's in shock, he'll be OK soon."

In room 302, she sat Dean down in one chair and pulled up the other next to Griff's bed. Griff's eyes were open and he appeared to recognize her.

"How are you feeling, my love?"

"I ish a bittle lit grogsy, but I feels good."

"Do you remember what happened?"

"I falsh down and mad a boo boo."

"Do you know where you are?"

"Hoshpittle—they got good drugsh."

"Lie back now, honey, and let's get you comfortable. You were shot and you need to lie still. You've been medicated so your words are slurred but we can understand you. Is there anything you need?"

"My nursh—she's my budsy."

"There are lots of nurses, love, how do I know which one is yours?"

"Her name is Busty McNipples."

That was all it took to shake Dean out of his near catatonic state,

"What did he say? Who did he say?"

"What was it again, dear?"

"Busty McNipples, Busty McNipples," he said emphatically.

"OK Zoo, I'll see if I can find her for you. On the dry-erase message board on the wall of Room 302, was the notation: Betsy, Night Nurse. Judy left Dean to keep an eye on Griff while she strolled down to the nurse's station. "Excuse me, my boyfriend wants his night nurse but he's too medicated to use the call button. He's in 302, the nurse's name is Betsy."

A string bean of a nurse stepped forward, "I'm Betsy McNickels, you say he's asking for me?"

"That's right, by name." Betsy McNickels, that's close to Busty McNipples. Wait until I get back and tell everyone about his major faux pas, Judy thought. When she returned to the room with Nurse McNickels, Griff was sound asleep. Her services no longer needed, Betsy McNickels excused herself and went about her other duties.

Dean was wide awake so Judy told him about Betsy McNickels. Dean got a big chuckle about Griff's dyslexic handling of the name. "At least, he didn't call her Fuzzybutt," he said and they both laughed heartily.

"It's good to laugh," Judy said. "It breaks the tension of this stressful situation. You mentioned Fuzzybutt, where is Recruit?"

"Who would have guessed there were two Shriners Hospitals—one belonging to a Dr. Slater Shriner, DVM, a vet hospital. It worked out OK though, I was able to board Recruit there for the night. The big boy wasn't happy about it. He'll get me back later. Hey Judy, did they say how long Zoo is going to be in here?"

"Overnight for sure, we'll know more in the morning."

"You know that if he stays here more than one night, I'll contact the local boys and see if we can get a guard for him. He is a cop and he is being stalked by a killer!"

"You don't think Shotz would try something in a hospital, do you?"

"Don't be naïve girl, he just tried to kill Griff in a national park with a crowd around, why wouldn't he try again here?"

"That makes sense, Dean, I guess I was thinking like a girl and not like a cop."

"Get some sleep Judy. I'll sit the first watch and if he wakes up, I'll let you know." Griff slept through the night and through breakfast, which Dean enjoyed and was chastised for when he asked for seconds.

When Dr. Singer made his rounds to see Griff, the hungry deputy woke up Judy. The doctor gently woke Griff and checked him out. Griff was alert and no longer mush-mouthed. The questions from Dr. Singer were general. "Do you know where you are?"

"In a hospital."

"Do you recall what happened to you?"

"I was shot."

"Right, and you are a very lucky man. The bullet grazed your upper back across your shoulders. I put in 31 stitches, the wound is about 13 inches long."

"How long will I be in here, Doc?"

"You don't like our little resort?"

"No offense, Doc, but I'm on vacation and this isn't quite the accommodations that I had in mind. The sooner I can get back on the road, the better."

"Well, the wound looks good, your vitals are good, you have no fever and you don't appear to have any adverse effects from the anesthesia. If you promise to take the meds I prescribe and promise to have that bandage changed regularly, I can discharge you today."

"Yes, I promise, I'm outa here!"

"Good, any questions?"

"When do I eat?"

"Your tray is empty, you didn't eat?" They both looked at the large floral cat who swallowed the canary. He was studying the ceiling tiles. "Betsy, get Mr. Park some breakfast and then kick him out, we need the bed for a really sick person."

Judy spoke up. "You don't know him Doc, he is really a very sick person, mentally."

"Have a safe trip, and enjoy the rest of your vacation," the smiling doctor said as he left the room. While Griff ate his replacement breakfast, they all chuckled about Dr. Singer (the sewing machine) and the anesthetically induced "Busty McNipples." It was decided that Griff would recuperate at Dean Tolliver's place until he was strong enough to travel.

Betsy McNickels was going off shift and said that an orderly would be in shortly with his discharge papers and a wheelchair. "Good luck," she said as she erased her name from the message board.

"OK boys and girls, here's the game plan. We pick up Recruit, we go to breakfast, because Judy hasn't eaten and then we go to my place for R&R, agreed? Good, I'll go pull my truck around."

As Dean was leaving the room, the orderly was coming in with the wheelchair. He invited Judy to "Step outside please while Mr. Park gets dressed."

The orderly had Griff sign the discharge papers and then asked him to board the wheelchair. “Do you have a sense of humor?” Griff asked. The portly orderly said, “Oh yes sir, why if I was any heavier, I could be all of the Three Stooges.”

“Good, the Zoo man must leave his mark.” A moment later they were out the door and behind them, the message board now read, ‘Dusty Knees—Head Nurse.”

CHAPTER TWENTY-THREE

Just when they thought that their vacation had come to a screeching halt, they were welcomed into the home of Deputy Dean Tolliver so that fellow officer, Griffith Park, could recover in comfort. Thus started a mini-vacation in the resort that Dean Tolliver called home.

Several years ago, Dean, being new to the area of Deadwood, was in the right place at the right time and acquired the deal of a lifetime, his current home. The four-bedroom, two-story log home with a wrap around porch faced the most beautifully landscaped pond that Griff and Judy had ever seen. The home was modestly decorated and the guest room was as large and comfortable as any 4-star hotel; all R&R places should be so lovely.

With Griff in the capable hands of "Nurse Judy," Dean went back to patrolling the Deadwood environs and checking on the status of the Shotz investigation. Judy did some checking on her own by phoning her SWAT Captain, John Rockefeller at work.

"Judith, this is a surprise, how is your vacation?"

"Well," she hesitated, "it's been different. I've never been camping before."

Captain Rockefeller interrupted her. "Judith, hold on a second. I'm going to put you on speaker." One click later, he continued. "That's better, can you hear me OK?"

"It's a little bit echoey, but it's all right and Captain, would you please call me Judy? My mom used to call me Judith."

"Only if you call me John. No need to be formal. You're on vacation, relax. Just like an after work choir practice only no cussing, OK?"

"OK, I was going to send you a postcard but I just thought I'd call and surprise you. So, what's up at the department?"

"Same as always, Judy. The gang bangers tried to start another turf war but we settled it without anybody getting hurt. So, how's the Zoo Man?"

"What makes you think that I'm……"

"I'm no fool. I can put two and two together. You both took the month of August off. You're both camping and Sgt. Atrick has been getting an unsolicited play by play from a Sheriff Tolliver in Corinth County. So, how's Griff?"

"Oh, he's resting right now. He got a scratch across his shoulders, kind of slowing him down a bit, but he's all right.

Another voice said, "A scratch, huh, the national news said he got shot."

"Are you playing with me, boss?! What's going on? Who is there with you?!"

"It's just Ed, Judy."

"Ed who, we don't have any Eds on the squad?!"

"Ed Riley, Judy, you remember me don't you? The old man?

"Oh shit, does everybody know?"

"No wild rumors yet, but we would like the *Reader's Digest* version of what's been happening."

"Well, things were nice and ordinary until we accidentally ran into Steroid Sammy out here in Deadwood and he tried to kill Griff. We've pretty much been under armed guard and being used as bait to draw Shotz out. We've been assigned to, of all people, Deacon Tolliver's son, Dean. That's where his Daddy's getting the news from. Anyway, we were at the Little Bighorn Battlefield when Shotz nearly took out the bait and then he got away. Griff's recuperating here at Deputy Tolliver's place, but he's going to be OK. Other than that, everything's been just fine."

"It sounds like the Zoo man sure knows how to show a lady a good time, all right."

"Right boss, just a peachy time. It will be better when Shotz is caught so we can continue with our vacation in peace!"

"Shotz is a tricky bastard, he had us all fooled. He left all of his C.C.P.D. gear at his place when he took off. Left everything but his gun, badge, ID and handcuffs. If he flashes that badge and nobody checks farther, he's got a free ride to anywhere in the country."

"Well, that did a lot to make me feel better!"

"John's just speaking the truth," the chief said. "Until Shotz is caught, nobody is safe and unfortunately he has a raging hatred for Park because he killed his half brother. Right now, Park is the least safe of all and I'm afraid that because you're with him, you aren't safe either."

"I guess the truth hurts," Judy said. "Griff and I almost got married a few years back and we split up. Now that we're back together, I'll protect him with my life. I'll kill Shotz myself before I let Griff get hurt again."

"That's a strong sentiment, Judy, just you be careful. Just out of curiosity, what brought you two back together?"

"Why you did, Captain, when you sent me out with the rescue squad."

"I can't take credit for that. That was Chief Riley's order."

"Were you playing Cupid, Chief?"

"More like the devil, I'm afraid. I was miffed at the way you snapped at me on the phone and I was just trying to get back at you. Not very professional, I admit."

"Well, whatever the reason, I owe you a big hug."

"My door is always open to you, whenever you care to deliver."

"Hopefully, Zoo will be able to travel in a couple of days so we can continue our trip. In the meantime, I'm going to go out and get some sun. Dean Tolliver has a pond that's just waiting for a sunbather."

"OK, you enjoy the sun and you guys be careful. We're all pulling for you. Give our best to Griff."

"Will do, John, you take care. You too, Chief."

"I'll be waiting for that hug. Bye Judy."

When Griff awoke he went to the bathroom for some water to clear the cotton out of his mouth and that's when he realized that Judy was gone. He called out but got no answer. When he looked outside he saw his bronze goddess reclined on a wooden chaise sunning herself. "Be careful that chair doesn't bite you," he called out.

"No problem there, I just hope this towel prevents me from getting splinters."

"Do you want me to rub some lotion on you?"

"You just want to touch my body."

"Well, duh!"

"That's OK. I'm not going to stay out much longer, have a seat. How's the shoulder?"

Griff sat sideways on the chair next to hers. "It's a little sore but the stitches pulling are the least comfortable. Do you know if these are dissolving stitches?"

"The paperwork suggested that they should be removed in 12 to 15 days after the date they were put in. I called the department today."

"You what? Why?!"

"Just to see what's going on. You checked in with your partner and I didn't question it."

"You're right, Judy, I apologize for snapping. It just took me off guard. I didn't want them to know about us and this," he said as he poked his thumb toward his shoulder wound.

"They already know about both."

"How? Who did you talk to?"

"I called my boss, Capt. Rockefeller and as luck would have it, Chief Riley was sitting in his office at the time. It seems that you made national headlines by being shot in a national park. As for you and me, they put two and two together, and we're a couple. They both send their regards."

"Did you think to have them call Joe? If it's national news, he'll be worried."

"Sorry, love, I never thought of that. I can call them back."

"That's OK, I'll call him tonight when the rates are lower."

"SWAT doesn't have to worry about that. Capt. Rockefeller had an 800 number put in for emergencies and for CI's to call in tips. To my knowledge, our unit is the only one to have an 800 number. It's not common knowledge."

"That's always the way, the elite unit gets all the toys and the real cops can't even get decent cars to drive!" When he realized that Judy was staring daggers at him, he realized he'd said the wrong thing. "That didn't come out right, did it?"

"No."

"You think I should change the subject?"

"Yes."

Taking a different tack, Griff said, "It sure is pretty."

"Uh huh," she replied as she leaned her head back.

"The landscape's nice too," he said.

"Nice save," she said as she smiled and rolled her head to meet his gaze and smile. Griff leaned back in his chaise and they sat in silence holding hands until they heard Dean pull into the driveway. He honked and waved. Judy and Griff got up and walked toward the truck. Dean waved them back. "It's OK, we're coming in anyway, Judy said.

"C'mon inside then, I've got something interesting to tell you."

Judy bounced up the stairs to get a robe while the men took up seats in the living room. "I'm back, I didn't want to be a distraction."

"Gee whiz, thanks a lot," Dean said, feigning disgust. "How's the shoulder, Griff?"

"Tight, but not too sore, so what's this news?"

"Remember when I told you that the officers found a small hidden room in Shotz' place? Well, among the things they found was a dossier on a local tattoo artist who seems to be flying under false colors. He's really a convicted forger. The feds think that Shotz was going to blackmail him; they think they can use that to their advantage and draw Shotz out."

"How so?"

"They think that an agent can intimidate him into calling them if Shotz makes contact, and then set up a meet."

"If he'll go for their game, and that's a big if," Griff said.

"Can you introduce me to the Feds? I've got an idea on how I can help them," Judy said. When the men looked at her quizzically, she smiled and said, "Feminine wiles, gentlemen, feminine wiles!"

Dean Tolliver phoned the FBI agent from Pierre, who was working out of an office at the Lawrence County Sheriff's Headquarters and made an appointment for Judy to meet with the agent who was planning to approach the tattoo artist. At her request, Dean was to go along to act as a buffer between the local and federal ways of doing things.

The next day, Judy and Deputy Tolliver were shown into a wood and glass cubicle where they waited for the special agent. They sat in the only two chairs, which were placed in front of the agent's desk; the nameplate read Sp. Agt. Wohcowhcs.

A tall thin man in his 30s entered wearing a three-piece grey suit and horn rim glasses. His buzz cut and no facial hair made him look more like a teenager. The agent extended his hand first to Deputy Tolliver and then to Judy and introduced himself.

"I'm agent Michael Wohocks, how can I help you?" Deputy Tolliver introduced himself and Officer Stanhope, who produced her C.C.P.D. ID.

"We understand that you are going to try to enlist a local tattoo artist to aid you in capturing the murderer, Sam Shotz. We thought we might be able to help with various parts of this investigation."

"Yes, it is common knowledge between my department and yours that we are thinking in that direction; how do you think you can help?"

Judy jumped right in. "I've been a police officer for over ten years and for the last four on SWAT with Shotz, so I can give you insight on him and secondly, I thought that I could act as a distraction to keep this tattoo guy off guard. I'm assuming it is a guy?"

"Oh, he's a guy all right, his real name is Jorge dePrada, but his 'nom deguerre" is Cogs Gearsly, somewhat of a motor-head biker working at a place called S. T. Inkers. Miss Stanhope, at the risk of sounding like a chauvinist, you're already a distraction; you are quite lovely." Judy smiled and nodded once to acknowledge the compliment.

Tolliver said, "I've been in that shop, it's got one front room where he displays books and wall hangings of tattoo designs and a work area in the corner across from the front door. The main room is separated from the rest of the area by a heavy green curtain. Gearsly doesn't look like any biker I've ever seen. He looks more like a wimpy professor to me."

“So, what’s your game plan?” Judy asked.

“I was planning on confronting Gearsly with the information we found in Shotz’ home and see where it goes from there.”

“That’s not very imaginative, Agent Wohcowhcs. May I call you Michael?”

“Why, yes of course, Miss Stanhope, please go ahead.”

Dean Tolliver sat back and watched her work. “Call me Judy. What I had in mind is to go in ahead of you and get him so flustered that he won’t know which way is up—you know, soften him up for you. Then you come in and put pressure on him, threaten him with a search warrant if you have to. See if you can get him to take you into the back room while I check the front.”

“You sound like you’ve done this before,”

“Well, I’m a cop.”

“How do you propose to ‘soften him up’?”

“I was thinking I would dress provocatively and pose as a customer—give me five minutes and he’ll be so weak he’ll be putty in your hands, unless he’s a eunuch!”

“I don’t know if my boss will sanction this type of activity.”

“Then don’t tell him,” Dean said. “Be aggressive, take the bull by the horns, be the man!”

“I am the man! I can do this! When do we do it?”

“How about noon tomorrow, I’ll need some time to shop for a suitable outfit. You ride with Deputy Tolliver and if you need a uniform presence, he’s available. You come in a few minutes later and do your thing.”

“Sounds like a plan, let’s do it!” Agent Wohcowhcs said. The next day, Special Agent Wohcowhcs was seated in the front seat of Dean’s cruiser on Main St. around the corner from the tattoo shop on Pine. A street walker walked up to the passenger side of the cruiser and leaned in the window, showing off her ample cleavage. Wearing sunglasses, a black shag wig and a black leather mini skirt, the woman had the Special Agent flustered beyond belief.

“Miss, this is a police car, not a taxi. You’re making us look bad, we’re working here, move along please, move along!”

The harlot stroked Wohcowhcs’ chin and said, “But Mikey, if I move along, who’s going to soften up Gearsly?”

“Judy?! Is that really you in that getup?”

“The way you reacted, you’d better not be too far behind me or you’ll meet Gearsly as he’s melting out under the doorway; see you in five minutes.” With that, Judy swished and jiggled down Pine Street in 4” stiletto heels.

S. T. Inkers, read the name on the full front glass window. Inside was a little professor looking man who was smiling broadly with his eyes wide open. "Are you Mr. Inkers? What's the S. T. stand for?" Cogs was flustered from the get go. "I, uh, no, I mean, I uh bought the shop, name included. I just thought it was a play on words, stinkers you know. Now, what can I do with, uh, for you?" asked the drooling Cogs.

"I'm thinking about getting a tattoo or maybe a piercing," she said as she put her foot on the window ledge so that Cogs couldn't miss the black satin panties. "Do you do piercings?"

Cogs was so busy looking at Judy's thigh and beyond that he almost missed the question. "Uh piercings, yes I do piercings."

"Do you do naughty piercings?" she asked as she lightly stroked her inner thigh.

Cogs Gearsly was a sweating, babbling mess by the time Wohcowhcs entered and badged Cogs. "I'm Special Agent Wohocks." He got off to a slow start because Cogs didn't look like his mug shot; he initially thought he had the wrong man. Wohcowhcs quickly recovered and started putting the pressure on Gearsly.

Cogs saw the old ID photo and started babbling. "See, that's not me, that's not me, you got the wrong man, that's not me, that's not my photo."

Wohcowhcs stood his ground, bent down to look Cogs in the eye and said, "Faces can be changed but fingerprints never do, Jorge! Now look, you boob, I got this information from a file that we found in Sammy Shotz' house. He was going to blackmail you, he still can unless you help us!"

Cogs looked like a sweaty trapped rat looking about for a way out of a maze. "I don't feel right talking in front of that tart, make her leave!"

"I'm a federal officer, being a customer is not a federal crime so I can't make her leave. I guess we'll just have to talk in the back," he said as he pushed Cogs through the curtain while Cogs vociferously complained about his rights being violated.

"Whoa, what do we have here?!" Judy heard Wohcowhcs say. "I thought you were out of the forgery business; I guess you are now! You violated federal probation when you disappeared; you changed your face but couldn't change your fingerprints. You didn't use phony money to pay for that new face did you? Listen, I can't help you with the probation violation but I might be able to keep you from getting new charges <u>if</u> you play ball with me!"

Cogs (Jorge dePrada) Gearsly knew better than to look a gift horse in the mouth and agreed to cooperate in nailing Shotz if he called. By his cooperation, he could postpone his eventual jail time for some time.

Judy overheard Cogs say, "If that tart hadn't distracted me, I wouldn't have been taken so easily." Judy smiled.

Wohcowhcs had Tolliver call for a panel truck for the transportation and storage of printing equipment and related items for changing identities and for the counterfeiting of U.S. currency. Cogs was transported to Wohcowhcs' temporary office where he was debriefed; he also wrote out a statement about his involvement in changing Shotz' identity. Cogs was subsequently fitted with a monitoring device and returned to his shop.

It was believed by all involved that setting only one trap for Shotz probably wasn't going to be enough to catch him, but it was a start.

CHAPTER TWENTY-FOUR

While the dynamic duo, Dean and Recruit, were off saving the world, Griff and Judy were again sunbathing by Dean's pond. It had been two days since the take down of Jorge DePrada and Judy was again regaling Griff about her role as the sexy distraction and how it had worked to perfection. "Feminine wiles, remember when I said that? You and Dean just scoffed."

"I don't recall scoffing, but if I did, I apologize. By the way, did the Feds pick up the tab on your hooker duds?"

"Yes, they did and what's more, I got to keep them; if you're a good Zoo Man, I will model them for you later."

"I don't know if I can be good but I guarantee I can be great! I was talking with Dean and he said that the pond is safe for swimming. Just watch out for the snapping turtles. Want to take a dip?"

"Why not?" she said as they grabbed hands and ran down the dock and jumped into the water. "Sheesh," she said as they surfaced. "I didn't expect it to be so cold; I think my nipples are going to pop right through the fabric."

"Yeah! Now that's what I'm talking about!"

Judy splashed him with a handful of water and the two cavorted like horny river otters for about fifteen minutes. As they exited the water, Griff commented on how small her wet micro-mini bikini seemed. "It almost disappeared." Judy took the hint and removed the bra. "What do you want to do today?" she asked as she was toweling off. "After that!" she said as she looked at his drooling grin.

"You mean we have to do something else?"

"Assuming that you're up to it, yes."

"Let's go visit Boot Hill or whatever they call the cemetery here. I would like to see Wild Bill Hickok's grave."

"Well then, we'd better take care of the preliminaries first." They put on their sandals and raced toward the house.

Dean had not awakened them to let them know that Sammy had called Cogs and had set up a meet. He and Recruit just rushed out to meet with Agent Wohcowhcs.

"We received a call from Gearsly that Shotz had contacted him and is going to be at the tattoo parlor at noon. We're going to go in at about 11:00 and camp out in the back room. Who would have thought it would go down so soon? Where's our happy hooker?"

"She's on vacation, remember? I let her sleep in." As they laid out their strategy, the time ticked by. At 10:45, they mounted up and drove to Gearsly's shop.

The capture team stopped short and all that Wohcowhcs could think about was Judy's statement about Gearsly melting under the door. What they saw was red liquid seeping from under Cogs' door. Everybody drew their weapons and went in trying to carefully avoid stepping in the blood.

The front room scene was ghastly. Blood spatters everywhere, bloody drag marks leading behind the counter. On the floor, was a roughly hack sawed, double-barrel sawed-off shotgun. At the end of the barrels was a crudely made device that must have acted as a silencer.

The bloody drag marks led through the curtain and terminated with the remains of the former forger. The body had taken at least three hits, from what appeared to be .00 buckshot, to the torso. Two other shots had obliterated the forger's hands but the one that was the worst was when the killer had stuck the gun barrels in Gearsly's mouth and had blown out the back of his head. A pencil jabbed into the drywall held a rough handwritten rambling note:

you tried to steel my identity
you made my friend into a puppet
you made him turn on me
I am invincible I can't be stopped
I can't be caught I am a ghost
I am the sord of damaclese
No enemy is safe
You violated my home
The old me is gone
You know me I am the New Man
But you can't catch me

Dean Tolliver had a strong constitution but he had to excuse himself and joined several others already retching in the street. When he finally returned inside, he glanced down at the murder weapon and noticed some scrollwork on what was left of the stock. "Oh, shit!" he said as he raced from the building to his cruiser. Using his emergency radio frequency, he had a radio dispatcher patch through a call.

Judy and Griff were just starting out the door and almost ignored the ringing phone. Judy, wishing to be a considerate guest, answered it. A nearly breathless Dean Tolliver said, "Oh, thank God, you're all right!"

"What's the matter, Dean?" Judy asked.

"Cogs Gearsly is dead, horribly murdered by one of my own guns, the house must have been compromised." He paused to catch his breath and they continued. "Arm yourselves, lock yourself in the guest room, stay away from the windows, stay in there until I get there, I'm on my way – any questions?"

"No, we'll do as you say."

The panicked deputy hung up. "Recruit, if anything happens to those kids, I'll never forgive myself." Tolliver skidded to a stop in his driveway and raced inside. Recruit instinctively went upstairs while Dean ran to his gun cabinet. He had not checked his hunting guns in some time as they were in a downstairs work room. The door glass was intact but the doors to the gun cabinet had been pried; all of his long guns were gone.

The big man bounded up the stairs two steps at a time without using the handrail. As he turned to the left, he saw Recruit lying in front of the guest room door at the end of the hall. "Griff, Judy, are you OK?" No answer. "Griff, Judy, it's me, Dean!" Judy called out. "How do we know it's you? Prove it."

Dean paused and thought and finally said, "My Daddy has a fuzzy butt." Judy threw open the door and almost fell over the big guard dog. Dean approached as Griff appeared behind Judy. The couple had taken to heart his order to arm themselves. Judy looked like a big breasted, beautiful Pancho Villa wearing crossed bandoliers of ammunition. Griff had his .45 in a shoulder rig, a pistol in a belt holster and his Derringer tucked in his waistband. Behind Griff, Dean saw a mattress and box springs fortress.

Tolliver ruffled Recruit's ears and then put him on interior alert. As the Great Dane walked away to check the house, Dean stepped into the guest room, grabbed a chair from behind the fortress and sat down hard. "I'm at a loss, kids. Shotz is bolder than brass. He contacted Gearsly all right. He took him apart with a crudely hacked up sawed-off double barrel shotgun – mine! Somehow he got into the house and took all of my rifles and shotguns. Not only is he after you, but now he knows the layout of my house, now you're not even safe here. The good thing is he didn't find my sidearms. At least we have Recruit to warn us of intruders.

"I feel terrible about this, Dean," Judy said. "You've been so good to us and now you're in the crosshairs same as us."

Griff said, "Don't take this wrong Judy, but neither one of you would be in danger if I'd just slunk off to be by myself rather than endanger you on my fantasy vacation."

Judy put her hands on both sides of Griff's face. "Don't talk like that, even had we known there was going to be trouble, I'd still be here with you; we're in this together and we'll beat it together." Judy then lightly kissed Griff's lips.

"OK, you love birds, I don't want to be a wet blanket here but we need to strategize."

While they were making plans, work continued at S. T. Inkers. Because of the magnitude of this heinous crime by an unpredictable mad man, a perimeter guard of officers facing outward was set up to protect the investigators. A civilian looking at this would think they were guarding the President.

When the crime lab techs arrived, they were amused to find an area of vomit roped off. After a minute inside, one of the techs added to the area of disgorgement. The lab boys measured and photographed the scene from every angle. The pencil and crude note were sealed in separate plastic bags. The dangerous ordnance (aka sawed-off shotgun) was made safe and handled gingerly so as not to disturb fingerprints or the homemade silencer. Lastly, the locations of the spent shells were noted, numbered and collected. There were nine spent shells indicating that both barrels had been used at once, at a least several times.

Finally, the coroner's meat wagon arrived to remove the hamburgered corpse. The bagged and tagged body was removed and the news media got their obligatory shot for the evening news. All involved removed their rubber gloves and discarded them in the crime scene. They all rushed off to find a place to wash their hands.

Removing his hands from under the faucet, Griff dried them and prepared to fix salads. Thinking, planning and conniving is always easier on a full stomach. While they ate, Griff and Judy gave in to the notion that their vacation was now over. "Shotz came West to hide, we just stumbled on him. We're no threat to him if we're gone," Griff said. "Surviving and getting home is now priority one."

"Are you guys serious about calling it off and going home?" They both nodded at the same time. "This trip is ruined," Griff said. "We were having great fun and we got to make a great new friend, you, but the fun's over."

Judy added, "We can always come back, we couldn't have seen everything in one trip anyway. It's hard to enjoy looking at things while you're looking over your shoulder too."

Deputy Tolliver rose from the table. "I have an idea. I need to make a phone call." When he returned, he stated, "If your vacation is over, mine will just be starting."

"You lost me, Dean. What are you talking about?" Griff asked.

"I just called in and got permission to start my vacation right now. I'm going to personally escort you home and then I can visit with my Daddy."

Judy hesitantly said, "Uh, the camper sleeps two." Dean roared with laughter. "I wouldn't think of invading your personal space. What I had in mind was following you in the Suburban. Recruit and I can sleep in the back. We've done it before." As the afternoon wore on, the plan took shape. They retrieved Joe's camper from Dean's pole barn and packed it while Dean outfitted his truck.

Both trucks were given a thorough once over checking fluid levels and tire pressure. Everything was packed except the arsenals; the guns would be stored in the morning before they left. So that the "vacation" trip back wouldn't be a total loss, it was decided to take a different route home.

First thing in the morning, they gassed up the trucks, drove to Rapid City and stopped for breakfast. When they left the restaurant, none of them noticed the small pool of liquid under Judy's truck. From Rapid City, they took lesser known but more scenic roads to Buffalo Gap and then skirted the southern edge of the Badlands National Park and then back up to scenic route 40. The Badlands were barren yet beautiful and even calming as they stopped to view a very active prairie dog town. At Cactus Flat, they got back on I-90. With luck they would make Mitchell by nightfall.

The trip was a little slower than planned so they exited near Oacoma and took State Route 50 to Crows Creek to camp for the night. Judy noticed that the brakes felt a little "different," but didn't say anything.

The next morning it was a quick camp breakfast and off they went. About halfway to the interstate, a small herd of mule deer crossed the road in front of Judy's truck and she slammed on the brakes—there were none. The sudden brake pedal compression not only finished the cut in the brake line but also caused the truck to swerve. At 40 mph and with the trailer fishtailing back and forth, the brakeless truck passengers were in trouble. Judy fought hard and was finally able to use the unimproved shoulder to slow the truck to a stop.

Tolliver ran up. "Are you guys OK? What the hell happened?"

"The brakes went out," Judy said, her white knuckles still gripping the steering wheel.

"That was some piece of driving," Griff said praising Judy. "With my tight stitches, I couldn't have done that."

The Lawrence County deputy had been given permission to take a police band radio with him and with it he was able to arrange for a tow. At a local garage, Judy's truck was put up on the rack. The mechanic let out a whistle and said, "Who hates you?!"

"What do you mean?"

"C'mer, look at this." As the three of them looked, the mechanic pointed out the cut brake line. "You can thank your lucky stars that you weren't on the interstate. The back road's slow speed saved you." The mechanic replaced the brake line and gave the truck a thorough once over. To be on the safe side, Dean Tolliver had his truck inspected too.

The small-town, customer-friendly mechanic did not want to be paid for just checking the truck out, but Dean insisted on paying. Just before leaving, Griff spoke to the mechanic and again thanked him for his helpfulness; this time he slipped him an extra $20 for his trouble.

Mitchell, South Dakota was kind of a disappointment. Griff and Judy had both expected the Corn Palace to be a palace, it was instead a brightly corn-decorated auditorium. The shops were excellent though and they got back into the shopping spirit, buying lots of souvenirs for friends.

At Sioux Falls, they gassed up the trucks and then sat down in a restaurant to plan the next leg of the trip. During the discussion, Griff and Judy both looked at Dean and pleadingly asked, "Do we have to go through Iowa?"

CHAPTER TWENTY-FIVE

Tolliver, wearing a khaki shirt instead of his floral print, said, "We're as close to Minnesota as we are to Iowa, I vote for Minnesota."

"Why not? It's got to be better than Iowa," Griff said. Judy was a little more direct "ANYWHERE is better than Iowa." Griff trotted down the street to a service station and came back with a Minnesota state map. "Not their biggest seller, I'm guessing," Judy said, pointing to the map's faded front.

"They're all like that, the rack sits in the sunlight," Griff responded, as he spread the map out on the table. As they looked at the immensity of Minnesota, Griff was taken by the number of bodies of water across the state and pointed that out. Judy brightened up. "Water means beaches, which translates to sunbathing." A low-toned aside to Griff, "I'd better find a more conservative suit to wear. I don't know how strong Dean's heart is."

Griff whispered back, "Well, if he dies, he dies!" Judy playfully bopped him on the head.

"All right you two, what's going on?"

"Sorry, it's just a little private joke. We're just getting our relaxed side back."

"Right, Judy!" Dean said skeptically. "You two find a spot for us to spend the night, I'm going to feed my partner."

Judy had to keep smacking Zoo's hands as he was getting frisky under the table. "Settle down, big boy, and try to concentrate on the map." By the time Dean came back in, they had formed a plan. "Look at this Dean, we're just a short hop from here to Luverne and you can almost spit on the Blue Mounds State Park from there. State park means campsites and it's starting to get late."

"Sounds like a plan, Zoo Man. Hey, I made a rhyme." Judy let her head drop. "Good Lord, not another one." Griff, in his best John Wayne impersonation, said, "Saddle up pilgrims," Pointing to the door, he said, "Yo."

It was indeed a short hop to Luverne and the state park. The kids had done it, they had bypassed Iowa! Blue Mounds was perfect, not only was it rugged yet colorful, it offered a full range of activities; hiking, climbing, fishing and swimming. Griff said, "How about tomorrow we rent some fishing gear and wet a line? While we fish, Judy can work on her tan. We can leave Recruit to watch over her."

"I'm not a big fishing person but we can talk about it some more tomorrow. Right now, all I want to do is roll up in my sleeping bag, I'm getting tired." As if to punctuate his statement, he stretched and yawned and headed to his truck; his partner went with him. Griff and Judy talked for a while about the circumstances which shortened and altered their vacation, eventually they turned in too.

The next morning, Judy fixed bacon and eggs. Dean sat in the camper doorway with his back to his friends and his plate on his lap as there was only room for two at the tiny table. He said, "This sure is the life." Judy agreed, "No radio, no television, no outside distractions, just good friends and relaxation."

Dean passed on the fishing idea and they decided to head north to a large area of water on the map known as Lake Shetek State Park. Lake Shetek didn't exactly roll off the tongue with lyrical promise but it turned out to be a large and lovely state park. Dean had lanterns and both trucks had gallons of bottled water so they asked a ranger if they could stay in a primitive area, one with no water or electric hookup. With permission granted, they checked out various areas.

"Over there," Judy called out. "We're close to that lake and the hillsides are adorned with both wild flowers and cactus. This is lovely and so serene; I say we camp here."

"Your wish is my command, my dear," Griff said.

"I like the way that sounded, my love."

"All right, lovebirds, do you want to be left alone or are we going to explore this area, hmm? We're burnin' daylight, kids."

OK, we'll do the touristy stuff, besides we'll have a lifetime to do the he'in and she'in thing."

"Does that mean what I think it means?" Judy asked.

Griff replied is his best Don Corleone accent. "Someday, I will make you an offer you can't refuse."

"And when you do, I'll say yes."

"This is getting too mushy for me. I'm going on by myself."

"Hold on, Dean, we're coming. Is it my fault that your date is a real dog?" Dean started pelting Griff with gravel and they all laughed. Leaving the pick-up and camper behind, Dean drove. The day was perfect, hiking was invigorating, the sights were spectacular and the good friends enjoyed each other's company immensely.

They returned to the camper in mid-day and had a sumptuous feast of cold cuts and soda and then they strapped on their guns and went outside. It had become a habit that when possible and legal, they would all wear sidearms. Dean's weapon of choice was a .40 caliber Glock, Griff carried a department-issued S&W stainless model 4506, and Judy preferred her 6-shot .38 Colt Detective Special; no wimpy little pop-gun for her.

Griff and Dean were standing in the shadow of the camper talking about what a beautiful state Minnesota was and that it would be a good place to retire if the winters weren't as harsh as advertised. Judy sat in a lawn chair just outside the shadow, adding a little blush to her bronze tan.

The shot whistled between Griff and Dean's heads, broke the camper window and struck metal. As one, they drew and fired at the silhouette with the rifle on the hillside. Like a scene from a western movie, the body pitched forward and fell down the hill, bouncing and rolling and leaving a small dust trail.

Even before the body stopped moving they were on the move running toward the base of the hill. They found the body lying face down and turned it over. Most of the man's shirt had been shredded during the slide down the hill and they could see that the man was well muscled with six-pack abs. The face was heavily bearded and cut up and the long wig was coming off, but still they could identify the dead shooter as Steroid Sammy Shotz.

"We got him, Judy, we got Shotz, our nightmares are over." When Griff turned to face her, she wasn't there. Looking back, he saw Judy still sitting in the lawn chair. Maybe she doesn't want to see our nemesis up close, he thought, since they used to work together.

Dean took his red bandana handkerchief from his hip pocket, tied it to a stick and stuck it in the ground by the body. "This way, we don't have to come back here, we can point out the marker to the Rangers and they can go right to him. We'll let them hunt for the weapon too, no use further compromising the crime scene."

"I'm sure this will be a great weight off of Judy's shoulders," Griff said. They stopped about forty feet from the camper and saw Recruit with his front paws on the arms of the lawn chair; he was licking Judy's face. Judy was not responding, her arms were hanging straight down.

"Judy, Judy," Griff yelled as he broke into a run. He came up so fast that it frightened Recruit and the big dog jumped out of the way. "Judy, Judy!!" Griff screamed, but she was silent and her open eyes did not move to meet his. He fell to his knees. "Judy, Honey, what's wrong?" He put his arms around her and found that her back was wet. The jagged hole in the back of her skull was letting blood run down her back and into a pool behind the lawn chair.

"NO! NO! NO! NO! NO!!" he screamed. As Dean tried to put his arms around him, Griff threw him off like a rag doll and began to rail at God. "YOU UNCARING SORRY SON OF A BITCH, IF YOU WANTED A GODDESS, YOU COULD MAKE ONE—YOU

DIDN'T HAVE TO TAKE MINE!!!!! WHAT WERE YOU THINKING, HOW COULD YOU..."

The words trailed off as he fell writhing on his back, the hot bright sun shining down on his anguish-twisted face.

CHAPTER TWENTY-SIX

Griffith Park opened his eyes to the bright sunlight and heard the voice say, "Welcome back, Mr. Park, can you tell me what you were thinking?"

"I was reflecting on what we talked about, Doc. I cursed God for Judy's death. That was wrong of me. I realize now that God allows things to take their course, He didn't make her death happen, it was predetermined, like karma. I'm beginning to understand it now, but I still don't like it."

"You've made significant progress, Mr. Park. I believe you've finally turned the corner. You're almost ready to go home. Would you like to go home?"

"Absolutely! No offense, Doc, but these two weeks in here have seemed like an eternity."

Dr. Jules just smiled and asked, "Are you up to having a visitor? There's a big cowboy here to see you. Shall I show him out here?"

"Yes please, Doc, I'm almost ready to go home and I finally get a visitor." Dr. Jules thought—maybe he isn't really ready!

Dean Tolliver was shown through the etched, glass French doors and strolled out into the arbor. Griff was wearing a robe and was sitting in a wheelchair; Dean sat down on the stone bench next to him. "How 'ya doin', little buddy?"

"I'm not Gilligan, Dean. Don't treat me like a child!"

"I'm sorry, I just thought a funny voice would make you smile."

"I didn't mean to snap at you, it's been a rough couple of weeks since Judy...." He couldn't bring himself to finish the sentence.

"Two weeks? Zoo Man, you've been here for two months."

"Really?! I thought it was two weeks, thanks for stopping by."

"I've been here every day. So has Joe and your Sergeant and lots of others."

"How can everybody be here in Minnesota, they should be working. YOU should be working!"

"You're not in Minnesota son, you're right outside of Capitol City at the Cedar-Ash Rehab facility"

"Dean," Griff said grabbing the big man's forearm, "if I've really been here that long, then I missed the funeral and a lot of other things, too. I need to get caught up." Tears were running down his cheeks. "How did I get here?"

"The Minnesota Highway Patrol arranged for a military helicopter to fly you…." He paused to compose himself. "…and Judy's remains, to Capitol City after the autopsy."

"What exactly happened to her?" Griff sobbed.

"Shotz' only shot missed us both and struck an iron skillet in the trailer. The ricochet tore through the camper wall and struck Judy in the center of the skull. Dean was choking back tears but continued. "The odds of that happening were astronomical; I was assured that she uh, went instantly, no pain, she never knew what hit her."

The big men held each other and cried and couldn't care less who saw them. After they had collected themselves and sat in silence, Dean said, "I didn't come here to upset you, but you asked."

"Dean, I'll be leaving here soon. I want to know things before I leave. I don't want any surprises. I want you to tell me everything. Will you do that, my good friend?"

"Sit tight, Griff, let me find Dr. Jules and check with him, we don't want to do something that might prevent you from being released." Dean Tolliver found Dr. Jules in his office and explained the situation.

"By all means, tell him what he wants to know. Frankly, he will be more receptive of the truth if it comes from a friend. I've been hoping he would ask. I don't want you to think I'm making light of this, but the saying, "The truth will set him free" really does apply. Thank you for caring and helping."

When he returned to Griff, Dean said, "The Doc deputized me to fill in for him. I'm to answer all questions—fire away."

"Tell me about the funeral, Dean."

"You cut right to the tough questions, don't you? Because of the circumstances in that Shotz was trying to kill you two because you were cops, Capitol City Police deemed her loss to be in the line of duty. The service was with full honors. I'm certain you've attended others, but this was the largest police memorial that I've ever experienced. There were hundreds of officers from a myriad of jurisdictions present. Dad and Sis even brought the Fuzzybutts. They were well behaved, respectful and stood at attention and so did the Fuzzybutts."

Griff chuckled, "I needed that!"

Dean was patient, not wanting to push any issue, and waited for Griff's questions.

"When I'm better, Dean, we'll take a road trip to Minnesota and bring back Joe's camper and Judy's truck."

"Already done. I took your partner back to the shooting sight and then we picked up the rolling stock and brought them here. Joe unloaded the camper and is storing everything at his place. After the memorial service, Judy's parents picked up the truck. They left her guns, said you should have them. Joe said that there was a leather bag marked, "Toys." He didn't offer it to Mrs. Stanhope."

Griff nodded and stared at the ground. "Where is she…..?" he haltingly started to ask.

"They took her home to North Carolina to rest in the family plot. Her folks left a note for you, they said that directions to the cemetery are in there. I'll give it to you whenever you want. Her parents were really sorry that they couldn't have met you."

"Oh, right, 'allow us to meet the man who got our daughter killed,'" he said mockingly.

"Griff, look at me. They don't hate you, they don't blame you, they know you would have protected her if you could have. It was an accident, they understand that; so should you."

A loud bang nearby made both men jump. "You hear that, Dean? Another patient who couldn't come to grips with reality."

"That was a garbage truck, Zoo, what were they doing—hiding in a dumpster?"

A smile came across Griff's face. He was becoming his old self again. "I'm getting tired, Dean, can we talk more tomorrow?"

"Sure, but if you can hold on a little longer, there's a family that arrived while I was talking to Dr. Jules; they'd really like to see you."

"OK, I guess I'm up to it."

Dean waved a come-on to the family behind the French doors and the Beveltniks started out. Dean looked Griff in the eye and caressed the back of his neck. "I'll be back tomorrow my friend, you take care." And with that he took his leave. As he passed the Beveltniks, he said, "He's back Joe, and he's full of questions. The Doc said to tell him whatever he wants to know—see 'ya."

When Joe approached, Griff stood up and gave him a big bear hug. "Dean tells me you've been here a lot, I'm sorry I didn't realize it. Thanks for watching out for me."

"That's what partners are for. Besides, you're my best friend. If anything happened to you, I'd be lost. How's the gunshot wound healing?"

"OK, I guess, the stitches are out and I'm in no pain." Griff motioned to Bev, who stepped forward and hugged him. "Glad to see you up and around, Zoo. Joey and I were so worried." She kissed him softly on the cheek.

"May I hold Baby Beveltnik? I won't break him." He sat down in the wheelchair and received Junior, giving him a big kiss. With Joe Jr. safely held in the crook of his arm, he asked Joe, "How are YOU doing, are you back to work yet?"

"Not yet, but soon. I'm off injury leave so now we're going on vacation, you know, a chance to finally get away after the accident. We're so glad that we finally found, you awake and alert. I wouldn't want to leave town without saying goodbye. When are you going to be sprung?"

"I'm not sure, but I think it's going to be soon. What's the scuttlebutt about the jewelry scam that Shotz had going?"

"You're not going to believe this. Rev. Wagner was the middle man in that mess, he was storing jewels in the soup kitchen. Wagner was an alias, his real name is Wanker (the Spanker). He was a child molester. The mission is kind of running itself until someone else takes over. The City sealed up the Tri-Way Warehouse and somebody put up a sign which reads, "The home of Joe's Hole." It's too high for me to take down."

"Why bother, partner, you've been memorialized, you're famous, be proud!"

"You're right, Zoo, I should be glad it didn't say something like 'Here's where a clumsy, flatfooted stumblebum fell through the floor.'" Joe noticed that Griff was starting to nod. "You're getting tired, Zoo, we should be going." As he was retrieving Junior he said, "We will get in touch as soon as we get back. It's good to see you doing so well. You'll be back in your old ride before you know it."

"Bye guys, thanks for coming."

Bev Beveltnik told a nurse that Griff was wilting and the nurse went out to check on him.

On Friday, Griffith James Park was discharged from Cedar-Ash. Sgt. Atrick picked him up and took him home. Monday evening, the Zoo Man would be back to work.

CHAPTER TWENTY-SEVEN

During the ride home, Griff's boss grabbed a box from the back seat and handed it to him. "I thought you might want these." Inside was a new shield, a new name plate and all new award ribbons already in frames and on three row bars. Also, there was a new hat with his hat badge already on it.

"Thanks Sarge, I wouldn't have thought about these until it was time to get ready for work."

"The ribbons are GPS FREE. So far, none of the law enforcement agencies out west have been able to find Shotz' stash. Your badge, Tolliver's hunting guns or anything else has surfaced. Shotz may have buried them in the desert for all we know. If and when any of the stuff is found, they'll let us know."

"It's a good thing that we have a contact out there."

"Who's that, Zoo?"

"Dean Tolliver at the Lawrence County Sheriff's Department."

"Didn't anyone tell you about Tolliver?" He left the Sheriff's Department out west and came back to work for his dad. Dean's been watching over you like a mother hen. Now that you're going back to work, he'll be heading over to Corinth County. He said to tell you that he'll stop by to see you before he goes."

"I guess I have some catching up to do. Just pull in here. Sgt. Atrick pulled his van into the loading zone in front of Griff's apartment building. As Griff was getting his suitcase out of the backseat, he commented, "I'm surprised that an orderly didn't slap an 'I visited Cedar-Ash' bumper sticker on my bag. Thanks for the ride Sarge, I guess I'll see you Monday night."

"Whoa, Zoo, you're not getting rid of me that easy. Take your bag up and come back down, there's more stuff to unload."

Griff had no idea what else that Jerry might have but he would do as he was told. Griff almost hated to open the door of his little apartment, after three months empty, the stale air and dust would just be depressing. When he opened his door, the scent of flowers wafted out. Confused, he double-checked the apartment number. The apartment was clean, neat and had vases of cut flowers. "I've been burglarized by a neat freak," he thought. Bev Beveltnik had always been a whiz with flower arranging, he was pleased by her thoughtfulness.

"Hey Sarge, did you know anything about this?"

"About what, Zoo?"

"About Bev and Joe cleaning my apartment while I was away."

"Sorry, don't know anything about it."

"My partner's the only one with a key to my….wait a minute, how did you get in to get my clothes?"

"I got the key from your partner, silly."

"You still got the key?"

"Hell no, I made copies for everybody in the unit and then I gave it back to Joe."

"That good old Jerry Atrick humor, you gotta love it. Now what else is there that has to be unloaded?"

"Just these, I'll help you with them." Griff looked into the back of his sergeant's van and asked, "What am I supposed to do with four boxes of copier paper, write a book?"

"You? Write a book? I can't hardly get you to write a ticket! But seriously though, I had to scrounge these boxes—your mail is in there."

"You've got to be joking, I haven't gotten that much mail since I've been alive."

"You have a lot of friends, Zoo, I don't know if they're get well cards or if they've started a Zoo Man fan club. Three of the boxes contain cards and letters that were dropped off at the precinct house, the other contains departmental mail and sentiments that were mailed to headquarters.

After lugging up a couple of boxes to Griff's apartment, Sgt. Atrick said, "See you Monday night. Don't forget to recycle," he said pointing to the boxes.

"The first thing I'm going to do is call my partner's wife and thank her for the flowers and the clean up."

"You'll have to wait on that. Joe and Bev are out of town on vacation. OK Zoo, I'll see you in a couple of days."

Alone in his apartment, Griff went to his trophy and memento shelf and looked at a photo of his Judy's beautiful smiling face. He extracted a medium size hex nut from his pants pocket and placed it in front of the photograph. "Oh well," he said to himself, "I probably couldn't have made a ring out of it anyway. Might as well get started on the cards."

After getting a cold soda, Zoo put the first of the boxes on a kitchen chair next to him so that he could use the table for sorting. Right on top of the stack of cards in the first box was a cigar box wrapped in butcher paper. The printing on the paper read, "Just something to remember me by, Ma." Griff unfastened the tape and opened the box. When he lifted the lid, the whirring cardboard paddles attached to a wound up rubber band threw out dozens of sugar and sweetener packets. A note on the interior of the lid read, "Sorry, I couldn't help myself, get well soon, Ma." Griff couldn't help but laugh as he looked at the sugar packets everywhere. Ma got me good, he thought as he brushed packets onto the floor and proceeded to open envelopes.

At the precinct house, Sgt. Atrick was addressing his troops at one of his standard sit-down roll calls. "We are now going to discuss the enhancement of manpower effective Monday night. Since I'm off on Saturday and Sunday, we'll cover this now. The Zoo Man will be back with us after a three-month hiatus. He's been through more than any man can be expected to endure and it almost broke him, but he's OK now and we're lucky to get him back. He is not to be looked at, or treated differently because he has been hospitalized. He is not nuts." The table erupted with hoots and hollers.

"All right, all right settle down, you all know what I mean. We are all nuts for wearing this costume and being under-appreciated. Griff is not insane. I defy any one of you to endure what he went through and come out unscathed. He is to be treated as if he'd only been away on vacation. We wouldn't do any less for you."

The table was silent, with everyone nodding with thoughtful looks on their faces. "That being said, let us prepare for his homecoming; J.B. are you up for this?" He received a hearty thumbs up. "OK men, fifteen minutes early on Monday and J.B., don't forget the ammo. All right men, hit the streets."

Sgt. Atrick was an excellent street supervisor, and everybody from the Chief on down knew it. His discipline was fair, firm, and to the point without being belittling. He took care of his men. On his own, he wrote to the ballistic vest company about how one of their vests had saved Officer Beveltnik from being skewered. His letter was so well received that they sent a new vest for his officer, accompanied by a framed citation. The vest he stored in his locker, the citation was hung in the roll call room as a reminder to others to wear their vests. They will be presented to Joe when he gets back to work.

Griff found that there were many ways people had shown their sentiments. Some sent get well cards, some sent sympathy cards, and others sent checks or cash. To some, money is the answer to everything. All monies collected would be sent to Judy's parents. And of course, there was Ma's sense of humor. Why is she always throwing things at me?

Griff had worked in the same area for fifteen years but was still shocked by the number of people who knew him or knew of him, and would take the time to send a card. He paused for a second to recall who Geofrey Brieson was when he got to that card. “Duh,” he said to himself, Old Breezy. Enclosed with Breezy’s card was a copy of a flyer soliciting money to save Harry’s teeth. Griff thought, ALL of that money doesn’t have to go to Judy’s folks. Maybe I can help out, that would be a good thing to do. Just about everybody on the department had sent him a card by inter-office mail.

The Zoo Man had to start a new pile when he got a card from the staff at the Qua King Duck. In the envelope were a half dozen coupons and probably twenty fortune cookie fortunes.

One box contained nothing but packages of notes and cards written in pencil and crayon. Apparently almost every teacher in the city had given their pupils an assignment to write to the policeman whose train had jumped the track. Funny, he thought, get the Medal of Valor and no one cares. Get your girlfriend killed and go bananas and everybody takes notice.

A packet envelope from the Justice Center of Corinth County caught Griff’s attention. It was postmarked nearly three months ago. In the envelope were photos and a letter: From the Desk of Sheriff Deacon Tolliver.

My Dear Griffith,

Enclosed are copies of the photos we took when you and Miss Stanhope visited last week.I suppose these photos will be anti-climactical after your western trip.

I was very pleased when you called wanting to visit and show off your traveling companion. I get few repeat visitors and to have such a celebrity as yourself return was very special.

My daughter and I both noticed that there was a special electricity between you and Judy. If I may be so bold, I sense wedding bells in your future. If I am correct, and you need a honeymoon getaway, I have just the place. I own a very nice, very clean secluded cabin which I would gladly offer to you if and when the time comes. That’s all I’m going to say on the subject, son.

Please keep in touch. It’s always good to hear from special friends.

Good Luck my Friend,
Deke

Tears were clouding Griff's vision, it was time to take a break. This would be a good time to check his uniform and put it together. The shirts still fit, that was a relief and he only had to put one additional hole in his trouser belt. Griff went to hang his uniform shirt on the back of his open closet door when he found one of Judy's 40 DD bras hanging there. He sighed deeply and then meticulously started adding attachments to his shirt.

On the right side of his shirt and centered above the pocket, he pinned on his new name plate, below that on the pocket flap he added his shooting badge. To finish off the look, he added three rows of award ribbons. It was an impressive rack, better than most—he had been lucky. The Zoo Man polished his new shield to a high luster and attached it to the left side of his shirt. Polishing his hat badge and shoes would complete the ensemble.

On Monday evening, after a bachelor's dinner of Ramen noodles and crackers, Griff dressed for work for the first time in months. "Another death before the holidays," he sighed out loud. After putting on his ballistic vest, shirt and tie, he strapped on his gun belt.

From the lock box on the closet shelf, he retrieved his departmental weapon. After the incident in Minnesota, his .45 had been collected as evidence. The weapon was later returned to C.C.P.D. where the ordnance section's gunsmith cleaned and inspected it. Griff put in a full magazine and racked the slide to chamber a round. He automatically dropped the magazine out, added one bullet to it and replaced it in the weapon. With his side arm now combat loaded, he secured it in his holster.

Time to hit the road, he thought as he picked up his war bag and jacket and headed for the underground garage. Griff pulled the cover off of his Vette and stowed it behind the seat. He then piled his gear into the car and fired it up. It sounded pretty good for having sat so long. As he pulled out of the garage and stopped on the sidewalk to wait for traffic to pass, a pedestrian said, "Now there's a classic. You don't see many Chevettes around anymore." Griff drove on wondering if the man was just being nice or was laughing at him. Zoo made an impromptu stop at St. Thomas Aquinas church for his first attempt at making peace with God.

Everybody arrived early for last minute instructions. Zoo, as usual, showed up at the very last minute. He had butterflies in his stomach. This was like his first day on the job. Would his co-workers shun him for being bad luck? Oh well, time to face the music. When he walked in the door, he was home. Everybody welcomed him back with handshakes and pats on the back.

When Sgt. Atrick came out of his office, he nodded to Griff and then called his men to attention. When the officers were lined up, the sergeant gave them an "about face" order. While his mens' backs were turned toward him, the sergeant got a box from under a table and prepared his surprise. The good sergeant shrugged into a long black tail coat, popped open a top hat and placed it on his head. When the sergeant gave them another "about face" his men were dumbfounded to find him in formal attire.

"Tonight, men, we are having a formal roll call." Sgt. Atrick couldn't keep a straight face and neither could his men. "Tonight we honor one of our own, Zoo Man, front and center."

Officer Griffith Park hesitantly stepped forward and stood in front of the sergeant. "In recognition of your unflappable behavior in the face of muck, mire, mayhem, murder and kidnapping, I hereby confirm upon you a quasi provisional field promotion."

Zoo asked, "Sir, a crazy promotion?"

"No, that's quasi!"

Zoo replied, "That's the quasi-est thing I ever hoid."

"If I may continue, from this day forward, you will no longer just be Zoo Man; I thereby promote you to Zookeeper." Gales of laughter could be heard even out in the parking lot as a red-faced Griff was roasted. When the laughter died down and Sgt. Atrick caught his breath he said, "Griff, your first assignment as Zookeeper is to present his framed ballistic vest citation to Officer Beveltnik."

"Yes sir, I'll do that as soon as he gets back. He's off somewhere vacationing with his wife and son."

"Are you trying to tell me that you have no knowledge as to the whereabouts of your best friend and partner?"

Sheepishly, Griff answered, "Yes sir."

The Sergeant slowly removed the top hat and said chidingly, "Can you believe it? The Great Zoo Man has no idea how to find his partner. Would anyone here like to help our new Zookeeper find his partner?"

"I would," came a voice from the sergeant's office. As Griff turned around, a smiling Joe Beveltnik stepped out of the office dressed in a brand spanking new uniform and said, "Are you ready to go to work partner?"

Griff ran over to Joe, grabbed him by the upper arms and said, "You're damned right I am, welcome back!" Griff then put his arms around Joe and gave him a big bear hug.

"Hey Zoo, you're not going soft on me are you?"

Misty eyed, Griff said, "Heck no, I'm just checking to see if you have your vest on."

As chaos had already become rule, the sergeant yelled "Roll call is dismissed!"

Joe and Griff were headed for the exit door to patrol together for the first time in months when someone yelled out, "Hey Zookeeper."

When Griff turned to look, every officer pelted him with a handful of peanuts.

Another voice called out, "Welcome home, Brother."

While they walked to their cruiser, Griff asked, "Why does everyone keep throwing things at me?"

"I dunno, Zoo Man. Just give me the keys so I can drive."

"Not this time partner. I'll drive. Just don't let your mind wander!"

DEADLY WIRED

CHAPTER ONE

As we left the precinct house and marked in service Joe said, "I sure hope this is a dead night, I'm tired. Bev was gone all day and I had to babysit little Joe."

Radio: "Patrol 17."

"Patrol 17. Go ahead."

Radio: "Patrol 17, check on the well-being of an elderly man at 819 Galveston Ave. An out of town relative hasn't heard from him in some time."

"Patrol 17. What is the gentleman's name?"

Radio: "The name is Wallace Keeper. If you make contact, we have the caller's information."

"Patrol 17. We copy, 819 Galveston."

Galveston Avenue was pretty and tree lined, made up primarily of two story brick homes, 819 being one of them. The mailbox was full and the porch was littered with newspapers and circulars – not necessarily the best sign.

Joe knocked on the front door and called out for Mr. Keeper, no answer. I tried the knob. The door was unlocked. The nauseating stench of death hit us in the face when we opened the door. You half expect this when someone wants you to check on a relative that hasn't been heard from in some time. Even if you expect it, the foul smell is still startling. This kind of run makes or breaks new officers. My partner and I have faced this type of thing before; we stepped back onto the porch to regroup.

I took my small tin of camphor cream from my pocket and rubbed some on my upper lip below my nostrils. I passed the medicated vapors to my partner, and he also partook. After donning powder free latex gloves, we ventured back into the house. The smell was so bad it was hard to locate the source; had it been warmer, the flies would have pointed out the way.

After the fiasco where my partner fell through a rotted warehouse floor, we checked out everything together. With a broad stance so as not to step on the center of the stair runner (just in case there is a need to gather evidence) we walked upstairs.

"Zoo Man, I think our search ends up here. The smell of death is getting stronger."

In the bathroom we found an elderly clothed black man in the bathtub. None of the pictures that we had noticed were of black people and his features were European; the days since his death had caused him to discolor. A blue steel revolver lay on the bathroom floor below his dangling hand. The gunshot wound to the right temple had gone all the way through, and the cracked ceramic tile was dried blood and brain matter spattered.

Joe called radio from his walkie and advised them of the probable suicide. He also requested homicide detectives to investigate and related to them to bring cigars.

We checked the bedrooms and closets and then proceeded to check the rest of the house. The first floor was cluttered and disheveled. The basement was dark and dusty and also cluttered but devoid of further bodies.

"Looks like your typical suicide to me, don't you think, Joe?"

"I don't know, Zoo. I didn't see a note, and that back door looks forced."

"Good call partner. I missed the door. Let's position ourselves in the dining room so we can watch both the front and back doors. Might as well turn the lights on. It'll be dark by the time the suits get here."

"Zoo, don't you hate getting a run like this, first thing out of the chute? You smell of death the rest of the night."

"I know what you mean. My first errand after I get up will be to take this uniform to the cleaners. If I had a house with a garage, I'd leave it in there 'til I had to go to the cleaners."

When the homicide detectives showed up and Griff went out to meet them, he didn't recognize them. "You guys new to homicide?"

"Yeah, we transferred over from Special Ops. I'm Rick Hunter and this is my partner, Lem Tople."

"I'm Griff Park. My partner, Joe Beveltnik, is inside."

"Griffith Park? Like the zoo? You're the Zoo Man! Damn, you're a legend and boy, do you stink! Thanks for the heads up about the cigars. I may have to fire one up just to mask your smell! So what have you got?"

"Possible homicide, found a male D.O.A., days dead in the bathtub with a head shot. No suicide note and the back door's been pried, front door was unlocked, too."

"We'll check it out and let you know."

The detectives each lit an aromatic cigar to try to make the stench bearable and went inside.

Joe came out and said, "Even though I don't smoke, I wish I had a cigar. The camphor cream works O.K., but the cigar smells a lot better. Who were the suits?"

"Transferees from the Secret Shit Squad. I hope they know what they're doing. I don't feel like training them!"

Det. Hunter came out and said, "You called it right. It's a homicide; we'll need a written statement."

"What were the deciding factors?"

What you said, plus he was left handed; watch band mark on his right wrist; watch and rings were gone and his pockets were inside out. It's a homicide staged to look like a suicide."

When Joe went back inside, I sat in the cruiser writing out a statement of what we found and did. The suits called for the lab boys and had a perimeter guard set up. We were relieved an hour later.

"How are we supposed to work smelling like this?"

"Joe, I think this is a decision for the Sarge."

We cleared the scene and requested that our immediate supervisor, Sergeant Jerry Atrick, meet us at E. 21st and Trent. We waited for the sergeant at Doc Hock's Outdoor Barbecue.

When the sergeant arrived, he found us standing in the smoke talking to Doc Hock.

"What are you doing?!"

"Trying to make ourselves smell better. We just came from a ripe one. What do you think maybe we should go home since we smell so bad."

"When I promoted you to Zookeeper, that was ex-officio, it didn't confer upon you any real supervisory ability. I, on the other hand, have already assessed the situation and have a decision in mind."

Sergeant Atrick called for the district paddy wagon to meet at our location before they go on to their dispatched run.

"Sarge, you have a mean streak, making those guys smell our stinkiness," Joe said.

When the wagon arrived, Will Dorsem and Reggie Likens bailed out and thanked the sergeant for delaying their run.

"What's that smell? Was there a fire at the funeral home?"

"Very cute, Will. You don't like our new cologne?"

"All right you guys. Stop bickering. I've got some sergeanting to do. I hate to do this to you, but I think this will work out best. Reggie, Will, I want you two to switch rides with Joe and Zoo. You guys can finish out the night in Patrol 17. In the morning you can meet up and exchange gear.

A befuddled Zoo Man said, "Wait a minute, Boss. What's going on?!"

"I'm supervising, Zoo. You guys already stink. You might as well take the wagon run. Fourteenth and Sturdevant, Homicide Lt. Dingell has requested transport of four ripe homicide victims to go to the morgue and since you are already odorous, this will work out perfectly "

"Do not expect a Christmas card this year," Zoo said.

Joe said, "And don't you cowboys mess up our ride!"

"Don't you stink up ours," Reggie yelled as the wagon pulled away.

Griff looked back in the mirror and saw Will and Reggie laughing and dancing.

At Fourteenth and Sturdevant a patrol officer directed them to the alley. When they were about a quarter block from the other officers, they could smell their destination. They pulled the wagon past the open garage door and were met by Lt. Barry Dingell.

"Zoo Man, what are you doing in the wagon?"

"We're already stinky from one ripe one so Sarge thought we might as well handle this haul, too. What have you got L.T.?"

"We've got four to go to the morgue. Neighbors called about a bad smell coming from the garage; it was locked from the inside."

"Murder suicide?"

"It appears to be four homicides. Four males were playing cards in this locked garage behind the vacant residence. My guess is that they all accused each other of cheating and shot each other as they sat at the table; all were shot in the front and all died. All weapons and monies are here, but no I.D.s as yet. Just when you think you've seen it all," Dingell said, shaking his head. "How many body bags do you have?"

"Don't know. Just switched rides – let's take a look." As Zoo and Joe checked the truck, Lt. Dingell lit up a fresh cigar – it helped, but not much.

"We've got two body bags, one good one and one disposable."

"O.K. then, take two now and pick up more body bags at the morgue. They'll be expecting you. If you've got booties, wear them. It's a mess in there."

Lt Dingell wasn't kidding. It was a mess! Not only was the floor covered in sticky body fluids, but the bodies had been there so long, they had also burst. The camphor and everyone else's cigars did little to help the smell. There was also evidence that some officers had vomited both inside and outside of the scene. Latex gloves from the wagon's supply were given to officers who would be assisting in the bagging and loading of the bodies.

The first body was the easiest. When the player was shot he fell straight back with the chair collapsing under him. With assistance, Joe and Zoo were able to roll the remains into a body bag. Three officers were needed to load the sagging corpse into the back of the wagon. The second body had fallen to the floor in the fetal position. Fortunately rigor mortis had long passed so the body was flexible. Work had to be stopped momentarily because the crime scene boys had failed to bag the hands. With the use of a snow shovel found in the garage, body number two was scooped into the body bag and put into the truck.

While the first two card players were taken to the morgue, lab tech guys and street officers would attempt to remove the last two from their chairs and position them for bagging.

Like any bad smell, you eventually get used to it to some degree. Such was the case with the putrid poker players. The stench became tolerable. We backed the wagon up to the morgue doors, rang the bell and waited.

"I imagine some Lurch-looking character is sleeping on a table in cold storage and we'll have to wait."

"Don't be a cynic, Joe. Some poor med student who's working off his tuition will probably open the door soon."

After several minutes of ringing and pounding, a sleepy-eyed kid, dressed in light green surgical scrubs, emerged from a break room, yawned, scratched and then wheeled a crash cart to the door.

"Are you by yourself?" Zoo asked.

"Nah, I've got plenty of company here – my silent partners. What have you got?"

"The first two members of the poker shootout, we have a reservation."

The three slid a body onto the cart and then repeated the task when Joe College brought up another gurney. One by one the loaded carts were pushed onto a floor scale and weighed. The morgue kid briefly looked inside of each body bag and then filled out file cards for each. A John Doe tag was tied on one handle of each bag. We picked up two more body bags, and we were free to do it all over again.

We used the phone in the morgue office and called Ma's Diner. Ma herself answered.

"Ma, it's Zoo. Can I ask a favor of you? What we need is two coffees to go, one black and one doctored up like Joe likes."

"I don't run no delivery service, Zoo."

"I know Ma. We were hoping for a little curb service. We smell so bad we'd empty out the diner just by walking in. Thanks, Ma. I knew you'd understand. We'll be out in front in five minutes."

We pulled up in front of Ma's and she carried out two cups of coffee.

"Here's your special deliv--- Judas Priest! You guys stink!! What did you fall in?!"

"We've been swimming in ripe bodies. Pretty bad, huh?"

"Pretty, no. Bad, oh yeah. Here, take these and go. You can pay me later. Zoo Man, I think you captured a skunky." She was pointing at Joe. Ma laughed her way back inside and we pressed on. For some reason we couldn't smell the coffee and it didn't taste that good either.

Back at the garage the other two bodies had been laid out on the floor ready for pick up. Near one of the bodies was a big skid mark and a rookie with a stink soaked backside was grumbling in a corner.

The next body was probably the worst. This player apparently had been sitting across from the player with the sawed-off shotgun. It must have been held sideways when both barrels were fired. One shot took out the center of the man's chest while the second tore through his neck and lower jaw. The head tilted back like a Pez dispenser. When we moved him, two aces fell out of his left sleeve.

After the first three, number four was a piece of cake. With the last of the bodies in the paddy wagon, the crime scene boys finished their measuring, photographing and evidence gathering. Only one cruiser officer was allowed to touch the guns and money; that way the chain of evidence is preserved as he turns the evidence in to the property room.

Our last trip to the morgue was a carbon copy of the first. The bagged and tagged bodies were signed for and put in cold storage. We grabbed two new body bags and a box of latex gloves from the supply closet and headed out. We stopped by an all night gas station and purchased a can of floral air freshener through the window and emptied it into the back of the wagon. By the time we returned to the precinct house the paddy wagon smelled more like a whorehouse than a hearse.

We showered and changed into civvies before we went home, our uniforms tightly tied in plastic bags. The dry cleaners are going to love us!

As we walked to our cars I said, "Joe, they've got a system in South Dakota where the coroner has its own pickup wagon and crew. Too bad we don't have that kind of system here. Maybe I'll put that idea in the suggestion box. Another suggestion, Joe. Don't wish for another <u>dead</u> night!"

CHAPTER TWO

"Patrol 17 in service, two officers."

Radio: "17 copy."

"Did your dry cleaner give you a hassle over cleaning your uniform because of the smell?"

"I'm not sure, Zoo."

"You're not sure?! They did or they didn't, Joe!"

"The lady that runs the cleaners is Oriental. When she opened the bag she was very vocal and quite animated, but I couldn't understand a word of what she said; but she did charge me double when I picked it up. How about you?"

"I washed mine at the coin laundry and then took it to the drycleaner to make it look professional."

Radio: "Patrol 17."

"17. Go ahead."

Radio: "Patrol 17 see the man at the carnival set up at the SeaView Mall. The caller's name is Billy Yellowknife. He runs the petting zoo."

"Patrol 17. We copy."

"Headline news – 'Zoo Man goes to petting zoo.' Good, huh?"

"Just drive, Joe. Leave the humor to me."

"I love carnivals. This is a great opportunity to check it out."

"They'll be here for two weeks partner. You'll have plenty of time to be a kid again."

Joe pulled their black and white into the south entrance of the mall where the carnival was set up. He drove very slowly toward the petting zoo, taking in all of the sights. A large man dressed in a fringed buckskin shirt, blue jeans and cowboy boots was waving frantically. He was in front of a banner which read 'PETTING ZOO' in large letters. The big man lumbered over to the cruiser as Griff and Joe were exiting.

"Are you Billy Yellowknife?"

"That's me," said the tattoo covered carnie.

"I'm Officer Park and this is my partner, Officer Beveltnik. What can we do for you?"

"I want to report the theft of a pig."

"You want to report a purloined piglet?" Griff asked smiling.

"It was the sow," said stone-faced Yellowknife. She's a big 'un, three hundred pounds. The piglets rely on her for milk."

"When did you find her missing?"

"When I came to open up the petting zoo for the evening, she was gone. Are you guys going to put out an APB or something?"

"We have to take a report before the department starts scouring the city," Joe said. He was working on the report as they spoke.

"Could she have wandered off?"

"She might coulda shouldered the gate open. But she couldn'ta closed it up. It was closed up tight."

"OK. What did the sow look like?" Joe was really getting into this and enjoying himself immensely.

"She's a big pig, a big pink pig!"

"Does she have any marks, scars or tattoos?"

"She's got spots," he drawled.

"If we find her, how can we contact you?"

"I'll be right here for the next two weeks." Billy Yellowknife picked up a pitchfork and started arranging straw bedding in the pens while baby farm animals looked on.

As they drove off, Griff said "OK, hotshot, what kind of report did you take? Missing pig?"

"Nope. Just your standard lost or stolen catch-all report." Joe reached for the mike and Griff stopped him.

"What are you doing?"

"I'm going to air an APB, an All Pigs Bulletin."

"Oh, no you're not! We'll be the laughing stock of the whole department! Trust me, if someone finds a big pig, we'll hear about it."

Joe smiled and drove on. Griff cleared the run. There were no other runs pending.

The slack time between runs allows street officers to do real police work, often in inventive ways. Joe and Griff always varied their patrol areas so as not to establish a pattern or routine. There were a number of churches and schools near the SeaView Mall. This would be an opportune time to check them.

"Joe, did you ever wonder where the name SeaView Mall came from? There's no sea and not much of a view either."

"They had to call it something," the quick witted Joe Beveltnik answered as he drove down church row. Church row is actually Mark Road, but it has five churches and two schools in a three block stretch. The first two checked out all right.

"There's been a rash of thefts from churches across the city lately. Electronics, microphones and amplifiers seem to be the target. You think maybe there's a battle of the bands coming up?"

"Could be, Joe," Griff said as they exited the property of St. Paul's Episcopal. "St. Paul's looks good and the Chinese church is also tight. Waterford Elementary is the next to check, middle of the block."

While Joe drove around the school, Griff walked along checking the doors and inspecting the windows. The cruiser turned into an alcove and stopped abruptly. The headlights picked up an anomaly.

"What's with the planks leaning against the wall, Zoo, a homeless shelter?"

"Doubtful, Joe. It does look like an impromptu lean-to, but the school wouldn't allow it. Let's take a look."

With the door post spotlight trained on the planks, they approached. In the space under the leaning boards was the three hundred pound pink pig, gutted.

"You're the Zoo Man. What do you think?"

"I think she built this shelter, gutted herself and laid down to die."

"She could have used straw, sticks or bricks. I wonder why she chose boards."

"Joe, I think you're crazier than I am! I don't see any ritual signs or symbols. I'm guessing it's just a sick prank. I'll nose around here. You can pick up Billy Yellowknife and bring him back here."

While Joe was going back to the petting zoo, Griff was using his flashlight to examine the area. Faint drag marks were found leading out of the alcove to a nearby dumpster. An old painter's drop cloth and pig's intestines were inside. Whoever had done this was thoughtfully neat. Griff had just finished examining the dumpster when Joe returned. Joe walked Mr. Yellowknife to the area of the ultimate good news, bad news scenario.

"We found your pig," Joe said emphatically as he shined his flashlight under the planks.

"That's not my sow," the petting zoo owner said. "Granted it looks like my pig, but mine was alive. Since this hog is dead, I am not claiming ownership." Yellowknife folded his arms and looked smug.

"I think I can wrap this up in a *snap*," Griff said while nodding to his partner. Zoo walked Yellowknife over to the carcass and was uncovering the pig by removing the planks when Joe walked up.

"Hey guys!" Joe snapped a flash picture of them with the big pig when they turned to face him.

"What's that for?" Billy demanded.

"That, my good man, is a photo of me returning your pig to you. The photo will be attached to the report, case closed. How soon can you get your pig out of here?"

The trapped carnie said he could get some carnival workers with a cart, but didn't think he could find his way back. To solve Yellowknife's problem, the C.C.P.D officers drove him back to the carnival. The carnie got two of his buddies with a cart and a garden tractor to help him in the removal of the big pig.

With beacons on, Joe and Griff escorted the mini parade to the school and once the cart was loaded, back to the carnival. Billy was steaming about having been bested when Zoo said, "Doc Hocks' Outdoor Barbecue is at Twenty-first and Trent. If Doc can't help you out, you at least have the main fixings for the world's largest B.L.T. Have a good day." As the cruiser pulled out, Billy Yellowknife waved, but he didn't use all of his fingers.

Patrol 17 cleared and finished checking church row. Bethany Baptist and St. Raphael's Catholic Church checked OK except that some tagger had put a stylized Ninja turtle on St. Raphael's garage since the last time they checked. John F. Kennedy High School checked out OK, too. The cleaning staff was working late.

The last church stood quite a bit off the road and was fronted by a huge asphalt parking lot. The God's Little Acre of Hope, Inc. was also tight. When Griff's flashlight shone on a vertical brass pole in the sanctuary, he thought that he might attend a service sometime and jotted down the worship times.

When Griff got back in the cruiser, Joe said, "I'll bet I could write a play about tonight's incident."

After about three blocks of silence Griff responded, "OK, I'll bite. What would you call your play?"

"How about 'Pig-malion'?"

"How about we get some coffee?" Griff asked, shaking his head.

At Ma's Diner, their favorite watering hole, Joe regaled the four hundred pound owner with his take on the pig incident.

"You boys didn't think of poor old me?" Ma asked. "That big pig would have made a lot of pork chops."

"Ma, I've always been a little suspect of your meat," Griff commented.

"My meat is prime, Zoo Man!" Ma smacked her butt and waddled away laughing. The coffee fueled officers went out to their cruiser and returned to patrol.

"I love this job. No two days are ever alike and it's always something interesting."

"I agree, Zoo, even the smelly runs."

"You know it's ironic, when I was knocked out and kidnapped last year I was held at an old pig farm and never saw a pig. I come back to the city and voila, a pig run. Go figure."

"It kind of STYmies the imagination," Joe said. He was so proud of his pun that he laughed out loud.

"That was bad," Griff groaned. "Too bad I didn't think of it. Now tell me more about that girl you want me to see."

Joe was telling Griff about the pretty barista working at The Last Drop Coffee Shop when they got a call.

Radio: "Patrol 17."

"17. Go ahead."

Radio: "1617 Floral Garden Way, shots fired, no injuries. The shots apparently came from a light green car, possibly a Firebird. The vehicle has left the immediate area."

"17. Copy, 1617 Floral Garden." Griff repeated the address. "I'll bet that waitress is a dog. You're just messing with me."

"I'm not trying to sell her. I was just telling you about her," Joe said as he wheeled their Crown Vic cruiser toward the Floral Circle subdivision. As they approached Babylon Terrace, the main drive into the subdivision, a light green Camaro exited in front of them. The Camaro quickly turned left on Christen Drive passing Patrol 17 which was going in the other direction. The male white driver looked wide eyed at the cruiser and punched the accelerator.

"Hold on, Zoo. As hinky as those guys are they've got to be our shooters." While he spoke, Joe B. made a u-turn to follow the suspect vehicle which was rapidly pulling away. Griff activated the beacons and siren and grabbed the radio mike.

"Patrol 17. In pursuit eastbound on Christen from Babylon Terrace, light green Camaro, occupants may be armed."

Radio: "All units stand by. Patrol 17 is in pursuit."

"17. He's still eastbound on Christen, just ran the light at Fern. Male white driving."

The sports car narrowly missed colliding with a crossing vehicle at Fern. Joe, having to safely play by the rules, slowed and checked for traffic before running the light.

The cruiser was again closing when a figure leaned out of the passenger side window and then there were a series of yellow flashes. Thud! Thud! Spang! The cruiser had taken some hits. One slug ricocheted off of 17's hood and chipped the windshield which started to star immediately. Joe pulled the cruiser as far to the left as possible to cut down the shooters angle.

"Patrol 17. We're taking gunfire – continuing eastbound on Christen passing Dale. Radio, do we have a chopper available?"

Radio: "Negative 17. Air support is not available."

Patrol 2 was westbound on Christen and had the Camaro doing 105 mph by moving radar. When Unit 17 passed, he joined the pursuit as the secondary vehicle. The eastbound Camaro showed no signs of slowing or stopping and was rocketing toward Fleckner.

"Suspect vehicle approaching Fleckner. The light is red."

An 18 wheeler, unaware of the fleeing shooters, entered the intersection from northbound Fleckner to turn westbound onto Christen.

"17. The intersection at Fleckner is blocked." Griff yelled into the mike, "Emergency! Emergency! The bogey just hit a semi!" As soon as they stopped, Griff and Joe ran up to the wreckage.

"Patrol 2. I'm with 17. Roll C.C.F.D and heavy rescue. Also start A.I.S this way as well as a supervisor and units to divert traffic. This has got to be a D.O.A."

Radio: "Already rolling, Unit 2. Keep us advised."

On his walkie Griff said, "Radio, the fleeing vehicle is wedged under the semi. If there are survivors, we're not going to know about it until they get the car out."

The whole area was soon ablaze with flashing lights from the cruisers, the squads, the fire engines and a big boy wrecker that radio had dispatched.

Patrol Sgt. Jerry Atrick coordinated his officers while they directed traffic away from the scene. Other officers cordoned off the area so that the rescue effort could be undertaken without interference from the gore hungry public. Television and radio news crews were kept at bay at a distance that was safe and reasonable.

Battalion Chief Glenn Barron directed the work of the fire responders. Paramedics and heavy rescue, with help from the oversized big boy wrecker, extricated the once pristine Camaro from under the 18 wheeler. An engine company stood by to assist and put out any fire that may erupt.

While a squad treated the semi's driver for shock, several members of the C.C.F.D Heavy Rescue Unit used the Jaws of Life and pry bars to peel the roof and to open the driver's door. When the door opened, a bloody mass fell to the pavement. A fireman rolled it over with his foot revealing a face. An A.I.S. investigator had the head returned to the vehicle. When it was determined that there were no survivors, the decision was made to tow the wreckage, bodies and all to the morgue and continue the investigation there.

Sgt. Atrick sent Patrol 18 to the original Floral Gardens address. The men of unit 18 took damage reports on the residence and on three unrelated vehicles. They also collected shell casings and took witness statements.

Before the car was towed an A.I.S investigator took photos. So did Joe B. His trusty Polaroid was getting lots of use. Joe tried to take a photo of a visible blood covered semi-automatic pistol, but it didn't come out so that you could tell what it was. The red blood on the light green car made a gruesome but pretty color photo though.

"Boss, do you think we'll ever find out what this was all about?"

"I don't know, Zoo. L.E.A.D.S shows the plate to have been taken off of a Jeep in Michigan. I'm guessing the car is hot, too. But we won't know that until we locate the V.I.N number. After the accident investigators and the lab boys go over the car and the bodies, I'm sure we'll know more."

As they were walking back to their cruisers, Griff said, "I'll bet those two have long rap sheets – which end here. Did you see what that S.O.B. passenger did to our ride?"

Joe joined them as they inspected Unit 17 and took pictures.

"That was some pretty good shooting from a moving car," the sergeant said. "Hood, windshield, bumper and fender. Don't be surprised if the body shop only replaces the windshield. Monies are tight for cosmetic work. Go ahead and lay your ride in at the body shop, transfer your gear to a relief car and then head in to A.I.S. and write out statements about the chase. I'll meet you two back at the substation. Good job, men. You get to go home in one piece."

CHAPTER THREE

A financial advisor was available for overlap shift officers on the first Monday of the month, and Joe wanted to take advantage of it. Since Patrol 17 was in headquarters, Griff headed for the Accident Investigation Squad on the fifth floor to find out what had turned up regarding the shooters in the light green Camaro. Griff took the stairs and was glad to think he was exercising. He paused to catch his breath before he went in.

Lead investigator, Danny Chan saw Griff and buzzed him in. "The elevator broken again? I saw you come out of the stairwell."

"Nooooo! Just trying to get some exercise, Danny," he said with heart racing. "What's up with the semi bad guys from the other night?"

"Zoo Man, this case gets curiouser and curiouser. The driver and his passenger were small time local gang bangers; cause of death, according to the coroner, was 'decapitation due to a traffic collision.' I should run for coroner. I'd already made that call. Identifications were made through I.D.s they carried and confirmed through fingerprints. That Camaro turned out to be a rolling arsenal of guns taken out of a burglary at Sol's Pawn Shop. Burglary Detective Delbert 'Bob' Barker is handling that aspect of the case." When Danny referred to Barker as "Bob" he made quote marks with his fingers and his voice held an obvious disdain for the detective. "To further muddy the waters, the Camaro was taken out of a homicide. Lt. Dingell is heading up that part of the incident.

"Sounds pretty convoluted all right. Do you mind if I look at the package, Danny?"

"No problem. Go ahead, Zoo."

Griff carefully went through the A.I.S. file studying the photographs and accident scene diagram. Next he read a transcript of the radio traffic that went on during the chase. Zoo thanked Danny and proceeded down one floor to the homicide squad. A sign next to a door read "Dingell, Barry – Lieutenant". Griff smiled to himself and wondered if that read as funny to others as it did to him.

Griff knocked on the frame of the open door and Lt. Dingell looked up from his newspaper. "Hey, Zoo, what can I do for you?"

"I was just upstairs talking with Danny Chan. He said that the Camaro we chased the other night was used in a homicide."

"Not used in," Dingell said as he got up and came around his desk, "Taken from!" The lieutenant walked by Griff and he followed.

They stopped at Lem Tople's desk and the lieutenant picked up a package marked Keeper, Wallace!

"Keeper, the staged homicide on Galveston?"

"You know something about this case, Zoo?"

"Joe and I were the first responders. We found the body but weren't aware of any car. I didn't see it listed on any hot sheet."

A computer check of Keeper's name came up with a Camaro registered to him. The neighbors said he didn't drive it much and assumed it was in his garage which was padlocked. My guys were still trying to locate relatives to see if any of them had the car when you guys chased it!"

"We think there was more to it, but we're not sure what. I don't think those young punks were smart enough to stage a murder by themselves; too bad we can't interview them. We do know that the gun used was taken out of a burglary at Sol's Pawn Shop and more of the guns were in the Camaro."

"That's what Danny said L.T. I'm going to call down and see if Barker is in."

Joe was finished with his meeting with the advisor and called Griff on his walkie. "You about ready to go?"

"Not yet. Meet me on two. I'm going to meet up with Bob Barker in burglary. He's waiting for me."

Griff walked down the two flights and met Joe as he was getting off the elevator. "You rode up one floor?" he asked.

"Sure. When I start getting paunchy, I'll start taking the stairs."

Griff filled Joe in on the latest goings on while they walked the hallway to the burglary squad; he was still stinging from Joe's barb. As they entered the squad they saw Barker on the phone. He acknowledged their presence and motioned them over. When Barker finished his call, he said, "Zoo, what have you and your partner gotten yourselves into this time?"

"What do you mean, Bob?"

"Sol's Pawn Shop had a break in and one of the stolen guns was found at the Keeper homicide where you boys found the body. Then more of the guns show up in Keeper's vehicle which you chased into the side of a semi. It just looks funny, that's all."

"What looks funny? What are you trying to suggest, Bob?"

"Don't get your hackles up, Zoo Man. It does seem pretty coincidental, don't you think?"

"Coincidental yes, but that's all!"

"Let me pick your brains a bit. Frankly I'm getting nowhere in my investigation and you guys seem to be a common denominator."

"A common denominator?! We were sent on a run and found a dead body. Then we were sent on another run and wound up chasing the victim's car, which nobody knew was stolen. I think the radio room is more of a common denominator. They sent us on those runs!" Griff was livid. "How about those stolen guns. Isn't that a connection?"

"I'm asking for your help boys, not making accusations. I'm just trying to put the pieces together. Barry gave me a copy of your statement regarding finding the Keeper body. Is there anything else you can remember?"

"Like what?" Joe asked.

"I don't know. Did you guys examine the gun?"

"No reason to. That's the detectives' job."

"Did you see any other guns?"

"Nope. If there were some lying about, I'm sure we'd have seen them. We didn't go nosing through drawers or anything!" Griff was starting to get steamed again.

"How about the shooters that you ran into the semi, did you know them?"

Griff came up out of his chair and slammed his hand down on Barker's desk. "What are you trying to imply?! We chased some shooters who tried to drive under a truck – their fault, not our fault!! What is your problem?!"

A stunned Barker replied, "I don't have a problem. I have an unsolved burglary that I'm trying to solve; you're supposed to be a team player. Why won't you work with me?"

"A team player?! You put us on the other team. You want to question us any more, you had better read us our rights – we're outta here."

Griff stormed out of the door. Joe shrugged his shoulders and said, "I dunno," in answer to Barker's quizzical look.

"Come on, Joe!" Griff barked with spittle flying.

"I'm coming – where are we going?"

"Back up to homicide," Griff said through clenched teeth. He nearly broke his index finger punching the up button on the elevator. On the fourth floor Griff stormed into the lieutenant's office without knocking; Joe was trying to keep up.

"What the hell is going on?" yelled Griff.

Barry Dingell stood up, startled, nearly spilling his coffee on his crossword puzzle. "Have you lost your senses, Zoo Man? What burr do you have under your saddle all of a sudden?!"

"That crazy sawed off runt, Barker, in burglary seems to think we were in cahoots with Keeper's killers somehow. What do you think?!"

"I think you should switch to decaf. I've never seen you this wired."

"Do you think that Joe and I had anything to do with Keeper's murder?"

"Hell no, and I'm sure Barker doesn't think so either. There must be some kind of misunderstanding."

"I'll say there is! Barker added two plus two together and came up with twenty-two. He can piss up a rope before he'll get any help from us. Do you think we're suspects in anything?!"

"Of course not. I'll have a talk with Barker. Now get out of here before my detectives come back and find me goofing off talking with you guys."

Without saying goodbye, Griff left the office. As Lt. Dingell returned to his crossword puzzle, Joe said, "Nice talking with you lieutenant." Joe gave Dingell a Stan Laurel finger wave and followed his partner. Dingell followed Joe with his eyes and thought, "He's crazier than the other one."

Griff started to enter the driver's door of the cruiser when Joe stopped him. "I'm not sure what popped your cork, but you're in no frame of mind to drive. Give me the keys." Griff relented with no argument.

On the silent drive back to their district, Griff eventually started to open up. "Can you believe that pin head Barker? He can't solve a crime so he starts grabbing at straws and we're the straws."

"I didn't quite get that feeling. I think he was frustrated and was thinking outside the box; that's all."

Griff couldn't believe what he was hearing from his partner. They'd been partners for over four years and they had never been this out of sync. "Maybe Joe was right," he thought. "Maybe I'm just too thin skinned and didn't understand the line of questioning." Griff did not admit to Joe that he might be wrong. After about five more minutes of silence, Griff spoke. "Where are you headed, Joe?"

"You'll just laugh."

"No, I won't. It's the SeaView Mall, isn't it?

"It couldn't hurt. You know I love carnivals and they need protection, too."

"I agree, Joe. Besides I could use a little break. I've been a little surly lately."

Patrol 17 marked busy at the mall, locked their cruiser and proceeded to walk through the temporary carnival. It wasn't a big carnival, but it was a source of stress relief. Joe stopped at a booth on the midway and played a game; two of three darts broke balloons – he won the choice of a small prize. He consulted with a small child who had been watching and chose a small stuffed monkey. Joe gave the monkey to the child, much to the delight of the child's mother.

"Why didn't you take that toy home to your son?"

"Don't you think it would look kind of strange walking around with a monkey?"

"I'm doing it, and it doesn't seem strange to me," Griff quipped.

A familiar voice from behind them said, "Did you pigs come to work in my petting zoo? I'm down a big pig, you know!"

Griff and Joe turned around and found Billy Yellowknife backed up by four overgrown carnies.

"Hello, Billy," Griff said. "I see you brought an audience with you. Is there something you want to say?"

"You did me wrong when my pig was took!"

"How do you figure, Billy?"

"You made me look foolish in front of my friends and now we're going to make you pay. I can't believe you're dumb enough to come back here."

Joe turned his walkie to a dead channel and then made an exaggerated count of Billy and his four friends. Joe keyed his walkie and spoke to the inactive channel. "Patrol 17. We're going to need five ambulances at the carnival at the SeaView Mall. We're going to have five to go to area hospitals."

"Nobody's that good," Billy sneered. But as he spoke, his backups were all backing up with their empty palms facing forward. The carnies could not afford to go to jail or worse. Billy was on his own. "There'll be another time," he said with false bravado as he walked away.

"I don't think he's quite ready to change his last name to Badass. By the way, that was an interesting stunt with the walkie. Why didn't you just call for backup?

"Why? I had every confidence that you could take them. Besides I would have helped if you had needed it."

Patrol 17 cleared and was immediately dispatched to see a Mr. Sol Goldman at Sol's Pawn Shop.

"I smell a rat," Zoo said. "This feels like a set up. Keeper's murder weapon and the Camaro shooters' guns all came from Sol's, and now someone is trying to draw us in further. This can't be a coincidence!"

Sol's was located on Slough Avenue in an ever changing part of town, changing for the worse, that is. It was flanked on one side by a small Caribbean Café and on the other by a coin laundry which was on its last legs. Many store fronts were boarded up. The area was in a state of decay. Sol's door was locked, they rang the bell and were buzzed in.

"Bet you don't get a lot of walk-in traffic with that buzzer system," Griff said.

"Almost more than I can handle. What can I do for you boys? Need a cheap throw down gun or something?"

"We're to see a Sol Goldman."

"I'm Sol Goldman. What can I do for you?"

"We were sent here to see you. You didn't call?"

Goldman shrugged his shoulders and shook his head.

Joe called radio and was advised that the caller was anonymous but had asked for unit 17. It was assumed that it was Mr. Goldman.

Griff requested the use of Mr. Goldman's phone and was given access to the broker's cage. While he phoned, Joe looked for bargains.

"Burglary, Barker."

"Barker, this is Park. What the hell are you up to now?!"

"Whatever do you mean, Mr. Team Player?" Barker asked with an obvious sneer in his voice.

"For some unknown reason you're trying to put us in the jackpot for your pawn shop burglary. Now we get sent out here to Sol's Pawn Shop by an *anonymous* caller. Mr. Goldman did not call for us. He doesn't need our help and frankly we don't want or need to be here. If you want to play guilt by association so can we. Why did you send us here?"

"I didn't have you sent there!" Barker barked. "Why would I do that? What would I have to gain by messing with you?"

"I'm not sure but………

The explosion from the back room of the pawn shop rocked the block. The back wall blew out, scattering bricks and pawned items into the alley and surrounding properties. The old wooden garage across the alley collapsed. The front wall of the back room blew over and collapsed onto the frame of the pawn broker's cage. Griff survived the blast because Goldman's body broke his fall – Goldman's body, just broke. Griff was out cold as was his partner who was buried under as avalanche of drums, guitars and other musical instruments in the front of the store.

The concussion did not cause a fire, but hot wires were arcing. The first responders from the Capitol City Fire Department charged lines and stood by in case a fire started while they were waiting for the electricity and gas to be shut off. Once the utilities were made safe, firefighters with helmet mounted lights began their search for bodies. The café and coin laundry were closed and sustained heavy damage. The pawn shop had a history of being occupied at night. While the rescuers worked inside, looters were carting off nearly everything that had been blown out of the building.

The firefighters' first discovery was discouraging. The remains of a person at the blast point were so shredded that the sex could not be determined. When the back room wall was breached, they found a crumpled police officer under the broker's cage; under him were the remains of the elderly Sol Goldman.

The street and alley were swarming with police and fire personnel. When Sgt. Atrick arrived he saw one sheet draped body in the alley and another sheet draped over what appeared to have been a workbench. Griff was carried out on a backboard and was being placed on a stretcher when the sergeant approached. "We think he fared pretty well, all things considered, Sarge. X-rays will tell the tale."

"How about his partner?"

"Partner?!" A firefighter asked, "Was he in uniform, too?" Sarge nodded.

"Heads up, men. We've got another one inside!"

A further search ensued, and several minutes later another backboard was rushed in, and
Joe was removed. The officers were stabilized and put in separate squads.

The paramedics saw that Sgt. Atrick was very concerned and one said, "Don't worry, Sarge, we'll get them to 'The Falls' in short order."

"That's great, Stella Niagara Hospital is the best!"

Much work lay ahead. The remains of the back room blast recipient needed to be removed and identified. Arson investigators needed to scour the scene. Structural engineers had to decide if the building as well as the adjacent structures was safe for occupancy and salvaging. The scene had to be guarded, traffic diverted and looters kept at bay. It was going to be a busy night and day, but the two central characters would not be participating. The boys of Patrol 17 would be told about it later.

CHAPTER FOUR

Capitol City has two hospitals with varying reputations. One is St. Anthony's, a certified hospital, but most patients were thought to be certifiable for going there; it wasn't dubbed St. Agony's for nothing. The other is Stella Niagara, the hospital of choice for many residents and the required place for treatment for fire and police personnel.

Everybody notices when a uniformed police officer is wheeled into the emergency room, but when two are wheeled in, the worst is expected. Neither officer appeared to be bleeding, but both were unresponsive. A hospital security officer took charge of the police officers' hardware until a police representative relieved him of it.

With speed and precision the doctors and nurses in the emergency room removed the officers' uniforms and ballistic vests. The sadists at St. Agony's revel in cutting off clothing, but Stella Niagara personnel are more respectful when it's not a full blown trauma case.

Both officers were prepped and ready in short order and sent for x-rays and CAT scans before Sgt. Atrick arrived at the E.R.

Both officers had received concussions and would be spending at least twenty-four hours for observation; both had bumps and bruises but no broken bones; they were assigned to a common hospital room. Griff regained consciousness first and lay there confused and with one hell of a headache. The attending nurse bombarded him with questions apparently designed to ascertain how scrambled his brain was. Griff couldn't hear the questions but could read the nurses lips on some. He answered to the best of his ability while indicating that he was having difficulty hearing. Joe Beveltnik underwent the same inquisition when he came around and fared only a little better. Written communications indicated the belief that the hearing loss was not expected to be permanent.

A police guard was posted outside of their hospital room as a precaution, in case they were intentional targets of the blast. One of the two hour guard shifts was pulled by Officer Jake Matuska who stuck his head into the room and jokingly chided the boys for being malingerers.

"You'll have to speak up, Jake. It's hard to hear you. What's the scuttlebutt about the pawn shop? Do they know exactly what happened?"

Officer Matuska spoke louder and slower. "As I understand it, Joe, the late Sol Goldman was more than just a pawn broker; he was more of a crime boss than anything else. One of Sol's employees, a local gang banger, was making pipe bombs in the back room when something went wrong making him part of the room decorations." He repeated the information to Griff who was straining to hear. Joe finally came over and stood by Zoo's bed.

"You said Goldman died?" Griff asked.

"Yeah, he was crushed under some heavy weight."

Joe said, "That's probably pretty close to what happened. He was crushed under a heavyweight." He chuckled, pointing a finger at his partner.

"The word is that a full blown investigation is under way focusing on the Goldman family. They think Goldman made a false report of a burglary to account for lost guns he was furnishing to young gang members. Detectives also think he may have been responsible for at least one murder."

Over the next two days the boys' hearing slowly returned and they had a fairly steady stream of visitors. C.C.P.D. personnel got a free pass. Others like Bev Beveltnik got the third degree by a guard officer before being allowed admittance. Even Detective Bob Barker came by to make amends for doubting Griff's loyalty. Griff cupped his hand behind his ear just so Barker would have to repeat his apology. Joe tugged on Barker's sleeve so that he, too, could hear the apology. They scammed the detective and loved seeing him sweat.

Three days was plenty of time for the officers to bounce back, and the nurses begged the attending physician to release the frisky jokesters. Besides the inappropriate writings on the message board, Griff indoctrinated each employee with a whoopee cushion that an equally twisted officer had brought to him. Griff gave the fake vomit and molded rubber crap to Joe.

The department insisted that Zoo and Joe take an extra two days off before returning to work, to make sure they were good to go.

Griff found a hole in his uniform shirt and mended it before taking it to the dry cleaners. The lady working the desk at the cleaners gave him a cautious look. Ever since he brought in his death soaked uniform, she was wary. On the way out he ran into his partner.

"Changing dry cleaners?"

"Had to. The Chinese laundry refuses to handle my uni's after I brought them in sealed in a bag. I tried to argue with them, but I don't speak the language."

Griff cupped his ear and said, "What?"

They were talking and laughing in front of the cleaners when a teenager approached and offered to sell them a car stereo. It still had Sol's For Sale tag on it. As they spoke, Joe eased his jacket open revealing his shield on his belt. The wide eyed wannabe gangster took two steps to run, but Griff's iron grip on his shoulder prevented him from fleeing. The kid tried to plead his case but to no avail. A call to the burglary squad confirmed that they wanted the kid brought in for questioning; they sent a black and white to pick him up.

Joe convinced his partner to leave his beater Chevette parked and come with him to take a look at the damaged pawn shop. Griff folded himself into Joe's wife's old beat up V-W bug and grumbled that it had less room than his subcompact car.

The section of Slough Avenue where the pawn shop was located looked like a war zone. Repairs were underway at Rastas' Caribbean Café. A For Sale or Lease sign was tacked to the front of the boarded up coin laundry. A host of workers were feverishly trying to get Sol's up and running. The man directing the work must have been one of Sol's family members; the similarity was strong.

"Is working on Saturday kosher?" Griff asked.

"It is when you're trying to put your business back together," replied the Sol look alike. "I think the police should pay for this, they blew it up and didn't stop the looters from carrying away all of the inventory."

"I heard that a guy working in the back room making pipe bombs blew this place up," Griff said.

Before the anger-eyed Goldman could respond, Joe said, "What happened to all of the musical instruments? They couldn't have taken them all."

"There's nothing left. The insurance company is going to have a shit fit!"

"Who are you insured with?"

"Mutual of Mendicino; for what they charge in premiums you would think those lazy bastards would at least send a representative out. They'll pay plenty for making us send damage and inventory claims to them. By the way, what can I do for you fellas?"

Griff couldn't resist. "We were just in the neighborhood and thought we'd drop by. We're from Mutual of Mendicino."

The insurance belittler gasped so hard that his upper plate came loose and dropped. While he stuttered and stammered, Griff said, "Just kidding," and the boys rapidly walked on. A barrage of comments followed them as they quickly walked down the street, but they couldn't understand the language.

"You know who I'm going to call?" Griff asked.

"Mutual of Mendicino?"

"Let's do it together. You can give them a firsthand account about their musical instruments inventory and then we can call the burglary squad and inform them of the upcoming insurance fraud." The boys chuckled all the way back to the old Zoomobile.

Monday night roll call for overlap shift officers was punctuated with jabs at Patrol 17.

"I went out and got bombed the other night and nobody gave me a week off."

"Heard you guys had a blast!"

"I heard that the hospital said that you two jokers are to go to St. Agony's in the future."

Sgt. Atrick finally got his men under control and held roll call. "Joe and Griff are taking a lot of guff from you guys and let's be thankful they can. They could have been hurt a lot more, or worse. In this job things happen fast and can be deadly. You never know what's going to happen, so it behooves you to live a clean life. I'm not trying to sound like an evangelist. I just want you to be careful. That's all."

"Amen, preacher, amen."

"Get out of here you guys. Criminals are waiting."

As they were prepping their cruiser, Griff found a small black box under the driver's seat. It appeared to have been bolted down. Griff flagged down another cruiser and checked under that seat: no box. Griff apologized to the other officers for holding them up and then he and Joe went in to see the sergeant.

"Got a minute, boss?"

"Are you guys still here? I hope you're not going to ask for another week off."

"Sarge, are Joe and I under investigation for something?"

"Not that I'm aware of. Why do you ask?"

"We just found a black box mounted under the driver's seat. It's never been there before. Do you think it's a monitor of some kind?"

Sgt. Atrick had a puzzled look on his face and got to his feet. "Let's take a look at it." The three went to the parking lot and Sgt. Atrick, using Griff's flashlight, looked under the seat. Sgt. Atrick also looked under the car. When he stood he started walking backward away from the cruiser and indicated that Joe and Griff should join him in the substation. The sergeant used the phone to call the radio room.

"We need the C.C.F.D bomb squad at the substation A.S.A.P., and call all cruisers and have them immediately check for unusual devices mounted under their seats or elsewhere in their cars. Tell them this is not a drill!"

Joe and Griff were wide-eyed while listening to the phone call. Sgt. Atrick said "It's better to be safe than sorry, but unless I miss my bet, there's C-4 packed under your car. You guys go out to the driveway and keep everyone but the bomb squad from coming in and direct those bomb guys to your cruiser."

While Griff and Joe were taking up their positions Sgt. Atrick was ordering cruisers to block off nearby intersections so that the public could not come close to the substation. Other cars were assigned to evacuate buildings in a one block area.

The bomb squad truck and disposal trailer arrived with a blaze of beacons and a blare of sirens, accompanied by a full complement of fire personnel, pumpers, paramedics, etc. While the disposal team suited up, Griff and Sgt. Atrick were debriefed on what they saw and the device's actual location. They were thankful that by nature of the parking lot's fencing, the area was already cordoned off. As the curious arrived to see what the bomb squad was doing, they would be held at bay by officers and firefighters.

The two man disposal team, dressed like heavily padded spacemen, cautiously approached the vehicle. Using lights and mirrors, they slowly assessed the job at hand. The job was going to be trickier than usual due to the suspected explosive being under the car and the detonator above and inside of the car. A large inflatable bag was used to raise the rear of the car. The inflatable thus afforded the "boom boys" easier access without causing sparks. After conferring, it was decided to attempt to remove the plastique first and then tackle the detonator. The pair retreated to their truck and retrieved a large heavy lidded box with four extended handles for carrying like a stretcher. The lid was removed and the box slid under the explosive.

The work was slow, precise and nerve wracking as it was being done seemingly in slow motion. The suspected explosive material was removed and placed in the box. Like earthbound astronauts, the bomb squad boys slowly and gingerly carried the covered box to the bomb trailer. A collective sigh of relief could be heard once the box had been secured in the blast proof trailer. The bomb disposal boys started to step away from the trailer to go back to remove the detonator when it exploded. The cruiser shook and smoked. The shredded driver's seat and interior shrapnel was blown out of the open driver's door.

Griff sat back against the bomb squad truck. He was breathing hard and beads of sweat were forming on his brow. "I guess it was no hoax. I was hoping it was," he said to the battalion chief who was standing nearby. Joe had turned a pasty pale and was escorted to a squad where he sat on the floor with his legs dangling out of the rear doorway.

The substation parking lot was now a crime scene. Arson investigators were joined by lab techs as they scoured every inch gathering up each small fragment which might be used in reconstructing and identifying the detonating device. After the gathering was complete and photographs taken, the rest of the car was checked. Griff and Joe were finally allowed to retrieve and examine the remains of their belongings. The departmental shotgun was removed from the trunk to be returned to the ordnance section to be checked for damage.

Patrol 17's cruiser was the only one that had been tampered with. After the cruiser was towed to the body shop for estimates and repairs, and the lot was cleared for returning cruisers, a new player showed up on the scene.

CHAPTER FIVE

The tall young man entered the substation, his F.B.I. windbreaker had Wohcowhcs embroidered on left front breast. Griff pushed his chair back from the roll call table and suddenly stood up.

"Agent Wohocks, what are you doing here?"

At the sound of his name the special agent wheeled and came face to face with his old acquaintance. "Zoo Man? Why am I not surprised to find you here; trouble follows you." The two shook hands and then embraced.

The rest of the officers followed the conversation like it was a tennis match; they knew that Griff had friends in high places, but this really surprised them. Joe had heard about Agent Wohcowhcs through Griff but never expected to meet him.

"Mike, this is my partner, Joe Beveltnik. Joe, Michael Wohocks." Joe looked at the name on the agent's jacket and said, "And I thought I had a tough name to pronounce."

"What's up, Mike?"

"I'm here in response to the cruiser bombing. I'm supposed to meet a Sgt. Atrick, Jerry Atrick."

"C'mon, Mike, I'll take you to him. Did you transfer from South Dakota?"

"It was the Director's idea, shuffle people around the country so they can get different experiences. I never thought I'd be running into you again; by the way, my condolences on the loss of your girlfriend. She was a damned good officer. I heard you went through a rough time over it. Are you O.K. now?"

"Right as rain, Mike, although I still owe Judy's parents a visit; I guess I've been putting that off, nerves you know." More quietly he said, "Maybe I should have said 'Right as acid rain'."

They stopped at the sergeant's office and Griff rapped on the window of the closed door. The sergeant called out "Come on in, Zoo." As Griff and the special agent walked into the office, Sgt. Atrick asked, "Who have we here?"

"Sgt. Atrick, this is Agent Michael Wohocks from the F.B.I."

After pleasantries were exchanged Agent Wohcowhcs explained his visit. "Our local office received an anonymous call just prior to the cruiser explosion saying that a police car was going to be blown up, occupied or not. The caller hung up before we could get a trace. Our best guess was that someone was trying to ground the whole fleet so that he, or they, could carry out some plot."

"There are other police agencies locally. Why one of our cars?" Jerry asked.

"Why my car?!" Griff demanded.

"We don't know. When was the last time the car was used?"

"It hasn't been used for a week. Griff and Joe were hospitalized out of a pawn shop explosion."

Wohcowhcs suddenly looked up from his notes with greater interest. "I just got into town yesterday. Nobody told me about another explosion."

"That one wasn't planned," Griff said, "but there may be a connection. Pipe bombs were being made in the back room of a pawn shop. We just happened to be there when one accidentally went off killing the owner and the bomb maker. Investigations point to the late pawn shop owner as being some type of local crime boss. Joe and I went by there Saturday and the owner's family is now running the business."

"I'll get the pertinent information from you and look into it until we hear back from your lab boys. They are trying to reassemble the detonator."

"Joe and I have to hit the bricks; we'll let you two alone to talk. By the way, boss, what are we supposed to drive? There are no relief cars available."

The sergeant tossed his keys to Zoo. "Take my unit. If I'm needed out there someone can pick me up. In the meantime, I'll try to scrounge a ride for you."

"Hey, Zoo, here's my number. It's the main office number. I'm not settled in yet."

As Mike was handing Griff the number, the Sarge said, "Don't blow up my car."

Joe and Griff, both being a little gun shy, went over the sergeant's cruiser with a fine tooth comb. Griff drove off of the substation lot while Joe marked them in service; they were immediately given a run. They were the last car to be dispatched on a burglary alarm at Exotic Meats on the private Exotic Drive.

Patrol 7 was already on scene and Patrol 5 was just pulling up. The front door glass had been broken out. Patrol 17 roared to the rear to cover the back door. A large black man burst out of the rear door as the cruiser pulled up. He dropped his arm load of white paper wrapped packages and ran for the rear fence. Joe was on him before the car stopped and easily closed the gap on the lumbering man. Joe caught him as he was unsuccessfully trying to scale the chain link fence. The big man was breathing heavily and Joe had no problem affecting the arrest. Joe hooked two pairs of handcuffs together, because the man's shoulders were so wide. Patrol 17 called for a paddy wagon, because the supervisor's car that they were driving had no interior screen and the perp was so large.

Patrols 5 and 7 caught two more miscreants inside and two of the officers brought them to the rear of the store to wait for the detectives. While their partners watched the front and interior, each suspect occupied the rear of a separate vehicle to keep them separated. They would also be interviewed separately.

The burly Jamaican that Joe had nabbed had dropped his loot onto a parking block and one of the packages split open. The "meat" was green and leafy and did not look like oregano. Burglary detectives and narcotics were both called to investigate. A narcotics dog hit on all of the packages that the Jamaican had brought out.

Griff sat in the paddy wagon with the Jamaican. Before rights could be read or questions asked, the suspect started making rambling spontaneous utterances in an effort to save his skin. He said his name was Tomas Domingue but people called him Rasta. He was the owner of Rasta's Caribbean Café and that his freezer was destroyed when a bomb went off at the pawn shop next to his restaurant, ruining all of his meat. Two of his customers talked him into doing this break-in and told him he could have all of the meat he could carry. He knew it was wrong, but he was desperate; he had no insurance and could get no line of credit for fresh meat to keep his restaurant open. "Please have pity on a poor emigrant jus trying to get along, mon."

Griff told him that he couldn't promise anything, but he would tell the detectives what he had said and maybe they could give him a break if he cooperated with them. He didn't ask the crying Jamaican about the drugs, no need coloring or tainting his testimony. Griff was still taking notes and filling out the arrest report when word came down that Municipal Court Judge Robert Climes had been located and had signed warrants to search the entirety of the Exotic Meats company for drugs and fruits of the crime.

The first assault on the building was with a narcotics K-9 unit. The dog hit on just about every package of "meat" that he came in contact with. While the search was taking place, the owner showed up in response to the alarm.

The short stout man wearing a camel hair coat and fedora approached the supervisor's car. "I'm Izzy Goldman. What exactly is going on here?! I saw the front door broken out and another cop standing in front."

"Are you the owner of this fine establishment?" Griff asked.

"I certainly am, and what is that filthy dog doing in my business?! I've got tons of exotic meats in there and I don't want the health department shutting me down due to flea infestation or something!"

"We don't think that will be the case, do we, Zoo?"

"You're right, Joe." Griff turned his attention back to Mr. Goldman. "We caught three burglars trying to rip off your merchandise. Do you wish to prosecute?"

"Hell, yes, I want to prosecute. I'm a tax payer and I want to get my money's worth," he said indignantly.

"Not to worry," Griff responded with a smile. "You may get more of your money's worth than you want. By the way, that dog is a flea free narcotics officer and he seems to be very interested in your packaged meats."

Goldman started to pace and wring his hands. "What a time I'm having. My brother dies, my business is broken into and the gate at my property malfunctions; that's the reason I'm late getting here."

"I don't suppose your brother was in the pawn shop business?"

"Did you know my brother, Sol?"

"I can honestly say we were very close at the end. Who's running the business now?"

"That would be my other brother, Daniel; he looks a lot like Sol. That business is having its share of problems, too."

A tall thin bearded narcotics sergeant, dressed in faded ragged denims, strolled over to the pair and introduced himself. "I'm Sergeant Hendershott from narcotics. Are you a representative of this company?"

"I'm the owner, Izzy Goldman. Why isn't a burglary cop talking with me?" He was nervously looking around as if expecting another detective to appear.

"He'll talk to you, too, but I want to speak with you first. Walk with me; we'll talk inside your business." The two walked from Griff's cruiser to the rear door of the business. Izzy Goldman saw the dropped packages and bent down to pick them up. Mr. Goldman suddenly stood like he'd been given a shock. He looked over his shoulder at the packages as he and the narcotics officer entered the building.

Wherever the K-9 alerted, his human partner marked the area or package with a round red sticker. The marked areas would be given primary search attention. The dog was tiring and starting to act confused, so he was replaced with a fresh dog that had been waiting outside in a plain car, a dog that had not been overworked.

Mr. Goldman wanted to know what was happening.

"Every place the dog alerts to narcotics, a red dot is placed; frankly it looks like your business has the measles. We need to have a serious chat."

"In that case I want my lawyer here!"

"Conversation's over," Hendershott said.

Mr. Goldman was given a copy of the search warrant and was escorted to his car and told to stand by. He would be interviewed at headquarters later. Narcotics sergeant Hendershott called for a panel truck in which to load the seized narcotics.

The diminutive Izzy Goldman was a nervous wreck; he couldn't stand waiting and got out of his silver and black Bentley to walk around. At first he just paced the parking lot but eventually walked toward the police vehicles. When Mr. Goldman passed one cruiser, a handcuffed suspect turned his head toward the slightly open window and sheepishly said, "Hi, Mr. Goldman."

Goldman stopped suddenly and glared into the back seat of the cruiser. "What's this young man doing in here?!" he demanded.

Officer Kevin Jenks jumped out of Patrol 5 and confronted Goldman. "Step away from the cruiser, sir. Do you know this man?"

"Of course I do. He's Harold Butz. He works at my brother's pawn shop. Why is he being kept in there like a prisoner?"

They had been joined by Jack "The Terrier" Russell who interjected, "And Louie Arnett, do you know him, too?"

"Why, yes, he works at Sol's too. Why? What's going on anyway?"

"They are two of the suspects we caught burglarizing this business," said Officer Jenks.

An astonished Goldman blustered, "That can't be right. There must be some mistake. These are trusted employees of my brother. Louie and Harry both work at Sol's Pawn Shop. It keeps them off the street and out of trouble."

"Well, they're in trouble now; they broke out your front door glass to make entry and we caught them inside. Hey, Jinx, do you really have a Harry Butt in your car?" Jenks and Russell both laughed. Goldman just walked away. A worried Izzy went back to his Bentley and sat down.

While the crime scene boys were photographing and fingerprinting, the narcs were examining every red stickered package and then loading them into the panel truck. Before they were all loaded, the open package of suspected marijuana was photographed along with the others that had been dropped.

Hendershott walked out and over to Patrol 7 and asked them to keep an eye on Goldman so that he wouldn't leave. The sergeant then sauntered over to Patrol 17 and said, "If you guys can spare a minute, I'd like to show you something inside." As they walked toward the Exotic Meats building he explained that there were actually some exotic meats in there, just enough to satisfy the name. Most of the packaged "meat" had been loaded into the truck. As they entered the nearly empty building Hendershott said, "I thought this might interest you guys since I heard about your pig caper." Both officers blushed, expecting further ribbing.

Sgt. Hendershott opened the walk in freezer to reveal row after row of carcasses. "Notice anything strange?"

"I give up," Griff said. "It's a meat store. What did you expect?"

"Goldman is Jewish. Don't you think there are an inordinate number of swine carcasses? Take a closer look." As the boys stepped forward, they noticed that the carcasses were packed with bricks of suspected marijuana. Joe whistled.

Griff said, "It looks like Goldman may be a major distributor."

"I was thinking that there might be some kind of connection with the carnival pig you found."

"If there was, it must have been planned for an incoming shipment because the pig's guts were found in the school's dumpster."

"I'm sure we'll get to the bottom of this, what with the big Jamaican's help. By the time we sweat the two they caught inside, Goldman's really going to need his lawyer! I wonder how he'll try to explain the pot. This is one major bust! Once Del Barker gets here, I'll give him the low down and then we'll all go into headquarters. It's going to be a long night."

"You know who's really going to have it rough? It's your boys who have to unload, weigh and check in all of that pot at the property room," Griff said.

"Are you guys volunteering to help?"

"Sorry, Sarge, someone has to work the street; can't be tied up on this all night," Joe said.

Griff said, "Once Barker gets here, we'll give him our notes and then get back to work. When you guys have this all wrapped up, be sure to tell Barker he was a 'team player'. He'll appreciate it."

"I'll do that, Zoo. We'll let you know how this all shakes out."

CHAPTER SIX

The week following the Exotic Meats burglary could be categorized as mundane. The evening overlap shift is usually quite busy so a respite from the hectic is well enjoyed. After a full seven days there were no updates on the recently uncovered Goldman crime family. Charges will be filed by detectives and street officers won't necessarily be subpoenaed immediately, unless of course there is a motion to suppress the evidence. Patrol 17 started out the next week by making a trip into H.Q. to find out what was going on with the investigation.

As the investigation was unfolding, it was found that the freak set of circumstances had unearthed a long hidden and carefully guarded secret, the crime inter-connections of the Goldman's. The Goldman brothers had all been well respected entrepreneurs in Capitol City.

Izzy Goldman was a procurer of rare, exotic and kosher meats. As a humanitarian he would donate 15 percent of his profits to the poor from the Safari Club's Annual Exotic Foods Dinner. Goldman was able to furnish everything from gator to gnu, pigeon to puma, and wombat to wallaby. God only knows what else was brought in with his exotic meats. His meat of choice currently was stuffed pork.

Sol Goldman had run a pawn shop. It served the needs of the declining area, providing money for goods until people could get back on their feet financially. Some of the customers probably used their money to purchase brother Izzy's products. If it weren't for the unexpected explosion in which one of Sol's clumsy employees set off a bomb he was making, Sol would still be alive and in business. The back room of the pawn shop had held a cache of pipe bomb parts; all of the gunpowder disappeared when "Fidgets" Poe made an ash of himself.

Brother Danny ran a thriving landscape business which gave his crew members access to many of the nicest properties in Capitol City.

Besides being brothers, the common thread connecting all of the businesses was their employees. So far as it could be ascertained, all of the subordinate workers belonged to a hither- to overlooked gang of youths known as the Lone Strangers.

Chief Ed Riley allowed the use of his conference room as a center of operations for the coordination of the interconnected investigations. Large easels had been set up, one for each Goldman brother with strings attached linking each of the Goldman brothers and their employees. A separate easel held the names of known Lone

Strangers gang members known to have been associated with the cases. Thus far the list showed:
Louis Arnett
Harold Butz
Graham Casterly (deceased – auto accident)
Jason Casterly (deceased – auto accident)
Frankie "Fidgets" Poe (deceased – explosion)

There was one additional board which was like a family tree of the Goldman crime family. Someone had made up a sign and tacked it to the top of the board. It read:
All that glitters is not Goldman!

The way things were shaping up, the eldest of the Goldman brothers, Sol, had been the godfather of the family. He ran the pawn shop, a thriving business which hired local boys as gofers. Sol was also a small time employment service providing workers to Izzy to help with the unloading, packaging and distributing of "exotic meats".

Brother Danny Goldman used more of the gang members as day laborers in his landscaping business and groused every time he had to pay a stipend to Sol for their services. Danny taught the agile gang members how to case and burglarize pricey homes.

Brother Sol had filed a false burglary report to cover the loss of all of his missing handguns in case the owners returned to reclaim them. Sol had apparently furnished the guns to the gang members.

Thus far Izzy Goldman was in custody and was being held on felony counts of possession of narcotics and possession for sale. His brother Sol's greedy employees, Louie and Harry, were also held pending indictment on felony drug charges as well as burglary of the Exotic Meat shop. Rasta Domingue agreed to turn states evidence and was given immunity from prosecution for his upcoming testimony. Rasta will also gladly do community service as part of the deal.

Det. Del Barker was very thorough in his investigation. With the cooperation of the meat burglars, he was able to clear up numerous upscale residence burglaries. He was also able to flesh out a list of Goldman gang members and employees.

The Wallace Keeper homicide was out of the norm for the gang members. It was learned that the retired Keeper was having trouble financially and apparently had been hocking some heirlooms and antiques to get by. The supposition was that the Keeper residence was targeted to look for more heirlooms and that he probably wasn't expected to be home. Lem Tople and Rick Hunter were working with "Bob" Barker to tie up loose ends in the Keeper caper. Some of the loose ends are: Why was Keeper silenced; why was the victim posed to make it look like a suicide; and who was smart enough to decide to do that? Whatever went wrong, the answers may never be known since the suspects lost their heads while running from the police.

A team of detectives were gradually rounding up other Lone Strangers in an effort to build a case against Danny and Izzy Goldman.

Due to phone calls from Zoo and Joe, the insurance investigators determined that their company, Mutual of Mendicino, should not pay for any of the claims, thus shutting down Sol's Pawn Shop.

The wide spread and complex nature of these investigations did not escape the notice of F.B.I. Special Agent Wohcowhcs who was getting to be very well known in the detective bureau. He attacked the explosive side of the investigations which was greatly appreciated, because it freed up other detectives. His work uncovered a storage locker in which there were enough explosives to make the pawn shop "bombing" look like it had been done by a firecracker.

Being new to the area and using old fashioned methods he personally visited all of the local storage facilities and checked their rental records for the last name Goldman; he found three. All of the storage facilities' owners and representatives were cooperative and were certain that their customers were legitimate. Wohcowhcs needed probable cause to enter storage units which were sealed with customers own locks. When his list of Goldman lockers was complete, he borrowed an off duty airport security officer and his bomb sniffing dog to walk by each of the suspected lockers.

A storage unit at the Lok, Stok and Stor that was leased to Candace Goldman of the Goldman Art Gallery got no reaction from Boomer, the aptly named bomb dog. A second unit at the same facility belonged to Solomon Goldman of Sol's Pawn Shop. The special agent was almost dumbfounded when the dog failed to react. He made a special note of that locker for further investigation later while checking the Goldman crime syndicate.

The third storage locker at Campbell's Lock and Store made the dog go crazy. The dog's handler said he'd never seen his dog act like that before. The locker, in the middle of back to back locker rows, was rented by a Rabbi Seth Goldman who was six months in arrears on his rent. Scotty Campbell had no qualms about cutting the lock off of the ten feet by ten feet storage facility. The lock was removed and the door was slowly and minimally raised. The men cautiously peeked under the door and were surprised to see elephant feet. When the door was fully raised and the entire contents were revealed, they could not believe their eyes.

As they cautiously retreated, the agent ordered Mr. Campbell to quickly check for customers and employees on the grounds and to evacuate them immediately. From a safer distance Wohcowhcs used his walkie to contact his office to put out a seldom used all-call alert for state, county, municipal and federal law enforcement personnel to evacuate the area to a distance of half a mile. All available bomb disposal teams were called out and the military was assigned to lead the assault on the locker.

A battalion of officers from many jurisdictions showed up to cordon off a major amount of real estate. Surprisingly it only took slightly more than three hours to evacuate all of the businesses and residences in the urban area. A robotic camera was sent in so that the men could ascertain the scope of the problem ahead of them. It was getting on toward dusk and the decision was made to not start the removal until daylight. It was going to be an inconvenience for businesses and residents, but the risk had to be minimized. The heat from the powerful work lights was a serious concern because of the unstable explosives.

The images from the robot camera were a little grainy but discernable. The amount of explosives involved would have left new bomb squad workers weak in the knees. The ten feet by ten feet storage unit was packed from floor to ceiling with boxes of clearly marked C-4 military grade plastique, dozens of cases of weeping and unstable dynamite and boxes of blasting caps and detonators. Also found were a dozen cases of firecrackers and two elephant foot umbrella stands containing oversized bottle rockets. Short of blowing the stuff in place, a phalanx of astronaut looking bomb disposal specialists built many small sandbag bunkers by the light of the moon. Not only would these be used for the protection of the waiting workers, but also they could provide a safe area to set down the explosives if they shifted or became too cumbersome on the walk to the waiting units. By sunrise most of the bunkers were in place and plans formulated. Bomb disposal teams from many communities had responded and many different looking bomb disposal trucks lined up between two of the long rows of adjacent lockers. As bomb boys from other jurisdictions arrived they were briefed on the problem and the route to Fort Hopewell which had a large storage bunker.

The first of the heavily padded and shielded workers began the long and arduous task. The first team drew the easiest assignment. The first items to be removed were the fireworks and large bottle rockets. Due to the nature of the rest of the contents, these items were also treated as being fragile as eggs. The other units in turn removed the detonators and blasting caps and then the boxes of old unstable dynamite, probably the trickiest of all. As the day grew longer the cases of C-4 were removed in the slow meticulous manner. Agent Wohcowhcs watched the proceedings from a mobile command station on screens which showed what the now stationary robot camera was seeing. As a courtesy the robotic images were also fed to the TV networks. As the final wall of explosives was dismantled, it became obvious that this was not the end of the project. Behind the final cases were a cache of shoulder mounted disposable rockets and two cases of nitroglycerin. Nothing is ever easy. A section of the back wall of the storage unit had been removed and replaced by a locked makeshift door which led to a locker that abutted the rear wall.

Scotty Campbell reluctantly returned to the site to check his records and identify the lease of the other locker. The file indicated it had been rented five years earlier to one Creighton Gentry, a private citizen. The address of Mr. Gentry was relayed to C.C.P.D. for follow up; hopefully this address will not be bogus like that of Seth Goldman. The illegal door was sealed from the inside. The inside of the Gentry locker was examined by flashlight. The interior held no visible explosives but turned out to be a workshop. A large wooden workbench was along one wall and a shelf above held dozens of books and pamphlets on bomb making and terrorist activities. On the opposite wall were maps of the city and locations of all law enforcement facilities and their related properties. A large box of pipe and pipe ends gave further evidence that this was a bomb making facility. Agent Wohcowhcs' hunch had paid off big time; a major terrorist facility had been uncovered. Lab techs would soon be going over this place with a fine tooth comb. Further follow up and investigations were in order.

While the long line of bomb disposal units was being escorted to Fort Hopewell, a C.C.P.D unit was being sent to check on Creighton Gentry.

CHAPTER SEVEN

Radio: "Patrol 17 check the address at 912 Galveston Avenue. If it's a good address, try to contact one Creighton Gentry and invite him to accompany you to H.Q. to the chief's conference room.

"Patrol 17. We copy 912 Galveston Avenue. Is there any information that we can use to persuade Mr. Gentry?"

Radio: "It's part of the Goldman investigations, the explosions aspect, I've been told."

"Patrol 17. We copy."

"Galveston Ave., that's where Keeper lived. Do you remember the address, Joe?"

"Not sure, Zoo, it was the odd side of the street though, got to be pretty close."

"Nice houses, I'll have to watch for FOR SALE signs. I'm seriously considering moving out of Zoo's Zoo. My one bedroom apartment is just too confining. I need to find a house."

Joe was excited. "Oh boy," he said while rubbing his hands together, "a new game in town! Find Zoo a house. We can spot the FOR SALE signs while we're working and you can check them out during the day."

"Cool your jets, Sparky. I'm just in the thinking stage. It's not a necessity, just something to think about."

"I just can't check out every FOR SALE sign I see. I need to know just what you're looking for."

"I don't know. I'll probably know it when I see it. When I get serious I'll get a real estate agent."

Zoo pulled their cruiser to the curb in front of 912 Galveston. It was a lovely two story brick which sat back from the street and had a porch across much of the front of the house; it sat nearly across the street from the Keeper house. As they walked up the neatly landscaped brick walk to the house, they realized that there was an elderly man rocking in a rocking chair behind the brick railing. Griff approached the gentleman who was illuminated by a yellow porch light; it almost made him look jaundiced.

"Excuse me, sir. Is this the Gentry residence?"

"Yep."

"Are you Creighton Gentry?"

"Nope."

"Is he here?"

"Nope."

"This is going to be a long night," Griff said in an aside to Joe. "Do you know where I can find him?"

"Yep."

"I'd like to speak with him. When can I do that?"

"You can't," he answered, never missing a beat in his rocking chair.

"Keep at it, Zoo, you're making progress. You got a two word answer that time."

Griff just stared at Joe and then slowly turned his attention back to the old man.

"Why can't I speak with him?"

"Been gone forty years." The old man started to sound perturbed by the questions.

"Forty years! Are you sure?!"

"Yep, he's dead."

"He's dead?!" Griff blurted.

"Buried him myself."

"Is there another Creighton Gentry?"

"Nope."

A voice from inside the house increased as the speaker approached the screen door. "Who are you talking to, Pops?"

"No one," he said and stuck his tongue out at Griff.

As the speaker stepped to the door, Griff and Joe both saw a fetchingly beautiful redhead. "Oh I'm sorry, am I interrupting something?"

Griff removed his cap. "Good evening young lady. I'm Officer Griffith Park and this is my partner Officer Beveltnik. We were just seeking information from your grandfather."

The thirtyish redhead half chuckled. "He's not my grandfather. I'm Mr. Gentry's nurse."

"Didn't introduce himself to me," the old man grumbled to himself.

"And he doesn't normally remove his hat either," Joe thought, "unless he's speaking to a dead person's relative."

"My apologies, Miss, I just assumed. We are trying to locate a Mister Creighton Gentry."

"Did you say your name was Griffith Park? Like the Zoo?"

"Yes ma'am, like the zoo."

"They call him the Zoo Man," Joe interjected.

"Do you believe in fate, Officer Park?"

"Please call me Griff. What's this about fate?"

“My name is Giselle Parker, same initials, G.P. We wouldn’t even have to change the towels. I didn’t see a wedding ring. I assume you’re not married.”

“Would you like me to wait in the car?” Joe asked.

“Stay right here!” was the whispered reply.

“No ma’am, I’m not married.” He glossed over the towel remark. We’re here to locate a Mr. Creighton Gentry, but the older gentleman tells me he’s passed on.”

“He’s dead I told you!”

“Be civil Pops. I’ll handle this. Let’s talk inside,” she said as she held the screen door open. “Right this way Griff and please call me Red. Ma’am sounds so matronly. I’m only thirty-two,” she said with a toss of her long red hair.

As they sat in the parlor Griff said, “O.K., Red, we’re trying to find out about Mr. Gentry. He rented a storage locker, the contents of which detectives would like to speak to him about.”

“I’ve only been here four years, but Pops told me about Creighton. He was Pops’ only son. He died about forty years ago. That’s a long time to keep a storage locker.”

“They didn’t have storage lockers forty years ago. This was a rental of only a few years.”

“Maybe it’s another Creighton Gentry,” Red said.

“He gave this address.”

“Did you rent one in his name?” Joe asked.

“Why no, why would I?”

“I don’t know, the question hadn’t been asked. Do you know anybody who might have done this?”

“No, it’s very strange, isn’t it Officer ....”

“Beveltnik, but you can call me Joe. Do you know of any homes for sale in this area?” Griff shot him a look.

“No,” Red said, “but I am a part-time real estate agent. Are you looking to buy?”

“Not me, the big guy with your initials is looking for a bigger place,” he said pointing to his partner. “You see, I <u>do</u> believe in fate.”

While Griff was glaring at Joe, Red retrieved some business cards from her purse. “Here, give these to your friends,” she handed Joe about a dozen. “Here’s one for you, too,” she said. As she pressed the card into Griff’s hand she looked into his softened eyes, “My number is on there. If I find something you might be interested in, is there a number where you can be reached?”

Griff fumbled through his wallet and found a generic departmental business card and wrote in the substation’s phone number and his work hours. Griff then did something that he'd never done before. He put his home phone number on the back. When he handed it to Red, she smiled. So did he.

Griff and Joe made their goodbyes. As they passed the elder Gentry he mumbled, "Flatfoot."

"Buzzard bait," Griff said through clenched teeth, never looking at the old man. They reported to radio that there was nothing to report and went back to work.

"Nice girl, eh Griff?"

"She did seem nice, didn't she, and she's a realtor, too. That's always a plus. If we don't get a run, let's get some coffee."

Joe and Griff entered their favorite coffee stop, Ma's Diner, and were surprised to find it empty, no customers, no clerk and no four hundred pounds of Ma. Griff called out, "Ma?" Ma, are you here?"

Joe grabbed his walkie and advised radio that something may be amiss at their location; radio started another car their way.

Griff called out again and then went behind the counter to check the kitchen area. Joe checked the restrooms and then caught up with Griff. The kitchen was empty and the rear door was bolted. Zoo's heart dropped when he realized that the walk-in freezer was the only place left to check.

Cal Rich and his partner burst in the front door and Cal called out, "Zoo Man?"

"Back here, Cal," he answered as his fingers folded around the freezer door's handle. When he opened the door, his worst fears were realized. There on the floor, on her back with her feet to the door, lay four hundred pounds of ebony goodness and goodwill. While Griff knelt to feel for a pulse, Joe called for a squad. Cal and his partner cleared tables and chairs out of the way to make room for the paramedics and their gear. Griff walked out of the back room grim faced and crying. His favorite barista was cold and had no pulse; the squad's job would be to confirm and pronounce. "She must have been in there for some time, as cold as she is," Griff said. "I'm surprised nobody called in about the diner being open and unoccupied."

"Maybe she had no customers, nothing is disturbed and there's still money in the register," Joe said.

The paramedics arrived and rushed their equipment to the back room. They dragged Ma's body out of the freezer and put defibrillator paddles on her chest. With the machine running they can get an E.K.G. readout. The cold body had a flat line reading. The paramedics made an official death pronouncement and left.

Joe found a phone list tacked to the wall next to the phone and called Ruby, his favorite waitress, to see if she could come in and take over. She said she could and would be there in 45 minutes.

When Ruby arrived she took over and called Ma's relatives. Griff spoke with them and told them that Ma would be taken to the morgue and that the funeral home of their choice could call the morgue and make arrangements to pick up her remains after the autopsy.

The obituary notice read that Sister Marabelle Perkins, owner of Ma's Diner, was seventy-two years old and had had a heart attack. The service was to be held at Saint Jude's church of the Lost Souls at twelve noon; relatives would greet friends from 10 A.M. until time of service.

A hush fell over the predominantly black congregation as the six foot tall white uniformed cop entered, hat in hand. As Griff walked to the front of the sanctuary, an elderly nurse dispensing tissues, encouraged the crowd to part. Griff went to the casket to say his last goodbyes to Ma. While he was saying a silent prayer, he felt a touch on his arm and turned to meet a fiftyish woman dressed in black. As he wiped tears from his eyes, the woman asked, "Are you Officer Zoo Man?"

"Yes ma'am, Griffith Park, they call me the Zoo Man," he answered.

'I'm Belle, Ma's daughter. Thank you for coming," she said as she hugged him. "Ma talked about you all the time, said you were one of her favorite customers. She used to chuckle about how you two would heckle each other."

"Your mother was a well loved member of the community. I'm going to miss her a lot."

"She's in a better place," Belle said.

"I hope God likes his coffee strong and black. Nobody could make better coffee."

"Wait 'til you taste mine," she said. "I'm going to take over the diner. I may not be as big as Ma, but she taught me how to cook. I hope you'll continue to be a customer."

"I promise I will, but it just won't be the same."

"Don't worry, Officer. She taught me how to heckle, too."

Griff felt like a member of the family. As he was going back to his car at the cemetery, he was jolted back into the reality of the present as a bomb disposal truck drove by the cemetery. Driving out of the Whispering Pines Memorial Garden, he again mentally said goodbye to his old friend.

That night, Griff was extra quiet. When he did speak, it was about Ma's funeral and about how her daughter was going to take over the diner.

"I'm going to miss her," Joe said. "She gave us grief, but she was good natured."

"We gave her grief, too, but you're right. I'm going to miss that big girl, too. Can you believe she was seventy-two? Ma's daughter, Belle, is going to take over the diner. It'll be interesting to see if she'll still serve your favorite dish, 'radioactive' chicken."

"She'd better. I miss it when my stool doesn't glow."

"That's it! Pull over, that's more graphic than I can handle. I'm going to shake some doors. You can drive down the alley." This was as close to old fashioned street cop police work as Griff could come; walk, clear your head and see if anything jumps out at you. While he was trying doors and peering into closed store windows, he became aware of a dark, blacked-out sedan slowly moving down the street behind him. Griff discreetly keyed his shoulder mike and told radio and his partner that he was being shadowed. A second blacked out car appeared behind the first. It was Patrol 17 and he lit up the dark blue sedan as Griff wheeled and drew down on the driver.

Agent Wohcowhcs threw up his hands and froze. When Griff saw who it was, he holstered his weapon and approached. "What the hell are you doing, Wohocks?" he screamed, "trying to get yourself shot?"

The embarrassed G-man sheepishly exited his car. "I've been looking for you, Guess I found you," he said.

"You could have called on the radio, Agent Wohocks!"

"New car, doesn't have one yet."

An exasperated Zoo Man said, "So now that you've found me, what-do-you-want?!"

"Guess who showed up at Campbell's storage place today? None other than Seth Goldman himself, madder than a wet hen that someone had cut the lock off of his locker and cleaned out all of his stuff. The clerk stalled him until an agent arrived and took him into custody. It turned out to be a kid, a Lone Stranger, was sent there to renew the rent. When he saw that the locker was empty, he played it by ear. From what we can gather he gets his marching orders from Rabbi Seth Goldman. He even had cash to re-up the locker rent."

"But we know that Seth Goldman doesn't exist," Griff said.

"Not where he put on his application, but he apparently does exist. The gangbanger claims not to know him personally – got the money from Danny Goldman.

"Wohocks!!!"

"Calm down. We checked with Danny Goldman who says he is helping out his cousin Rabbi Seth who lives in Chicago. He used to live here and stored his furniture when he left and forgot to renew his lease. Danny G. knows nothing about the address snafu or the explosives of Creighton Gentry."

"Well, you know he's lying!"

"Our experts don't think so. Our Chicago office is going to check on Seth Goldman. Until then we'll just sit tight. We've got the explosives, you know. If we can confirm that Seth Goldman exists, that's a start. Still nothing on Gentry though.

"Christ, I thought this whole mess was screwy when old man Keeper was murdered with a Goldman gun and others were found in that Camaro."

"Who's this Keeper fellow?" Wohcowhcs asked. "I need a program just to keep up."

"It's far too complicated to go into now. If this whole mess ever gets straightened out, it might make a good novel."

"Nah," Joe piped up, "too many twists and turns. It's not believable."

"It is unbelievable, but we're living it, Joe. We're living it."

Patrol 12 radioed that a green and gold garden tractor had just been boosted from in front of the Ranchmart about five miles away.

"Hey Wohocks, care to do some real police work?"

"Sure, Zoo. What have you got in mind?"

"Just follow us." Griff jumped in behind the wheel of Patrol 17, buckled up and made a u-turn; he readjusted the seat on the fly. It took about three miles to catch up to the pick-up truck that had passed them while they were talking. Joe activated the beacons and the pick-up truck carrying the green and gold lawn tractor pulled to the curb.

The nervous driver handed over his license and registration at Griff's demand while Joe and Mike watched him work.

"Nice lawn tractor," Griff said as he walked the driver to the back of the truck. "Just pick it up?"

"Why, yes," answered the driver, Tommy Timmons.

"Thought so, still has the Ranchmart price placard attached to it."

"I'm picking it up for a friend. It's paid for. They were holding it for him."

"Must have held it pretty good. You needed these bolt cutters here to cut the chain."

“I don’t think I want to talk about my buddy’s lawn tractor any more. May I go now?”

“Sure, Tim, as soon as you give me your license.”

“I gave you my license!”

“That was your driver’s license. I want to see your hunting license.”

“Hunting license! Hunting license? I don’t have a hunting license.”

“In that case I’ll have to take you to jail,” Griff said.

“For what?!” Timmons demanded.

“For taking a Deere without a permit.”

Patrol 12 pulled up and witnessed Joe and a man in an F.B.I. jacket applauding Griff as he was cuffing the tractor thief.

CHAPTER EIGHT

Patrol 17, being team players, turned their collar over to Patrol 12. While Timmons was being transported to jail Griff and Joe impounded the pick-up and returned the garden tractor to the Ranchmart. If Tommy Timmons doesn't plead out, Joe and Griff will eventually receive summonses; with no night court, a court appearance means overtime pay. Agent Wohcowhcs turned down a chance to receive a subpoena, no overtime is afforded him.

Wohcowhcs headed to his temporary hotel room digs thoroughly impressed with the speed and efficiency of the stop and arrest that had gone down. Most of his college work had prepared him for his work as an F.B.I. agent and academy scenarios were good training, but he still marveled at the thoroughness of veteran cops.

The next day, two follow-up reports made their way to the agent's desk. One indicated that the detonator that had gone off under the seat of unit 17 had been set off by remote control and did not resemble anything found in the locker full of explosives.

The other report was more disturbing to the federal agent. The large find of military C-4 was traced to, of all places, Fort Hopewell, where nobody seemed to know it was gone. Considering the red tape it took to have civilians transport the confiscated explosives into the fort, the question that begged to be asked was, "Who was able to get the explosives out and why?" Even more disturbing was the ho-hum attitude of the fort personnel; they did however say thank you for returning their "misplaced" goods. The attitude was so cavalier that Wohcowhcs felt that the base big wigs were being groomed for political office, a thought that he kept to himself.

As if there weren't enough pieces to this ever expanding jigsaw puzzle, another piece came from Chicago. Special Agent Mitch West phoned to say that he had located Rabbi Seth Goldman. Goldman had said he stored his furniture and household goods in one of Campbell's storage units and had given a false address to throw off his anti-Semite enemies. He had also said he was sorry if he inconvenienced anyone. Seth Goldman knew nothing about anything but his precious furniture. He also wanted to know who he could sue for his losses.

Agent Wohcowhcs was now thoroughly frustrated and in a rare fit of rage. He swept the papers from his desk into the corner of his cubicle. He scrawled out a crude Do Not Disturb sign and tossed it on the pile before he stormed out. He had to clear his head and start thinking outside the box.

In Zoo's Zoo, Griff was sleeping soundly and thought it was the alarm clock going off that had awakened him at 2 P.M. It was the telephone.

"Park!" he answered brusquely.

"I'm sorry, did I wake you?" Red asked.

"That's O.K.. I had to get up to answer the phone anyway." It was one of his automatic situational responses.

"I didn't know how late you slept in. I waited. Was 2:00 too soon?"

"3:00 would have been better, but I'm flexible. What can I do for you?"

"I think I found us a place."

"Us?! That sounds like a trap. What do you mean, us?"

"Us, you the prospective buyer and me, your real estate agent – us. I know you didn't specifically ask me to find a house for you, but I've been looking; I'm a take charge kind of girl. So, do you want to see what I found? It's a real steal and it will go quick, but that's all I'm going to tell you until you see it. Is this afternoon O.K.?"

"Sure, Red, just give me the address and I'll meet you there."

"Nope, we go together. That's my rule. Now tell me where you live and I'll pick you up."

"Things are happening way too fast. This girl is too aggressive," he thought, "but that might not be too bad either."

"Tell you what, how about I stop by your place and we'll go from there? Does Pops allow you to have callers?"

"No problem. I'll put on a pot of coffee. You do like coffee, don't you?"

"I sure do. Strong and black! How does 3:30 sound?"

"Sounds great. See you in a little while."

Normally Griff wouldn't shower and shave until it was time to go to work, but he wanted to make a good impression. One of Griff's quirks was his love of super hero tee shirts; he just had to decide which one to wear. After studying on it, he decided on one of his rare finds, a blue shirt with a yellow batwing symbol on the front. He would tuck the tee shirt into beige Dockers and wear a matching blue blousy sport shirt to conceal his S & W model 4506. He suspended his belt clip badge holder from a chain under his tee shirt. The metal belt clip was cold against his chest. Beige Hush Puppies completed the ensemble. Too bad his old Chevette didn't look as good as he did.

On the ride over to the Gentry place, he tried to envision the type of home Red had found for him. He guessed that she was going to show him a vine covered cottage with flower beds, manicured lawn and a white picket fence – just the kind of place she would like. He pulled up in front of 912 Galveston Avenue and could smell the coffee. Griff looked across the street and saw that the Keeper house was for sale. "No way!" he thought.

Giselle Parker literally skipped out of the house to his car, red hair bouncing in a pony tail. Red was wearing blue converse sneakers, white denim slacks and a Batgirl tee-shirt. This was carrying Karma too far.

"Nice ride," she said as he got out of his old Chevette. "Coffee's ready. Come on in."

As they walked past the rocking Pops Gentry, Zoo greeted the old man, "Nice day isn't it, Mr. Gentry?"

"It was!" grumbled the old man.

Griff thought, "I'm going to make that old man like me if it takes the rest of my life. Uh oh! Red flags! Trap!" Over coffee Griff asked, "Is Pops always that surly or does he just hate cops?"

"Yes," Red answered as she stirred sugar into her cup. They sat in silence as Griff waited for an explanation. It never came.

"Your partner said they call you the Zoo Man. It sounds like a super hero name, so I wore my Batgirl tee shirt. Impressed?"

Without thinking he unbuttoned his overshirt to reveal the Batman symbol. "Good choice," he said.

Red stared at the shirt and squealed, "Oh my God," and quickly covered her mouth with her hand. "Karma, good Karma!"

As Griff drained his cup he said, "So, about this house…?" He let the question trail off.

"Right, it's not too far. Shall I put some coffee in a thermos?"

"Sure, don't want to waste good coffee and this is good coffee!"

After filling a thermos she said, "C'mon, I'll drive."

"What about Pops?"

"The neighbors will watch out for him. We won't be gone too long."

Zoo followed Red out the back door. Her car was parked on the garage apron. It was the cleanest Chevette he'd seen in years. "What are the chances?" he thought.

While driving, Red Parker described the house they were going to see. "It's a lovely post war one story modern with two bedrooms, 1 and a half baths and a finished full basement. There is no garage, but its carport can be converted later as an option. The whole house has been painted inside and out. It's free of liens and it's priced to sell. The owners are asking a ridiculously low price. It hasn't been listed yet so if you're willing to make a snap judgment, you could get a real steal.

As they pulled into the driveway at 1212 Romero Street Griff was silent. He got out of the car, leaned his back against the passenger door and just stared. His right hand came up to his face – his hand covered his mouth and his index finger pressed against his upper lip. The Zoo Man appeared to be studying the home.

A flood of memories came rushing back. He knew this house all too well. This was the Toscic residence. Ruth Toscic's only son, Leon, had been an addict. He'd been in and out of psyche units and drug rehab programs. Nothing had worked for Leon. When his demons had gotten too much for him he acted. Leon took one of his father's shotguns, a ten gauge single shot goose gun, put the barrel under his chin and pulled the trigger. Griff recalled the gruesome sight. There was flesh, blood and brain matter throughout the bedroom. Not only had Leon killed himself, he'd blown his face off in the process.

"What a day that was," he recalled. After he had consoled Ruth Toscic, he had gone to a warehouse on an unrelated follow-up investigation where he was ambushed and kidnapped. Oh he knew this house all right, all too well!

When Red was sure that Griff had studied the exterior long enough, she took his hand and led him onto the front porch. Red retrieved the front door key from the realtor's lock box which was locked to the door knob. She opened the front door and with a flourish, invited Griff to enter. The interior was larger than he remembered and new thick carpeting covered the floor. The velvet paintings were gone and all of the walls had been painted in soft pastels. Leon's room was spotless. The master bedroom was much bigger than he'd remembered and the kitchen was fully furnished with appliances. He'd never looked at the house from a buyer's perspective before and he was pleasantly surprised.

The full basement was very masculine. With only wall hangers left, Leon's father's trophy heads were gone. There was a gun cabinet built into one wall with a curtain rod above it. A drape would hide it.

"What do you think, Zoo Man?"

"I don't think this house would have been my first choice, but I like it and the price is right. Let's see what Leon thinks." And with that he bounded up the cellar steps. Red went up and found Griff in the smaller bedroom and she heard him say, "You know me, Leon. Do you think we can live together in peace? If not give me a sign." Red didn't know who or what he was talking to, but she watched and waited also.

Griff was surprised to see Red standing in the doorway. The new thick carpet had muffled her footsteps.

"Who is Leon and what did he say? Is Leon your spirit guide on something?"

"I've been here before. This used to be Leon's room. Leon died in this room and he, how can I say this, he didn't die well. Maybe with Leon gone, it can be a happy house again."

"Did Leon say anything about the kitchen? That's where most people congregate."

"The kitchen is adequate if that's the appetite you're trying to feed," he said as he smiled and Groucho'd his eyebrows knowingly. Let's get this baby under contract and see if I can get financing. I want first shot at this place. This is a good neighborhood; good people and I ought to know." Griff couldn't believe how fast things were happening and he couldn't remember the last time he'd made a snap decision on a major purchase. "Maybe there is something to Karma after all," he thought.

"Red, you've gone above and beyond. How can I ever thank you?"

Giselle Parker took Griff's hand and led him over to the larger master bedroom. "I came by here last night and put these in the closet," she said as she removed a bundle of blankets from the closet shelf. "I know how you can thank me," she said as she spread a blanket on the thick carpet.

Griff hadn't been with a woman since Judy had been killed and even if it was a trap, it felt right. As the two smiled and embraced he said, "I think I can provide a proper thank you, but I'm going to have to make a drugstore run first."

"Thought of that, too," she said as she produced a box of sealed necessities. While Red made sure that the doors were locked, Griff put his badge and gun on the closet shelf.

The couple took their time getting to know each other, hugging, kissing and caressing. As they slowly undressed each other, they let their hands explore each other's bodies. When Griff removed Red's bra he was surprised to find that she had a nipple ring. As she stepped out of her panties his eyes were drawn to her shaved mons.

Red took down Griff's shorts. She was pleasantly surprised by the size of his manhood. She opened a foil pouch and said, "I hope these are big enough. We wouldn't want to impede progress." And with that the modern woman took over. With shaking and unpracticed hands, Red gleefully fit Griff with his latex protection.

Over the next two hours the couple cavorted like otters with a new toy. Griff, being ever the gentleman, went slowly at first so he wouldn't hurt the little nurse, but he needn't have worried. Red Parker was a wild child and Griff almost had trouble matching her intensity. Delightfully spent, they finally just lay on the blanket and held each other in blissful nakedness.

"Do you treat all your real estate clients like this?"

"No, but then again, I've never met anyone quite like you. I couldn't just ask you to hop into bed. You're a great lover and selling this house was a nice fringe benefit."

"You don't have any fringe," he quipped as he lightly stroked her bikini area.

She playfully slapped him and said, "That was a bad pun, but you <u>are</u> a great lover!"

"If you think that was good, wait until we get a bed in here." Even though he meant it, Griff could not believe how easily the words tumbled out of his mouth. This day was just full of surprises.

Park and Parker got dressed and headed for Red's car. Before they left, the frisky part- time real estate agent took a FOR SALE sign from the hatch of the Chevette and planted it in front of 1212 Romero Street. She topped the sign with a smaller one which read IN CONTRACT. Griff looked at the sign and commented, "How appropriate." The sign indicated that Red worked for the Lovey-Dove Real Estate Agency.

No sooner had the couple returned to Pops place, the Zoo Man called in and took a personal day. There was no way he could get to work on time. He hated to put his partner in a lurch, but he'd understand. The Sarge would probably partner him up with another officer.

Griff took a cat nap while Red changed clothes, fixed Pops supper and then they headed out to eat.

"I'll fly, you buy." Red said and Griff agreed.

"Do you like Chinese?"

"I love Chinese, especially Wor Su Gai."

"Good, I know the best place," and he directed her to the Qua King Duck.

CHAPTER NINE

Before leaving for the restaurant, Giselle Parker used Pops Gentry's old rotary phone and called Lila Dove, one of the main partners of Lovey-Dove Real Estate and told her to put a hold on 1212 Romero Street. She told Lila that she had a buyer and she was going to draw up the contract papers and bring them by the office in the morning. She would do the paperwork at dinner. Lila Dove was very proud of her new part-time agent for showing such initiative. Fortunately Capitol City wasn't so large that things couldn't be done loosely, all of the rules and regulations of the home buying business would be taken care of, in due time.

Ling Po, the owner of the Qua King Duck, saw the couple enter his restaurant and rushed to greet them. "So good to see you again, Officer Zoo Man," he said as he shook Griff's hand. Griff, being a semi-regular at the restaurant, was friends with the good natured owner.

"Ling Po, this is Giselle Parker. She wanted the best Wor Su Gai in town, but I brought her here instead.

"Ha, ha, very funny! Would you like your regular booth or something a little more intimate?" Mr. Po gave Griff a wink and a devilish smile.

"The booth will be fine, Ling. The light's good there and we have a lot of paperwork to do."

"One of the girls will be with you shortly," he said as he patted Griff on the shoulder. "It is so good to have you back. You gave us quite a scare."

"What did he mean by that?" Red asked after Po walked away.

"Oh, nothing much." Griff offered no further explanation. He thought, "If this relationship blossoms further, then I'll tell her about my kidnapping and Judy's murder." If it comes to that, soul searching conversations would come later. "Here comes the waitress. Let's order."

They both ordered the Wor Su Gai dinner with Won Ton soup, and they shared a pot of tea. Over the years Giselle had eaten Wor Su Gai, her favorite dish, many times. This by far was the best. The lettuce was fresh, the chicken was tender and moist and the gravy was superb. After the meal was over and the table was bused, they ordered coffee and got down to the business of filling out the real estate forms.

Part way through the paperwork, their concentration was broken by the sounds of emergency vehicles screaming by the restaurant. More emergency vehicles came by and more could be heard in the distance.

“Something major must be going on,” Griff said. “We’ll know soon enough. Ling religiously listens to a scanner in the kitchen.” As if on cue, Ling came running out of the kitchen and approached the booth.

“What is it Ling? What’s going on?!

“It’s bad Mr. Zoo, very bad, it just blew up; people had to be hurt,” he said breathlessly.

“Catch your breath, Ling. What blew up?”

“A police car, over at the SeaView Mall!”

“Pack up these papers, Red, while I pay the check. We’ll finish the paperwork later.” At the register when he paid, he discreetly asked the owner if they gave the unit number of the cruiser that was lost. He was told that the radio had not aired that information. At the booth Griff left a tip and collected his dinner date. On the brisk walk to the parking lot he asked, “May I drive? I’ll be careful with her!”

“I was going to suggest it,” Red said as she gave Griff the keys. She put her brief case in the back seat and barely got her door closed before Griff headed for the exit.

“I know some back ways to the mall. I don’t know how close they’ll let us get, but I’ll bet they won’t turn down the volunteered services of a nurse at the scene. God, I hope nobody was killed.”

“I’m glad I ‘volunteered.’ I hope I can help.”

The back entrance to the mall was still open and from there on he badged his way through the chaos. They were able to get within ten parking rows of the action before they had to hoof it. Griff suspended his badge outside of his shirt. Red dug her nurse I.D. badge out of her purse and clipped it on to her blouse.

A wide area around the scene had been cordoned off with scene tape and they were stopped six rows from the blast site by a uniformed officer that Griff did not know. “I’m sorry,” he said, “but you can’t go any further.”

Griff extended his badge chain to its full length so that the officer could see his badge up close. “I’m an officer and she’s a nurse!”

“Orders are orders, brother, Chief’s orders!”

“Who can I talk to. I need to check on my partner and see if anyone’s hurt.”

The uniformed officer asked to see Griff’s photo I.D. and then called in on his walkie. “Unit 25 to Command 1.”

“Command 1. Go ahead.” It was Chief Riley’s voice.

“Unit 25. I have an Officer Griffith Park here and a nurse. They’re seeking permission to enter the crime scene.”

"Command 1. That's a negative. Tell Park that Joe B. was not involved and there are no fatalities. Tell him also to be in my office at 10 in the morning, in civvies. That is all!"

"Command 1 says..."

"I heard him, I heard him." Griff said as he and Red retreated to her car. Griff was not pleased about being put off but he was not about to question the chief's thinking. He should know best.

"Let's go to your place and finish the agreement paperwork so I can go loan shopping tomorrow."

"Why don't we do it at your place. I'd like to see your bachelor pad."

"Several reasons come to mind. My place is a mess, we really need to finish this paperwork and my car is at your place." He pressed her keys into her hand after unlocking and opening the driver's door. Griff noticed that Red was a bit pouty, but he'd make up for it in the future.

When they arrived at the Gentry residence, Red parked in the back. After checking on Pops, she spread the real estate papers out on the kitchen table, made some fresh coffee and she and Griff got back to work.

"This is why we did this here. We wouldn't have finished this if we'd been at my place, too much temptation." When they were finally finished, Red turned out the kitchen light and they said good night, passionately, for fifteen minutes.

On the drive home Griff recalled his good fortune. "What a day," he thought. "Found a wonderful woman, got back in the saddle, got my pipes cleaned and bought a house. Oh, yes. What a day!" He was still concerned about the cruiser explosion, but he'd get the skinny on that at headquarters in the morning.

Griff slept fitfully. He didn't know why. Perhaps it was the news of the cruiser explosion and the fact that he was nearly taken out that way earlier. Giving up on getting a relaxing full night's rest, he arose early and showered.

Feeding time at Zoo's Zoo consisted of a meager breakfast of coffee and buttered English muffins, too much butter on the warm muffins, but that was the way he liked them. He turned on his T.V. in the living room and turned up the volume hoping to hear news of last night's fiasco. When the news came on he took his cup and plate and sat down on the sofa in front of the set.

The morning news anchor, Charlotte Carolina, started out with the day's weather forecast. Griff didn't pay close attention, but he did like looking at the perky blond with the obvious stage name. When the cruiser story came on it was less than desirable coverage. There were no photos and it was reported that for some unknown reason a patrol unit was heavily damaged when some type of explosion took place at the SeaView Mall. Two unnamed officers had, moments before, left the vehicle to attend to a domestic dispute. The investigation was ongoing.

"Well, that told me nothing new," Griff thought. As he went back into his kitchen for another muffin, he neglected to turn off the TV set. Another news story caught his ear and his chair fell over as he got up suddenly to rush back to the TV. It was the reporting of the death of local entrepreneur, Izzy Goldman. When Mr. Goldman failed to come home from work at his Exotic Meats shop, his wife asked his brother, Daniel Goldman, to check on him. Izzy Goldman had been found shot to death in his office. Authorities refused to speculate on the motive, but did indicate that the late Mr. Goldman had been a person of interest to the police department for some time. It was also reported that Mr. Goldman's company had been burglarized recently, resulting in a great loss of exotic product. "You can say that again," Griff mused. He probably got his "exotic product" on consignment and couldn't pay for it since the C.C.P.D. impounded his humungous stash of drugs.

Griff finished breakfast and got dressed for his meeting with the chief. A green and black checked shirt over a Green Lantern tee shirt looked good with his olive drab chinos. The checkered shirt helped break up the outline of his gun. The drive to H.Q. was mundane. Because of lack of parking near headquarters, he had to park blocks away and hoof it. Being early, Griff went to the basement Cop Shoppe coffee shop which was operated by a couple of disabled former C.C.P.D. cops.

"What's shakin', Otis?"

"Not much, Zoo Man. What brings you to God's little corner of heaven? Haven't seen you around in forever."

"Got a special invite from the chief – any idea what that may be about?"

"Word has it that the black and white that blew up was the last straw, another too close for comfort incident. The chief wants this figured out and stopped before someone gets killed or maimed."

"Any officers get hurt last night?"

"No, but that's not for want of trying."

"Thanks, Otis, I'd better get upstairs. Here's a couple of bucks for the coffee."

"Keep it, it's on the house."

He pressed the money into Otis' hand. "Then put this in your pocket, brother."

"Thanks, Zoo. Here let me refill that cup, might as well take a full one with you."

At 10:00 sharp Helen Steiner, the chief's secretary, showed Griff into the chief's office; there were others already there.

"Good morning, Chief," he said and then gave a nod to Agent Wohcowhcs.

"Good morning, Park. Have a seat. Gentlemen, I've convened this meeting because last night's incident was similar to the one that damaged Park's other unit, only this one was more successful. A few seconds earlier and we'd be making funeral arrangements for two officers. For those of you who don't know him, this is Special Agent Michael Wohocks of the F.B.I. Mike, what can you tell us?"

"Thank you, Chief. The device that destroyed last night's cruiser was apparently set off by the same person or persons as the one that took out Officer Park's unit. As with the first incident, the bureau got an anonymous call stating 'We're going to blow up a cop tonight and you can't stop us.' The agent who took the call feigned that he was having hearing aid trouble and asked the caller to hold on and he did. The call was traced to a landscape company; the building was closed and padlocked from the outside when my people arrived."

"Let me guess," Griff interrupted, "Danny Goldman's landscaping business?"

"Bingo. Another Goldman connection. Last night's blast was so heavy, I doubt they'll recover the detonator parts, but it, too, I'm sure, was set off by remote control and the explosives were under the driver's seat. Coincidentally, Danny Goldman found his brother, Izzy, shot to death earlier in the evening. Officer Park, is someone out to get you?"

"Yes, and she is succeeding," he said grinning widely.

"Be serious, Zoo. I'm talking about enemies."

"Not that I can think of." After a pause he yelled, "Don't tell me it was my cruiser again!" As the chief and Wohcowhcs both nodded, Griff jumped up, "What about my partner? Is he all right?"

"Calm down, Zoo," Chief Riley said. "He's O.K. Atrick put him on the wagon last night with a rookie. Dorsem and Likens were working Patrol 17. They're both O.K. By the way, the domestic run they were sent on was a phony."

"A couple of questions jump out at me," Griff said. "First, I'd like to know who had the time and the availability to tamper with my unit? It hadn't been laid in for work, so it had to have been done on the substation lot. Secondly, I don't want to get Likens and Dorsem in trouble, but why didn't they check the unit per your directive after the last explosion? Also, why do they screw with my car? If it's as badly damaged as you say, I won't be able to salvage any of my gear or the department's shotgun! I wonder what old piece of junk they'll outfit for my next cruiser!" Griff was steamed and he didn't care who knew it.

Chief Riley said, "I spoke with Dorsem and Likens at the scene. They said that they inspected Patrol 17 very thoroughly in light of the first explosion. Maybe the mad bomber is getting more sophisticated in hiding his handiwork. Let's repair to my conference room. We can add this new info to what we already know and see if anything jumps out at us."

As the men walked into the conference room, Griff saw a detective working on a new easel. When the detective stepped away he saw that it was labeled Cruiser Bombings and sported pictures of his former rig. There was a section already waiting for pix from the latest blast. The new easel gave Griff an ominous feeling. They are getting ready for more bombings.

The other members of the meeting, Lieutenant Dingell and A.I.S. Investigator Danny Chan, joined the others in the conference room. The men were all looking at the easels when the lieutenant said, "Danny Goldman seems to be in the center of this whole shootin' match. He's apparently the burglary king pin of the family, pays the locker rent where the explosives were stored and found his brother shot to death. My gut feeling is that he actually shot his brother, Izzy, so that he could be the lone head of the Goldman crime enterprises."

"For somebody that devious, he's been cooperative. Wohocks' men confirmed that Seth Goldman does exist and that he did rent the locker that Danny Goldman was paying rent on. The locker initially held household goods," Griff said. "What I'd like to know is what happened to the Rabbi's furniture and how could that storage unit then be jam packed with explosives without anyone seeing it happen?"

"People minding their own business," Chan suggested. "It was probably done in broad daylight. People are only worried about their own items and don't pay any attention to other lockers contents."

"If Danny Goldman wanted to kill Park or any other officer, why didn't he just do it? No offense meant, Park, but both explosions happened to unoccupied cruisers – I don't think that was an accident. I think somebody was watching and blew the cars as some type of warning," Chief Riley said. "We know that the first detonator was set off by remote control after the explosives were removed. This time was the real deal but after the officers were away from the cruiser. No, blowing up the empty cruisers was deliberate; I'd bet your paycheck on it," he said as he pointed to Lt. Dingell.

Dingell responded, "I say we bring Danny Goldman in and sweat him. We know he's dirty. I say we sweat him 'til he cracks and spills everything."

"Barry, you know we can't do that. This isn't the Thirties. Modern police work has come a long way; we're above that sort of thing. Off the record, it did sound like a good idea though."

"Gotcha, Chief."

"Have you got anything else Wohocks?"

"No, Chief, not really."

"Zoo, as of now you're on special assignment since you don't have a cruiser. I want you to work with Agent Wohocks, brainstorm this thing together from the federal and the normal angle." At this the F.B.I. agent raised an eyebrow. "Any questions?"

"What about my partner? Joe and I make a great team and he lost his half of the cruiser, too."

"O.K., Joe, too, starting tonight. I'll square it with Atrick."

Griff and Mike Wohcowhcs walked out together.

"I hope it won't interfere with things, Mike, but I just signed for a house and I'm going to be needing some time to try to get financing.

"That's the beauty of working a special assignment. You can do such things while you're working. You can't do that in a marked cruiser."

Later that afternoon Griff called his partner, filled him in on their new covert assignment and the fact that he was buying a house. He would fill him in on the details later.

CHAPTER TEN

It was decided that Mike, Griff and Joe would work Friday night on Patrol 17's hours and switch to daylight variable hours after the weekend. Griff and Joe would receive their regular salary from the city and everything after 40 hours would be picked up by the Feds. It seems that Washington is more than willing to fund such an enterprise. You've got to love this country!

Griff called Sgt. Atrick at home to make sure that Chief Riley had informed him of the plans so that he wouldn't be blindsided when the dynamic duo failed to show up for roll call.

"Park, are you suggesting that the Old Man might have forgotten to call me?"

"Not at all, Sarge. I just wanted to make sure that you were completely in the loop and that you knew you were going to be shorthanded for an indefinite period of time."

"Thanks for your concern, son. You and Joe be extra careful; I fear that you are going into the belly of the beast. Are you sure this Wohocks fellow is seasoned enough to keep you safe? He seems to me to be a lightweight."

"He's pretty squared away, but we'll keep our eyes wide open just in case. Listen, Sarge, I'm really sorry to have bothered you at home, but I wanted to make sure that you knew what the score was before I leave to pick up Joe."

"I appreciate the call, Griff. Be sure to keep me up to date on what's happening."

"Will do, Sarge. Oh, and make sure you stay on the guys about thoroughly checking their cruisers; we don't need any dead officers. Bye."

Joe and Griff arranged to join up with Mike Wohcowhcs at Joe's favorite coffee shop, The Last Drop, located at Race and Cane. Mike arrived first and spotted three outlaw bikers' tricked out motorcycles in the parking lot; the dynamic duo arrived a few minutes later. Mike waved to them from a table which was next to the three bikers. An odder looking half dozen people couldn't be found, the dirty leather clad bikers and the neat and clean cops in plain clothes. Mike had been eavesdropping on the bikers' conversation. Even though they had been talking in hushed tones, Mike was able to get the gist of what was being said and wrote on a napkin for Griff and Joe to read. "Bikers are talking about robbing this place – stay on your toes."

Griff went to the order station and got a cup of Bolivian dark roast, the strongest they had and a Peppermint Patty for Joe. Mike already had his drink. The stunning barista, Cheri, who had seen Griff and Joe walk in said, "Remind Joe that his drink is hot. He has a tendency to burn his lips." Griff nodded and winked at the girl.

"I thought you were bullshitting, Joe," Griff said as he sat down. "That Cheri really is a knock out.'

"Told ya," Joe said.

As they were talking about going to the F.B.I. field office to get the boys a car to drive, the biggest biker approached Cheri; the other two sat in silence. Wohcowhcs was like a shadow. No one saw him move. The heavyset bearded biker bought a cup of coffee, tasted it and spat it out on the counter. In a voice loud enough for everyone to hear, he said, "This shit is terrible. Give me everybody's money back." When Cheri hesitated, the biker pulled a very menacing twelve inch long sawed off shotgun from under his leather jacket, pointed it at her and said, "I'm not kidding. Give me all of the money and don't alert any pigs."

"Too late!" Agent Wohcowhcs said through clenched teeth as he pressed his pistol barrel to the side of the biker's temple. "Put the gun on the counter and step back away from it."

The suspect's partners started to draw guns and rise to join their buddy but they were met with guns staring them in the face. "Sit down unless you're growing!" Griff barked an old Joe Friday Dragnet line.

The robber was taken into custody as well as the accomplices. Officers Likens and Dorsem answered the call for a wagon to take the miscreants to the county jail.

"How do you do it, guys?" Likens asked. "Stop for coffee and make a major arrest."

"We're just back-up, this is the F.B.I.s play."

Joe said, "If it's O.K. with you boys, I'll ride in the back of the wagon with the prisoners. I'll complete the arrest forms while Griff and Wohocks file the charges. Have the jailers put them in separate interview rooms; my partner and Wochocks will meet me there."

To their knowledge the bikers were not involved in the investigations they were working on, but it was a productive way to start their assignment.

Cheri, the barista, wrote out three permanent discount cards and handed them to her three heroes. "Sorry about the sloppy writing. I couldn't keep my hand from shaking. I'm sure glad that you boys were here."

As the wagon pulled away, Agent Wohcowhcs had Cheri write out a witness statement while Griff gathered the names and addresses of the customers in case witnesses were needed for trial. As they were exiting, the remaining customers gave them a round of applause. Mike and Zoo then headed to the Clerk of Courts to file charges.

At the jail each of the bikers were placed in individual interview rooms after they were slated in. The interview rooms were six feet by eight feet with a metal table bolted to the floor and a hand-me-down office chair on each side. The prisoner's seat was facing the door; a leg shackle bolted to the floor could be employed if the subject was overly hostile. The wall facing the prisoner had a mirror of one way glass behind the interviewer. In the hallway, the window was covered with a drape so as not to make the prisoners suspicious; although most certainly they all knew what it was.

In the interview rooms, the boys would pair up briefly to read and witness the Miranda rights; all of the bikers declined attorneys. Each officer took a different biker to interview.

Wohcowhcs took the biker that he had surprised. He would get the attempted robbery charge. The gruff know-it-not-enough biker opted not to cooperate. Mike noticed a tattoo on his left forearm which read LS/MFT. "Must be a Lucky Strike smoker," he thought. He then joined Joe in an adjacent interview room.

All of the bikers were in their mid to late 30s. The second biker was cooperative and as Mike was walking in Joe was asking, "Do you smoke Luckies?"

The biker answered, "Shit no, that stuff'll kill ya."

"So, what's with the LS/MFT tattoo on your forearm?" Joe asked.

The cooperative prisoner said, "Hell, that's a leftover from my younger days. I used to belong to a gang called the Lone Strangers." He pointed to the tattoo, smiled and said, "Lone Strangers / Make Fine Terrorists, pretty clever huh?" Upon hearing this Mike went to the third interrogation room where Griff was having no success.

The long sleeved biker sat with folded arms and glared at the F.B.I. agent when he walked in. "Any luck, Zoo?"

"No, Billy Badass here 'don't know nuttin!'"

Wohcowhcs stepped over to the biker and asked him to roll up his sleeves. The biker replied, "Fuck you."

The G-man then grabbed his left arm and pulled it away from his body; the biker instinctively pulled it back. Mike again snatched the arm and this time pinned it to the table. In the same move he stuck his elbow under the biker's chin, putting pressure on his Adam's apple. The moves were so fast in the tight quarters that Griff could hardly believe what he had just seen.

Mike yanked up the badass' left sleeve and revealed a like LS/MFT tattoo. "This tattoo tells me that you're just a punk," he said.

"Fuck you, pig. You don't know shit! The Lone Strangers breeds nuttin' but the best, and I'm living proof of it."

"Goldman must be so proud," Mike said under his breath.

The biker had 20/20 hearing and replied, "Those old boys are the shit. We was going to pay our respects before you stopped us from emptying the piggybank. You got some balls for a pinko Fed."

"So, what do you know about the Goldmans?"

The surly biker realized that he'd said too much and uttered, "I don't know nuttin' – fuck off!" He folded his arms and became stoic once again.

Mike returned to Joe's prisoner and offered him a deal if he'd cooperate. The biker agreed and told him how the Goldman brothers started the Lone Strangers years ago, and all things were supposed to be low key, but things had gotten out of hand lately. He said that he and his buddies were living out of town now and weren't currently aware of what was going on, but would keep an ear open and contact Wohcowhcs if he heard anything.

As the trio drove to the F.B.I. offices Mike related his good luck about finding a Goldman connection and a cooperative source of information.

Like most police departments, the Feds used impounded and confiscated vehicles for undercover work. Joe and Griff had their choice of a select few, a pea green Yugo, a distressed red Firebird or a high mileage frost green Explorer; they chose the Explorer. The radio was mounted in the glove box and a plug-in tear drop dash beacon was in the console. The car's radio was not set up to interphase with C.C.P.D., but the walkies were. Before signing out the car the boys examined it thoroughly, inside and out. F.B.I. personnel are no different from regular cops when it comes to maintaining undercover cars; the boys removed a whole bag full of newspapers, coffee cups, fast food wrappers and miscellaneous junk. "No wonder we're called pigs," Joe said.

After all of the arrest paperwork was done, I.D.s were issued, payroll forms filled out and cars and walkies signed out, Griff called the C.C.P.D. I.D. section. He inquired if any of the known Lone Strangers had LS/MFT tattoos. They all did. Griff asked to be transferred to the war room where the Goldman investigations were centered.

"Detective Topel. How can I help you?"

"Lem, this is Griff Park. I've got some new info for you."

"Damn, you guys work fast. What have you got?"

"I've got three names for you to add to your Lone Strangers list. These are former gang members who are currently in town. They're in the county jail actually. Are you ready to copy?"

"Fire away, Zoo"

"First is Landon Bosworth A.K.A. Lando or Bozo. Second is Robert Johnston A.K.A. Johnny or Knuckles. Third is Leslie Johnson, no 'T', A.K.A. Lee or Les.

"Is that it, Zoo?"

"Almost, Lem. These three are outlaw bikers who ride together but are not currently affiliated with any gang. They used to be Lone Strangers. The Lone Strangers were founded by the Goldman brothers years ago. All of the members are tattooed with LS slash MFT on their left forearms. It stands for Lone Strangers make fine terrorists. Lem, you may want to check with the gang unit and see if they know of anyone else who carries this mark plus you might want to issue a department wide notice for everybody to watch for this tattoo on suspects."

"Hell, Zoo Man, with this new information we ought to have this whole mess cleared up by the time I retire."

"That's the spirit, Lem. Keep at it."

While he had been talking on the phone, he doodled Giselle Parker's name over and over. He was shocked to see that the last few times just read Giselle Park. Griff figured that he just must have been too engrossed in the conversation and that this was not an outpouring of his subconscious, but he could be wrong. He had been thinking more and more about the pretty redhead, especially how she took charge and got him into the sack. What a lovely ride it was – she had taken him to new heights and brought sex and love back into his life.

Joe went to retrieve his partner from the Fed's impound office where he had been using the phone. He looked in the window and saw his partner seated with his eyes closed and a winsome smile on his face. Joe knew this look from Griff's relationship with Judy Stanhope. This would be a good time to broach the subject of Zoo's new girlfriend and his sudden house purchase. There had been no time to discuss it until now.

Joe entered the small office without Griff noticing. "Ahem! In La-La Land?"

Griff blustered, "I didn't know you were here. I was, uh, daydreaming."

"From the look on your face, I'd say you were daydreaming about that new girlfriend – tell me about her."

"OK, Joe. Sit down and strap yourself in. You're not going to believe this." He gave Joe the blow by blow of the day he bought his house and fell in love with Giselle Parker. He glossed over the specific intimacies of the lovemaking session.

"You really bought the Toscic place?"

"Yep. Granted it's not as great as Casa Beveltnik, but for a first house, it's a perfect fit for me."

"Sounds like our real estate agent was a perfect fit, too."

"Yeah," Griff sighed as he stared into space like a moon calf.

Joe snapped his fingers in front of Griff's face. "Snap out of it, partner. Time to go back to work."

"Work! We just popped three felons! That wasn't enough work for you for one night?"

"What? Mr. Workaholic is going to slack off? Not going to give a full eight hours?"

"Joe, I thought we might knock off early and get some sleep. Mike has to appear in Federal Court tomorrow, so I thought we'd think outside the box and take a road trip.

"A road trip? Do you want to interview the personnel at Fort Hopewell?

"That is an excellent idea, Joe. Write that down. We'll put that on our future agenda. No, what I had in mind was to pick the brains of a cagey old veteran sheriff and see how he'd approach our investigation."

"Corinth County? Sheriff Tolliver?"

"You got it. Any objections?

"No. Ever since you told me about him, I've wanted to meet him. I saw him of course at Judy's funeral, but I never got a chance to talk to him."

"That's good because I called him at home, and he and Dean are going to meet us at his office at noon and then go to lunch. I'll pick you up bright and early Monday morning, say 6 A.M. – you can buy breakfast."

"Aren't you forgetting something? You picked me up tonight. That gives me the plain car. Do you want to drive to my place or shall I pick you up?

Griff had been daydreaming so much about Red and had forgotten about the driving arrangements. "OK, you can pick me up and still spring for breakfast."

"We'll discuss breakfast when I pick you up."

Griff hadn't had a particularly tiring weekend, but 6 A.M. seemed to come early. Griff had hit the snooze alarm so many times that the clock had given up. He awoke to a pounding on his apartment door. Annoyed, he jerked the door open with gun in hand. A startled Joe Beveltnik jumped to the side at the sight of the gun.

"Ease up on the hammer, brother. It's just me. Did I wake you?"

"Yeah, I guess the alarm didn't go off. Sorry about the gun. I should have invested in a peephole for my door."

"From across the hall his matronly neighbor gave an attempted wolf whistle and said, "Nice outfit, stud."

"Thank you, Miss Boltshoff." It was then that Griff realized he was standing in his doorway, gun in hand, stark naked. He made an immediate about face and grumbled, "Close the door, Joe!"

"Does she really know you well enough to call you Stud? She's got to be eighty if she's a day. An old flame?"

"Shut up, Joe, and let me get dressed."

Joe looked over the Zoo Man's memento shelf and sighed deeply when he saw the photo of the late Judy Stanhope. He also looked closely at the photos of Zoo and Judy with Deacon Tolliver, the object of today's visit. "Hmm, he never did answer the question about his neighbor," Joe thought.

"Ready, Joe? How about breakfast at the Golden Arches? I'll buy."

The dynamic duo ate a quick breakfast and then headed for Corinth County. Joe drove and Griff navigated.

"That picture that you have of Sheriff Tolliver doesn't do him justice. When I saw him at Judy's memorial service, I'm sure he had even more trappings on his uniform than General Patton. Are those really pearl handled grips on his six guns or just plastic?"

"I don't know, Joe, but I'm not going to ask, and don't you ask either. I don't want you to embarrass my friend."

During the four hour drive Zoo kept Joe in stitches with stories about his previous visits with the colorful sheriff. As they passed a farm that was for sale, Griff had Joe pull in.

"Going to buy a farm, too?"

"Nope, just remembering. This is where Sammy Shotz held me captive. The large barn was standing open and they ventured inside. Griff pointed out the pass-through where he got his meals and where the cameras had been placed in the ceiling corners. The barn was now devoid of vehicles and fixtures and seemed even larger than he'd remembered. After a quick look around, they drove on.

The plain frost green Explorer was parked in the lot across from the Corinth County Justice Center. The boys walked up to the marble steps of the former mansion. They stopped at the base of the steps and Joe looked up and whistled. He admired the old five story home which was fronted with white columns. "This sure looks a lot nicer than the brick and steel monstrosity we have for a headquarters building. I'll bet it's a bitch to heat."

Upon entering, they approached an older deputy who was leaning on the counter and thumbing through an auto parts catalog.

"We have an appointment with Sheriff Tolliver," Griff said before the deputy could speak.

The lackluster deputy pushed the sign-in log at the visitors, pointed to it and said, "Sign in." The deputy checked the signatures and demanded to see their I.D.s. Satisfied at what he'd seen he strolled over to the intercom, exhaled audibly and punched the button. "Two cops from Capitol City to see you, sir."

"Send 'em in Russell, send 'em in."

Deputy Russell pressed the door button and Deacon Tolliver's office door unlocked and popped open.

CHAPTER ELEVEN

Sheriff Tolliver stepped through the door and approached. When Griff offered his hand, Deacon Tolliver grabbed it and pulled Griff to him, giving him a hearty hug. "How are you doing, son? You're looking better than the last time I saw you, in that hospital." Without waiting for an answer, the big sheriff put out his huge hand to Joe and welcomed him. "You're Joe, right? Been lookin' forward to meetin' you, young man. Come on in."

The sheriff stood aside as the boys entered his office. He was dressed in a standard sand colored uniform shirt devoid of ribbons or badge, only the shoulder patch to denote the Sheriff's Department. Joe had expected to see the personification of General Patton as he'd seen in the photographs at Griff's; he was disappointed with the stark look.

The sheriff's office was even more than Griff had described. Commendations, awards and photos of the sheriff with well known people were on every wall; there was even a framed photo of him shaking hands with the Zoo Man. When Sheriff Tolliver sat, it was behind a huge fancy desk with an even bigger U.S. flag on the wall behind him. Joe and Griff sat in overstuffed leather chairs across from him.

"This is a subdued look for you, Deke. Where are all of your awards?" Griff asked motioning to the sheriff's shirt.

"My daughter, Caroline, finally convinced me that I looked too gauche on a daily basis. Besides it was a pain in the ass pinning everything on each time I changed my shirt. Everything is now on my formal uniform jacket. If I need to make an impression I just slip the jacket on; even an old war horse can learn new tricks."

"Speaking of your daughter, I expected her to be out front. Deputy Russell is a poor substitute." Griff said.

"She's on maternity leave, going to make a grandfather out of me. Believe it or not, I inherited Russell when I took over thirty odd years ago. He's gruff but dependable, just not Mr. Congeniality. Dean will join us shortly. He's out on a run just now. What's this problem you guys are wrestling with and how can I help? Your phone call was almost cryptic."

The subject broached, Griff said, "Capitol City is going to shit. Under everybody's noses and apparently going undetected for years was a criminal enterprise run by three well respected businessmen; they were brothers. Two of them died recently and the third brother is our main suspect in the amassing of explosives and the bombing of the police cruisers. We're having a hard time sorting it all out and pinning it on our main suspect. It that's not enough, the brothers apparently started a low level gang years ago, and it thrived without anyone taking notice. We think that this gang is the center around which most of the criminal activity revolves. The gang calls itself the Lone Strangers and has adopted as their own the old Lucky Strike logo, LS/MFT which stands for Lone Strangers / Make Fine Terrorists. The members even have the logo tattooed on their left forearms. Joe and I are part of a task force to clear up this cancer and we've been assigned to work with a federal agent. We're trying to take a fresh approach, to think outside the box – four hours outside of the box. We've come seeking your wisdom, knowledge, expertise and ideas."

"Gosh darn if you haven't said a mouthful. What we need is an old fashioned brain storming session. When Dean gets here you can lay out all of the details and we'll see what we can come up with. Anything else on your mind?"

"Have you made nice with the county commissioners? I haven't seen any of the Fuzzybutts around?"

A black cloud of doom seemed to fall over the sheriff's face. "The dogs are out at my place. To my knowledge we have the only family of law enforcement trained Great Danes in the country and they're not allowed to work. The dogs are frustrated, and frankly so am I. The only dog that the commissioners will accept is Dean's Recruit; he rides as a K-9 but isn't allowed in the buildings."

Twenty minutes or so later Dean Tolliver showed up. Recruit stayed outside. The situation was repeated for Dean and his father, but this time in more detail. The Tollivers listened intently and Deacon opened his mouth to speak, but his son did not notice.

"I had contact with a biker last week who said he was on his way to Capitol City for a funeral; he had that LS/MFT tattoo on his arm. I figured he was a Luckies smoker.

"Do you remember his name?"

"Not right off, but I have his name in a file box in the cruiser; I hear that someday computers will be small enough that you can carry them with you. That will be a blessing."

"If you have an extension cord long enough," Joe chimed in.

"I'm sure by that time they'll have that part of the problem fixed, but don't hold your breath until it happens," Dean said.

Deacon Tolliver realized that his son hadn't noticed that he was going to speak and did not feel snubbed. With his elbows on his desk and his fingers tented he said, "Your department is big enough to form a task force; we never had that luxury. But on the other hand sometimes 'too many cooks spoil the broth' if you catch my meaning.

Too many factions, too much chance of communications break down if you ask me."

"The task force method worked good when Griff was kidnapped," Joe said, "and we got him back O.K.!"

"We're all glad you did, son. I'm not arguing with you, just musing, that's all. Maybe you shouldn't rely so much on others and get more 'hands on', that's what I'm suggesting."

"That's a good idea, Deke, we're already making progress just coming here; any other ideas?"

"Has anyone interviewed the base personnel at Fort Hopewell? Something stinks about the way their explosives disappeared and nobody said anything."

"The top brass has been interviewed but it's on our list to go out there again. I think Mike Wohocks is going to handle the interviews there since it's a government installation."

"The Mike Wohocks?" Dean questioned, "the one from South Dakota?!"

"The very same. He got transferred to Capitol City and his first assignment was the first cruiser bombing; an anonymous caller tipped that off, to the F.B.I. Since both cruiser bombings were to Patrol 17, our cruiser, we were assigned to work with Mike since we no longer had a ride. He's the one who uncovered the large cache of explosives."

"He's a good man," Dean said. "While he is conducting interviews at the fort, maybe you could print the explosives cases, if it's safe to do so and you have the stomach for that kind of gamble."

"That is an excellent idea! I'm sure Joe here would want to tackle that."

Joe shot Griff a look which basically said, "Are you nuts?" But then that was a given.

"Say, have you boys had lunch?"

"No," Joe said, "we came right here."

"Well I'm starved, boys. What say we get something to eat."

"You're the boss and it's your jurisdiction. Where do you suggest?"

"My favorite spot is the Punch Bowl. It's a bar, but it's got a good kitchen and an extensive sandwich menu. I'll ride with Dean and Recruit, you guys can follow."

It was a five minute drive from the Justice Center to the bar. The lot was packed and the vehicles could not park together. When they exited their respective vehicles Griff and Joe noticed that the sheriff had pinned his custom ordered oversized badge to his shirt and had strapped on his six guns with the pearl grips, the belt buckle was a large U.S.A.

The sheriff and his son are both big men and a hush briefly fell over the lunch crowd when they entered the bar. Deacon Tolliver removed his Stetson and waved it. "This is not an official visit boys and girls. Enjoy your meals."

An audible exhale could be heard and things returned to normal. "To have such a command presence was awesome," Griff thought.

The men were seated in a booth which had a reserved sign on it. To Griff's knowledge the sheriff had not called ahead, leaving him to believe that the head lawman was a regular with a booth permanently reserved for him. This type of action was counter to Griff's own; vary your routine and keep your enemies guessing was better than having them know where to find you. Maybe big city thinking doesn't apply in rural America. This was re-enforced when father and son both ordered without using the menu.

Deacon and Dean both ordered garbage burgers, extra large burgers with every type of topping and condiment in the place. Deacon had them hold the mayo and Dean ordered double fries. Griff ordered a more traditional cheese burger with bacon, Swiss cheese and sautéed mushrooms with a side of coleslaw. Joe ordered a plain burger and fries. Colas all around.

While they ate, the lawmen discussed the intricacies of the case. Griff was only half paying attention, because his eyes were drawn to a Dolly Parton look alike who was seated cattycorner from him in another booth. She kept smiling and winking at him. Suddenly and apparently not caring who noticed, the woman hiked her skirt up to her waist and shimmied out of her black and red panties. Griff, who was seated across from the sheriff, couldn't believe the display he was watching. Without bothering to put her skirt down, the natural blond put her fingers in the elastic waistband and shot the bikini panties like a rubber band; they landed on Deacon Tolliver's head.

Without undo reaction, the sheriff reached up and retrieved the undies. He brought them to his nose and inhaled deeply. "Not now, Scarlet, I'm on duty," he said and tossed the panties over his shoulder to the blond who caught them like it was a practiced routine. Scarlet smiled at Griff and then slowly put the panties back on, still not caring who was enjoying the show. Joe hadn't seen the show that Griff was watching and Dean acted like this was an everyday occurrence. The Tollivers kept eating.

A somewhat flustered Zoo Man returned his attention to his meal and the conversation about Capitol City's problem. The main suggestion to come out of the luncheon meeting was that Griff, Joe and Mike double check everything that the task force members had done. "I know it's a lot of work, but you'll find clues and connections that they've missed. I'll bet my star on it."

After the meal was over Griff motioned for the waitress to come over and then asked for the check. The waitress, Doris, just smiled and went on her way. "What's that all about?" he asked almost to himself.

"Your money's no good here, son. She'll put it on my tab."

"That's not right. I called you and picked your brain for suggestions. The least you can do is let me pay for lunch."

"Nope, and that's final!"

"O.K., but I'm leaving the tip," and he put a $20 bill on the table."

When the big sheriff slid out of the booth, Scarlet reached over, patted the sheriff on the butt and said, "See you later, Sweetcheeks."

As the blushing sheriff reached the door he was met by a chorus of, "See you later, Sweetcheeks."

The sheriff stopped and turned slowly as the patrons grew silent. "That's Sheriff Sweetcheeks," he bellowed. The crowd laughed as he exited.

While Joe, Deke and Dean were talking, Dean gave Joe the biker's information. Griff went to the Explorer and retrieved a bag from his briefcase. He extracted a large dog biscuit and gave it to the appreciative Recruit. "I brought enough for all of the Fuzzybutts," he said as he turned the bag over to the sheriff.

As the boys were saying goodbye the Zoo Man said, "Deke, give Scarlet a big hug for me and thank her for the show."

"Hell, son, I'll have her come out so that you can hug her your own self."

"No, no, no, no, that's OK! To paraphrase a Mel Brooks line though, 'It must be good to be the king'," he said as he winked at the big sheriff. Deke smiled and nodded.

Handshakes and hugs completed, Joe and Griff walked over to the Explorer. Joe questioned, "What was that about thanking Scarlet for a show?"

Griff explained what went on in vivid detail. Griff asked his shocked partner, "How are you feeling, Joe, tired?"

"No, I'm good to go."

"Good, you can drive. I'm going to take a nap. Tomorrow we'll meet with Mike and plan our next move."

Good to his word, Joe's partner was soundly sleeping in short order. Joe drove without benefit of conversation and took in the beauty of the rural countryside while he pondered Sheriff Tolliver's advice. He also listened to instrumental music on a local P.B.S. station, a luxury not afforded them in C.C.P.D. cruisers as the new cars are ordered without radios. God forbid that C.C.P.D. officers should have an opportunity to get any culture.

Halfway home Joe took advantage of a roadside rest so he could stretch his legs and relieve himself. Zoo was out. It would be a waste of time to wake him. In the restroom Joe stepped into a stall to rearrange himself and tuck in his shirt tail. Graffiti on the back of the door caught his eye. The foot wide drawing was that of a cigarette with an exploding end. On the cigarette was written LS/MFT. This was either a random act of a gang member passing through or the Lone Stranger's sphere of influence reached beyond the borders of Capitol City. Was this the first sign of territorial markings? Rather than wake his partner, Joe retrieved his trusty Polaroid and photographed the drawing. Joe also jotted down the exact location of the rest area in case it needed to be plotted on a state map.

As they neared Capitol City Joe changed stations to pick up the local color. A news item about another suspected bombing jolted Griff from his sleep; he put the reclining passenger seat back to its original upright position and listened intently. The gist of the newscast was that an explosion had done extensive damage to the offices of Lovey-Dove Real Estate. Griff had Joe pull in at a convenience store. He needed to use a pay phone.

Griff placed a call to the Gentry residence. After seven or eight rings the phone was answered with a gruff, "What do you want?"

"Pops, this is Griff Park, is Red there?"

"Who?"

"Red, Giselle, your nurse."

"She's not my niece!

"Not niece, Pops, nurse," frustrated he blurted out, "Is she there?"

"She didn't answer the phone, did she? That's one of her jobs, to answer the phone."

"Pops, where <u>is</u> she?!"

"She's at the hospital, left me all alone again."

"Why did she go to the hospital, Pops?"

"Who?"

"Your nurse, Pops, why did she go to the hospital?"

Griff tried to remain calm, but this was starting to sound like a comedy routine.

"One of her friends got hurt; took her to Niagara Falls."

"Do you mean Stella Niagara? Who got hurt?"

"Some girl. Damn you're as nosey as that big dumb cop she's dating. I'll tell her you called. Who the hell are you anyway?"

"It's the big dumb cop. It was nice to finally hold a conversation with you. We must do it again sometime." Griff hung up, not waiting for a reply.

"What's up, Zoo?"

"Red works for Lovey-Dove. She's not home. Buzzard Bait says she's visiting someone who got hurt. She's at Stella Niagara."

"So you want me to head for the hospital?"

"No, Joe, let's go to the damaged real estate office instead."

Joe changed course and headed the Explorer for the offices of Lovey-Dove Real Estate.

CHAPTER TWELVE

The blast site was cordoned off with crime scene tape and sawhorses for about a half a block in every direction. The real estate office is in a residential area, so only a handful of people were truly affected by the blockade. Griff and Joe were recognized by one of the uniformed officers and waved on through. None to their surprise, the pair spotted Mike Wohcowhcs at the center of the action.

"Whatcha got, Mike?"

The kneeling G-man didn't look up but answered the familiar voice, "Not sure, Zoo, pretty destructive, but it appears to be just an accident as first aired." He pointed to a badly damaged silver sedan that was on its side on the other side of the parking lot. The story is that a car cut the driver off, she over steered, jumped the curb and struck this propane tank causing it to rupture. There's obviously extensive damage to the car and office but only minor injuries to the driver, thanks to her seatbelt. No other injuries. The office wasn't open yet."

"Does the driver work here?" Griff wanted to know.

"Yeah, Zoo. She's a fairly new employee. She refused treatment by the squad, but another employee who showed up took her to the hospital as a precautionary measure. I'm going to have an arson investigator check it out, but for now we can cross this one off of our list. So what were you guys up to on this fine day?" Mike asked as he stood and stretched to get the kinks out.

"We took a road trip and picked some brains," Joe said. We met with an old friend of yours, Dean Tolliver, and his father."

"It really is a small world. I'd heard that he'd left Deadwood to go home and work with his father, but I guess I didn't realize that this was home."

"It's half way across the state, Mike, but picking the brain of an old war horse like Deacon Tolliver was worth it. Plus we got this! Joe, show Mike your photograph of the latest gang artistry."

With a flourish Joe produced the Polaroid photo from his inside jacket pocket. Mike studied the LS/MFT exploding cigarette.

"Where did you spot this, Joe?"

"Half way between here and Corinth County, in a stall at a roadside rest.

"What do you think guys, are the Lone Strangers recruiting out of town?"

"Might just be someone passing through. Dean Tolliver stopped a former gang member who was on his way back here for one of the Goldman's funerals. For now we'll just add the characters name to the Lone Strangers list and pursue other clues. O.K., Joe, I know that look, what are you thinking?"

"I'm thinking, if it hasn't already been done, someone should check the jackets on all of the known Strangers and see who their running buddies are. We may considerably widen our base of information. I know, I can tackle that while you guys are at Fort Hopewell."

"Am I missing something?" Mike asked.

"An idea that was tossed around with the Tollivers. While you're interviewing personnel at the fort, Joe and I can check the explosives cases for latent prints. Joe's afraid that we may do a bang up job of it."

"It sounds like a project for tomorrow. Why don't we talk about it in the morning? I'm about ready to wrap up here and I could sure use some shut eye."

"Good idea, Mike. Zoo, why don't we stop by your place, you can grab a change of clothes and bunk at my place. In the morning we can meet up at The Last Drop." It was agreed, the three would meet at 9 A.M.

Seven thirty A.M. seemed to arrive all too quickly. Zoo was happy that he'd napped on the way back from their visit with the Tollivers. By the time he'd showered and dressed in the guest room bath, Bev Beveltnik had breakfast ready. Bev had fixed one of Joe's favorite breakfasts, scrambled eggs with cheese, mushrooms and asparagus tips. Griff was quite surprised how good the combination was, but passed on adding hot sauce like his partner. Juice, toast and coffee rounded out the meal.

"That was great, Bev. I don't get too many home cooked meals."

"Maybe you should settle down, get married. That should insure home cooked meals. Joey, don't give me that look. I'm allowed to speak my mind!"

Joe, indeed, had shot a look at his wife as if to say, "Why are you opening a can of worms?"

Before he could speak, Griff said, "It's O.K. As a matter of fact, I've been thinking along those lines myself." He stuck up his hand to ward off any questions and said, "That's as much as I'm going to say on the matter."

Bev's face lit up at the thought of the Zoo Man settling down. As the boys were leaving to meet with their G-man partner, they could hear Bev whistling. Griff couldn't place the tune, but he was sure it was from some Disney musical.

At The Last Drop coffee shop the crime fighters presented their permanent discount cards to the wary eye of the substitute barista, Gwenn. Mike hadn't eaten and ordered a toasted bagel with cream cheese to go along with his coffee. The three sat at the same table as their last time there.

In anticipation of doing follow-up work at Fort Hopewell, Agent Wohcowhcs called ahead and was told that they would have unencumbered access to whatever they needed. It was decided to take both vehicles. Mike would go first to interview the brass and anyone else of interest. Griff and Joe would go by headquarters to pick up a fingerprint kit and Mike would meet them at the ammo bunker when he was through. Joe had obviously not talked his way out of the venture.

At C.C.P.D. headquarters Griff and Joe were questioned in depth about why they needed to sign out a fingerprint kit. They were getting static until they dialed up Lt. Dingell. "Give them whatever they need," he barked. "Those officers are doing serious police work. You're just a clerk!" Lt. Dingell slammed his phone down. The injured officer, working light duty in the I.D. bureau, was stunned and sorry he had put the phone on speaker.

Zoo half apologized for the lieutenant's gruffness. "He must be having a bad day. He's really a nice guy."

The humbled officer now bent over backwards to give them what they needed and even got them a pair of lab coats. "That powder's really messy and wearing rubber gloves will save your hands." As they were leaving with the tackle box fingerprint kit, the officer said, "Don't get blown up." That did not help the already apprehensive Joe Beveltnik.

Zoo was driving and kept glancing over at his nervous partner. "What are you doing? Your hand is moving a mile a minute in your jacket pocket!"

"I'm praying. I've got rosary beads in here."

"But you are not Catholic!"

"These are Bev's. Praying couldn't hurt, we'll be working with dangerous explosives, you know."

"Hopefully we'll have base trained personnel helping us. If you feel like something is wrong, hold the explosive to your chest, your ballistic vest will absorb the shock."

"Zoo, you're an asshole. It would still blow my hands off."

"Must you always look at the dark side?" Griff was smiling broadly but inside he too had reservations about the upcoming task.

At the Fort Hopewell gatehouse, their I.D.s were checked against the incoming visitor's roster and then they were directed to the welcome center just inside the gate. Again their I.D.s were checked and their itinerary was noted. They also had to surrender their firearms. Griff and Joe were given limited access passes and a map of the base. The desk officer made a call and assured them that two munitions officers would meet them at the ammo bunkers. He also confirmed that Agent Wohcowhcs was also on base.

The map was fairly clear and they could eventually see their destination on the horizon at one of the furthest outposts. The series of large mounds were shaped like Quonset huts, but all were covered with sandbags. Some had sparse foliage growing on them. They had little trouble finding bunker No. 2. It was clearly marked and an occupied jeep was parked there. As they parked the Explorer and got out, they were met by two G.I.s in camo fatigues. One of the G.I.s playfully tossed a dummy grenade to them – "Think fast," he said. Joe caught it in his right hand and in one motion side armed it back striking the startled G.I. in the side.

"What did you do that for," he yelled. Griff shrugged his shoulders and responded, "Joe's got no sense of humor."

Starting over with more civil introductions, Griff and Joe explained to Saunders and the playful LaPorte that they needed access to the explosives from the Capitol City raid.

Bunker No. 2 was unlocked by Saunders and the printing of the explosive cases was begun. Saunders and LaPorte wore rubber gloves and handled the contraband while Park and Beveltnik printed the items. Some usable prints were lifted off of the Bazooka type portable rocket cases, but none off of the explosives boxes with the exception of one which was garnered from a stick-on label. Griff also printed the lacquered toe nails on the rough hide elephant foot umbrella stands where one clear fingerprint was obtained.

It was hot and sticky in the ammo bunker and the ballistic vests made it worse. The G.I.s stripped to the waist in an effort to cool down. Griff noticed the LS/MFT tattoos as did Joe a moment later.

The boys were just finishing up when Mike met up with them. "Any luck?"

"Surprisingly few prints for as much powder as we used, but we did find something else of interest," Zoo said, pointing to the G.I.s tattoos.

"Looks like you guys may have struck gold. I merely struck out," Mike said. "By the way, where are your space suits?"

"What space suits?" Joe asked looking at Mike as if he were a space alien.

"Those heavy padded suits that the bomb squad guys use to keep themselves from getting blown up?!"

Joe looked at Griff. Griff looked at Saunders and LaPorte who were looking at each other. When they looked forward they shrugged their shoulders. In unison they both said, "Oops, we forgot."

After they had all retreated to a safe distance, Mike introduced himself to Saunders and LaPorte. He then individually took them aside for interviews. The story he got from both men was basically the same but was different from what was expected. Both Saunders and LaPorte admitted growing up in Capitol City and both had been loners. They said that they were taken into the social club of Lone Strangers by Sol Goldman who provided employment and camaraderie with other boys. The LS/MFT tattoos were a requirement and stood for Lone Strangers Make Fellowship Terrific. The tattoos were meant as an introduction to other members. Apparently the scope of the gang changed since they were members 10 years ago.

When asked about how the explosives were taken from Fort Hopewell, they didn't have a clue. Both men indicated that they had been transferred to munitions when their predecessors went A.W.O.L. Neither Saunders nor LaPorte knew the names of the previous munitions men but were sure that base personnel would have that information.

A call to personnel indeed produced the names of the men in question, but it was not known if they had Lone Stranger tattoos. Personnel files did not carry tattoo or other body markings information. Joe became the keeper of the A.W.O.L.s info; he would cross reference the names with C.C.P.D files.

Mike suggested that before they leave, they should do an inventory check to make sure all of the inventory from the storage locker was still complete. Joe wasn't too thrilled about going back into the bunker. He'd already been in there today and had, as he put it, "cheated death". After being properly suited, Zoo and Mike did the hands on check while Joe handled the clipboard. The inventory was intact. Nothing was missing. LaPorte relocked the bunker and Agent Wohcowhcs then added a tape federal seal which he signed. Joe took a documentary photo of the explosive inventory while the door was open and another of the closed and sealed door.

At the welcome center Griff and Joe signed out and were relieved of their base access passes while Mike was in the restroom. Joe thought they were done but noticed that Griff was in a staring match with the officer behind the counter and Griff's eyes were narrowing. Finally the G.I. blinked. "Alright, alright, I wasn't going to let you leave without them. I just wanted to see if you would remember!" He bent down and unlocked the under counter cabinet, removed the boys' weapons and handed them over. Joe's face blushed. He had forgotten.

"What's the next move, boys?" Mike asked as he was clipping his holstered weapon inside of his waistband.

"If we have time today maybe we can check out the property that was taken from the locker that was used as a workshop."

"I think we can do that, Griff, but I need to grab something to eat on the way back. That bagel from this morning has given up the ghost. I saw a greasy spoon called The Mess Hall on the way in. My guess is they cater to hungry service men."

The ever thinking frugal Joe said, "Let's make sure our federal I.D.s are visible. Maybe we'll get a discount."

Griff had a snide grin on his face and remarked, "You better hope so partner. It's your turn to buy." To his surprise, he got no negative feedback from Joe on that suggestion.

At a little past two the boys parked side by side in The Mess Hall parking lot. A half dozen cars with local plates were already there. At the front door Joe said, "I changed my mind. Let's not worry about a discount. Stow the I.D.s. This might be hostile territory and we don't want to tip our hands." Griff and Mike agreed with Joe's thinking.

The Mess Hall was dimly lit and they had to let their eyes adjust to the dim interior. They were back lit by the sun as they walked through the doorway. A deep but friendly voice bade them to "Sit anywhere. I'll be with you shortly."

Like most cops, they sat at a wall table so that they could keep an eye on the door and the other patrons. They gravitated to that spot without even thinking about it. The mimeographed sheet on the table read like a grade school menu except for the reference to "Shit on a Shingle" as a breakfast item.

The jovial owner of the deep voice came to the table. "Howdy, fellas, welcome to The Mess Hall. I'm Slim, the new owner. I don't have a liquor license yet, but I make decent coffee and I've got iced tea and soft drinks. What can I get you to drink while you're looking over the menu?" Mike and Joe chose iced tea; Griff went with the root beer.

"Friendly sort, isn't he." Mike said.

"Sure is and he looks familiar. Too bad his sleeve isn't a little shorter. The bottom edge of his tattoo looks familiar, too," Griff mused.

Slim returned with the drinks and Griff saw the full LS/MFT tattoo when he was handed his root beer.

"You look familiar," Griff said. "Are you from Capitol City?"

"I was. Are you still a cop, Officer Park?" every head in the place popped up at that question.

"You have me at a disadvantage, Slim. I take it we've met before. Was it on a professional basis?" Griff inquired in a hushed tone.

In a lower tone Slim said, "You busted me for boosting car stereos about seven years ago but there's no hard feelings. I was young and dumb and you were just doing your job. In fact I should probably thank you; that stretch in jail changed my life. I found Jesus, got my G.E.D. and have stayed out of trouble ever since."

"How about we order and we can chat more while we eat?"

Slim thought that was a good idea.

The three ordered sandwiches and fries and talked among themselves until the food arrived. When it did Slim doled it out and then went to check on his other customers. Once all of his handful of customers was taken care of, he returned to the table.

"Sit down, Slim, if it won't offend your other customers."

"They'd better not be offended. I sit and talk with them, too, when it's not busy. So are you still with the C.C.P.D.?"

"Yes, I am, but I still can't place you."

"I'm not surprised. You deal with so many people and I wasn't 'Slim' then. The name's Jim Mess. You caught me and Wally Burke breaking into cars at the SeaView Mall."

"Were you that pudgy kid who tried to run with an armload of stereos?"

"Yep. But that's all in the past. I'm a legit, yet struggling businessman now. So, what are you up to?"

Slim seemed so genuine that Griff opened up to him. "We're trying to stop a crime spree in Cap City. That's what brought us out here. These are my partners, Joe and Mike." Slim and the boys shook hands.

"Saw the tattoo," Joe said. "Were you a Lone Stranger?"

"Used to be but it didn't take with me; back then they were too legit for my tastes. I didn't last."

Griff said, "The Lone Strangers are no longer legit. We think that they are in the middle of this whole mess. Who was in charge when you were a brief member?"

"Four older guys: Danny, Izzy, Pops and Sol. I didn't stick around long enough to get to know them all. I worked some for Sol in his pawn shop, but I didn't like it. Being a young thug was easier. I had to learn the hard way. Excuse me. I have to check on my other customers – you finish eating. Can I bring you any dessert when I return?"

The three opted not to get dessert but requested the check when Slim returned to the table. Griff gave Slim a C.C.P.D. business card and got Slim's phone number. He'd call him later. Slim promised to keep his eyes and ears open for any information regarding Capitol City crime and the Lone Strangers.

The refueled lawmen continued on to Capitol City. Their next destination was the C.C.P.D. property room.

CHAPTER THIRTEEN

Checking out the confiscated materials at the property room would make it a full day, but the boys were in a groove and chose to continue.

The old property room had been in the basement of C.C.P.D. headquarters for as long as anyone could remember and was a pretty antiquated facility. In 1988 the city loosened its purse strings and built a new freestanding building on a piece of city property about five miles from headquarters. The two cars pulled up to the fort-like property room's guard shack and the security guard let the officers pass through the chain link fence topped with razor wire. The guard called ahead and a civilian property room clerk met them at the door. Joe Standish knew Beveltnik and Park but thoroughly checked Agent Wohcowhcs' I.D. Once satisfied, Joe Standish led the boys past the secure property drop off counter and into the inner sanctum. The C.C.P.D. sergeant on duty gave them a half hearted wave of acknowledgement from his office.

Due to the large amount of items taken from the storage locker, one corner of the large items warehouse had been set aside just for them. Like items had been separated onto separate tables, and all items were cross referenced to the same property number. The volume of the items necessitated various approaches. Joe B. donned a lab coat and latex gloves. He would be in charge of seeking out latent prints. Mike Wohcowhcs checked the bomb making books and periodicals for marked pages, notations and anything that might point to the persons involved and their intentions.

Griff started studying the charts and maps showing the city, its infrastructure, utilities and the various marked police facilities and buildings. The materials looked as if they belonged in a combat general's war room. While he was going over the materials, Joe was busy playing I.D. tech.

The pieces of pipes and caps used for making pipe bombs yielded numerous fingerprints. Not knowing what handling procedures had been used, the on file fingerprints of the officers on the crime scene log as well as the property room clerks would have to be checked for elimination purposes. The identification and elimination process would be handled by real I.D. techs.

Griff got more confused the longer he studied the maps. The city map had all of the police facilities' locations circled along with all of the other city government buildings. A county map had all of the utilities circled. Griff could understand the government buildings and utilities if there were a vendetta against the establishment, but other markings stumped him. A variety of unrelated areas were starred with red pencil and some were labeled. For instance, five outlying restaurants were marked with their names written in; five different eateries and no correlation seemed evident.

Miniscule printing on the city map was almost missed by Griff's scrutiny. A magnifying glass revealed a cryptic symbol on the green area representing the Phideaux Dog Park. The oh so fine printing read LS/MFB. LS/MFT had two meanings; this was the first symbol alteration that they had seen.

"Hey, guys, what do you make of this? The dog park on the map is marked LS/MFB, any ideas?"

"B for bombs?" Joe asked.

"Maybe the whole thing is changed, a code based on the Lone Strangers logo," Mike suggested.

"Well that tears it, it's been a long day and this new wrinkle isn't helping. What say we knock off for the night. Maybe I'll get an inspiration if I sleep on it for a while."

"Sounds good, partner," Joe said. Let's meet back here in the morning and start fresh."

"You guys go ahead. I'm going to read a little longer. I'll meet you back here in the morning. How does 9 A.M. sound?" The boys both agreed and left for the night.

Griff reclined the passenger seat and closed his eyes as Joe drove in silence. Joe dropped Griff off in front of his apartment building with the admonition that he would pick him up again at 8:30 A.M. As soon as Griff entered his apartment, he called Giselle. If he were going to sleep on the map symbols, he might as well have company.

Red jumped at the opportunity to be with Griff, not only because she missed him and wanted him, but also because she would get to see his bachelor pad. It took her only thirty minutes to freshen up and drive to Zoo's Zoo. She parked her pristine Chevette next to his beater in the basement and walked up to his apartment. Zoo opened the door and snatched Red inside, smothering her with kisses as he kicked the door closed.

"Miss me?" she asked.

"Oh yeah, this case is tedious and I need a little R & R before I go to sleep."

"I can't promise that you'll get any sleep, but I can sure provide the R & R."

The apartment wasn't quite as Spartan as she had imagined, cozy but comfortable, kitchen and dinette, sofa, overstuffed chair, TV, stereo, a whatnot shelf displaying various pictures and a large portrait of John Wayne on the wall. The bedroom was a tribute to Griff himself. Two walls were nearly covered with medals, commendations and various framed certificates and diplomas. Red was impressed but surprised that none of his police trappings were hung in his living room. The bedroom was obviously his sanctuary and she did not question him about it. One wall had a large closet. The sliding door was shut.

Griff set the alarm clock for 8 A.M. and hoped it would wake Giselle, because he had a tendency to sleep through it. After a minimum of small talk, nibbling and foreplay, Zoo made love to the feisty minx like a man possessed. After a long hard day, the exhilarating romp left Griff drained and he was quickly asleep. Red snuggled against his nakedness and hoped that she had fulfilled his expectations in their brief but passionate interlude.

Eight A.M. came all too early for Griff as Red woke him up. The morning session was brief as she dressed and put her lover in the shower. Red's timing was perfect; as she walked down the stairs, Joe was riding up in the elevator.

After about five minutes of door pounding, Joe was greeted by a wet Zoo Man answering the door; he was covered with a towel. Miss Boltshoff, Griff's octogenarian neighbor, heard the pounding and waited for the show; she was chagrined to see the towel. "Nuts," she said as she closed her door.

"Thought maybe you overslept," Joe said.

"Nope, just washing the sleepy dust out of my eyes." Joe thought he caught a whiff of perfume, but he couldn't be sure.

A large coffee and a breakfast sandwich each, from a drive through window, would sustain them as they returned to the C.C.P.D. property room. Mike Wohcowhcs had not yet arrived.

Griff got back to studying the city map. As he stared at the map, a shape, like a constellation, became visible to him. Looking at the portion of the map as if it were a clock face, Griff drew lines from one locale to another and wrote down the names: Lower left, 7:00, Lou's Sandwich Shoppe. 12:00, Shoneys. 5:00 Mel's Diner. 10:00, Frank's Fish and Chips and at 2:00 was Tommy Tuckers. He drew a connector line from 2:00 to 7:00; the lines formed a star with the dog park in the center. The connected restaurants were:

Lou's Sandwich Shoppe
Shoneys

Mel's Diner
Frank's Fish and Chips
Tommy Tuckers

Reading from top to bottom, the first letters formed LSMFT.

Was the star a pentagram or satanic symbol and what was the significance of the dog park which now became the center of attention? Having found no other possible links to the occult during this investigation, Griff discounted that aspect but jotted a note to himself just in case. Griff showed his find to his partner.

As Griff and Joe were studying the star pattern, Mike Wohcowhcs arrived carrying a webbed folding patio rocking chair. "Whatcha got?" he asked.

"We're not sure, Mike. Zoo found an interesting symbol imbedded in the city map. It seems like the more we dig the more confusing things get. Did you do any good last night?"

Mike opened his folding rocker near the periodicals table and sat down. "I think I know how they took out the cruiser at the SeaView Mall," Mike said. "A pamphlet that I found last night had descriptions and diagrams for the pin point transportation of explosives and detonators on a light weight balsa wood bed mounted on a remote control car chassis. This would explain how the officers were unable to find the explosives by visual inspection. They arrived after the officers did on that bogus run. Our bombers are getting more sophisticated but they're still avoiding killing anyone. Hopefully we can solve this before anyone dies."

"That's our main objective," Griff reiterated. We know that Danny Goldman has to be involved, but we still aren't any closer to nailing him than the day we started."

"Have we looked into the background of the person who rented the storage locker where this stuff came from?"

"Early on, Mike," Griff said, "but the follow-up led nowhere. The alleged renter, Creighton Gentry, died forty years ago. The address given was that of Pops Gentry, Creighton's father, and he knows nothing about the storage locker or the explosives."

"What is Pops' first name?"

Griff looked at Joe who shrugged his shoulders. "We're not sure."

Mike asked, "Didn't Slim Mess tell us that there were four founders of the Lone Strangers, three Goldmans and a Pops?"

"I hope that's just a coincidence, but he has no love for cops," Griff said. "It looks like we need to do another follow-up with Pops."

As the three worked in silence, the possible Pops Gentry connection was eating at Griff.

"I'm done lifting prints," Joe said. "How about we break for lunch."

"Good idea, partner. While we're out you can drop the prints off at I.D. and then we can check out the dog park. If we've got time, we can interview Pops Gentry again. We'll call you tonight, Mike, to plan tomorrow's itinerary."

Mike had worked late and slept in and opted to stay behind and do more reading while Joe and Griff dropped off the lifted prints from Fort Hopewell and the property room.

At C.C.P.D headquarters the I.D. techs were visibly upset with the large task that had been dumped in their laps. It didn't help that the chief's office insisted that this project was to get priority preference. Joe quickly backed out of the I.D. section so that he wouldn't have to listen to the grousing. No one mentioned the fingerprint kit so Joe decided to hold on to it until the investigation was over.

Griff wasn't in the mood for another fast food sandwich and suggested that they visit their old haunt, Ma's Diner. It was their first time back since Ma had passed.

As they walked in, Ruby, Joe's favorite waitress, stared at them briefly until the spark of recognition hit. This was the first time she'd seen the boys out of uniform. Ruby was almost giddy as she seated them in a booth near the door. The three exchanged small talk as the boys perused the new menu and took in the altered ambiance. Joe and the Zoo Man both ordered Caribbean jerk chicken sandwiches with dirty rice. While the order was being prepared Griff asked to speak with Belle, Ma's daughter.

Belle was pleased to see Griff and thanked him for attending her mother's funeral. Griff then introduced Joe to the new owner of the restaurant. "I hope you boys enjoy the food. It's taken on a Caribbean flare. My new cook had some trouble and lost his own place. I was lucky to get him.

"That wouldn't be Tomas Domingue, would it?" Griff asked.

"Why, yes, do you know him?"

"We met once, but I've never tried his cooking."

Rasta Domingue himself served the meal but didn't show any sign of recognizing the lawmen. Belle must have given him a nod, because he also delivered a plate of conch fritters, "On de house, mon."

"I hate to admit it, but this food is even better than what Ma served."

"I agree, Joe, but I kinda miss the harassment. I'm certain that if we become regular customers again, we'll get our share. When we finish here, we'll check out the dog park."

The boys finished their meal in silence and relished every morsel, especially the conch fritters which were served with a slightly pungent dipping sauce. After a few words of praise to Belle and the paying of the bill, they left for the dog park.

Phideaux's Dog Park was either named for someone or was a terrible pun on a dog's name. Griff guessed it was the latter. The boys walked around the entire park checking it out and being careful not to step in or on any urban meadow muffins; nothing seemed strange. What were they missing? Why was this the focal point of the pentagram? They stopped at the monument in the center of the park. The plaque read: "For all our canine companions to enjoy. Remember, less stress means friskier dogs."

"Less stress means friskier dogs," Griff read aloud. "LSMFD, was the 'B' on the map a misprint? What the hell does it all mean?" In frustration Griff kicked the four sided aluminum column that held the plaque; it was hollow. An examination showed that one of the panels was hinged. There was no handle. Griff slid his pocket knife blade into the "door" edge opposite the hinge and forced it open.

"Now we're getting somewhere," Joe said. "I hope this turns out to be a treasure trove."

Joe peered into the blackness of the interior and wished they had brought a flashlight with them and said so.

"Good idea, Joe. Bring back some rubber gloves with you, too." Joe trotted off toward the truck; halfway there he wondered how his statement had become a mandate for him to get the light - oh well, someone had to do it.

The interior of the column was 3 feet to a side and 4 feet tall. The column sat on a concrete base. Joe's heavy duty flashlight lit up the interior as a woman and her Schnauzer stopped to watch. The interior was empty except for an envelope which was taped to the right panel. With gloved hands, Griff carefully pealed the white business size envelope from the panel and extracted a sheet of typewritten paper from inside. The letter inside read: "Congratulations, the time has come. Go to the Gentry locker for further instructions."

"What does it say, Zoo Man?" Joe was as excited as a kid in a candy store. His enthusiasm quickly faded when Griff responded.

"It says that we're in the middle of a wild goose chase; it directs us to the locker where we found the clue that sent us here. I'm beginning to think that this whole mess is just one big ruse. Maybe the explosives are even fake."

"You're forgetting that Patrol 17 wasn't blown up with fake explosives!"

"I know, Joe, but it's really frustrating, the more we uncover the less we know."

"Just you watch, Zoo, one of these days all of these puzzle pieces will fall right into place."

"That what I'm afraid of, an explosion is going to send all of these pieces into the air so that they can fall on us. We'll be crushed."

The two policemen sat on the pedestal's concrete base and stared into space as if willing the puzzle pieces into place. After a few minutes Joe, in his best British accent, asked "Where to now my dear Watson? Back to the storage locker contents for more instructions?"

"Let's talk to Pops Gentry first and then we'll head back to the property room."

CHAPTER FOURTEEN

The light green Ford Explorer drove down the alley behind 912 Galveston Ave. Red's pristine Chevette was not there. The boys parked in front; there would be no nurse to act as a buffer this time. As they walked up to the house they could hear the creak of the old man's rocking chair. Before Griff even put his foot on the porch steps, Pops growled, "What do you want, Flatfoot!"

"Fine, thank you, and how are you?" Griff said with menacing sarcasm.

"She's not here, so you might as well leave."

"Actually we came to speak with you – POPS!"

The crotchety old man said, "You don't know me well enough to call me that!"

"Fair enough," Joe interjected, "what should we call you?"

"Mr. Gentry!"

"Too formal, Pops. What's your first name?"

"If you must know, it's Clayton, but I have nothing to say to you!"

"We were hoping that you could give us some information on the Goldman brothers," said Griff.

"Who?"

"The Goldmans, you know, the men who were so instrumental in helping wayward youth, the ones who founded the Lone Strangers."

The old man clenched his teeth, hesitated and said, "I don't know who you're talking about."

Griff pressed on. "You know, the ones who designed the tattoo that you have on your forearm."

Pops instinctively slapped his right hand onto his left arm to cover the tattoo; that's when he realized he was wearing a long sleeved shirt. "You're a sneaky pig! So what if I got a tattoo, ain't no law agin' it."

"Calm down, Pops, two of the brothers are dead and we want to honor the remaining founder of the Lone Strangers, honor him for his impact on the community." Griff had driven the wedge in and the flood gates of conversation opened up.

"I knew they'd try to take all of the credit! I was a founding member, too! The LS/MFT logo and tattoos were my idea!" He rolled up his left sleeve to proudly show off his tattoo. "The club was a good idea, but I got out when the Goldmans took the club in a direction that I didn't believe in. They were more interested in turning a dollar than in helping youth; started turning them into petty criminals. Danny Goldman ain't worth honoring as a good citizen!"

"It's good that you got out when you did then – why didn't you call the cops and fill them in?"

"Had a bad experience with cops, - guess I carry a grudge."

The old man had not offered the boys a seat so Griff hopped up onto the brick railing and Joe sat on the edge of the porch with his feet on the top step.

"When did you leave the Lone Strangers?" Joe asked.

"A couple years ago. The Goldmans tried to make the experience more exciting for the kids by having them do criminal things. The doctors told me my ticker and lungs were going bad and my arthritis was gettin' worse; perfect reasons for me to bow out. Now I do nothing', but I do it well." The old man started to laugh and then had a coughing spell.

"Can I get you something," Joe asked, "a glass of water or something?"

"Some ice water would be nice," Pops said as he handed his glass to Joe. "You guys want anything, water, iced tea, beer?"

"I think I'll have some tea, thank you. Want anything, Zoo?"

"Just some water please."

Pops grabbed Joe's arm as he started in the door. "Would you empty this for me?" He retrieved a hospital type urinal from behind his chair and thrust it at Joe.

Joe looked incredulously at Griff who said, "To protect and serve!"

After Joe went inside Pops asked, "Why'd he call you Zoo?"

"My name – Griffith Park, is like the zoo in Los Angeles."

"Never heard of it!"

In just a manner of minutes the old man had mellowed into an almost normal person.

"Like you said, Mr. Gentry, I guess I was sneaky and I'm afraid, deceptive too; the only way we want to honor Danny Goldman is with a long prison sentence. Since you apparently have no more affiliation with the Lone Strangers, maybe we could get you to help in that regard." As he spoke, Griff leaned forward to look Pops in the eye with a hopeful expression on his face. "What do you say?"

Joe came back out with the drinks and the empty urinal. "Look who I found," he said as Giselle exited right behind him. "She came in the back door so quietly she nearly scared me into drawing down on her."

"I'm glad you didn't, partner. How are you doing, Red?"

"Better, now that I'm seeing you," she gushed. "Pops been behaving?"

Before he could answer, the old man said, "Red, could you leave us alone; we're talkin' police business here."

Griff gave her a quick wink and a nod to let her know that things were O.K. "I never thought I'd hear that," Red said as she backed through the door into the parlor.

Pops' face had softened and he looked thoughtful. He spoke haltingly; the words were hard to say. "Before we continue, I think I owe you guys an apology." He held up his hand to stop Zoo from speaking. "In my youth, a hundred or so years ago, I was a demon. I'd steal anything I could get my hands on and unfortunately when I got older and got married, my evil ways continued. I raised my son, Creighton, to be the same way. One night the dumb ass tried to bust into a bank and a cop shot and killed him. I've been carrying a grudge against cops ever since; thought they were all thugs, like the one who killed my boy. I see now that I was wrong. I treated you like dirt – you didn't deserve that. You're a decent guy, Flatfoot, and besides, my nurse has the hots for you. Did you know that?"

"I've had a feeling that she did," Griff said with a straight face.

"Anyway I hope you guys will accept my apologies."

Joe and the Zoo Man, in tandem answered, "Apology accepted."

A bleary eyed Clayton Gentry said, "Now that the air is cleared, how can I help you?" He pulled a faded blue and white bandana handkerchief from his robe pocket and loudly blew his nose. Joe looked toward the sky expecting that a flock of geese would be responding to the old man's honking.

Clay Gentry talked for a couple of hours about how a pharmacist, now long dead, had taken him under his wing and tried to help straighten him out. As an older man, he met the Goldman brothers and they all decided to help troubled boys just like the pharmacist had tried to help him. In his youth Pops didn't accept the help that was offered. As an older adult he had tried to make amends by forming the Lone Strangers.

The old man was a fountain of information, and Griff and Joe took many notes. At one point Griff excused himself so that he could phone Mike Wohcowhcs. He also wanted to speak with Red about the status of his house purchase. Joe took over the questioning of Pops.

Griff told Mike about Pops' admission to being a Lone Stranger's founder and how he was becoming such a wealth of information. Wohcowhcs said that he would go to the C.C.P.D. records and identification section to run Pops (Clayton) Gentry and the Goldmans to see if he could find any criminal links in their pasts and to see if they had matching running buddies. It was decided that the three would meet in the chief's conference/war room around 10 A.M. the next morning.

Red had been doing the legwork for Griff and was about to secure financing for him and set up a date for the closing. The inspections had been completed. Soon, hopefully, 1212 Romero would be his new address.

"Come up to my office area," Red beckoned. "It's on the second floor." Griff followed her up the stairs and soon realized that the layout was similar to the Keeper place, but without the smell of death.

"In here, Love, this is where I do my homework, at that old roll top desk that Pops is letting me use." What she had failed to mention was that her "office" was in her bedroom which overlooked the front porch roof.

"Is there really something that you want me to see or was that just a ruse to get me up here?" Griff asked the question with a wry grin spreading across his face.

"Yes to both," Red replied. "You've seen it before, but I'll bet you'd like to see it again!" Red playfully pushed her Zoo Man down onto the flowered quilt of her lace canopied four poster bed. She hummed a traditional stripper tune and proceeded to undulate like a snake as she wiggled out of her clothes. The light breeze blowing through the front window seemed to accentuate her erotic striptease. When she finished she gave him a naked curtsy and bade him to stand up. When he did, she sat down on the bed and giggled, "Your turn."

With a bewildered sigh, Griff removed his holstered side arm from under his over shirt and put it on the night stand. He then proceeded in a clumsy attempt to mimic the bumps and grinds while Red hummed. She applauded when his shirt came off to reveal a Green Lantern comic tee shirt beneath. When he had finally slithered out of all of his clothing, the Zoo Man stood facing Red with hands on hips. "Now what?"

"Now twirl that tassel, big boy!" she said, imitating Mae West.

The remark made Griff blush and he, instead, rushed the bed and jumped on for a session of love making.

An hour or so later Griff rejoined his partner on the front porch.

Joe, grinning smugly, asked, "How is the real estate deal going?"

"Going real well." Griff's red face and mussed hair accentuated the answer.

Pops couldn't hold it in any longer and blurted out, "I haven't heard bed springs sing like that since Ethel was alive. Ethel, that was my first wife; not only was she wild in bed, she was a screamer." A laughing Pops slapped his arthritic knee and winced in pain.

Trying to change the subject, Griff said, "Giselle was just showing me some interpretive dance moves; she's going to do Salome's Dance of the Seven Veils at church on Sunday. I'm going to go to church with her; care to come along, Mr. Gentry?"

"Heavens no! I about had a coronary the last time she danced in church."

"By the way, Pops, which church does she go to?"

"The God's Little Acre of Hope Church. I nearly had a heart attack when I saw her 'worshipping' on that brass pole they got." Pops made quotation marks with his fingers to punch up the worshipping part.

A smiling Giselle Parker stood on the other side of the screen door; she was wearing a very short robe.

After a little more small talk, Griff gave a nod and a wink to his lover/real estate agent, and then the boys made their goodbyes.

Even though they had made significant progress in getting Pops to open up about the Lone Strangers, the boys were still a little on edge. They knew that the timeline was narrowing. It was only a matter of time before there would be another bombing, possibly with deadly consequences. They must work faster and dig deeper.

Joe pulled the old Ford Explorer away from the curb and started heading for Zoo's apartment building to drop him off. As he accelerated away from the stop sign on Galveston to cross Reno Way, a loud bang jarred them both. Joe threw the old SUV into park and they both jumped out with guns drawn and ran to the curbs.

"Whoa, whoa, whoa, whoa, hold on there fellas!" the elderly gentleman on the sidewalk pleaded with hands in the air. "What's the matter?!"

"Didn't you hear that loud explosion?!" Joe asked.

"I heard that piece of shit you're driving backfire, that's all I heard!"

"Thanks, old timer," Griff yelled from the other side of the street. "Sorry if we frightened you!" The old man tottering with a cane continued on his way.

Griff and Joe holstered their weapons, composed themselves then continued on down the street. As they slowly passed the old man,

Joe heard him mutter, “I can’t believe that the Feds still own that clunker.”

CHAPTER FIFTEEN

Joe dropped Griff off at Zoo's Zoo and then headed for casa Beveltnik to spend some needed quality time with Bev and Junior. Griff had had his quality time at the Gentry place.

Griff fixed himself an old staple for dinner, a double portion of beef flavored Ramen noodles, extra watery and filled with snowed saltines. This bachelor delicacy served two purposes, one as a tasty meal and the other as a narcotic. With a satisfyingly big bowl of Ramen noodles in his stomach, Griff would sleep like a baby.

Griff lay in bed chuckling about how the F.B.I. had duped him into taking one of the oldest pieces of rolling stock that they had; apparently everyone knew that car. He also realized that he had gotten over-confident and lax in this plain clothes assignment. He had not been wearing his ballistic vest. The old Explorer's backfire had been an epiphany. He had worn his vest religiously while in uniform. He needed to wear it religiously now, too.

Griff had a good restful sleep and uncommonly awoke before the alarm clock went off. He arose, took care of the three esses and fixed himself an extra buttery English muffin before he dressed. He wore his vest over a Mighty Mouse tee shirt, and an extra blousy polo shirt covered the vest, sidearm and badge. Griff put on one of the only surviving mementos of his ill-fated vacation, his 7th Cavalry ball cap, and headed for his basement parking space.

Griff's camel colored beater Chevette was ugly compared to Red's pristine ride, but he didn't care. It still ran well. Because it was Saturday, Griff was able to find a parking spot within two blocks of headquarters. Joe had already signed in and Griff advised the info desk officer that Agent Wohcowhcs would be joining them in the chief's conference room.

Joe was studying the various easels when Griff walked in. Little had been added regarding Sol and Izzy Goldman. Their deaths slowed those segments of the investigation. When Mike arrived, they started adding new information, mostly about Pops Gentry.

Chief Riley walked in and asked, "How's it going, men?"

"We're making some progress," Joe said. "What are you doing here on Saturday, boss?"

"Working on the budget, trying to keep us in business. Your being subsidized by the Feds is helping, but it's not enough. If the city council doesn't come up with more money, I may have to farm you guys out to the Feds permanently."

"You can't be saving that much," Griff said.

"Between the overtime that you workaholics are racking up and their providing transportation and gas, it all adds up. I hope they gave you a decent car to use. You wouldn't want to get stuck with 'Whiskers'."

"Whiskers?"

"Yeah," Riley said. "It's an old green Explorer, seen more action than a $2.00 whore, might as well paint F.B.I. on the sides."

"Too late," Joe replied. "We call it The Green Monster, but Whiskers fits, too."

"Oh, well, if you need anything I'll be in my office." With that the chief turned and shuffled towards his office door.

"Nice slippers," Griff called out as the chief entered his office.

"It's Saturday! Jeez, Park, can't you give a guy a break?" he barked. The chief closed his door… HARD!

The three lawmen pooled their information and started fitting it in among the puzzle pieces.

"Did you know that Clayton's son was killed in a C.C.P.D. shootout?" Mike asked. "Pops seems like a prime suspect to me."

"So far we've ruled him out," Joe said

"…but we always have an open mind," Zoo added.

Joe called the I.D. section. "Any luck on my latents?"

"We'll call you when they're done!" The I.D. tech then slammed down the phone.

"They're not ready," Joe said, not mentioning the rude treatment he had gotten.

On the easel containing the names of the Lone Strangers, they added the founders information:

Danny Goldman		Bombing suspect
Izzy Goldman	:	Deceased
Sol Goldman		Deceased
Clayton "Pops" Gentry	:	No longer affiliated

To the list of current and former members they listed Jim Mess, the restaurant owner.

A message board had been set up for lesser information not necessarily connected to the investigation. A note on the board read, "Zoo Man, call Ling Po." The note was dated two days prior. Zoo punched up an open line and called.

"Qua King Duck," the female voice answered. She said she'd get the owner.

"Ling Po here."

"Ling, it's Zoo Park. I got your message, what's up?

"Officer Zoo Man, I need your advice. A man rented the vacant business next to mine and wants to open a bar."

"Afraid of the competition?"

"No! He have big idea, wants to cut a hole in the wall and sell my appetizers to his customers. What do you think I should do?"

Griff leaned back in the office chair, stroked his throat thoughtfully and then delivered his treasured advice. "I think if the city allows you to do it, you have an attorney draw up a contract for you to do business with the bar. I think it would be mutually beneficial to both businesses. Think of it, Ling, if his customers really like your food, maybe they'll come over to The Duck for a full meal."

"I had not thought of that. You always give good advice Officer Zoo Man. I just hope the neighbors don't blame my food."

"Blame your food for what, Ling?"

"The name of his place – he's going to name it after his old hound; he says he's going to call his bar The Flatulent Dog."

Griff laughed at the prospect of the name and told Ling not to worry. "He could have chosen a worse name," he said, though he couldn't think of one at the moment.

While Griff was finishing his call, Agent Wohcowhcs got a radio message to call his office right away. When he hung up he said, "Saddle up boys, our office got a call from the caretaker of the Pioneer Cemetery; says he's got information for our investigation. No use taking three vehicles, whose is closest?"

Griff and Joe spoke in unison, "Yours," they said while pointing at Mike. "Yours is newer and bigger," Griff said. "And I'll bet it's got working air conditioning," Joe added.

"O.K. I can take a hint; I'll drive and you guys can navigate; remember I'm new to the area."

The drive took them through Patrol 17's patrol area, through the flop house and warehouse areas and eight miles past the SeaView Mall.

The cemetery's wrought iron fence was partially overgrown and the permanently open gate was heavily rusted. To Griff's knowledge there had been no new burials there in years. As rugged as the exterior looked, the burial sites were just the opposite. The cemetery had obviously been maintained with loving care.

As they pulled in they were approached by a tall thin man in his 50s with a lined and chiseled face. His thin gray hair did little to hide the man's most prominent feature, ears that stuck straight out. The man's shoulders and chest were bronze, as he wore no shirt under his overalls.

"I'm Ignatious Wingler, the caretaker. How can I help you fellers?" he drawled.

The three flashed their I.D.s and introduced themselves; Mike took the lead.

"You called and said you have some information for us? We could use a break in our case."

"You fellers are all business aintcha. What I've got to show ya is back yonder; follow me." The caretaker grabbed his rusty two-wheeler which had been leaning against a headstone and led the way down a twisting lane. He stopped by an ivy covered mausoleum. "We're here," he drawled as he dismounted.

"You live in there?" Joe asked half jokingly.

"Shucks no, you must be joshin' me. I live in town. What I want to show you is in here. Aint got no nighttime security. That's when it happened, last night."

The bewildered officers waited for Wingler's next move. While they looked on, the caretaker unlocked the iron gate and opened up the large stone vault.

The interior was lit by skylights where large ceiling blocks had been removed. The crypt had two large altar style sarcophagi. The residents must have been prominent people to have such a resting place in an old pioneer cemetery.

"Who is buried here?" Joe asked.

"Lester S. and Mary F. Thomas, been here since the 1850s, that's what the outside plaque says." A check of the plaque confirmed Mr. Wingler's statement.

"I come in here every day to eat mah lunch. It's nice and quiet and I enjoy the Thomas' company. I was shore surprised to find that the tomb had been disturbed. It wasn't this way yesterday."

The men entered and saw dozens of burned down candle stubs dotting the tops of both crypts. Four of the stubs held down the following note printed with black marker on a plain paper grocery bag. "You are our heroes. You will be spared when the bombings start shortly. You may feel rumbles but you will be spared."

"See there, the word 'bombings', that's why I called. The news said to be on the lookout for bombs and explodables and the like. I figured this might be related."

"You did right to call, Mr. Wingler," Mike said. "Are you the only one with a key to the mausoleum?"

"Yep, that's why I eat lunch here. Neither of the other two vaults have keys, probably lost over the years. Nobody visits them anyway, no need to get in."

Griff asked, "What do you know about the Thomas family, Mr. Wingler?"

"Not a dang thing. Nobody visits here either."

"Another twist in the road. We need to find out who these people were and why they are heroes to our radical bombers."

"Partner, I don't think we'll have to go that far," Joe said. I think they chose this place just because of the residents' names, Lester S. and Mary F. Thomas. LSMFT."

"Could it be that simple?" Griff asked. "And how did the bastards get in here if Wingler has the only key?"

"Through the skylights would be my guess," Mike said as he pointed to the ceiling. The four trooped outside to take a look.

They found scuff marks on the back wall and Wingler found the 'key.' "Well, I'll be danged, looky here." In the underbrush he'd found about 30 feet of coiled knotted rope with a grappling hook on the end.

"Why wouldn't they a took this with 'em. It aint that heavy."

"Because they plan on coming back and we'll be waiting," Griff said.

"What do you mean, 'we'? Have you got a mouse in your pocket?"

"Easy, Joe, it was just a figure of speech. I'm sure we can find someone to stake this place out. We'll leave the rope so they won't think they've been found out. Mr. Wingler, have you looked in the crypts?"

"Violate the deads' resting place?" he asked in horror.

"I see where Zoo is going," Mike said. "What if the bad guys are hiding their explosives in there?" Wingler just stared at him. "What say we take a look," and with that Mike re-entered the mausoleum.

"Don't you need some kind of warrant for that?"

"We can get one if you insist! Do you have something to hide, Mr. Wingler?"

"Nope, nope, I just didn't want you guys to get in trouble or nothin'. If you want to peek, go ahead, I aint going to stop you."

Joe got his trusty Polaroid out of his bag, photographed the crypts and then the grappling hook.

Mike carefully checked the edges of the lids for trip wires or booby traps. Finding none, the four men grabbed the sides of Lester's lid. After several attempts they were able to move the lid. The men worked it around so that it sat across the top, allowing them to peer in at the ends. There were no explosives inside and the dust covered wooden coffin appeared to be in surprisingly good shape. The men replaced the lid and then lined up on both sides of Mary's crypt. They had to struggle more but finally were able to maneuver the other slab without disturbing the note. The men couldn't see anything, so Mike got a flashlight from his car. The light shone only on a dusty empty space. Apparently Mary had never moved in.

"Well don't that beat all. I wonder where Mrs. Thomas is?"

"She probably moved away after her husband died. Now you've got your own mystery to solve," Mike said to Mr. Wingler.

The men thanked the caretaker and exchanged phone numbers. Mr. Wingler would be contacted when they needed further access to the vault. As the undercover car was exiting the cemetery, Agent Wohcowhcs got a radio call. A fast talking caller had claimed that an explosion was about to happen at the SeaView Mall. Mike punched the accelerator and they headed for the mall.

As the team's car approached the main entrance, a large explosion at the rear of the mall sent debris flying and people running. Mike called it in and headed for the destruction. What was left of a contractor's mobile office was now just a burning pile of twisted wreckage. Hopefully the trailer had been empty.

"I'll bet Ichabod Wingnut heard that all the way back at the cemetery," Joe exclaimed.

CHAPTER SIXTEEN

In a very short period of time the mall was swarming with police officers, fire fighters and arson investigators. It would be days before the debris could be sifted through and any usable clues located. Fortunately the blast site was far enough away from other buildings so that there were no structural damages and there were no casualties.

The team was certain that this was the work of the Lone Strangers who now seemed content in upping the ante. But why the sudden shift from attacking police vehicles to blowing up an unoccupied landscaper's mobile office? Always more questions than answers!

The 'victim' of the latest attack was the Tri-State Landscaping Company, a large conglomerate which held the contracts for all of the government landscaping as well as most of the area shopping centers. Residential and small business landscaping was divided up among other area grounds keeping businesses. Tri-State had many regional on-site mobile offices and another would soon be moved to the SeaView Mall; Tri-State was well insured.

Zoo, Joe and Mike had already decided to take Sunday off; besides the site cleaning would take a couple of days anyway. Of immediate concern was finding someone willing to help with the mausoleum stake out. Griff knew the perfect choice, if he were available.

From a pay phone Griff called the Special Operation's office in an effort to locate John Jester; he had just walked out of the office. The secretary put Griff on hold, raced to the elevators and was able to catch Jester.

"Detective Jester here."

"Hey, Nimrod, Zoo Park, are you busy?"

"Up to my asshole in boredom, what can I do for you?"

Griff explained the mausoleum situation and wanted to know if he would be interested in staking it out. Griff knew which buttons to push. John (Nimrod) Jester was an outdoorsman who prided himself in hunting without being seen. A stakeout in an old cemetery would be a challenge to his camouflage skills, and Nimrod jumped at the opportunity. Griff gave Jester caretaker Wingler's phone number. He called and set up a meet at the cemetery for 6 P.M.

Nimrod drove his camo painted pick-up truck through the Pioneer Cemetery gate promptly at six and identified himself to the waiting Mr. Wingler. The caretaker gave him a tour of the ins and outs of the mausoleum and pointed out the grappling hook and skylights.

Jester had Wingler lock up the vault and told him that he would be hidden in the cemetery every evening until the trespassers returned. He told Wingler that he'd be in touch if there were any developments.

After the caretaker left, Nimrod Jester parked his truck next to another mausoleum and donned his turkey hunting camouflage suit. He silently crept among the graves until he found the best view of the mausoleum, then sat down against a shagbark hickory and proceeded to blend in. As dusk faded to dark, the ghost man disappeared among the shadows.

The experienced hunter/detective closed his eyes and let his other senses take over. Shortly after 10 P.M. he heard a vehicle approach and stop on the outside service road. The audible sounds were clear; four doors noisily closing and multiple parties walking through the weeds.

Jester let his eyes adjust to the available light and saw four figures with flashlights approaching the mausoleum and then a fifth hurried to catch up. The fifth man carried a large bundle. One of the individuals retrieved the grappling hook and with practiced skill snagged the flashlight lit skylight opening on the first toss. As Jester watched, the first miscreant scaled the outer wall and then hauled up the bundle behind him. As he straddled the skylight opening, he opened the bundle.

Nimrod Jester had been told the vault had been entered only once before, but the first man up made it look like an everyday affair. The first man unpacked and unrolled a metal emergency ladder and hung the hooks on the skylights opening; the ladder hung down inside of the mausoleum. One by one the nimble trespassers climbed up the rope and down the ladder. Candles were lit and the "party" was started. Thinking that they were alone in the old remote cemetery, the Strangers spoke in normal tones while Nimrod watched and listened.

"Man, I don't know why we have to come to this dump; my basement would have been just as good."

"Because I found it and I realized that the initials of these folks were just like our logo. It's perfect, it's us, and the residents haven't said a word! Now let's decide on our next target."

Nimrod found himself in the middle of a dilemma; should he stay and listen or should he move far enough away so that he could use his portable radio to call for back-up? While it would be nice to scoop up the whole bunch, he opted to stay and listen. Nimrod Jester did not have a tape recorder and he couldn't take notes in the dark. He would have to rely on his memory. Peering through the iron gate, Jester was able to get fleeting glimpses of the five white males who seemed to range in age from late teens to mid twenties.

"Why does Danny want us to target landscapers? I thought his beef was with the cops."

"Danny has a twisted idea that the cops are somehow responsible for his brothers' deaths. The cops are part of the government and he's angry with the politicos for not awarding him the government landscaping contract. The boss doesn't want a small piece of the local business; he wants the big contract; he didn't get it, so everyone pays."

"How can we pick a target if we don't know how much explosives he can get his hands on?"

"We'll pick a couple of targets based on the amount of explosives that we may be given. It's too bad the pigs found the storage locker; we'd never have to worry about a lack of boom. The main thing to remember is that there is to be property damage only; we're not out to kill people and go to prison."

The five argued back and forth and even beseeched information from the Thomases; it never came. Finally two targets were chosen, the large floral clock display in front of city hall and a lesser target being the Tri-State mobile office at the municipal utilities complex. An argument also ensued about the note that had been left at their previous meeting, with the author becoming very defensive.

"I thought it was a good idea to pay homage to our benefactors who are letting us use their 'home.' If you can think of a better way or for that matter, if you want to be the leader, just say so!" The speaker must have been very confident, because there was no further argument.

No date was decided for the next bombing, because it was not known when explosives would be made available. The next meeting in the tomb was scheduled for the following Saturday night.

While the five made their way up and out of the vault, Nimrod Jester quietly made his way through the weeds and jotted down the Strangers' license plate number. "Unless the station wagon was borrowed or stolen, the task force should be able to come up with one gang member's identification," he thought. Jester had lucked out on his first night; he would call the Zoo Man and report. He was instructed to wait until after 5:00 P.M. if he were going to call on Sunday.

Griff arose early on Sunday morning. He wasn't a regular churchgoer, but he'd been meaning to start going again. He wasn't sure how to dress but figured that sport shirt and slacks should be acceptable anywhere. He anticipated no problem but, as required, did carry his firearm concealed under his shirt. He was too nervous to eat. He was going to watch Giselle do her worship dance.

Griff drove to the Gentry residence to pick up Red; she drove from there. "This must be a very popular church," Griff said. "The huge parking lot is packed. I don't see any open spaces."

"I have a reserved spot in the rear of the church," Red said. At the rear of God's Little Acre of Hope was a section reserved for church personnel. Red gave Griff a peck on the cheek and then scurried into the CLERGY ONLY door with a small suitcase; Griff entered the door marked MAIN HALL.

The large interior was more like an exhibit hall than a church; hundreds of people were seated on folding chairs. Griff found a spot near the rear. A guitar, drum and flute trio softly played hymn music until it was time for the minister to come out.

With a drum roll that built to a crescendo and cymbal strike, the fiery five foot five Rev. Edford Blaisdale entered through the curtain at the rear of the sanctuary. The reverend gave an animated fire and brimstone heaven and hell sermon which would put any tent revivalist to shame. At the end of the sermon Edford Blaisdale made a plea for the congregation to be extra generous as the church was expanding into another venture for good, the acquisition of the God's Holy Mission homeless shelter, food pantry and soup kitchen. This announcement pleased Griff, because he knew that the shelter had been under chaotic interim management since the Rev. Wagner (Wanker the Spanker) had been arrested.

"Now for the interpretive part of today's worship service, we present Sister Giselle Parker with Salome's Dance of the Seven Veils.

Except for a minister's introduction of a newly married couple, Griff had never heard raucous applause in a church before. Red undulated through the curtain covered in long flowing veils while the congregation cheered. Slowly she twirled, glided and swayed back and forth across the sanctuary losing one veil after another, each veil shorter than the last, while the trio played on. After six veils, the mostly male congregation was whipped into a frenzy. It was no wonder that the church was so popular. The seventh veil covered a skimpy flesh colored outfit decorated with sequins which surely wasn't the garb of the day in Salome's time. The last veil wasn't removed but did cover Red's head when she turned herself upside down on the brass pole. While she hung there by one leg wrapped around the pole, the appreciative congregation dug deep into their pockets and filled the passed offering baskets with currency. The dance concluded with Red sliding snakelike to the floor and then cartwheeling her way through the curtain.

Rev. Blaisdale reappeared to thank and praise Sister Parker and requested that the audience be appreciatively generous as the baskets were once again passed among the worshippers.

Griff sat in amazement at the church service that he had just attended. Rev. Blaisdale had hit on the perfect combination, an entertaining religious dancer to bring in a generous congregation to hear his well delivered homily. Griff was grinning broadly when Red came out to meet him. “What do you think?” she asked.

“I think I could be talked into going to church here every Sunday. How often do you dance?”

“Once every other month, I’m not the only dancing religious zealot in this town, you know. Care to buy me breakfast?”

“Sure, ever been to Ma’s Diner?”

CHAPTER SEVENTEEN

Finally, thanks to the information from Ignatious Wingler and the luck of success on the first night of the cemetery stakeout, the picture was becoming much clearer. The beat up Buick station wagon used to ferry the Lone Strangers was registered to Francis Colgate, age twenty-one. Frankie Colgate had been in trouble as a youth, but his juvenile record had been sealed when he turned eighteen.

When Frankie's name was added to the list of Lone Strangers, several of the task force members said that they had known of him. In his youth Frankie Colgate had been a small time thief with pyrotechnical tendencies; just the type to be in a band of bombers.

It was decided to put a twenty-four hour watch on both the city hall floral clock and on the landscaping mobile office at the public utilities complex. Chief Riley approved the plan and authorized the additional manpower for this purpose. The chief also ordered that Danny Goldman himself be put under twenty-four hour surveillance in an effort to locate his explosives supplier as well.

Zoo, Mike, Joe and Cal Rich would take turns watching Goldman.

Daniel Goldman wasn't as flamboyant as his brother Izzy had been and didn't appear to be as greedy as Sol. The Goldman residence was located in the upscale Floral Circle subdivision, on Cactus Flower Lane. A drive-by of the property showed a driveway and garage off of the street; there was no alley. Few cars parked on the street, making stakeout cars very obvious. Griff spotted a sign which made him smile. Across the street and three doors down from Goldman's place was a vacant two story residence with a Lovey-Dove real estate sign out front.

"I have an in with that real estate company," Griff said. "I'll bet we can use that house for stake out duties."

"You also have an <u>in</u> with an agent, too," Joe said. Mike smiled broadly, but Calvin didn't get the significance.

Mike drove back to the entrance of the subdivision and dropped off the crew of Patrol 17. He and Cal would park down the street from Goldman's place and take the first watch.

Zoo drove towards the Gentry's in hopes of finding Red at home.

"Remember the last time we were out here, Joe?"

"How could I forget? We chased the shooters in the green Camaro. Any word on the Keeper homicide?"

"Not that I'm aware of. They're pretty certain that it links up with the Lone Strangers though."

A radio transmission caught their attention.

"Patrol 14 to radio. I've got one running."

Radio: "All units stand by. Patrol 14 is in pursuit, go ahead 14."

"Patrol 14. We're eastbound on Whitcomb from Fleckner trying to catch a black motorcycle, no plate, traffic only at this time."

Radio: "We copy eastbound Whitcomb."

A variety of marked units acknowledged that they were heading to assist. Taskforce 17 did not acknowledge, but did head that way. Zoo entered the freeway southbound so they would be in the area and assist if needed. Patrol 14's transmissions were spotty as it was a one officer unit, and the officer was obviously concentrating on his driving.

"Patrol 14. I've lost the rice grinder on the surface streets north of Whitcomb, request additional units to check the area."

"He's probably on his own turf, Zoo, those crotch rockets are really maneuverable, lots of places to hide. Holy Shit! What was that?!" Joe had pressed himself against the backrest.

"My guess is that it's Patrol 14's rice grinder."

It was indeed Patrol 14's Japanese Bogey; it had crashed through a freeway fence and had flown across the hood of the Explorer before impacting with the center median's concrete barrier. Joe aired the crash. The boys pulled over and ran back to the crash site. The bike was crumpled and broken, and so was the rider. The helmet helped to prevent head trauma, but the face shield was split open revealing the blank stare of lifeless eyes. The rider's down filled jacket had split open showering the freeway with feathers. Zoo felt no pulse, nor expected one. Their trip to see Ms. Parker would be put on hold as they had to write a letter of information for the Accident Investigation Squad who would shut the freeway down for several hours while they completed their preliminary investigation.

As Joe and Griff walked back to their SUV a shaken Joe said, "Another two feet and that bike would have hit us."

"I'm not sure it didn't partner."

Joe cocked his head toward Griff with a puzzled look on his face.

"What's that supposed to mean?"

"Look here, Joe," Griff said as they got to their vehicle and pointed out a tire smudge on the top of the left front fender about two feet from the windshield. We almost caught him for 14."

“He almost caught us. I don’t need another stint in the hospital,” he said as an uncontrolled shudder wracked his body. “Can we get some coffee before we find Red? I’m a bit shaken!”

“Sure Joe, I’ll just double back and head for Ma’s.”

Joe would have preferred to go to The Last Drop but that wasn’t close. He’d settle for Ma’s. The boys were greeted and seated by a new waitress with a Jamaican accent; her name tag read Saccharina.

“I will be right with you,” Joe’s favorite waitress, Ruby, called out. Two usuals coming up.”

Joe stopped her. “Make mine like Zoo’s,” he said.

“Honey, he likes his real strong, you won’t like it.”

“I need it!” he said, still visibly shaken.

While they waited for their coffees, they saw Rasta come out and talk to the new waitress. Before he returned to the kitchen he gave her a peck on the cheek and a playful pat on her backside.

“What’s up with them?” Zoo asked Ruby.

“That’s Rasta’s wife, she just started working here.”

Joe tried the coffee and winced noticeably. Ruby just shook her head as he loaded the cup with cream and sugar. She had known he wouldn’t like it strong.

Zoo used the diner’s phone and called Red. She was at home and said she’d put a pot of coffee on. Griff didn’t stop her; she made really good coffee. Twenty minutes later, they were seated in the Gentry’s kitchen.

“Where’s Pops? He wasn’t on the porch,” Joe asked.

“Pops is up in bed. He’s not feeling well today. Now what is this favor you want?”

Zoo laid out the details of his request to use the vacant house on Cactus Flower. Red called Lila Dove and relayed the request. Lila gave the O.K., “Helping the police is always a good thing,” she had said.

“Give me a day to get the keys and put an ‘In Contract’ sign in the yard and you’ll be good to go.”

“No blankets in the bedroom on this one,” Griff said. He laughed and Giselle turned beet red. Griff aired for Agent Wohcowhcs and told him that they would rendezvous later for the switch; tomorrow they would have the keys to the vacant.

“We kind of forgot to go over the house financing plans the last time you were here.” Red said coyly. “Want to do it now?”

“Might as well. I’m starting to get excited at the prospect of being a home owner.”

While Zoo and Red actually perused the loan application and other paperwork, Joe cooled his heels in Pops' porch rocker. Joe fell asleep and dreamed of the shooting in which Zoo had killed the shooter that had permanently scarred his face. He woke up with a start when the dream ended in a different way. Joe sat there shivering, hoping to regain his composure before his partner came out.

"Hey, Joe B., want to take a ride over and get the 50 cent tour of the new house? I've got my loan and the closing will be on Wednesday. Wilson Tennenbaum is going to send one of his associates to the bank to sit in on and review the paperwork during the closing; can't be too careful, you know."

While Joe was checking out Zoo's house, mischief was afoot at Fort Hopewell. Saunders and LaPorte, the newest munitions handlers, were looking for a way to spice up their commander's birthday. They remembered the oversized bottle rockets in the elephant foot umbrella stands in bunker No. 2 and decided to "borrow" some to give the party a bang.

"Maurice LaPorte carefully peeled away Mike Wohcowhcs' federal seal, and he and Saunders entered the bunker. To their recollection, the bottle rockets had been photographed but not counted so a few probably wouldn't be missed. Saunders grasped four of the rockets that were banded together and pulled up on them. The rockets appeared to be stuck so Saunders pulled harder. When he did both men heard an ominous audible click. Both men froze.

As Joe, Red and Zoo entered 1212 Romero Street, Zoo rapped on the door frame, "It's just me, Leon." Joe knew of Leon's passing in the house and did not comment on his partner's eccentric appeasement of the dead. As they viewed Leon's former room, which Griff had planned to make into a den, Red chimed in, "You know a roll top desk would look nice in here."

"You're probably right, honey, know where I can get one cheap?"

"I'm working on it, Zoo. C'mon, let's show your partner the rest of the house."

While Joe was looking in all of the cupboards and closets, Griff took a call on his walkie. "That was Chan in A.I.S.; they identified the victim of the motorcycle crash. It was Frankie Colgate. That makes another Stranger that we can't interview," he said with disgust.

The tour concluded with a look at the back yard where Zoo spotted a penny on the small porch's railing and picked it up. To Griff that was a sign of good luck. As the three stood talking in the back yard, the ground shuddered from a mighty tremor.

The next door neighbor ran out yelling hysterically, "What was that, an earthquake?"

"We're not sure," Red responded. "By the way this is your new neighbor."

Mrs. Browne looked up and recognized who it was. "Officer Park, we wondered who was going to move in. Ray will be so pleased; he always enjoyed your insights at the block watch meetings. Mrs. Browne was a full blown chatterbox and she spoke incessantly for minutes. Zoo didn't mind; he now knew all of the neighborhood gossip before he even moved in.

On the way back to the Gentry's a news bulletin on the radio told of a massive explosion at Fort Hopewell which could be felt as far away as Capitol City. A massive crater was found in a remote area of the fort and many people had been injured. Two munitions officers were reported missing and presumed dead; their names were not released pending notification of the next of kin.

"Damn," Griff said. "I have a bad feeling that that was our storage locker evidence that just went up in smoke."

"Good thing I brought my camera and documented everything, isn't it?" asked the beaming Beveltnik.

"Yeah, yeah, yeah, it was a good idea!"

Joe's purchasing on the Polaroid had been a good idea and Zoo was kicking himself for not having acknowledged it before now. "I wonder who got killed. I'll bet it was Saunders and that joker, what's his name, the grenade chucker."

"LaPorte," Joe said.

"I wonder what they were doing," Griff mused, "nosing around in the evidence bunker?"

"Maybe they came upon a booby trap that we missed, bad luck for them."

"If that stuff was deadly wired, I'm glad they found it and not us."

CHAPTER EIGHTEEN

While Griff was replenishing his stock of English muffins at Snavely's Corner Grocery, he picked up a copy of the Cap City Tribune. On page seven was the article about the mysterious explosion that destroyed much of Fort Hopewell and injured hundreds. The gist of the story was that two munitions handlers with local connections had died: Joe Bob Saunders of Texas and Maurice LaPorte originally from Louisiana.

The unexplained explosion had destroyed all of the fort's ammo and storage bunkers; the main point of ignition appeared to have been a bunker which had contained property confiscated by the F.B.I. from a storage facility in Capitol City.

An injured civilian employee at the fort had said that the outer area looked like a war zone and that many people had been injured when the concussion shattered windows and damaged fort buildings. An unnamed source at the base said that the situation was still under investigation, but terrorism had not been ruled out.

"That sounds just like a government spokesman," Griff thought, "covering up the screw-up of their munitions 'experts'. Mike and Joe will get a kick out of this."

Another article on the same page was about a local man who claimed that he saw a U.F.O. fly over the fort just prior to the explosions.

"Oh, that's rich," Griff said to himself, "blame the U.F.O.s." He thought about it and concluded that the government wouldn't do that – they claim U.F.O.s don't exist.

The phone was ringing when Griff entered his apartment. He answered it just before the answering machine message started, "Park here."

The voice at the other end was raging so much that Griff could almost feel spittle through the phone.

"Park, this is your Chief!! Why did I have to read about the loss of the locker evidence in the paper?! When in God's name were you going to tell me?! Made me look like a fool when I was asked about it!! I didn't even know about it!! Do you like making me look like a fool?! Well, do you?!"

In a nonchalant voice Griff asked, "I'm sorry, who did you say this was?"

"Do <u>not</u> be insolent with me!!" Chief Riley's voice was now two octaves higher. Through clenched teeth he asked, "Why didn't you call me?!"

“I was going to call you when you got into your office, but you got in five minutes early, didn’t you?”

“Well, yes,” Riley blustered, “but you still should have called me… should have called me at home!”

“We’re not supposed to call you at home!

“That’s not the point!!” Riley was now on his feet.

“What is the point?!”

“Don’t try to confuse me, just don’t let it happen again!!” and with that Chief slammed down the receiver.

Griff, too, hung up and threw up his hands; his chief was losing it. “Note to self, call the chief at home with minor information and damn the consequences.”

As he ate his buttered English muffin, his partner phoned. Whatcha doin’, Zoo Man?”

“Just getting ready to go to the hospital for a proctological exam.”

“Ouch! You having a problem?”

“Yeah, the chief just chewed my ass out for not telling him that most of our locker evidence is gone, said we kept him out of the loop.”

“We don’t know for sure that it’s gone.”

“It was in the Trib this morning. He called me before I could phone him. When you rang, I thought it was him calling back to apologize.

“Riley’s wrong! He should apologize! You should call him and tell him so.”

“Hows about you call him for me? Then we can go to the hospital together.”

“Uh… that’s all right, I’m sure it will all blow over.”

“Thanks, ‘Blood and Guts’, thanks for watching my back.”

“Anyway, the reason I called is that Bev is getting a little testy about all of the overtime I’m spending with you. I was thinking of taking a couple of days off to appease her. What do you think?”

“I try not to think; it clouds the brain. No, really, take some time off. We’ll manage to get along without you… I guess… somehow.”

“Thanks for that inspirational pat on the back, Zoo. Listen, don’t solve this sucker ‘til I get back; I want my share of the glory, too. Seriously, be careful and I’ll see you in a couple of days.”

Joe picked a good time to mend fences with his wife; the case had slowed, thanks to the big explosion and Zoo himself had a house closing to attend to.

At the closing things went smoothly thanks to Wilson Tennenbaum's whiz bang junior attorney, Darius Dean, who checked over everything before Griff signed. Red represented Lovey-Dove, of course, and all of her paperwork was perfect. At the end of the session the bank representative asked how Griff liked the bank's services. The wordsmith said he was disappointed that the bank man hadn't been wearing a mask; to accentuate the statement he veed his fingers in front of his eyes. Mr. Markham of the bank became very defensive and blustered, "Are you intimating that I robbed you?!"

"No, no, no, no, no, no, no," the Zoo Man quickly said, "I just expected the Loan Arranger to be wearing a mask, that's all."

Mr. Markham hung his head. He couldn't believe that he had not seen that old joke coming.

The new homeowner smiled and laughed heartily as he and Red left the bank arm in arm. After thanking Mr. Dean and shaking hands with him, Griff steered Red away from her car at the meter and walked her down the street instead. As they slowly walked, hand in hand, he stared straight ahead and started to open up to her.

"I had a girlfriend once and should have married her, but I let her go. When we did get back together she got killed before I had a chance to even properly propose."

Red stopped and patted his arm. "It's not necessary to tell me this. I can see that it's making you uncomfortable."

Griff faced her. "I just wanted you to know that I do have a serious side." They walked a ways in silence and then he stopped. He turned her to him and said, "I loved a girl and lost her. I don't ever want to make that mistake again." Griff suddenly dropped to one knee and took Red's hand. In front of all of the people on the sidewalk he said, "Miss Giselle Parker, will you marry me and make my new house your home?"

Red was completely taken aback and stammered, "Yes, oh yes, I'll be your wife. Now get up. Everybody is looking at us." When she said yes all of the "witnesses" applauded.

Griff had stopped in front of a jewelry store and gently pushed his blushing bride-to-be inside. "We have some shopping to do," he said.

That evening he met with Mike and Joe at the Qua King Duck and brought Red along.

"How did the closing go?"

"Real smooth thanks to Red. Not only did I have my closing but I also opened a new chapter in my life; show them the ring, hon."

As they celebrated Griff asked Joe to be his best man and Mike to be a groomsman; both readily accepted.

"Now let's wrap up this case. I, correction, we have a wedding to plan."

Later that night Griff and Giselle celebrated privately and intimately at Zoo's Zoo. In the morning Griff phoned Corinth county Sheriff Deacon Tolliver to see if he still owned that secluded getaway cabin that he had said would make a perfect honeymoon spot. He was pleased to hear that the cabin would be available for his friend whenever it was needed. With a renewed zest for life, Zoo sent Red home and went back to work.

CHAPTER NINETEEN

Giselle Parker and Lila Dove were good to their word and the vacant house on Cactus Flower Lane was made available for Griff and company. An upstairs corner bedroom turned out to be the perfect overlook of suspect Danny Goldman's residence. To make the ruse look real, small items were trucked in, thanks to the use of Jerry Atrick's van. Each of the men made contributions to the cause.

Griff brought, as did Mike, a pair of 10 x 50 binoculars. Cal Rich provided a card table and four chairs and Joe, thanks to his appeased wife, brought baked goods. Mike also brought his folding rocking chair and a tripod for the binoculars. Gradually the working refrigerator was stocked and a microwave oven was added. To the normal observer it would appear as if a bunch of bachelors had moved in.

The first time that Danny Goldman left his residence it was realized that it would look odd to drive out right after he did. To solve this problem, a rolling plain car containing a Special Ops officer was always working in the area. An F.B.I. stake out team was already established and would monitor Goldman when he arrived at work.

Days passed without a break in the case, and Ed Riley was getting more worked up. There were no meetings with nefarious characters and to Jester's disappointment, there were no more late night meetings at the crypt; Saturday night came and went. Goldman did not attend Frankie Colgate's funeral.

Early Sunday evening Cal Rich was manning the binoculars when an old, beat up, construction yellow pick-up truck backed into Goldman's driveway. When the driver exited he appeared to be old and somewhat hunched over. He straightened his hard hat and rang the doorbell. Goldman met him as the door and they both walked out to the truck. Goldman looked around to see if he were being watched. Even at a distance his eyes seemed to sparkle when he peered into the bed of the truck.

The driver, also shiftily looking around, reached across the closed tailgate and lifted out a wooden box by its rope handles. When one of the old rope handles broke, the driver froze like a deer in the headlights and then slowly eased the case to the ground by its good handle. When the rope broke, Goldman, too, looked like a deer, jumping over bushes; he moved super fast for an old man.

"I think this is what we've been waiting for," Cal said to Mike. From the way those old birds looked, my guess would have to be nitroglycerin."

"I'll bet your right. I'm going to contact special ops to have him stopped. We need to know who he is and what he's all about."

"Unless he blows himself up," Cal smirked.

When the box didn't explode, the driver sat down on the ground and wiped his brow with his sleeve while he stared at the box. Goldman slowly reappeared and went to the aid of the driver. The old man on the ground flailed his arm at Goldman's touch, not happy at having been brought so close to death. It appeared to the stake out crew that there was quite an argument brewing between the old men, but they were not close enough to hear. The driver appeared to get the upper hand in the argument as he was doing most of the gesturing and pointing. Eventually Danny Goldman retreated into the house and came out with some heavy rope which the driver used to replace both handles on the wooden box.

Once again Mr. Goldman entered his home; he electronically raised his garage door and emerged wearing a jacket and ball cap. Goldman backed a classic '57 Chevy Nomad out of the garage and the two men gingerly lifted the heavy box into the rear of the Chevy.

Mike Wohcowhcs made an executive decision to call the troops into readiness to stop Goldman if he moves. If he is carrying unstable nitroglycerin, the danger had to be minimized or eliminated.

Cal called the Special Ops Unit in the area to meet with a marked unit to find a pretense for stopping the pick-up. The Feds will call for some C.C.P.D. units to stop Goldman if and when he moves.

Things were happening fast, Cal radioed Griff.

Zoo and Joe had stopped by the Gentry place and were talking over basic wedding plans with Red. "What are you going to do about caring for Pops once you're married and living away?"

"I'm not deaf, Flatfoot, maybe you should ask me that question!"

"Hey, Pops, I didn't know you had 20/20 hearing," Zoo yelled out to the porch. "Why don't you come in and join in on the discussion?"

"Nothing to discuss," he yelled back. "Red had me start interviewing nurses shortly after she met you. As soon as she hits the bricks, I've got another one waiting in the wings – closer to my age – can't run so fast." Pops laughed so hard that he had a coughing spell.

"Is that so?" Griff asked Red.

She just shrugged her shoulders. "Guess I knew before you did – sorry."

"Don't be sorry, I'm glad that we both feel the same way."

The walkie crackled, "Taskforce 12 to Taskforce 17, come in."

"17 here, go ahead 12."

"Griff, we've got action. Goldman got a delivery of what appears to be nitro and it looks like he's going to move it. When the delivery man leaves we'll have him stopped, same for Goldman. Wohocks has called in the troops."

"17. We copy. We're on our way."

Griff gave his beloved a quick kiss and then he and Joe rushed out the door. "Got to go to work now, Pops, we may have Danny where we want him."

"You be careful, Flatfoot. You can't just think about yourself anymore."

Griff and Joe aimed the Explorer in the direction of Cactus Flower Lane and headed out. All units involved were instructed to work off of tactical channel 6.

The last vehicle in Goldman's driveway was the first to leave. There was only one way in and out of the subdivision and the Special Ops Unit and a marked cruiser, Patrol 74, were waiting.

The old yellow pick-up truck failed to signal his left turn onto Christen. "Special Ops to Unit 74, there is your probable cause, light him up A.S.A.P. If he tries to run we will block him."

"Patrol 74. We copy. Lighting him up at Christen and Applewhite."

The elderly driver was no stranger to being stopped; he immediately tossed his keys out of the driver's door window and threw up his hands. The driver was Slack Ledbetter whose information was readily available through N.C.I.C. He had outstanding warrants for illegal trafficking in weapons and explosives and readily admitted that he had just sold nitroglycerin to Danny Goldman. The sad old man who had spent over half of his life behind bars was going back to prison; he actually looked relieved.

From what Mike and Cal could see, it appeared that Danny Goldman was scurrying around like a mad man. He made numerous trips from the house to the station wagon, often carrying small items, other times nothing at all.

The final trip to the car found him carrying a blanket. From the way he carried it, it was concealing something. Goldman carefully placed the blanket covered item on the front passenger seat. Several times Danny Goldman did something with the wooden box, but his actions were not clearly visible. Finally the suspect stood still and looked off into the distance as if he were taking mental inventory. Danny Goldman entered his robin's egg blue Chevy Nomad, closed the garage door, tugged on the bill of his ball cap and backed out of his driveway.

"Taskforce 12 to all units, the bogey is moving; he's in a light blue Nomad."

Mike Wohcowhcs announced, "It has been confirmed; the car is carrying nitroglycerin. Give him plenty of room. We can't afford an incident in a populated area. I don't care if he knows that we are onto him, direct him to an open area." Griff and Joe were now racing towards the subdivision.

Daniel Goldman, originally unaware that he had been found out, exited the subdivision and turned right onto Christen. Local police and A.T.F. agents were closing in from all sides and were being apprised of Goldman's every move. When it appeared that he might be going to the Pioneer Cemetery, an unmarked unit raced past him and parked blocking the entrance to the graveyard. The unit activated its dash beacon and Goldman, who had braked to turn in, drove on by.

Marked units from all jurisdictions were putting themselves at exits to prevent the rolling bomb from exiting into populated areas. Goldman soon realized that he was being targeted and tried to out think the cops to get away. Christen had widened into a four lane divided highway and now even the median crossovers were occupied by either state troopers or local police units. No more vehicles passed Goldman and a look in his rearview mirror showed a phalanx of police cars with their beacons on.

The mobilization of troops had developed fast and Goldman was cut off no matter where he went. He was forced to stay on Christen and was now headed for the rural area. When Danny Goldman realized that he would not be able to get as far as the neighboring community of Whitley, he decided that it was time to make a stand. He slowed and then turned his car sideways under the Placer overpass which connected Placer with Benton, two upscale communities.

As the following police cars stopped at a safe distance from the bridge, Griff and Joe joined them. Griff called his radio room with instructions to have the Placer overpass shut off. "No cars, repeat no cars are to be allowed to cross over Christen; there is a risk of an explosion." Once that had been accomplished and the traffic stopped, law enforcement could engage the suspect. While marked units converged and blocked Christen from the other way, Park, Wohcowhcs, Rich and Beveltnik all moved forward; Mike and Zoo had bullhorns.

Goldman walked out of the dusky shadows of the overpass and spoke first. He was in fine voice and yelled, "Get back, I have enough nitro in my wagon to blow your precious bridge to smithereens."

Mike responded through the bullhorn, "Why would you want to do that? You could kill yourself in the process!"

"I've got nothing to live for anyway – might as well take as many pigs with me as I can when I go."

"You don't want to do that," Mike said. "Surely we can work something out; people don't need to die."

"Too late for that; you've gotten my brothers killed and now you want to kill me!"

"We don't want to kill you; we don't want anyone to die; let's see if we can't talk about this."

"Lies! All lies!" Goldman was starting to froth at the mouth – spittle was flying. "All I wanted to do was make an honest living, live the American dream! But nooooo!! You shot me down at every turn with all of those regulations and your being in bed with that big crooked landscaping company, Tri-State. You killed off my family and now you want to kill me!"

Mike whispered to Griff, "What is he talking about, Zoo?"

"Don't know. He didn't get the big landscape contract and his two brothers recently died. I don't know much more about his family."

"You have us at a loss," Mike answered through the bullhorn, trying to keep him talking. "What happened to your family?"

Mike must have hit a nerve; Danny Goldman was livid. "The cops went to my brother's pawn shop and blew it up! Then you pigs took all of my brother's drugs; he couldn't pay for them and that got him killed!! He was just trying to make a living! The Strangers are the only family I have left!"

"What about your wife?" Mike asked.

"She tried to stop me, too!"

Griff whispered to Joe, "Have someone check his house; his wife may be hurt or worse. Use the car radio."

"You might want to get back. I'm going to blow up this car and your precious bridge!"

As Danny retreated into the shadows, Mike trotted forward, "Don't do that!!"

A voice crackled in Mike's earpiece, "Don't go any closer or you will be in my sniper's line of fire – try to talk him out of the shadows."

Danny Goldman walked out from under the bridge and calmly yelled, "Talking time is over."

With that he raised a fully automatic Uzi-like machine pistol which he had been holding behind his back and sprayed the lawmen with bullets.

Danny Goldman bucked and fell under a barrage of bullets and dropped a small detonator from his left hand as he did so. In one last desperate effort, the dying Goldman stretched forth a shaky finger and pushed the button.

In one instant the classic Nomad was gone, the bridge was gone and also Zoo's hope for an early wedding was gone.

Agent Michael Wohcowhcs was dead. C.C.P.D. Officer Calvin Rich was dead. Another F.B.I. agent was dead and one was dying. Six C.C.P.D. officers suffered various wounds. Officer Joseph Beveltnik was spared; he was using the car radio. Officer Griffith Park was on the pavement writhing in pain, holding the sides of both thighs, two serious wounds, but no major damage; if the sweep of bullets had been slower he would never be able to father children.

Thanks to Daniel Goldman, deceased, it was a very black day for law enforcement.

CHAPTER TWENTY

Officer Griffith Parks' hospital bed had been rolled to the window. His many baskets and sprays of flowers wafted aromas about the private room and added to his funereal state of mind. Tears were running down his cheeks as he watched Calvin Rich's funeral procession pass by.

"Cal and I were good friends; we were in the same police academy class. I should be down there honoring his memory."

Griff's private duty nurse and fiancée squeezed his hand as they watched together. Giselle was not familiar with the pomp of a fallen officer's funeral and was amazed at the length of the procession; she counted the cars, 212 marked police vehicles from jurisdictions within the state and some from outside, 286 civilian cars. She, too, wept when the hearse went by and Griff saluted.

"You knew that the doctors wouldn't let you attend; the skin graft on your left thigh has to heal. You can hear all of the details from Joe when he comes by later."

When the final vehicles had passed by Griff said, "This should never have happened, Red; we should have figured it out sooner. What a terrible loss of life."

"Try not to think about it, love; it's not good for your blood pressure. In fact I'm going to insist that you get some rest now." Red rolled the hospital bed back to its main position and turned down the light. "I'll be back later, dear; now close your eyes and rest." Red kissed her man and then quietly left the room.

Griff closed his eyes but couldn't shut down his mind. He remembered going down in a hail of bullets and hearing and feeling the explosion; the aftermath had been told to him later. Tears again began to stream down his cheeks as he recounted the loss of life.

Calvin Rich had been killed. Another good friend, Mike Wohcowhcs, had also died along with two other federal agents. Six other C.C.P.D. officers had sustained various non-life threatenting wounds. He had been told that they were in the same wing as he; He would have to find out who they were and communicate with them.

The only bright spot was knowing that his partner, Joe, was O.K.; he had been in the car calling in a request to check on Mrs. Goldman – the late Mrs. Goldman. Griff finally fell asleep and dreamed of Joe and Bev watching their young son run and play. Sometime in his dream the little boy changed; he now had red hair.

Griff awoke with the realization that he was not alone. "Who's there," he called out.

"Just me," the voice boomed and the bigger than life Sheriff Deacon Tolliver arose from a chair and walked out of the shadows. "I didn't mean to frighten you, my friend; I didn't have the heart to wake you so I just sat down and watched over you."

Griff pulled the light chain and increased the light in his room. As the two men embraced, Griff asked, "Is your son aware that Mike Wohcowhcs was killed?"

"Dean knows and he is very troubled; he lost one good friend and nearly lost another. I, too, am upset by the loss of so many members of the law enforcement family. The one saving grace was your survival; Dean will be up to see you later."

The conversation was covering a myriad of topics, when Deacon noticed the writing on the room's message board. "Is Stella Niagara a military hospital? What is this private nurse business?"

Griff smiled, "That means that I have my own private nurse; she's very good. You will meet her later. She's my fiancée. She's the reason that I called about the availability of your cabin."

There was a tap on the door and Chief Riley stuck his head in. "Up to having visitors?"

"Sure, Boss, come on in."

"Deacon, you old war horse, do you know this guy?"

"The celebrated kidnapee of Corinth County? Are you kidding, everyone knows The Zoo Man!"

"Well, I see that no introductions are needed. I hope you didn't bring an anal thermometer with you. I'm not up for surprises."

"No, Park, I only bring good news, but first I want to know how you are doing."

"Well, the right thigh wound was through and through and the left thigh needed a skin graft because of the chunk of meat that was missing. I'm hurting some, but I'm O.K.; wish we could say the same about the others." With that he looked away and wiped a tear.

"Amen to that, Zoo Man, amen to that."

"Would you like me to step out so that you two can talk alone?" Sheriff Tolliver asked.

"Please stay," said Griff. "Now, Boss, about that good news."

"When we and the Feds entered Daniel Goldman's house, not only did we find his dead wife, but much more. It turns out that Goldman was a natural born archivist. He kept detailed notes and journals on all of the families' business ventures. With the info we found, Dingell's boys were able to solve the Keeper homicide and Bob Barker was able to clear many burglaries off the books. His writing also listed all of the Lone Strangers and their parts in various crimes.

The D.A. is ecstatic; once all of the information is gleaned, he is going to call a special grand jury. There's enough information to write a book. How do you like them apples?"

"It was a great break, Boss, but I wish we didn't have to have lives lost. It was too high of a price to pay."

"Agreed, but we have to go on. Officially I can tell you that you will again be one of the stars at the department's medals awards ceremonies in May. Any more medals and you will start to look like Sheriff Tolliver here."

"Sorry to disappoint you, Boss, but I'm not going to be available this year; I'm going to be on my honeymoon. Besides, I've been to enough of those; my appearance would only be a distraction. You need to focus on the real heroes, albeit posthumously, Judy Stanhope and Cal Rich and if you could say a few words about him, Mike Wohcowhcs as well."

"Can do, Zoo, can do."

EPILOGUE

With the Goldman crime families' investigation all but wrapped up, things started returning to normal in Capitol City.

Griff's bachelor party was held at the new Flatulent Dog and was co-hosted by the bar's owner, Beau Hemian and the Qua King Duck's own Ling Po.

On the first Saturday in May, Griffith Park married Giselle Parker in the God's Little Acre of Hope Inc. Church. The happy couple drove off in a rented replica of Adam West's Batmobile, to honeymoon at an undisclosed location deep in the woods of Corinth County.

And what of Joe Beveltnik, the Zoo Man's highly decorated sidekick?

Chief Riley gave him a special assignment to clear up one of the more puzzling loose ends of the Goldman case, "Find Seth Goldman's furniture!"

Made in the USA
Lexington, KY
25 July 2010